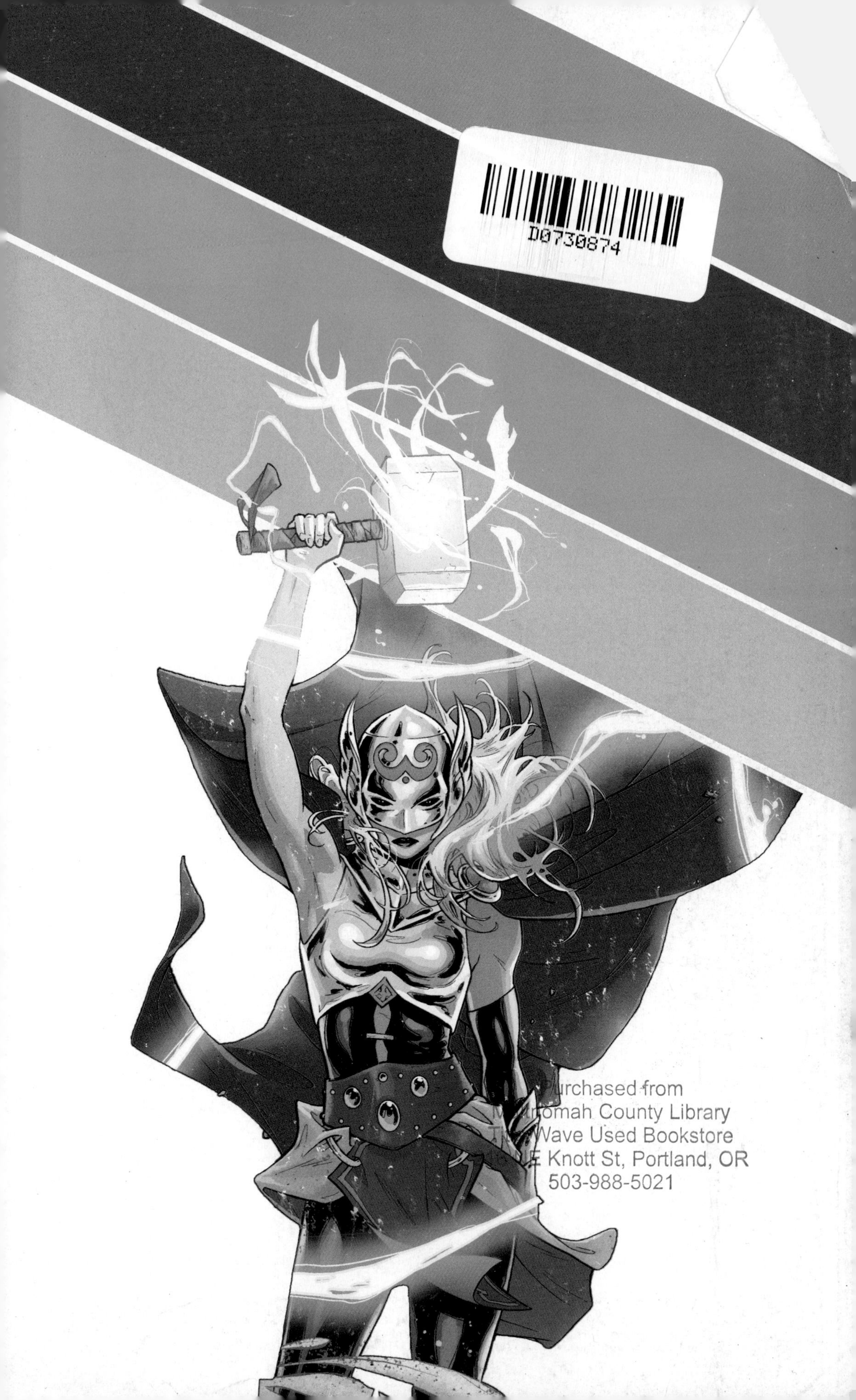

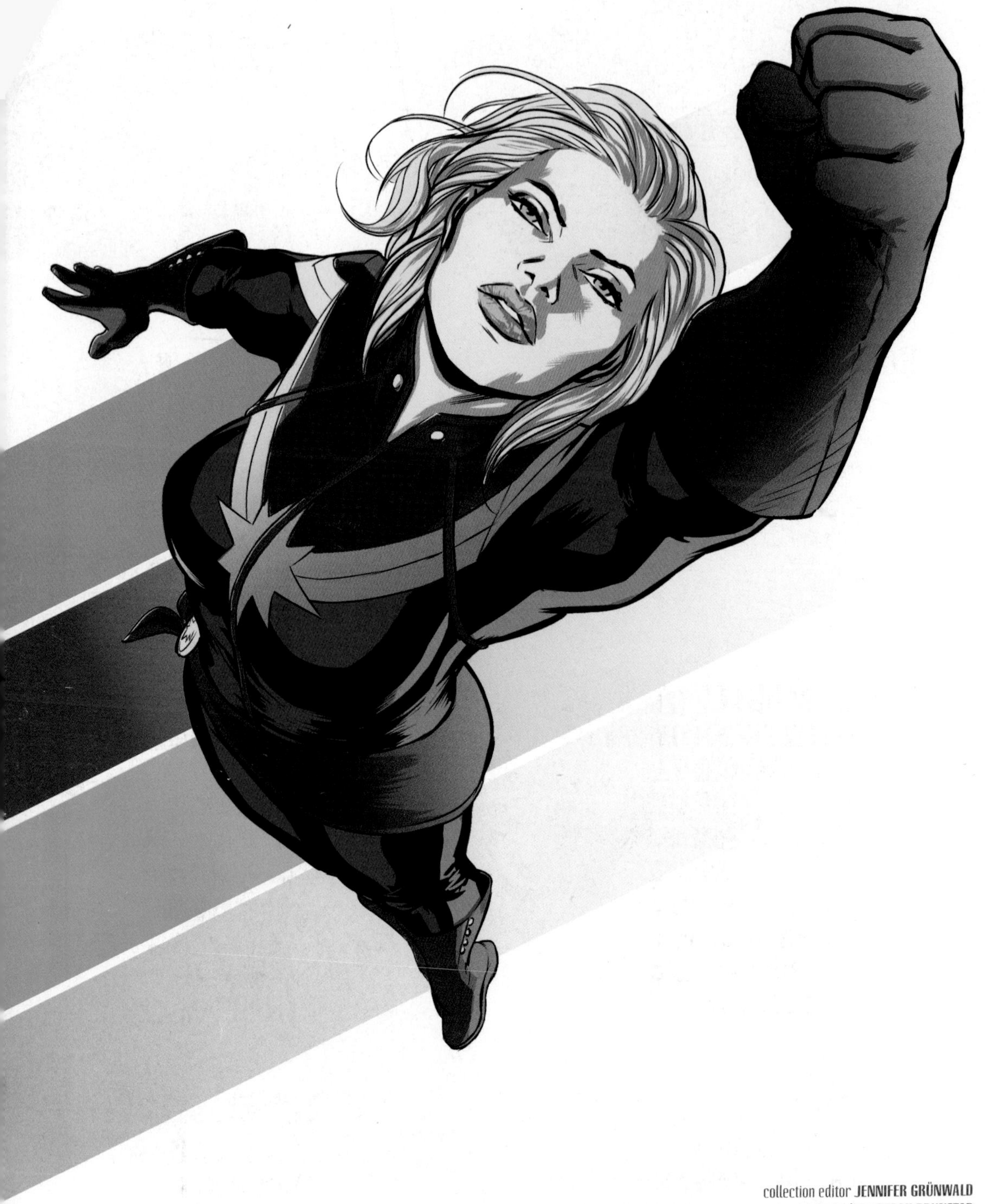

collection editor **JENNIFER GRÜNWALD**
assistant editor **SARAH BRUNSTAD**
associate managing editor **ALEX STARBUCK**
editor, special projects **MARK D. BEAZLEY**
senior editor, special projects **JEFF YOUNGQUIST**
svp print, sales & marketing **DAVID GABRIEL**
book designer **ADAM DEL RE**

editor in chief **AXEL ALONSO**
chief creative officer **JOE QUESADA**
publisher **DAN BUCKLEY**
executive producer **ALAN FINE**

A-FORCE PRESENTS VOL. 1. Contains material originally published in magazine form as BLACK WIDOW #1, CAPTAIN MARVEL #1, MS. MARVEL #1, SHE-HULK #1, THOR #1 and THE UNBEATABLE SQUIRREL GIRL #1. First printing 2015. ISBN# 978-0-7851-9898-7. Published by MARVEL WORLDWIDE, INC., a subsidiary of MARVEL ENTERTAINMENT, LLC. OFFICE OF PUBLICATION: 135 West 50th Street, New York, NY 10020. **Printed in the U.S.A.** ALAN FINE, President, Marvel Entertainment; DAN BUCKLEY, President, TV, Publishing and Brand Management; JOE QUESADA, Chief Creative Officer; TOM BREVOORT, SVP of Publishing; DAVID BOGART, SVP of Operations & Procurement, Publishing; C.B. CEBULSKI, VP of International Development & Brand Management; DAVID GABRIEL, SVP Print, Sales & Marketing; JIM O'KEEFE, VP of Operations & Logistics; DAN CARR, Executive Director of Publishing Technology; SUSAN CRESPI, Editorial Operations Manager; ALEX MORALES, Publishing Operations Manager; STAN LEE, Chairman Emeritus. For information regarding advertising in Marvel Comics or on Marvel.com, please contact Jonathan Rheingold, VP of Custom Solutions & Ad Sales, at jrheingold@marvel.com. For Marvel subscription inquiries, please call 800-217-9158. **Manufactured between 7/24/2015 and 8/31/2015 by R.R. DONNELLEY, INC., SALEM, VA, USA.**

10 9 8 7 6 5 4 3 2 1

A-FORCE PRESENTS

BLACK WIDOW (2014) #1
writer **NATHAN EDMONDSON**
artist **PHIL NOTO**
letterer **VC's CLAYTON COWLES**
cover art **PHIL NOTO**
editor **ELLIE PYLE**

SHE-HULK (2014) #1
writer **CHARLES SOULE**
artist **JAVIER PULIDO**
color artist **MUNTSA VICENTE**
letterer **VC's CLAYTON COWLES**
cover art **KEVIN WADA**
editors **JEANINE SCHAEFER** &
TOM BRENNAN

CAPTAIN MARVEL (2014) #1
writer **KELLY SUE DeCONNICK**
artist **DAVID LOPEZ**
color artist **LEE LOUGHRIDGE**
letterer **VC's JOE CARAMAGNA**
cover art **DAVID LOPEZ**
assistant editor **DEVIN LEWIS**
editor **SANA AMANAT**
senior editors **STEPHEN WACKER** &
NICK LOWE

MS. MARVEL (2014) #1
writer **G. WILLOW WILSON**
artist **ADRIAN ALPHONA**
color artist **IAN HERRING**
letterer **VC's JOE CARAMAGNA**
cover art **SARA PICHELLI** &
JUSTIN PONSOR
assistant editor **DEVIN LEWIS**
editor **SANA AMANAT**
senior editor **STEPHEN WACKER**

THOR (2014) #1
writer **JASON AARON**
artist **RUSSELL DAUTERMAN**
color artist **MATTHEW WILSON**
letterer **VC's JOE SABINO**
cover art **RUSSELL DAUTERMAN** &
FRANK MARTIN
assistant editor **JON MOISAN**
editor **WIL MOSS**

**THE UNBEATABLE
SQUIRREL GIRL** (2015) #1
writer **RYAN NORTH**
artist **ERICA HENDERSON**
trading card art **MARIS WICKS**
color artist **RICO RENZI**
letterer **VC's CLAYTON COWLES**
cover art **ERICA HENDERSON**
assistant editor **JAKE THOMAS**
editor **WIL MOSS**
executive editor **TOM BREVOORT**

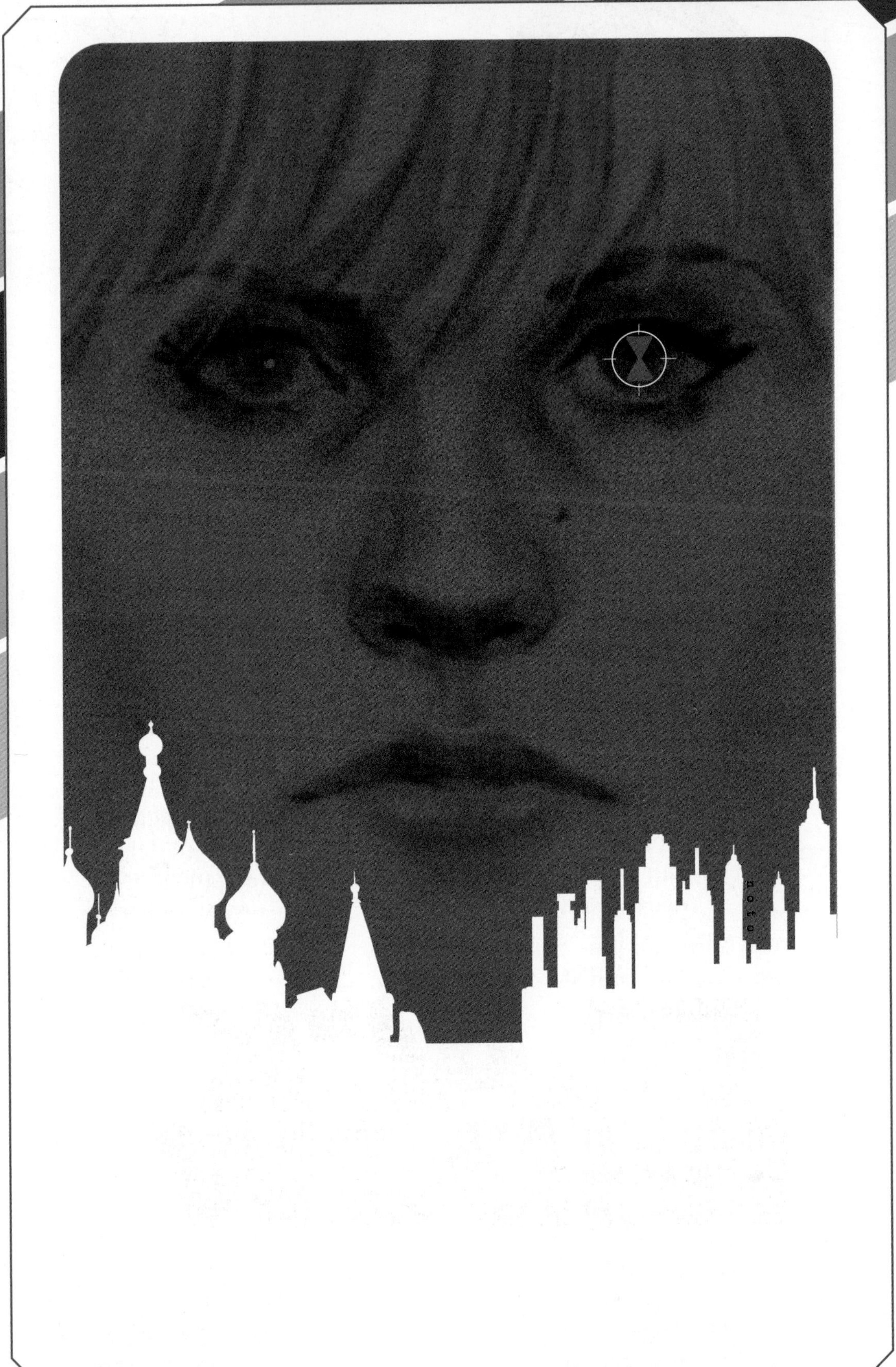

BLACK WIDOW #1

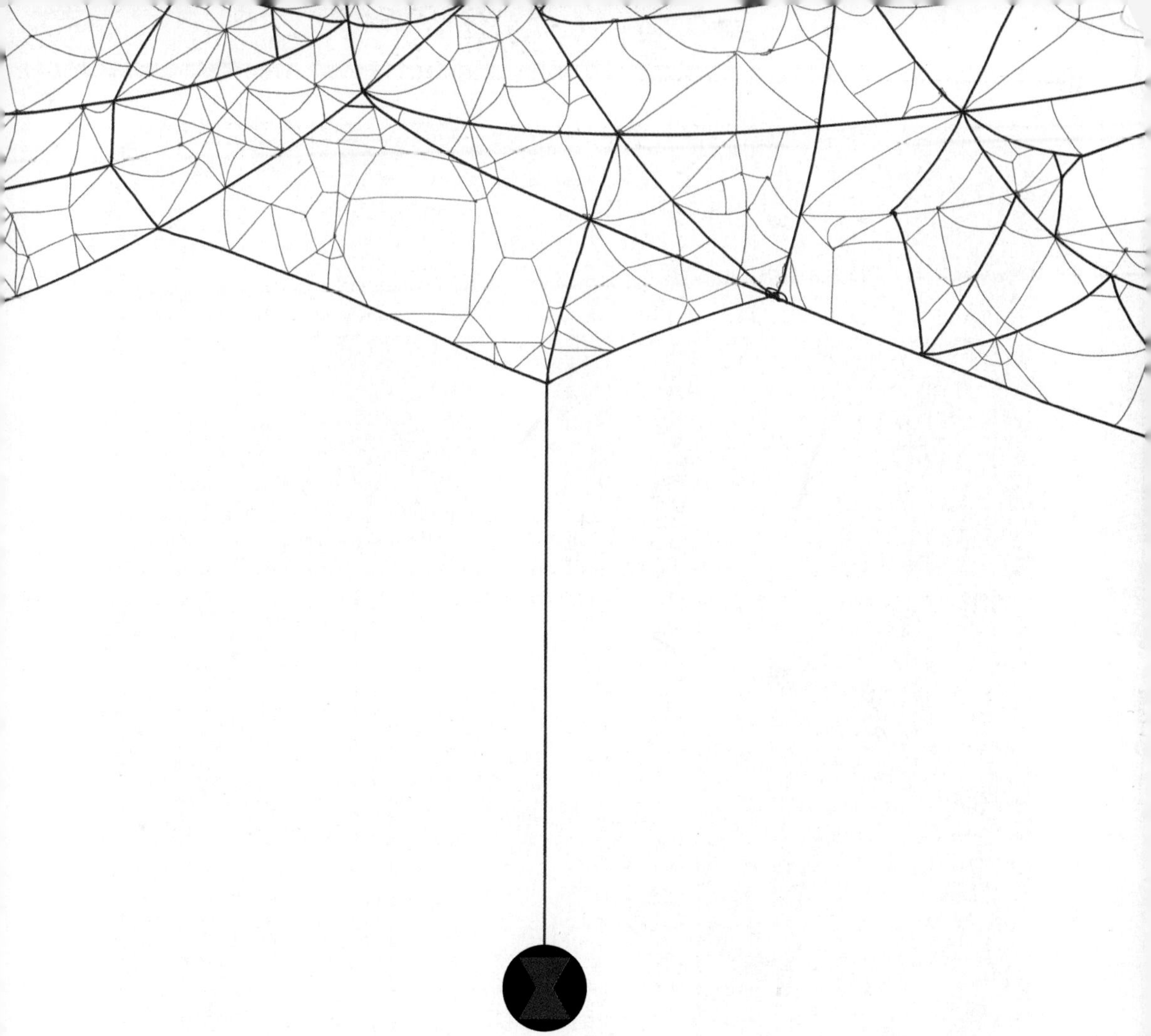

NATASHA ROMANOV IS AN AVENGER, AN AGENT OF S.H.I.E.L.D. AND AN EX-KGB ASSASSIN, BUT ON HER OWN TIME, SHE USES HER UNIQUE SKILL SET TO ATONE FOR HER PAST. SHE IS:

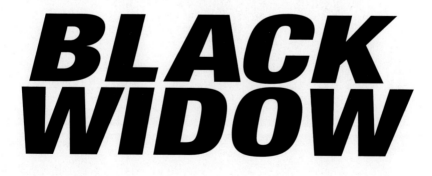

BLACK WIDOW

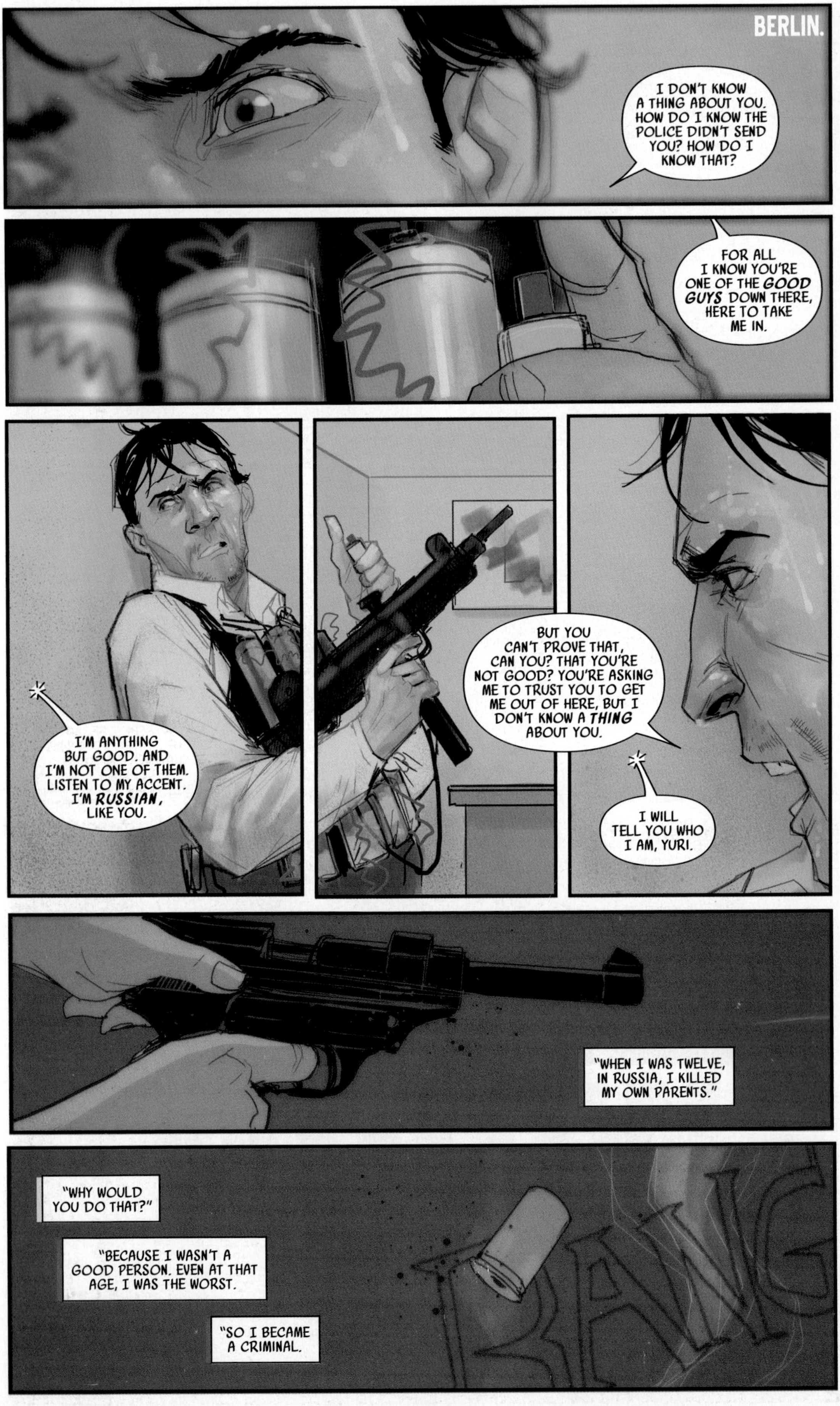
BERLIN.
I DON'T KNOW A THING ABOUT YOU. HOW DO I KNOW THE POLICE DIDN'T SEND YOU? HOW DO I KNOW THAT?
FOR ALL I KNOW YOU'RE ONE OF THE GOOD GUYS DOWN THERE, HERE TO TAKE ME IN.
I'M ANYTHING BUT GOOD. AND I'M NOT ONE OF THEM. LISTEN TO MY ACCENT. I'M RUSSIAN, LIKE YOU.
BUT YOU CAN'T PROVE THAT, CAN YOU? THAT YOU'RE NOT GOOD? YOU'RE ASKING ME TO TRUST YOU TO GET ME OUT OF HERE, BUT I DON'T KNOW A THING ABOUT YOU.
I WILL TELL YOU WHO I AM, YURI.
"WHEN I WAS TWELVE, IN RUSSIA, I KILLED MY OWN PARENTS."
"WHY WOULD YOU DO THAT?"
"BECAUSE I WASN'T A GOOD PERSON. EVEN AT THAT AGE, I WAS THE WORST.
"SO I BECAME A CRIMINAL.
BANG

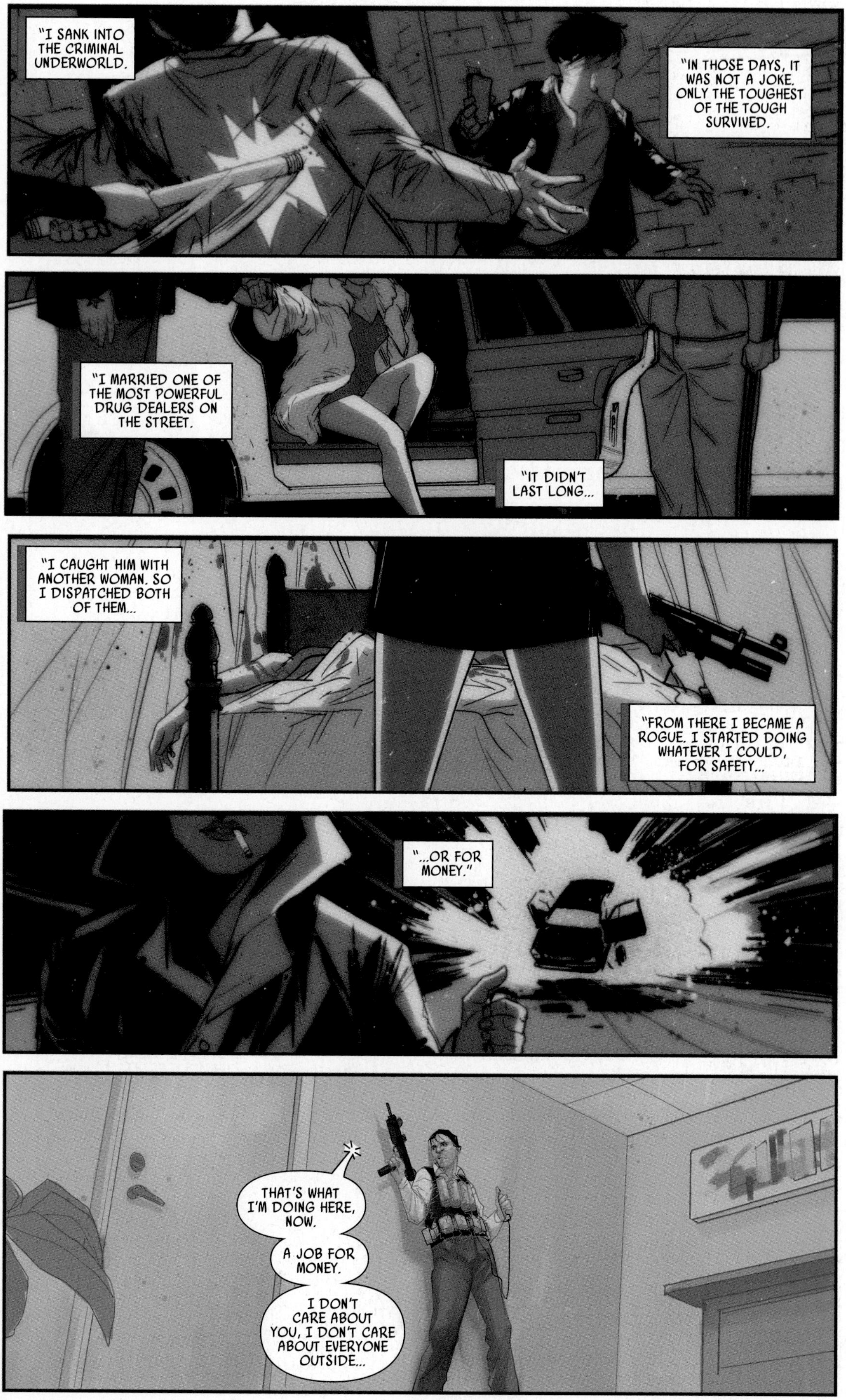
"I SANK INTO THE CRIMINAL UNDERWORLD.
"IN THOSE DAYS, IT WAS NOT A JOKE. ONLY THE TOUGHEST OF THE TOUGH SURVIVED.
"I MARRIED ONE OF THE MOST POWERFUL DRUG DEALERS ON THE STREET.
"IT DIDN'T LAST LONG...
"I CAUGHT HIM WITH ANOTHER WOMAN. SO I DISPATCHED BOTH OF THEM...
"FROM THERE I BECAME A ROGUE. I STARTED DOING WHATEVER I COULD, FOR SAFETY...
"...OR FOR MONEY."
THAT'S WHAT I'M DOING HERE, NOW.
A JOB FOR MONEY.
I DON'T CARE ABOUT YOU, I DON'T CARE ABOUT EVERYONE OUTSIDE...

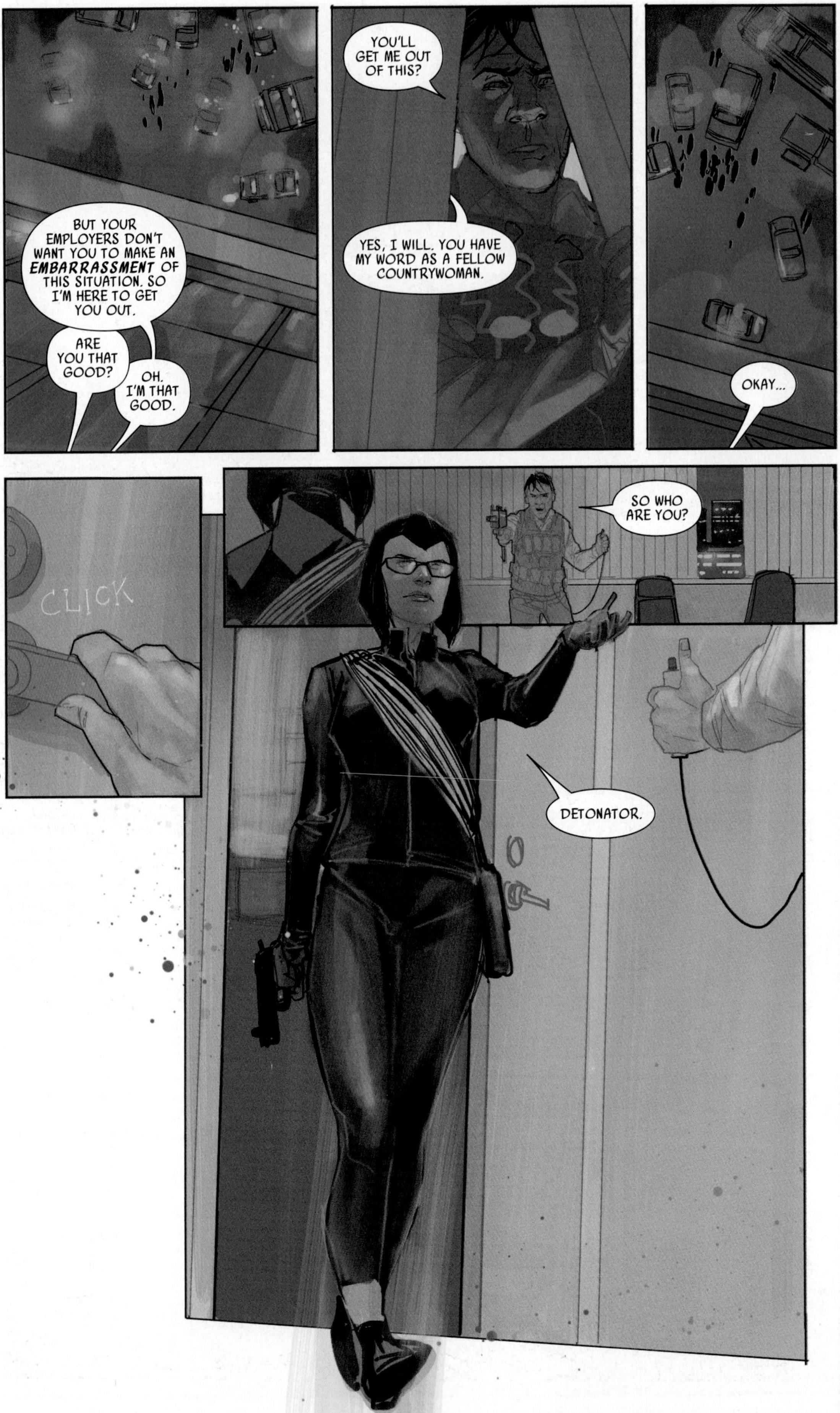

BUT YOUR EMPLOYERS DON'T WANT YOU TO MAKE AN EMBARRASSMENT OF THIS SITUATION. SO I'M HERE TO GET YOU OUT.
ARE YOU THAT GOOD?
OH. I'M THAT GOOD.
YOU'LL GET ME OUT OF THIS?
YES, I WILL. YOU HAVE MY WORD AS A FELLOW COUNTRYWOMAN.
OKAY...
CLICK
SO WHO ARE YOU?
DETONATOR.

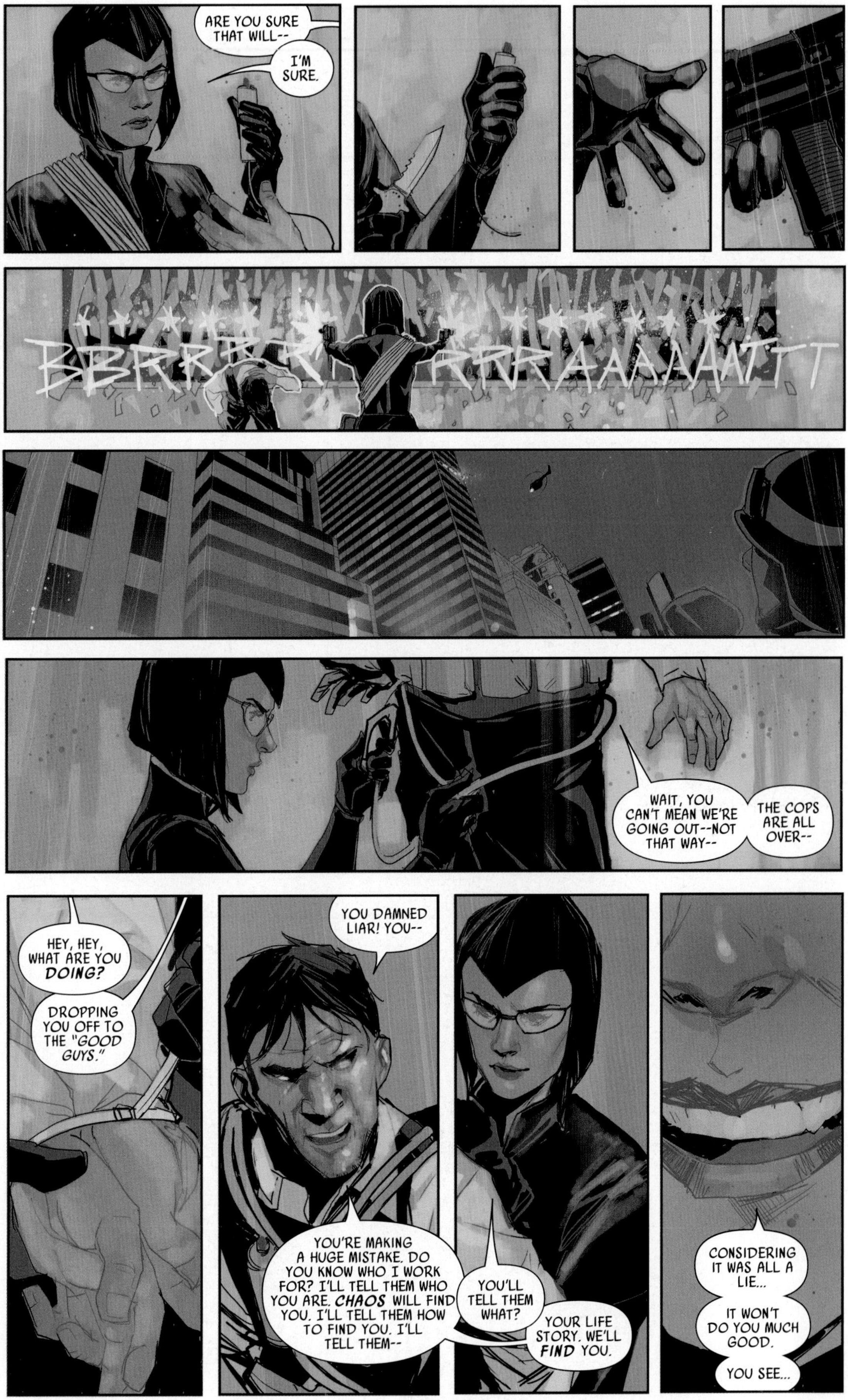
ARE YOU SURE THAT WILL--
I'M SURE.
BBRRRRRRRRRAAAAAATTT
WAIT, YOU CAN'T MEAN WE'RE GOING OUT--NOT THAT WAY--
THE COPS ARE ALL OVER--
HEY, HEY, WHAT ARE YOU *DOING?*
DROPPING YOU OFF TO THE "GOOD GUYS."
YOU DAMNED LIAR! YOU--
YOU'RE MAKING A HUGE MISTAKE. DO YOU KNOW WHO I WORK FOR? I'LL TELL THEM WHO YOU ARE. *CHAOS* WILL FIND YOU. I'LL TELL THEM HOW TO FIND YOU. I'LL TELL THEM--
YOU'LL TELL THEM WHAT?
YOUR LIFE STORY. WE'LL *FIND* YOU.
CONSIDERING IT WAS ALL A LIE...
IT WON'T DO YOU MUCH GOOD.
YOU SEE...

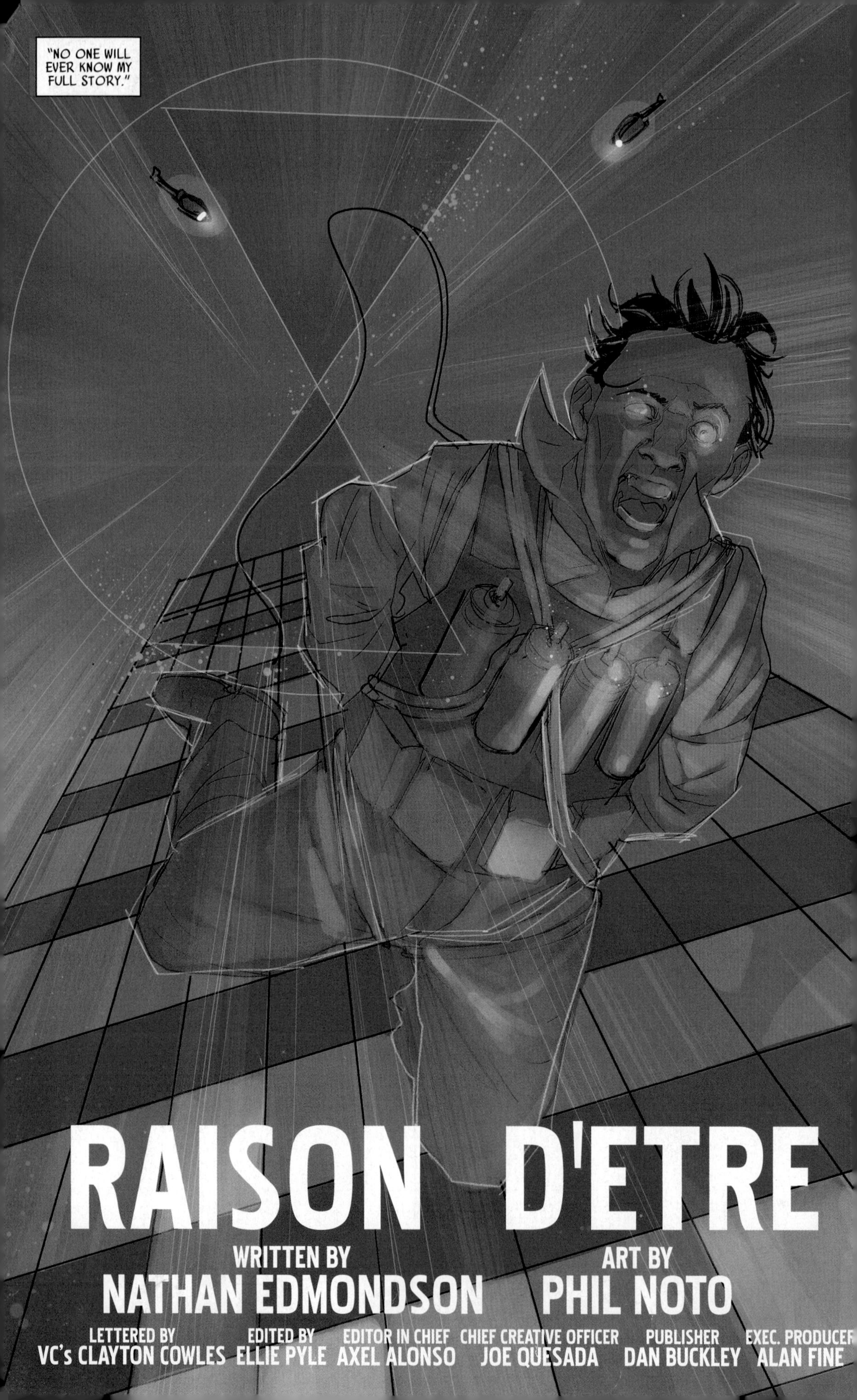
"NO ONE WILL EVER KNOW MY FULL STORY."

RAISON D'ETRE

WRITTEN BY
NATHAN EDMONDSON

ART BY
PHIL NOTO

LETTERED BY
VC's CLAYTON COWLES

EDITED BY
ELLIE PYLE

EDITOR IN CHIEF
AXEL ALONSO

CHIEF CREATIVE OFFICER
JOE QUESADA

PUBLISHER
DAN BUCKLEY

EXEC. PRODUCER
ALAN FINE

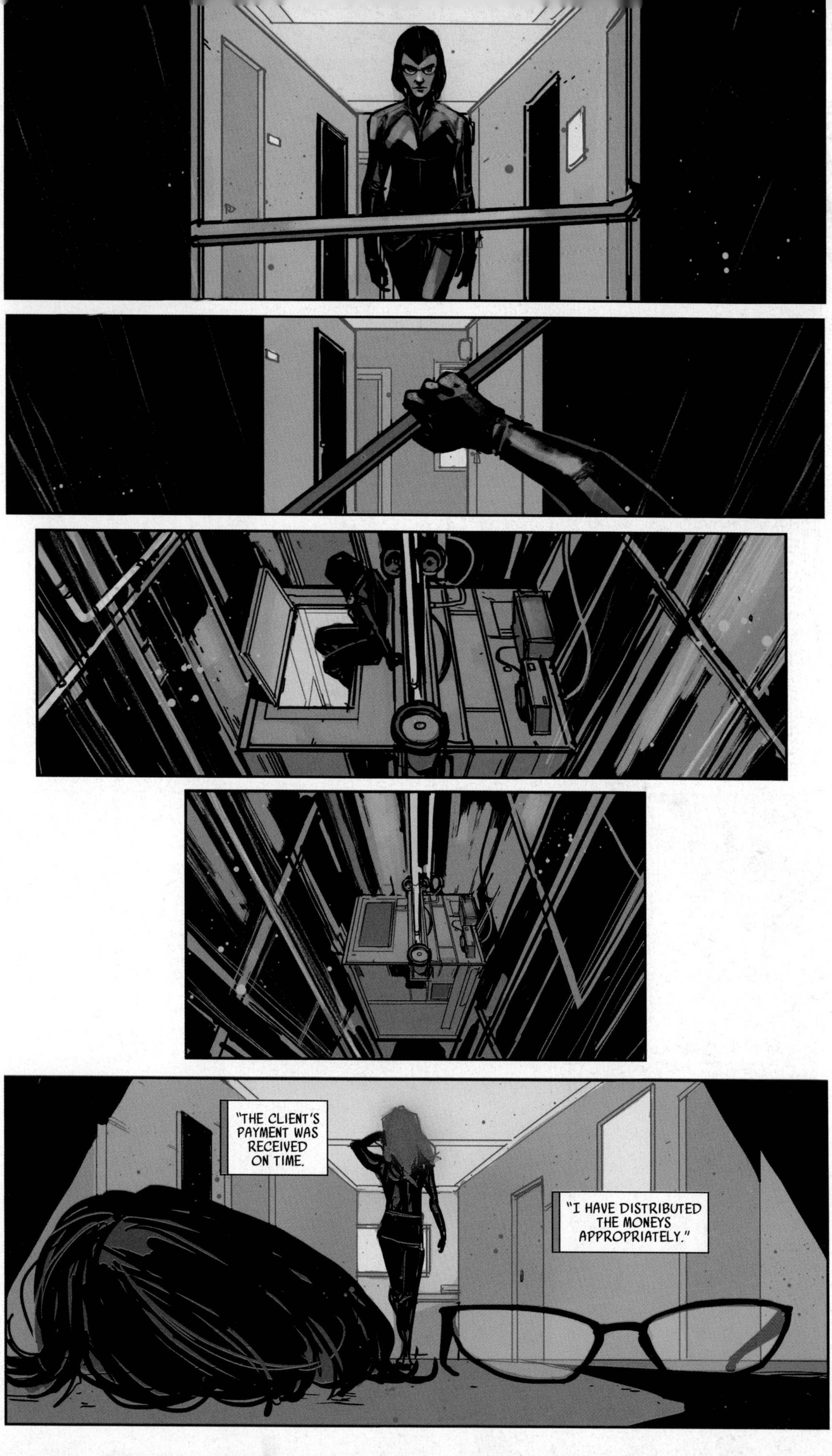
"THE CLIENT'S PAYMENT WAS RECEIVED ON TIME.
"I HAVE DISTRIBUTED THE MONEYS APPROPRIATELY."

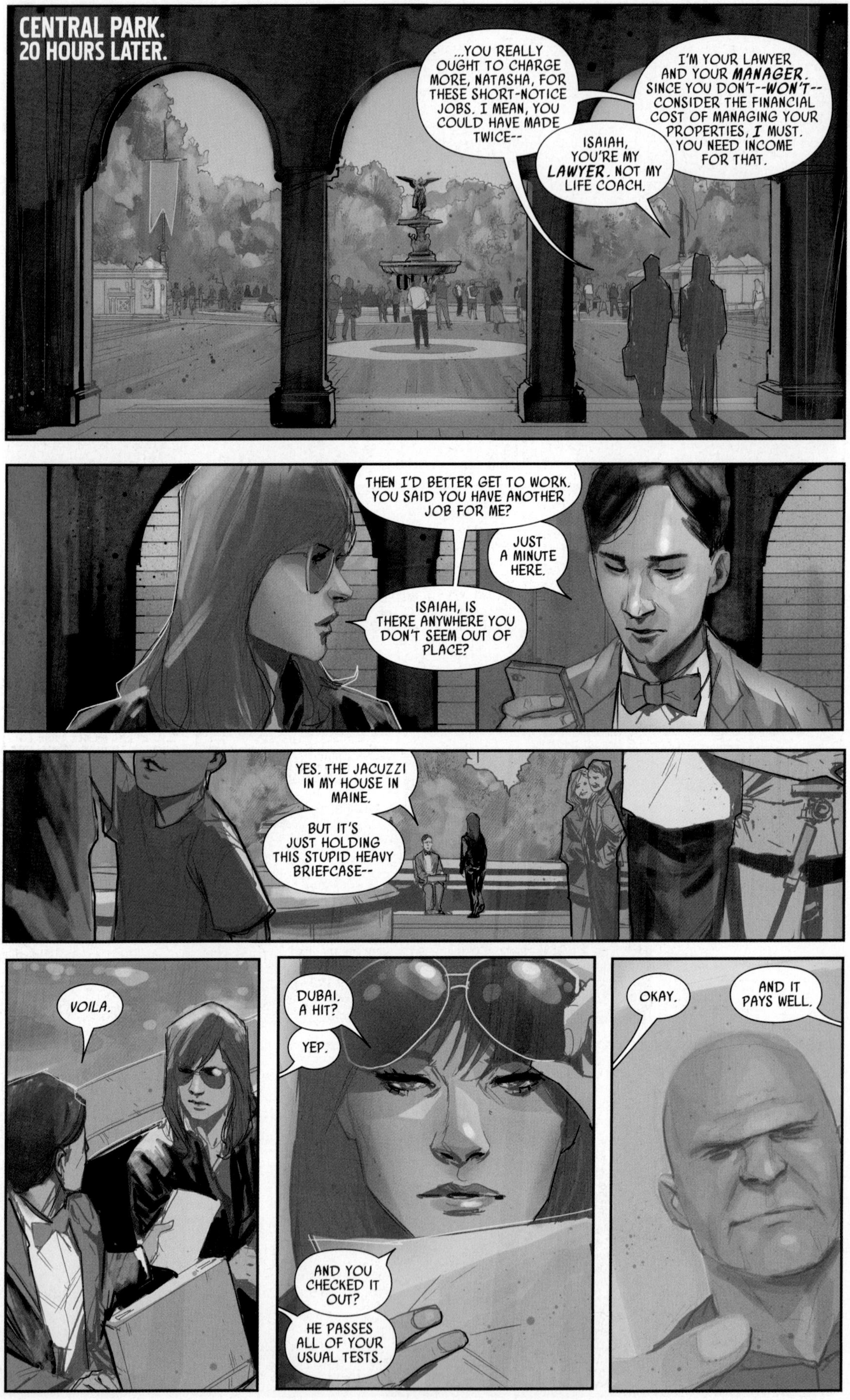
CENTRAL PARK. 20 HOURS LATER.
...YOU REALLY OUGHT TO CHARGE MORE, NATASHA, FOR THESE SHORT-NOTICE JOBS. I MEAN, YOU COULD HAVE MADE TWICE--
ISAIAH, YOU'RE MY LAWYER. NOT MY LIFE COACH.
I'M YOUR LAWYER AND YOUR MANAGER. SINCE YOU DON'T--WON'T--CONSIDER THE FINANCIAL COST OF MANAGING YOUR PROPERTIES, I MUST. YOU NEED INCOME FOR THAT.
THEN I'D BETTER GET TO WORK. YOU SAID YOU HAVE ANOTHER JOB FOR ME?
JUST A MINUTE HERE.
ISAIAH, IS THERE ANYWHERE YOU DON'T SEEM OUT OF PLACE?
YES. THE JACUZZI IN MY HOUSE IN MAINE.
BUT IT'S JUST HOLDING THIS STUPID HEAVY BRIEFCASE--
VOILA.
DUBAI. A HIT?
YEP.
AND YOU CHECKED IT OUT?
HE PASSES ALL OF YOUR USUAL TESTS.
OKAY.
AND IT PAYS WELL.

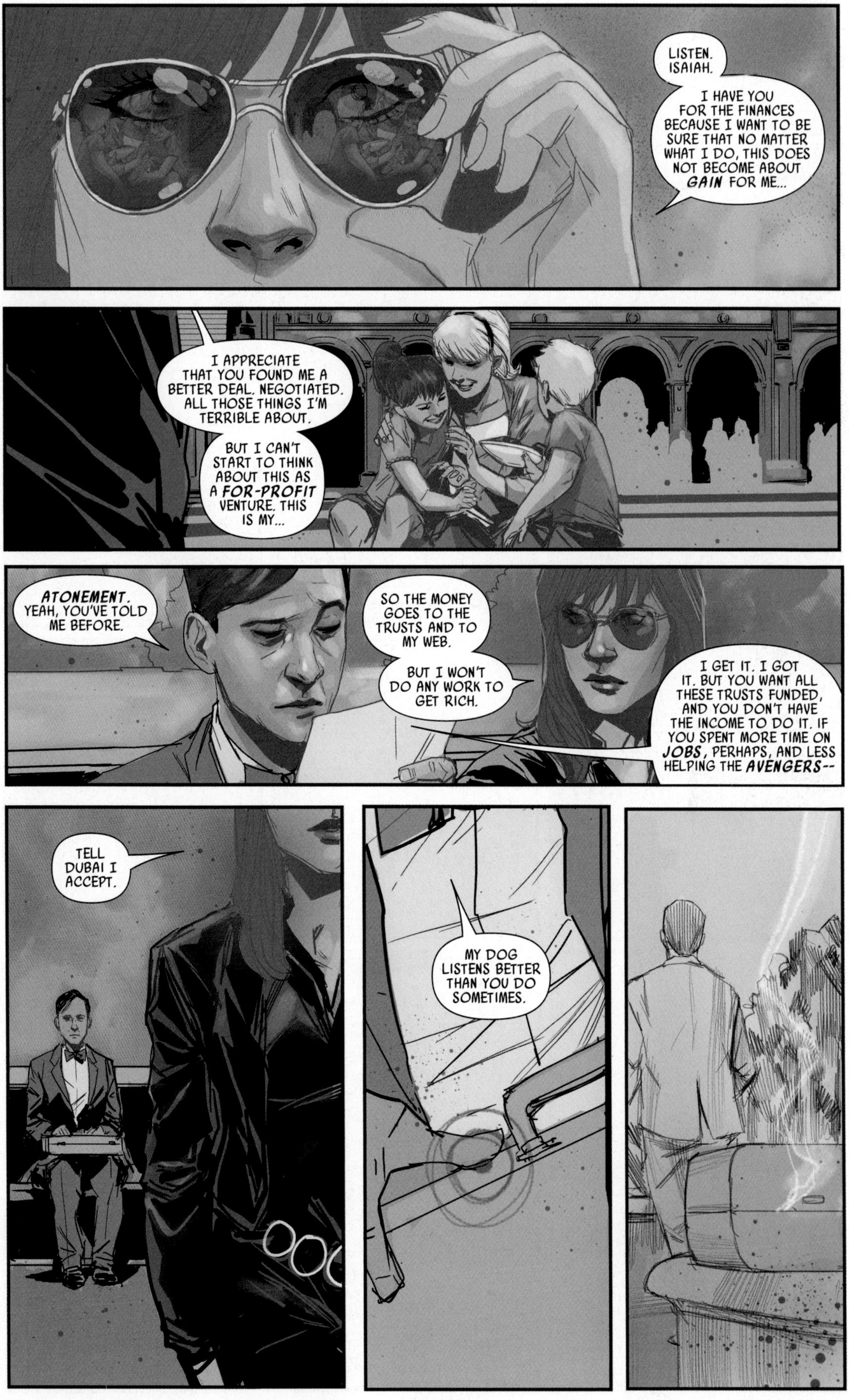
LISTEN. ISAIAH.
I HAVE YOU FOR THE FINANCES BECAUSE I WANT TO BE SURE THAT NO MATTER WHAT I DO, THIS DOES NOT BECOME ABOUT GAIN FOR ME...
I APPRECIATE THAT YOU FOUND ME A BETTER DEAL. NEGOTIATED. ALL THOSE THINGS I'M TERRIBLE ABOUT.
BUT I CAN'T START TO THINK ABOUT THIS AS A FOR-PROFIT VENTURE. THIS IS MY...
ATONEMENT. YEAH, YOU'VE TOLD ME BEFORE.
SO THE MONEY GOES TO THE TRUSTS AND TO MY WEB.
BUT I WON'T DO ANY WORK TO GET RICH.
I GET IT. I GOT IT. BUT YOU WANT ALL THESE TRUSTS FUNDED, AND YOU DON'T HAVE THE INCOME TO DO IT. IF YOU SPENT MORE TIME ON JOBS, PERHAPS, AND LESS HELPING THE AVENGERS--
TELL DUBAI I ACCEPT.
MY DOG LISTENS BETTER THAN YOU DO SOMETIMES.

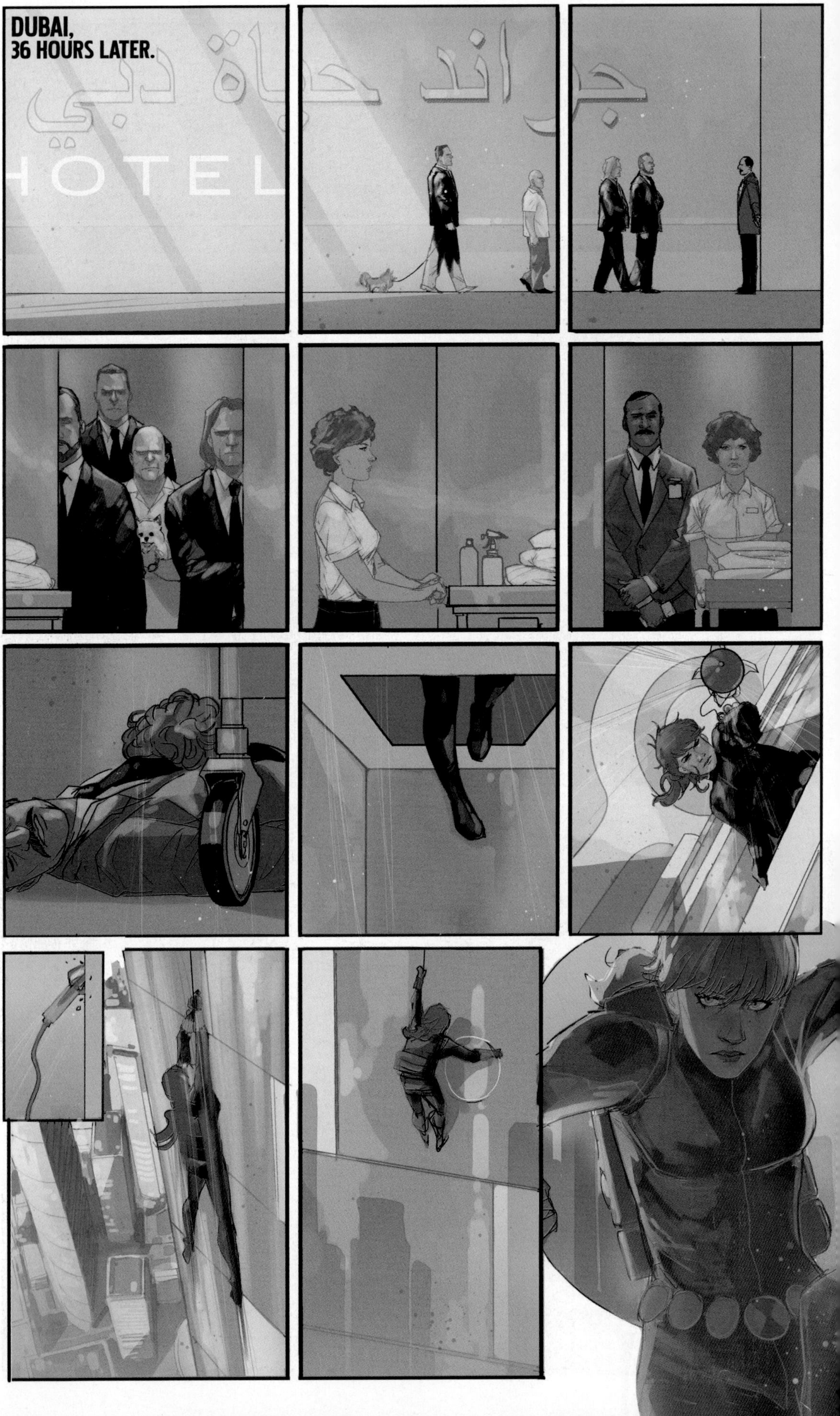
DUBAI,
36 HOURS LATER.
جراند حياة دبي
HOTEL

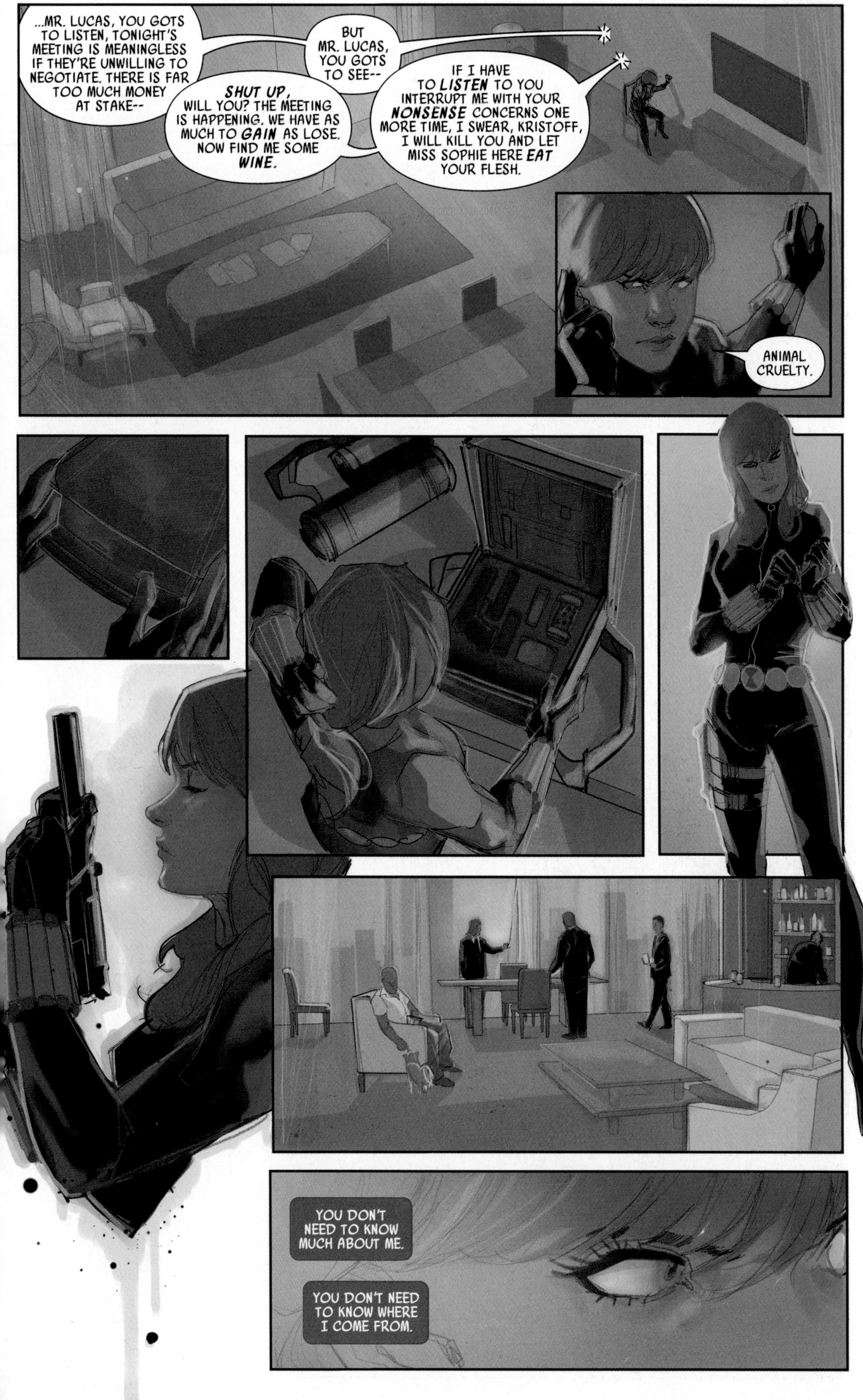

...MR. LUCAS, YOU GOTS TO LISTEN, TONIGHT'S MEETING IS MEANINGLESS IF THEY'RE UNWILLING TO NEGOTIATE. THERE IS FAR TOO MUCH MONEY AT STAKE--
SHUT UP, WILL YOU? THE MEETING IS HAPPENING. WE HAVE AS MUCH TO GAIN AS LOSE. NOW FIND ME SOME WINE.
BUT MR. LUCAS, YOU GOTS TO SEE--
IF I HAVE TO LISTEN TO YOU INTERRUPT ME WITH YOUR NONSENSE CONCERNS ONE MORE TIME, I SWEAR, KRISTOFF, I WILL KILL YOU AND LET MISS SOPHIE HERE EAT YOUR FLESH.
ANIMAL CRUELTY.
YOU DON'T NEED TO KNOW MUCH ABOUT ME.
YOU DON'T NEED TO KNOW WHERE I COME FROM.

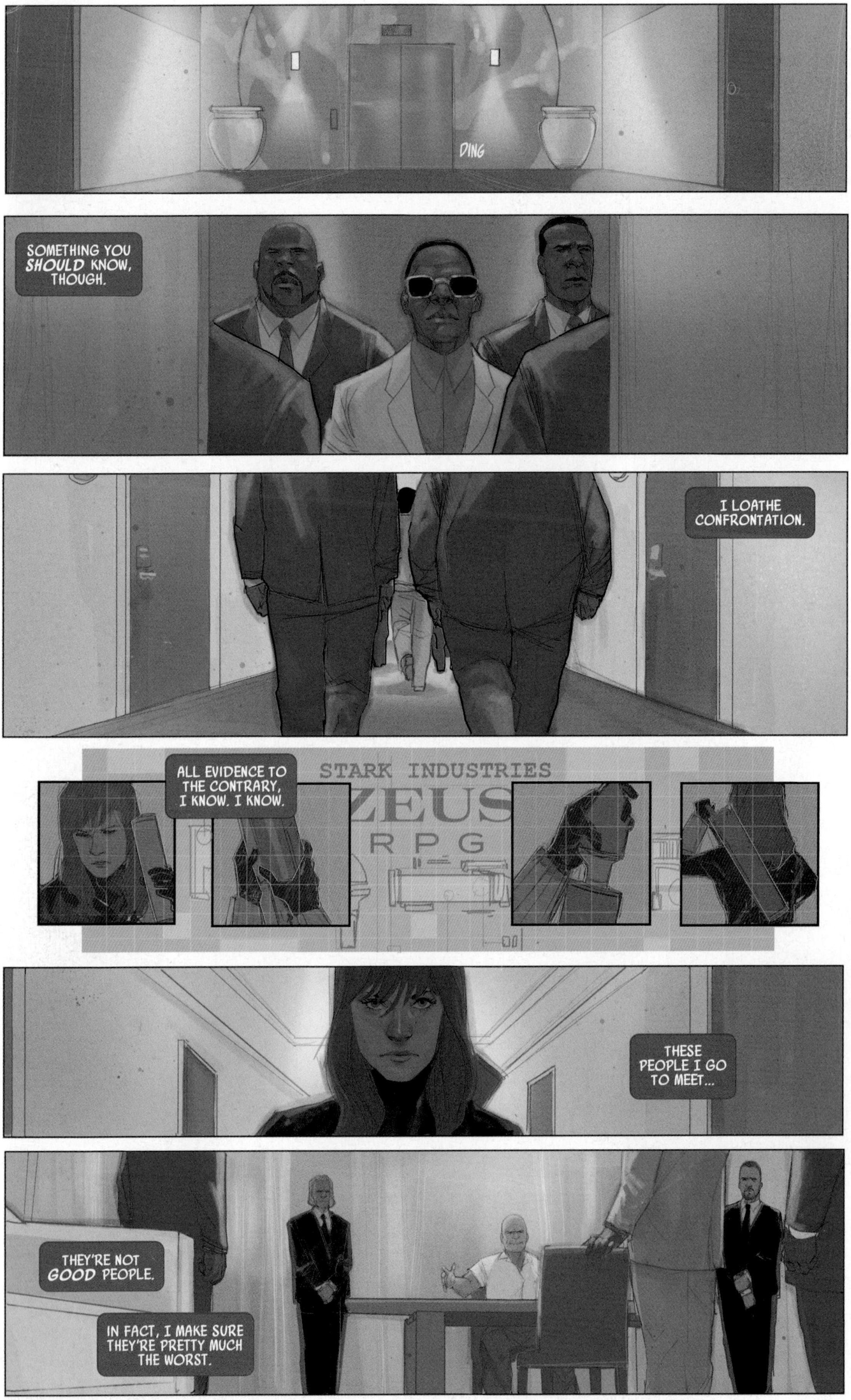

DING
SOMETHING YOU SHOULD KNOW, THOUGH.
I LOATHE CONFRONTATION.
ALL EVIDENCE TO THE CONTRARY, I KNOW. I KNOW.
STARK INDUSTRIES
ZEUS
RPG
THESE PEOPLE I GO TO MEET...
THEY'RE NOT GOOD PEOPLE.
IN FACT, I MAKE SURE THEY'RE PRETTY MUCH THE WORST.

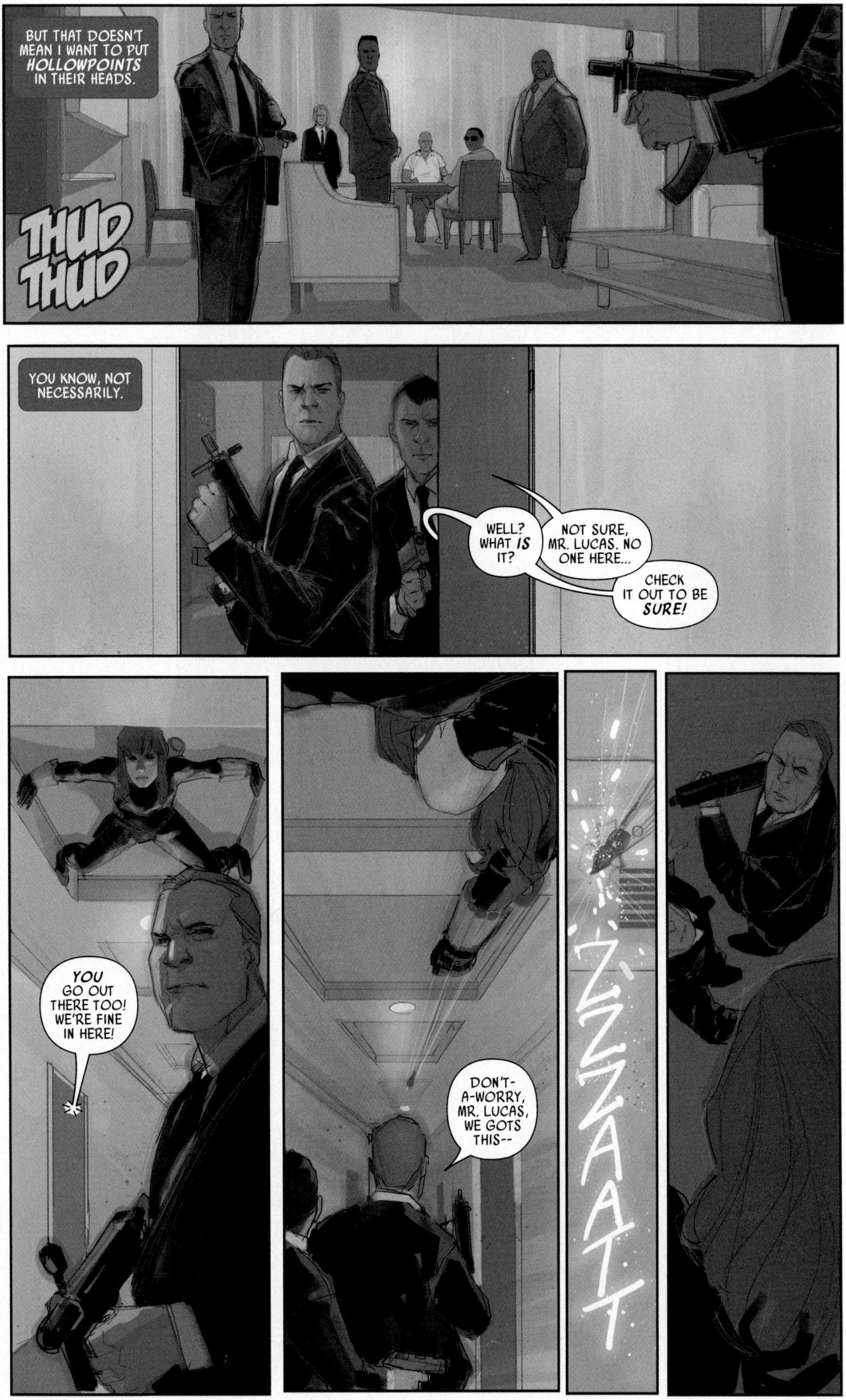
BUT THAT DOESN'T MEAN I WANT TO PUT HOLLOWPOINTS IN THEIR HEADS.
THUD THUD
YOU KNOW, NOT NECESSARILY.
WELL? WHAT IS IT?
NOT SURE, MR. LUCAS. NO ONE HERE...
CHECK IT OUT TO BE SURE!
YOU GO OUT THERE TOO! WE'RE FINE IN HERE!
DON'T-A-WORRY, MR. LUCAS, WE GOTS THIS--
ZZZAATT

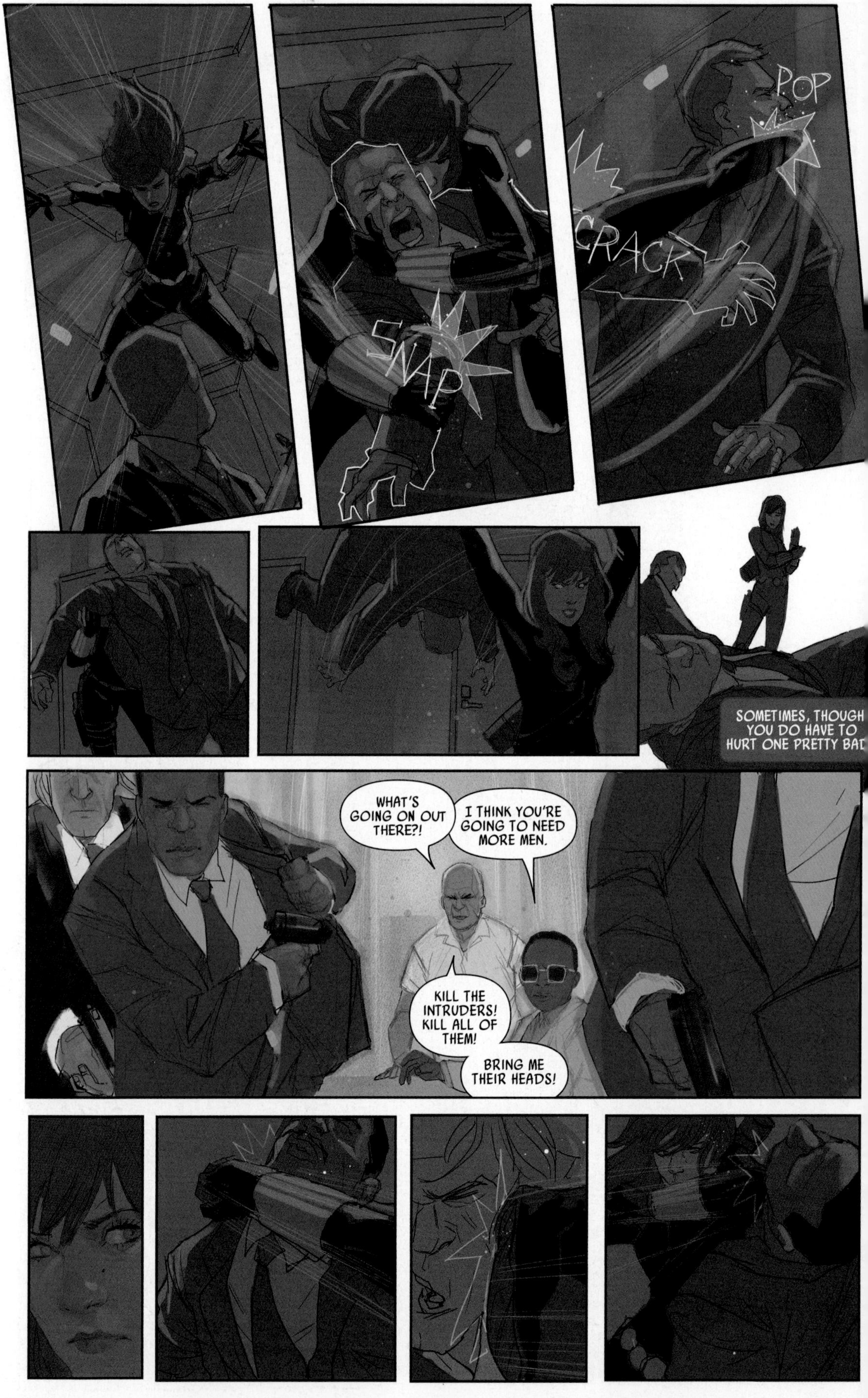
POP
CRACK
SNAP
SOMETIMES, THOUGH
YOU DO HAVE TO
HURT ONE PRETTY BAD
WHAT'S GOING ON OUT THERE?!
I THINK YOU'RE GOING TO NEED MORE MEN.
KILL THE INTRUDERS! KILL ALL OF THEM!
BRING ME THEIR HEADS!

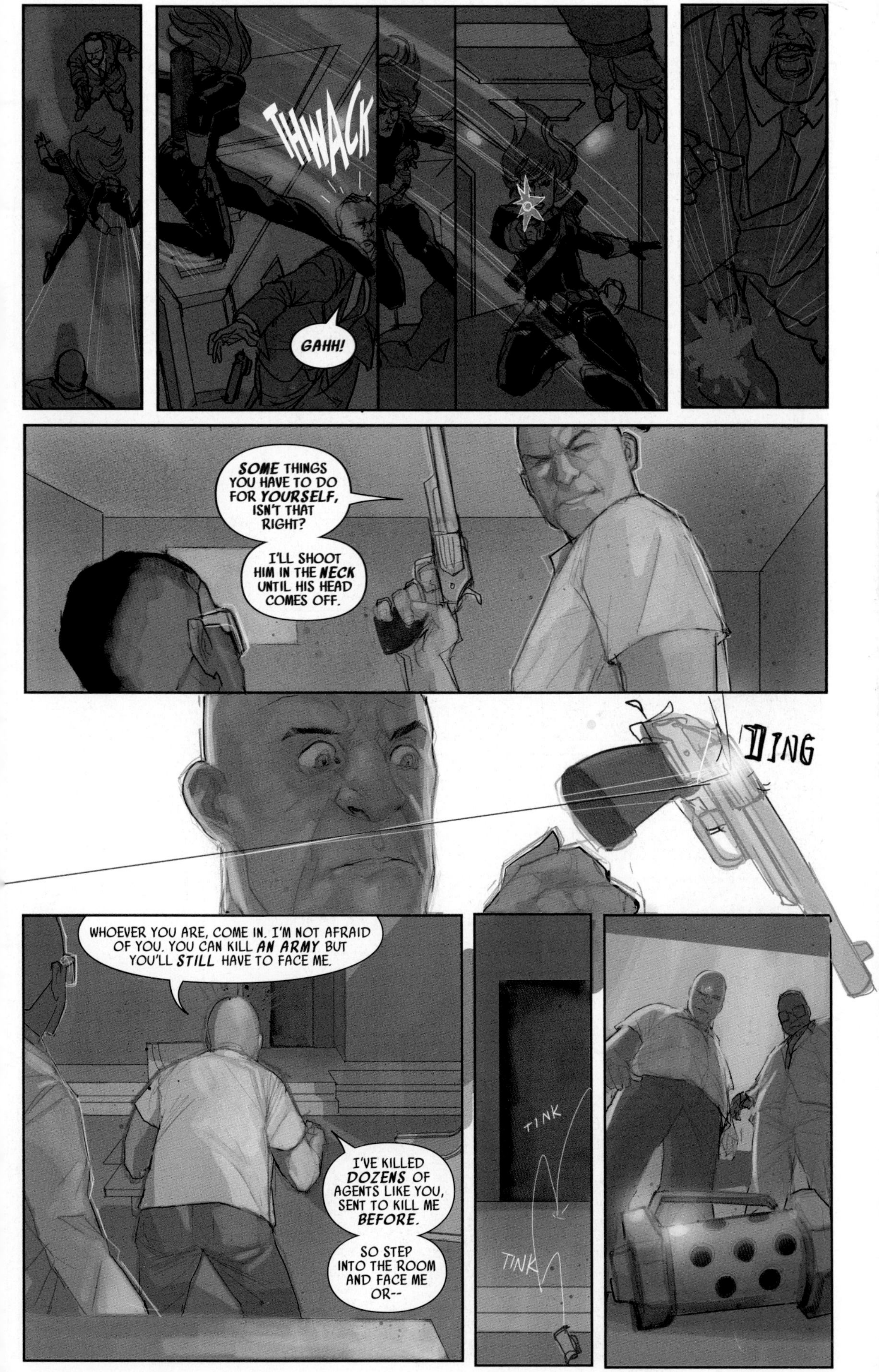
THWACK
GAHH!
SOME THINGS YOU HAVE TO DO FOR YOURSELF, ISN'T THAT RIGHT?
I'LL SHOOT HIM IN THE NECK UNTIL HIS HEAD COMES OFF.
DING
WHOEVER YOU ARE, COME IN. I'M NOT AFRAID OF YOU. YOU CAN KILL AN ARMY BUT YOU'LL STILL HAVE TO FACE ME.
I'VE KILLED DOZENS OF AGENTS LIKE YOU, SENT TO KILL ME BEFORE.
SO STEP INTO THE ROOM AND FACE ME OR--
TINK
TINK

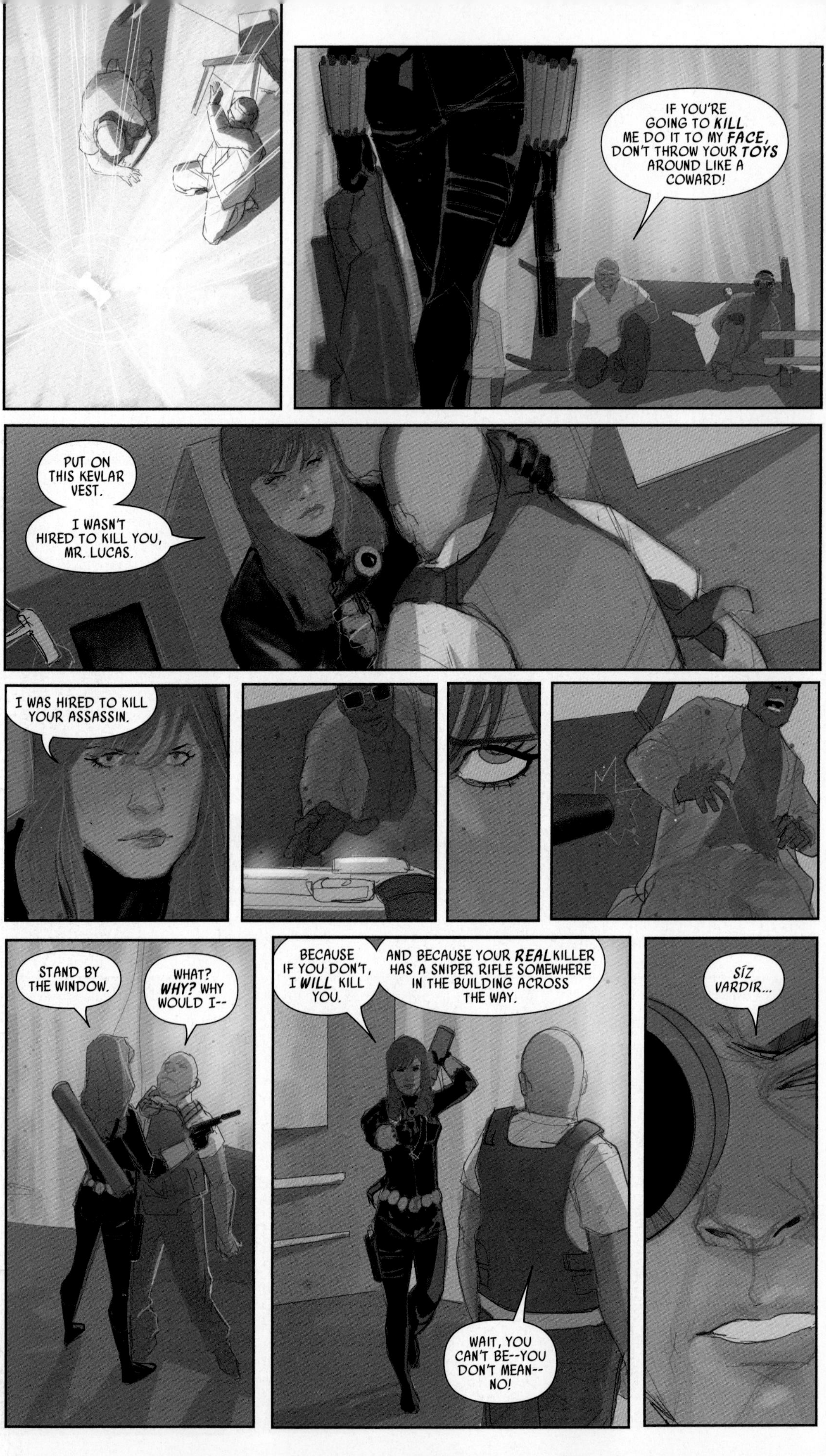
IF YOU'RE GOING TO KILL ME DO IT TO MY FACE, DON'T THROW YOUR TOYS AROUND LIKE A COWARD!
PUT ON THIS KEVLAR VEST.
I WASN'T HIRED TO KILL YOU, MR. LUCAS.
I WAS HIRED TO KILL YOUR ASSASSIN.
STAND BY THE WINDOW.
WHAT? WHY? WHY WOULD I--
BECAUSE IF YOU DON'T, I WILL KILL YOU.
AND BECAUSE YOUR REAL KILLER HAS A SNIPER RIFLE SOMEWHERE IN THE BUILDING ACROSS THE WAY.
WAIT, YOU CAN'T BE--YOU DON'T MEAN-- NO!
SÍZ VARDIR...

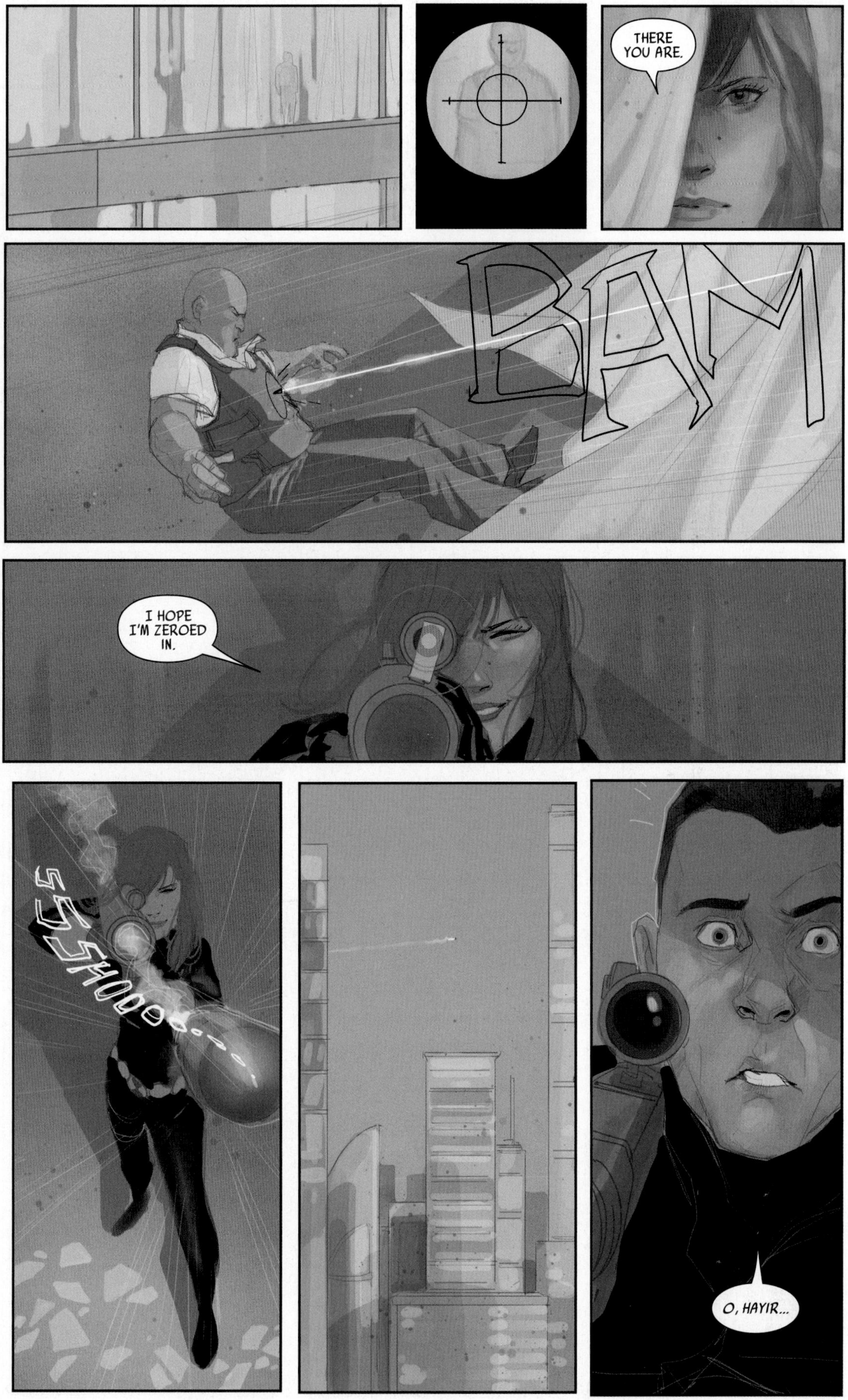
THERE YOU ARE.
BAM
I HOPE I'M ZEROED IN.
SSSHOOO------
O, HAYIR...

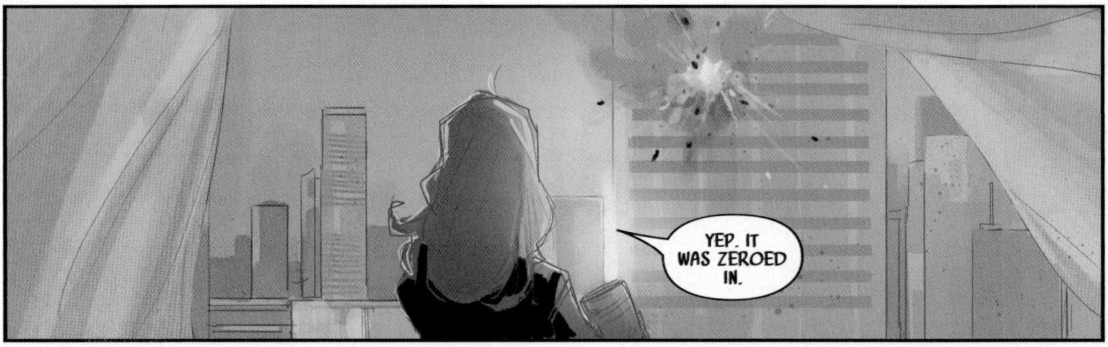
YEP. IT WAS ZEROED IN.

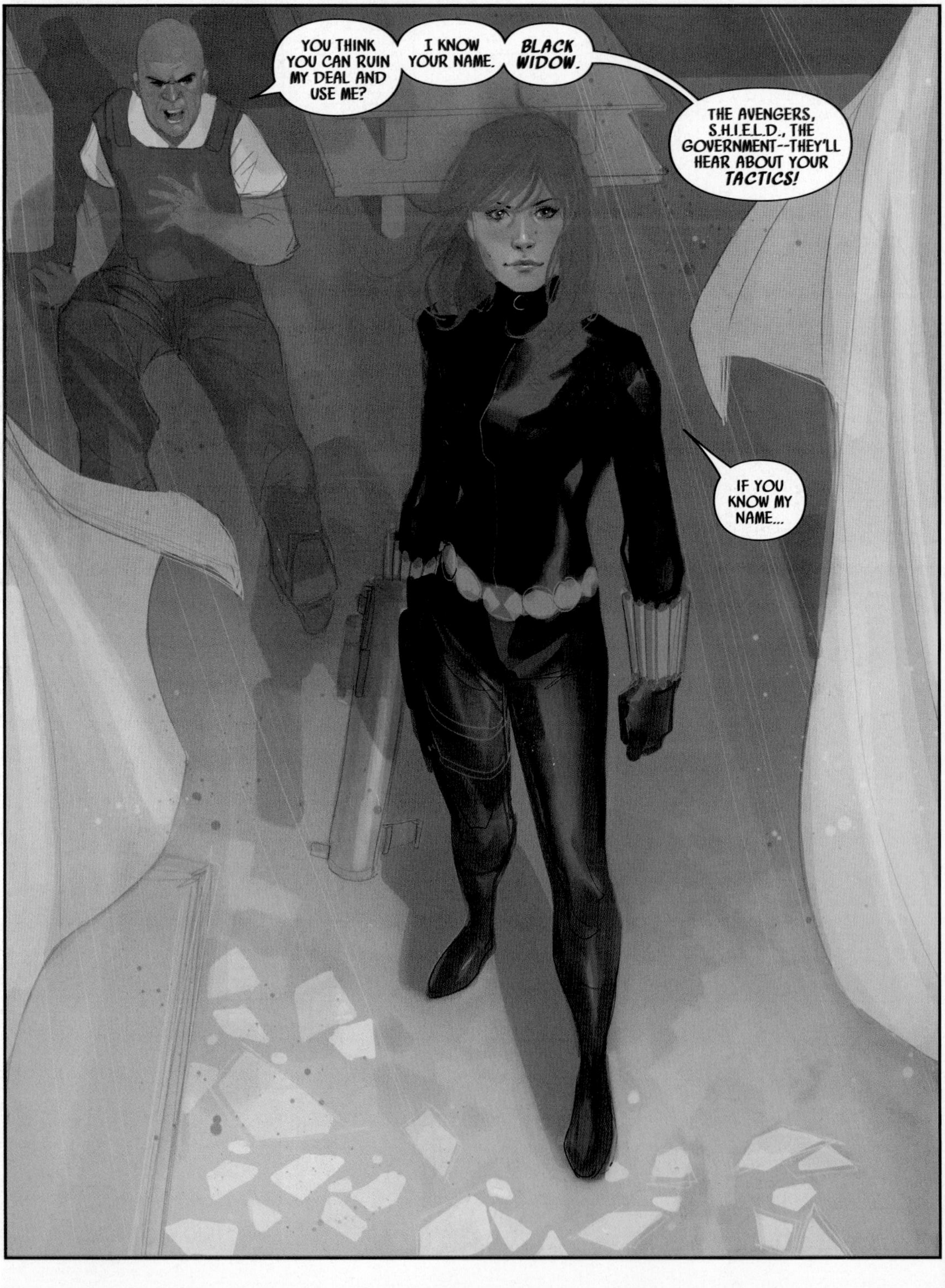
YOU THINK YOU CAN RUIN MY DEAL AND USE ME?
I KNOW YOUR NAME.
BLACK WIDOW.
THE AVENGERS, S.H.I.E.L.D., THE GOVERNMENT--THEY'LL HEAR ABOUT YOUR TACTICS!
IF YOU KNOW MY NAME...

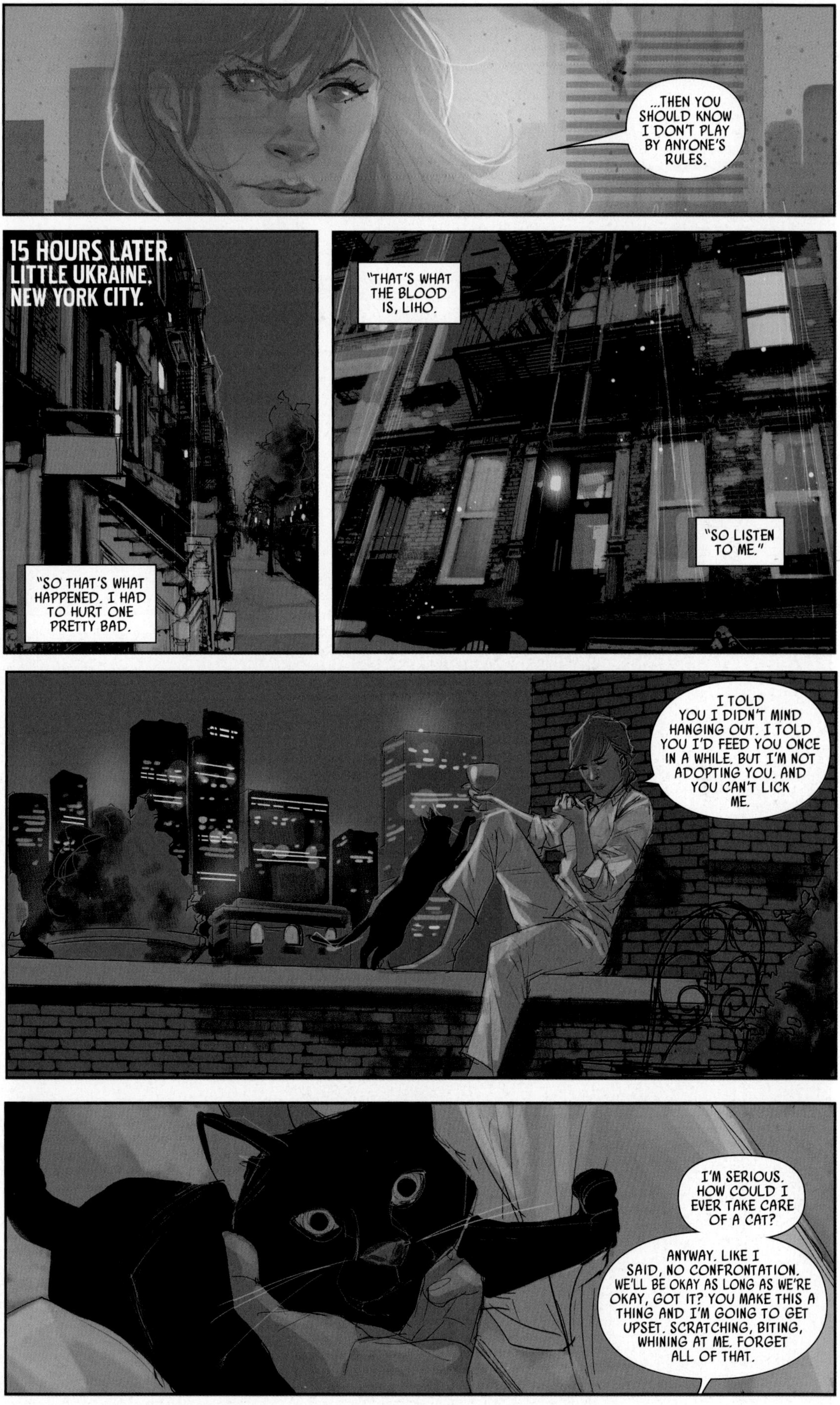
...THEN YOU SHOULD KNOW I DON'T PLAY BY ANYONE'S RULES.
15 HOURS LATER. LITTLE UKRAINE, NEW YORK CITY.
"SO THAT'S WHAT HAPPENED. I HAD TO HURT ONE PRETTY BAD.
"THAT'S WHAT THE BLOOD IS, LIHO.
"SO LISTEN TO ME."
I TOLD YOU I DIDN'T MIND HANGING OUT. I TOLD YOU I'D FEED YOU ONCE IN A WHILE. BUT I'M NOT ADOPTING YOU. AND YOU CAN'T LICK ME.
I'M SERIOUS. HOW COULD I EVER TAKE CARE OF A CAT?
ANYWAY. LIKE I SAID, NO CONFRONTATION. WE'LL BE OKAY AS LONG AS WE'RE OKAY, GOT IT? YOU MAKE THIS A THING AND I'M GOING TO GET UPSET. SCRATCHING, BITING, WHINING AT ME. FORGET ALL OF THAT.

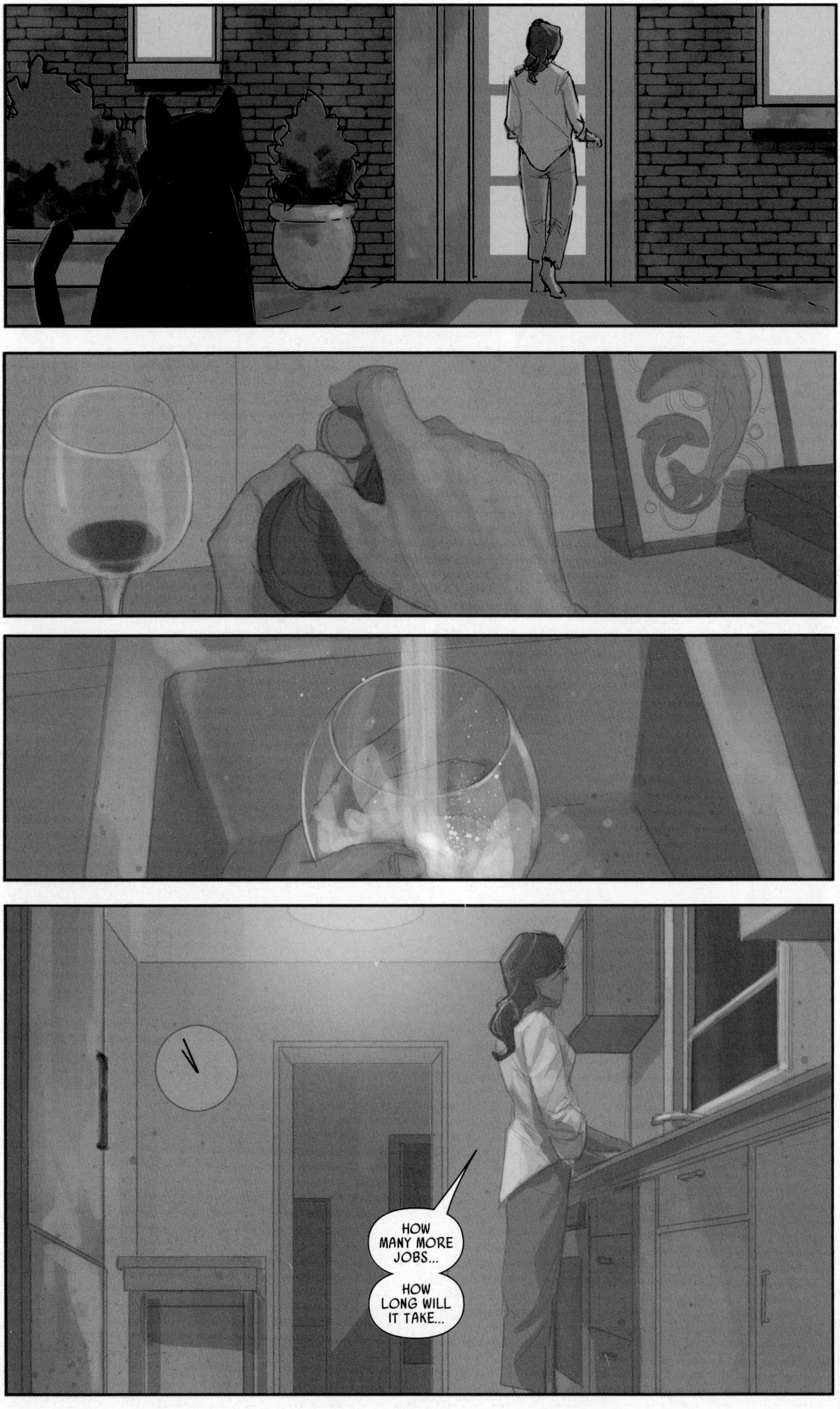
HOW MANY MORE JOBS...
HOW LONG WILL IT TAKE...

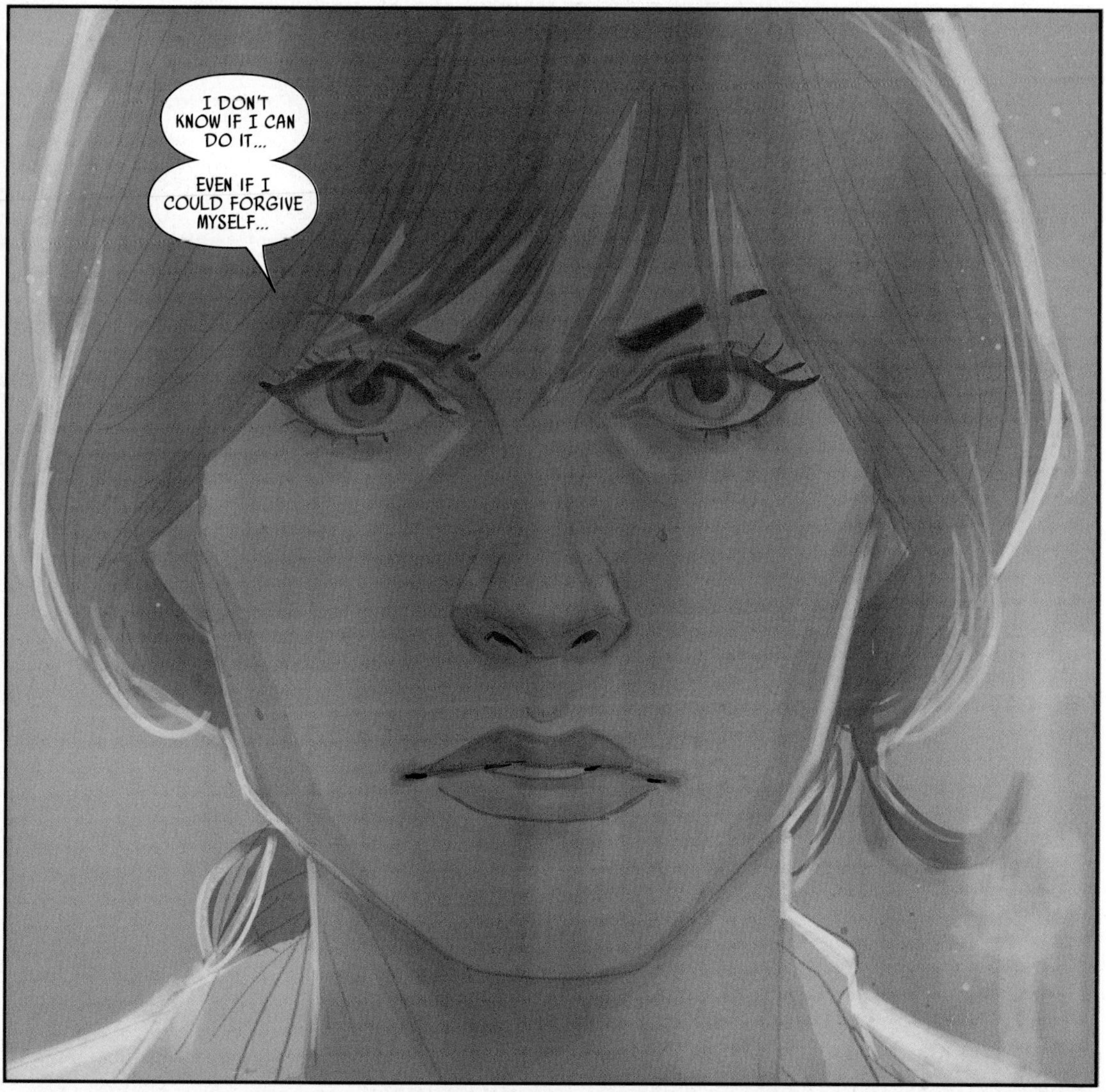
I DON'T KNOW IF I CAN DO IT...
EVEN IF I COULD FORGIVE MYSELF...

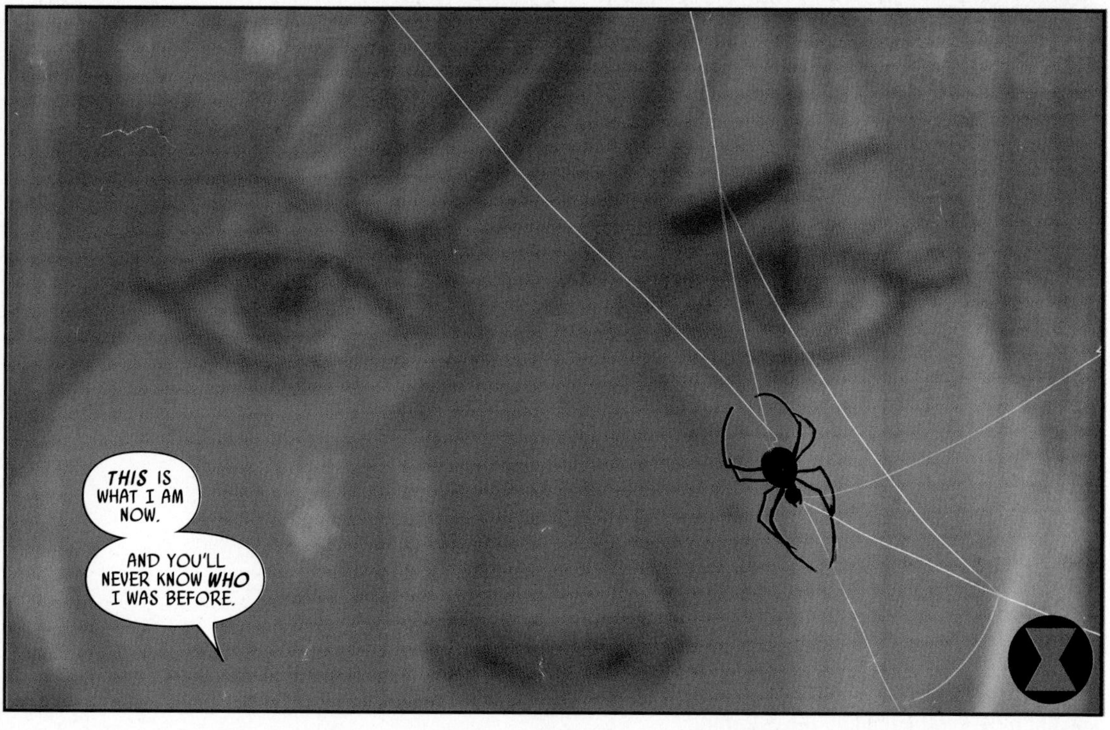
THIS IS WHAT I AM NOW.
AND YOU'LL NEVER KNOW WHO I WAS BEFORE.

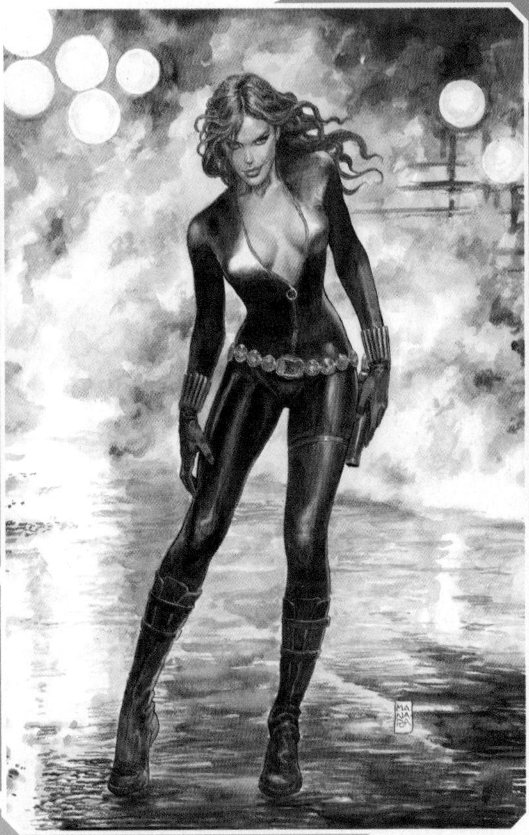

BLACK WIDOW #1
Variant by Milo Manara

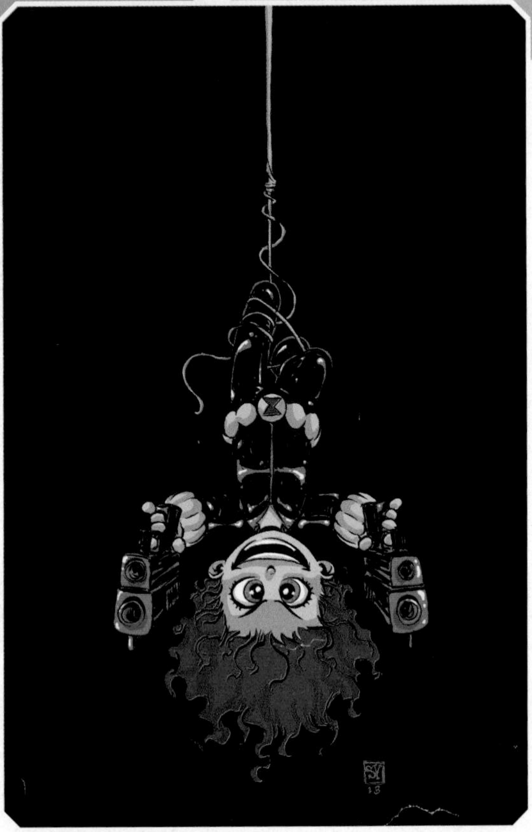

BLACK WIDOW #1
Variant by Skottie Young

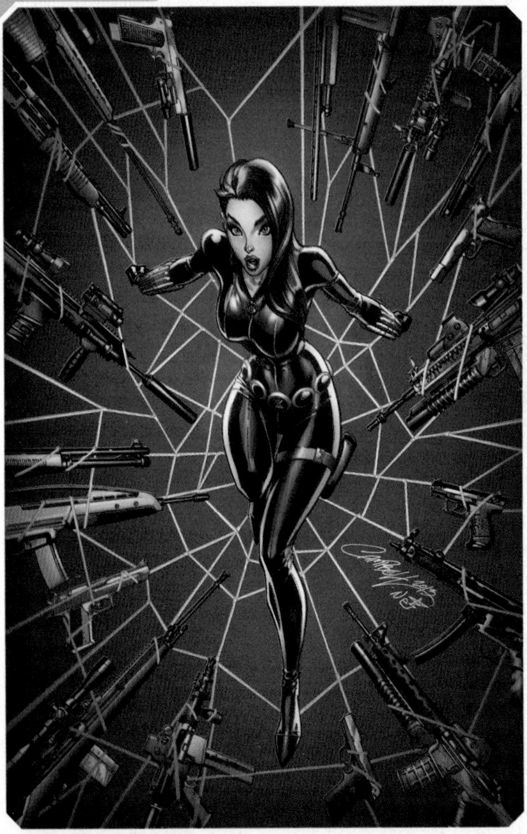

BLACK WIDOW #1
Variant by J. Scott Campbell & Nei Ruffino

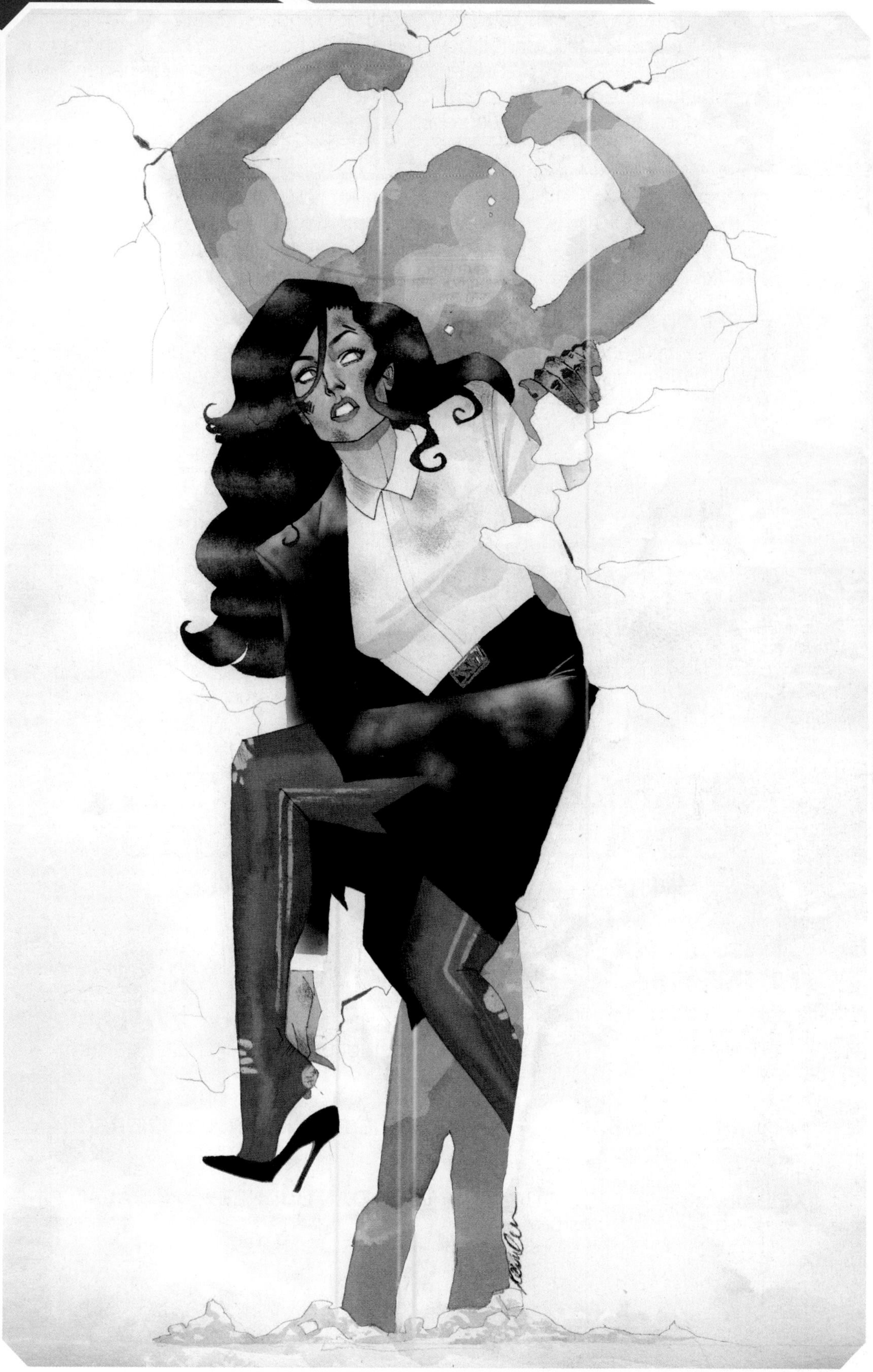

SHE-HULK #1

Jennifer Walters was a shy attorney, good at her job and quiet in her life, when she found herself gunned down by a crime boss. With her life on the line, only one person was close enough to donate the blood she needed for a vital transfusion: her cousin, Dr. Bruce Banner, who was secretly the gamma-irradiated monster known as the Incredible Hulk.

Bruce's blood saved Jennifer's life…but gave her the power to turn into a super strong, green skinned bombshell. Unlike her cousin, Jennifer Walters has managed to maintain her sanity and control over her superhuman form and even continued her career as an attorney – while also doubling as a member of the Avengers, the Fantastic Four, and a super hero known the world over.

Wherever justice is threatened, you can bet on the gamma-powered gal with the brain and brawn to right some wrong, the Sensational…

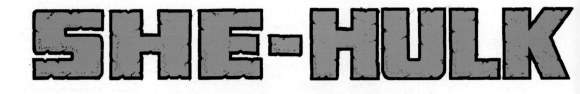

SHE-HULK

CHARLES SOULE
writer

JAVIER PULIDO
artist

MUNTSA VICENTE
color artist

VC's CLAYTON COWLES
lettering & production

KEVIN WADA
cover artist

FRANKIE JOHNSON
assistant editor

JEANINE SCHAEFER & TOM BRENNAN
editors

AXEL ALONSO
editor in chief

JOE QUESADA
chief creative officer

DAN BUCKLEY
publisher

ALAN FINE
exec. producer

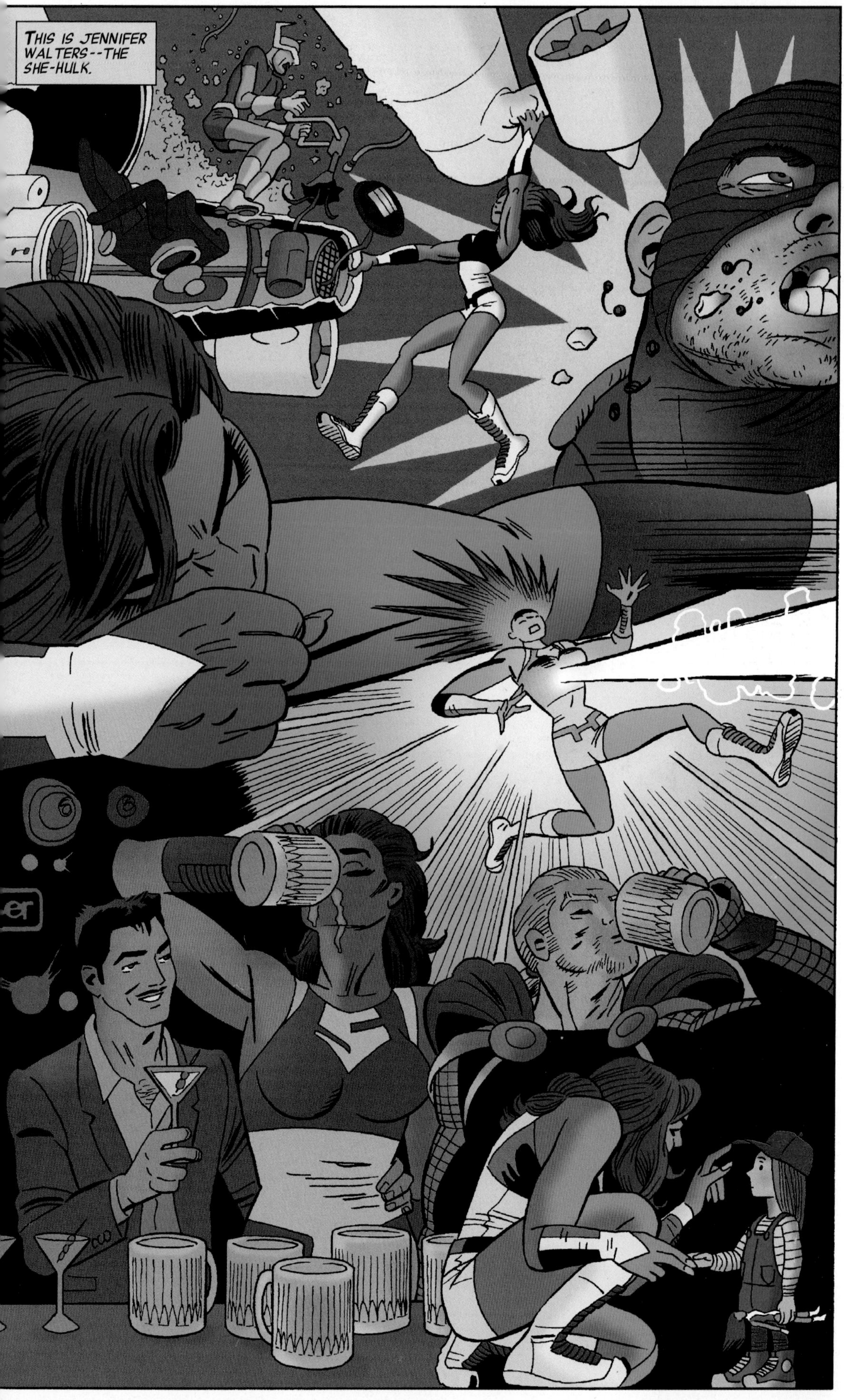
THIS IS JENNIFER WALTERS--THE SHE-HULK.

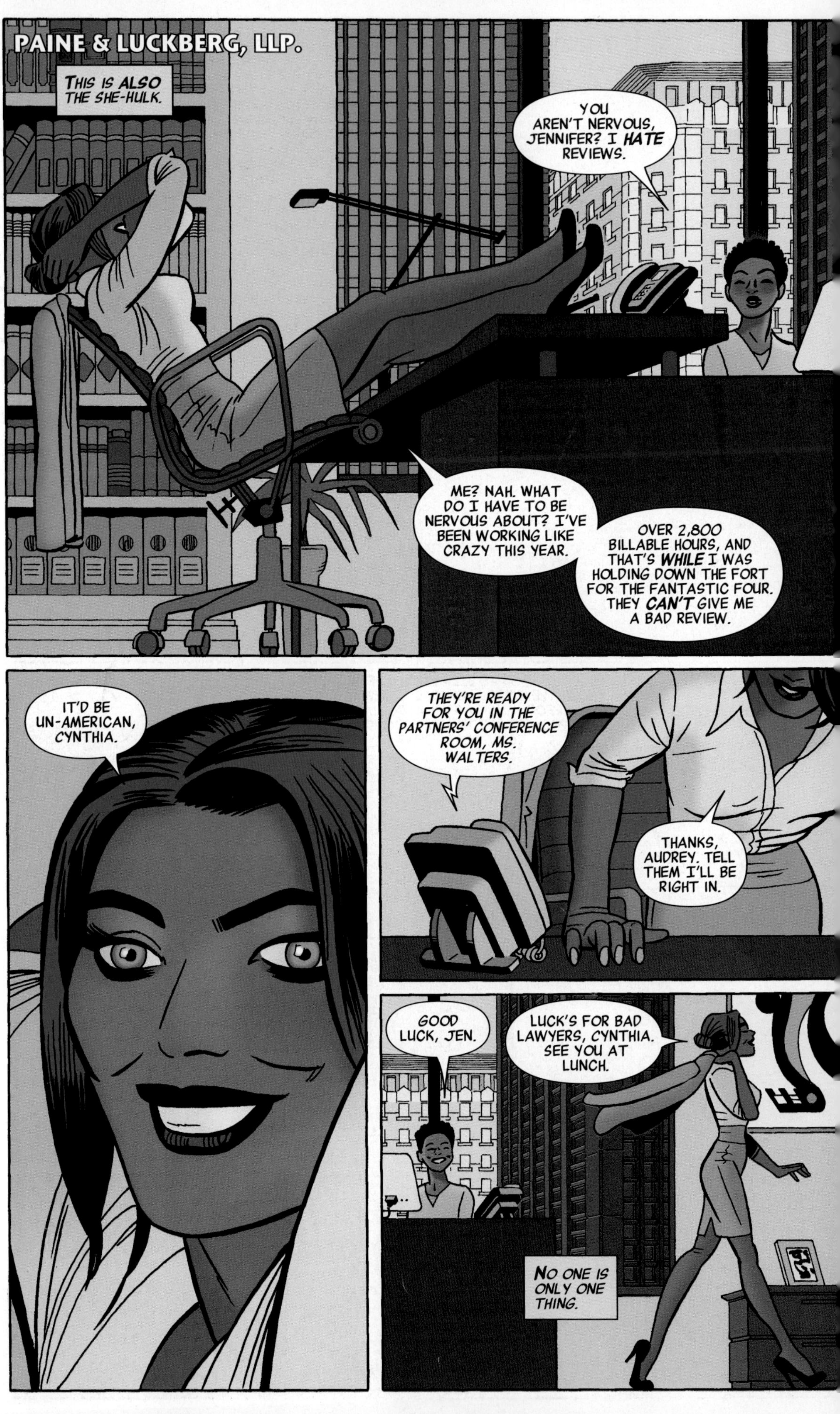
PAINE & LUCKBERG, LLP.
THIS IS ALSO THE SHE-HULK.
YOU AREN'T NERVOUS, JENNIFER? I HATE REVIEWS.
ME? NAH. WHAT DO I HAVE TO BE NERVOUS ABOUT? I'VE BEEN WORKING LIKE CRAZY THIS YEAR.
OVER 2,800 BILLABLE HOURS, AND THAT'S WHILE I WAS HOLDING DOWN THE FORT FOR THE FANTASTIC FOUR. THEY CAN'T GIVE ME A BAD REVIEW.
IT'D BE UN-AMERICAN, CYNTHIA.
THEY'RE READY FOR YOU IN THE PARTNERS' CONFERENCE ROOM, MS. WALTERS.
THANKS, AUDREY. TELL THEM I'LL BE RIGHT IN.
GOOD LUCK, JEN.
LUCK'S FOR BAD LAWYERS, CYNTHIA. SEE YOU AT LUNCH.
NO ONE IS ONLY ONE THING.

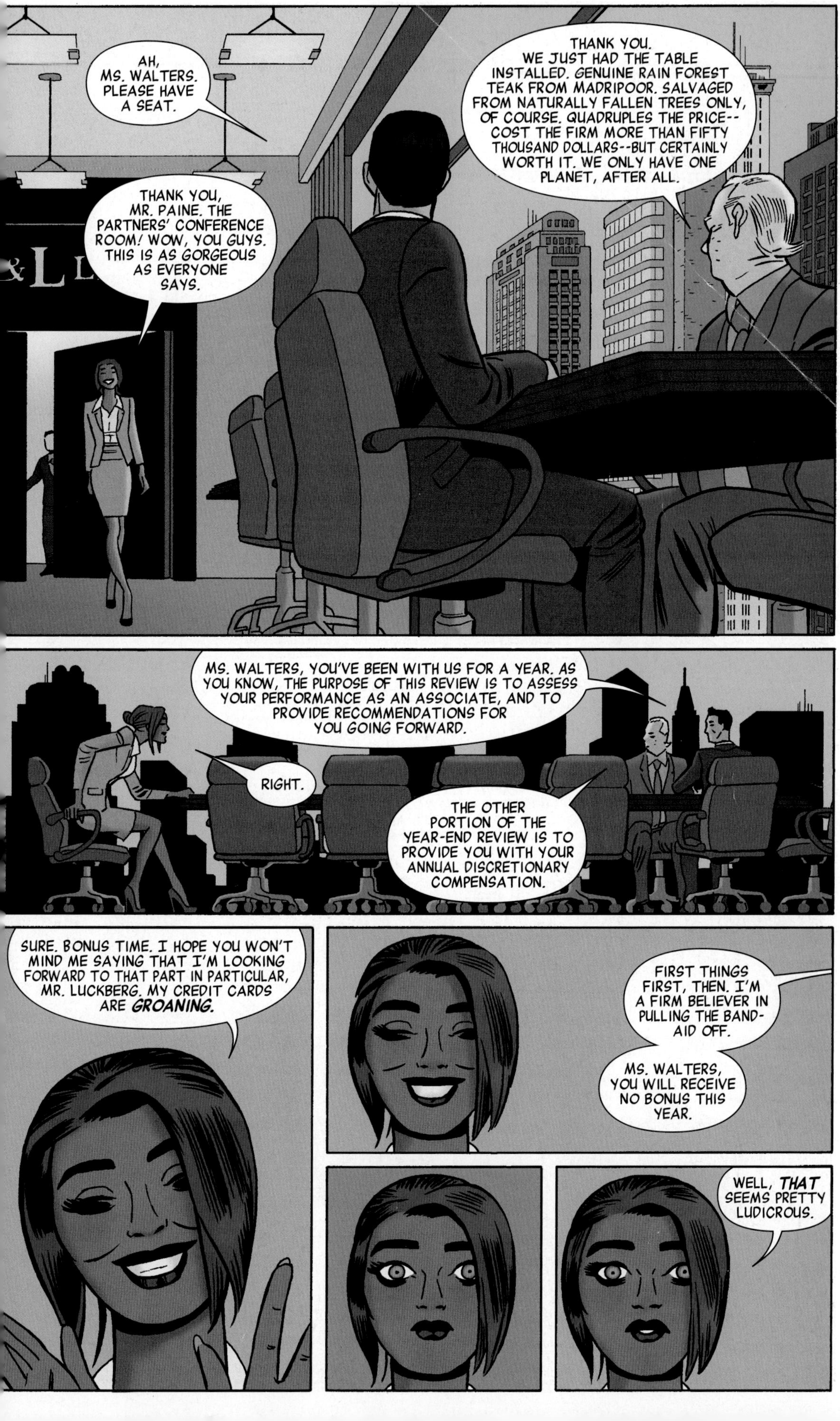
AH, MS. WALTERS. PLEASE HAVE A SEAT.
THANK YOU. WE JUST HAD THE TABLE INSTALLED. GENUINE RAIN FOREST TEAK FROM MADRIPOOR. SALVAGED FROM NATURALLY FALLEN TREES ONLY, OF COURSE. QUADRUPLES THE PRICE--COST THE FIRM MORE THAN FIFTY THOUSAND DOLLARS--BUT CERTAINLY WORTH IT. WE ONLY HAVE ONE PLANET, AFTER ALL.
THANK YOU, MR. PAINE. THE PARTNERS' CONFERENCE ROOM! WOW, YOU GUYS. THIS IS AS GORGEOUS AS EVERYONE SAYS.
MS. WALTERS, YOU'VE BEEN WITH US FOR A YEAR. AS YOU KNOW, THE PURPOSE OF THIS REVIEW IS TO ASSESS YOUR PERFORMANCE AS AN ASSOCIATE, AND TO PROVIDE RECOMMENDATIONS FOR YOU GOING FORWARD.
RIGHT.
THE OTHER PORTION OF THE YEAR-END REVIEW IS TO PROVIDE YOU WITH YOUR ANNUAL DISCRETIONARY COMPENSATION.
SURE. BONUS TIME. I HOPE YOU WON'T MIND ME SAYING THAT I'M LOOKING FORWARD TO THAT PART IN PARTICULAR, MR. LUCKBERG. MY CREDIT CARDS ARE ***GROANING.***
FIRST THINGS FIRST, THEN. I'M A FIRM BELIEVER IN PULLING THE BAND-AID OFF.
MS. WALTERS, YOU WILL RECEIVE NO BONUS THIS YEAR.
WELL, ***THAT*** SEEMS PRETTY LUDICROUS.

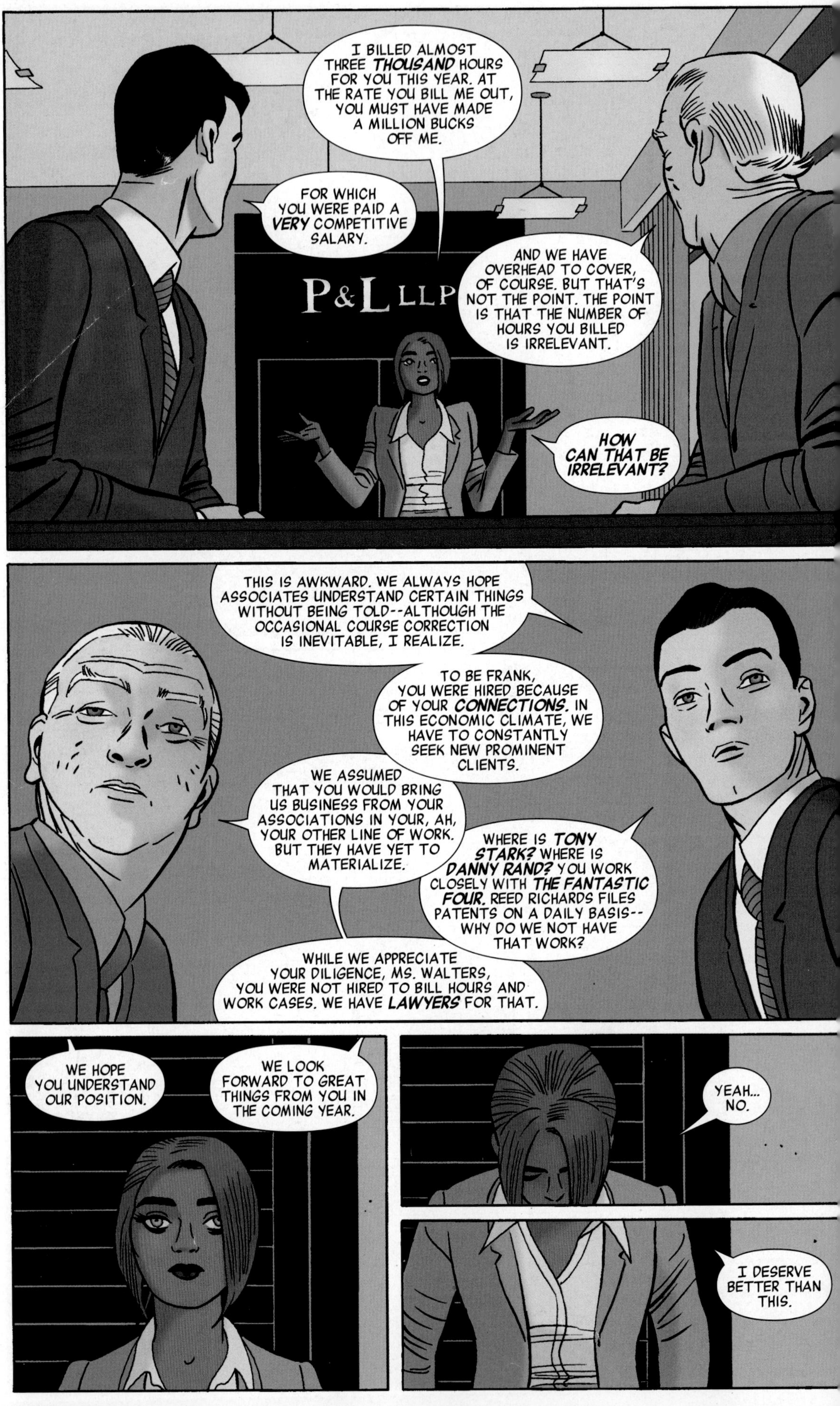
I BILLED ALMOST THREE THOUSAND HOURS FOR YOU THIS YEAR. AT THE RATE YOU BILL ME OUT, YOU MUST HAVE MADE A MILLION BUCKS OFF ME.
FOR WHICH YOU WERE PAID A VERY COMPETITIVE SALARY.
P&L LLP
AND WE HAVE OVERHEAD TO COVER, OF COURSE. BUT THAT'S NOT THE POINT. THE POINT IS THAT THE NUMBER OF HOURS YOU BILLED IS IRRELEVANT.
HOW CAN THAT BE IRRELEVANT?
THIS IS AWKWARD. WE ALWAYS HOPE ASSOCIATES UNDERSTAND CERTAIN THINGS WITHOUT BEING TOLD--ALTHOUGH THE OCCASIONAL COURSE CORRECTION IS INEVITABLE, I REALIZE.
TO BE FRANK, YOU WERE HIRED BECAUSE OF YOUR CONNECTIONS. IN THIS ECONOMIC CLIMATE, WE HAVE TO CONSTANTLY SEEK NEW PROMINENT CLIENTS.
WE ASSUMED THAT YOU WOULD BRING US BUSINESS FROM YOUR ASSOCIATIONS IN YOUR, AH, YOUR OTHER LINE OF WORK. BUT THEY HAVE YET TO MATERIALIZE.
WHERE IS TONY STARK? WHERE IS DANNY RAND? YOU WORK CLOSELY WITH THE FANTASTIC FOUR. REED RICHARDS FILES PATENTS ON A DAILY BASIS-- WHY DO WE NOT HAVE THAT WORK?
WHILE WE APPRECIATE YOUR DILIGENCE, MS. WALTERS, YOU WERE NOT HIRED TO BILL HOURS AND WORK CASES. WE HAVE LAWYERS FOR THAT.
WE HOPE YOU UNDERSTAND OUR POSITION.
WE LOOK FORWARD TO GREAT THINGS FROM YOU IN THE COMING YEAR.
YEAH... NO.
I DESERVE BETTER THAN THIS.

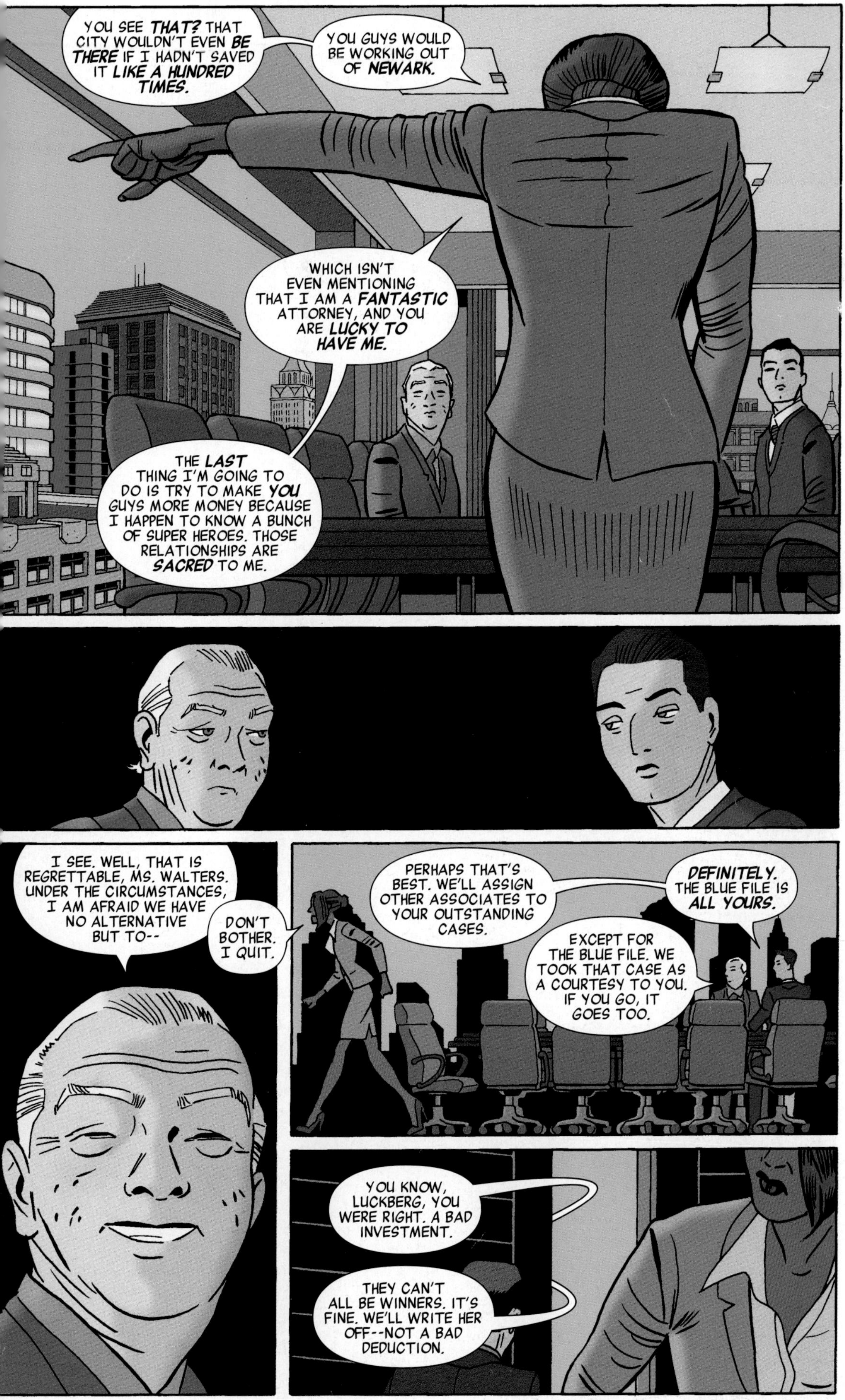
YOU SEE THAT? THAT CITY WOULDN'T EVEN BE THERE IF I HADN'T SAVED IT LIKE A HUNDRED TIMES.
YOU GUYS WOULD BE WORKING OUT OF NEWARK.
WHICH ISN'T EVEN MENTIONING THAT I AM A FANTASTIC ATTORNEY, AND YOU ARE LUCKY TO HAVE ME.
THE LAST THING I'M GOING TO DO IS TRY TO MAKE YOU GUYS MORE MONEY BECAUSE I HAPPEN TO KNOW A BUNCH OF SUPER HEROES. THOSE RELATIONSHIPS ARE SACRED TO ME.
I SEE. WELL, THAT IS REGRETTABLE, MS. WALTERS. UNDER THE CIRCUMSTANCES, I AM AFRAID WE HAVE NO ALTERNATIVE BUT TO--
DON'T BOTHER. I QUIT.
PERHAPS THAT'S BEST. WE'LL ASSIGN OTHER ASSOCIATES TO YOUR OUTSTANDING CASES.
EXCEPT FOR THE BLUE FILE. WE TOOK THAT CASE AS A COURTESY TO YOU. IF YOU GO, IT GOES TOO.
DEFINITELY. THE BLUE FILE IS ALL YOURS.
YOU KNOW, LUCKBERG, YOU WERE RIGHT. A BAD INVESTMENT.
THEY CAN'T ALL BE WINNERS. IT'S FINE. WE'LL WRITE HER OFF--NOT A BAD DEDUCTION.

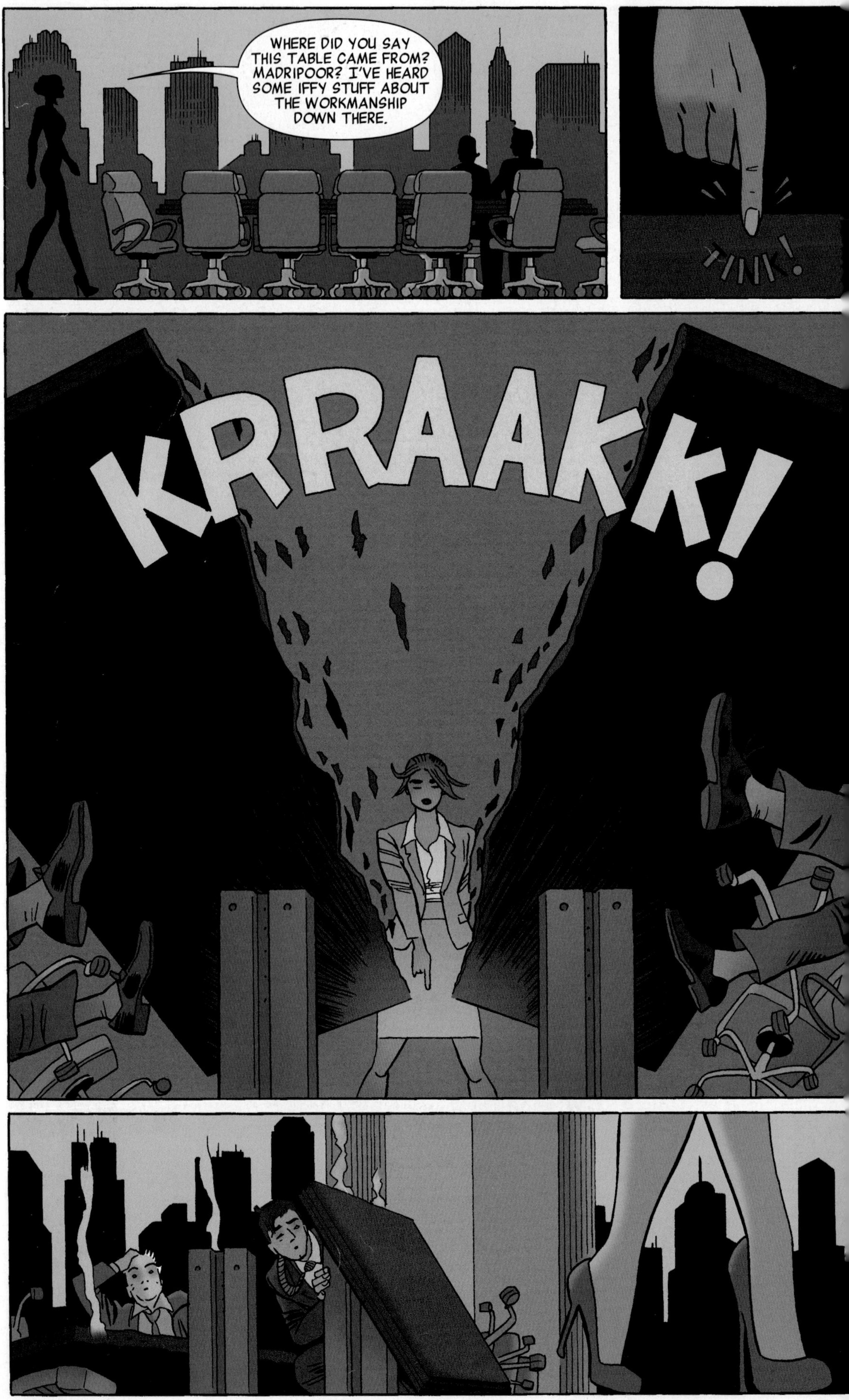
WHERE DID YOU SAY THIS TABLE CAME FROM? MADRIPOOR? I'VE HEARD SOME IFFY STUFF ABOUT THE WORKMANSHIP DOWN THERE.
TINK!
KRRAAKK!

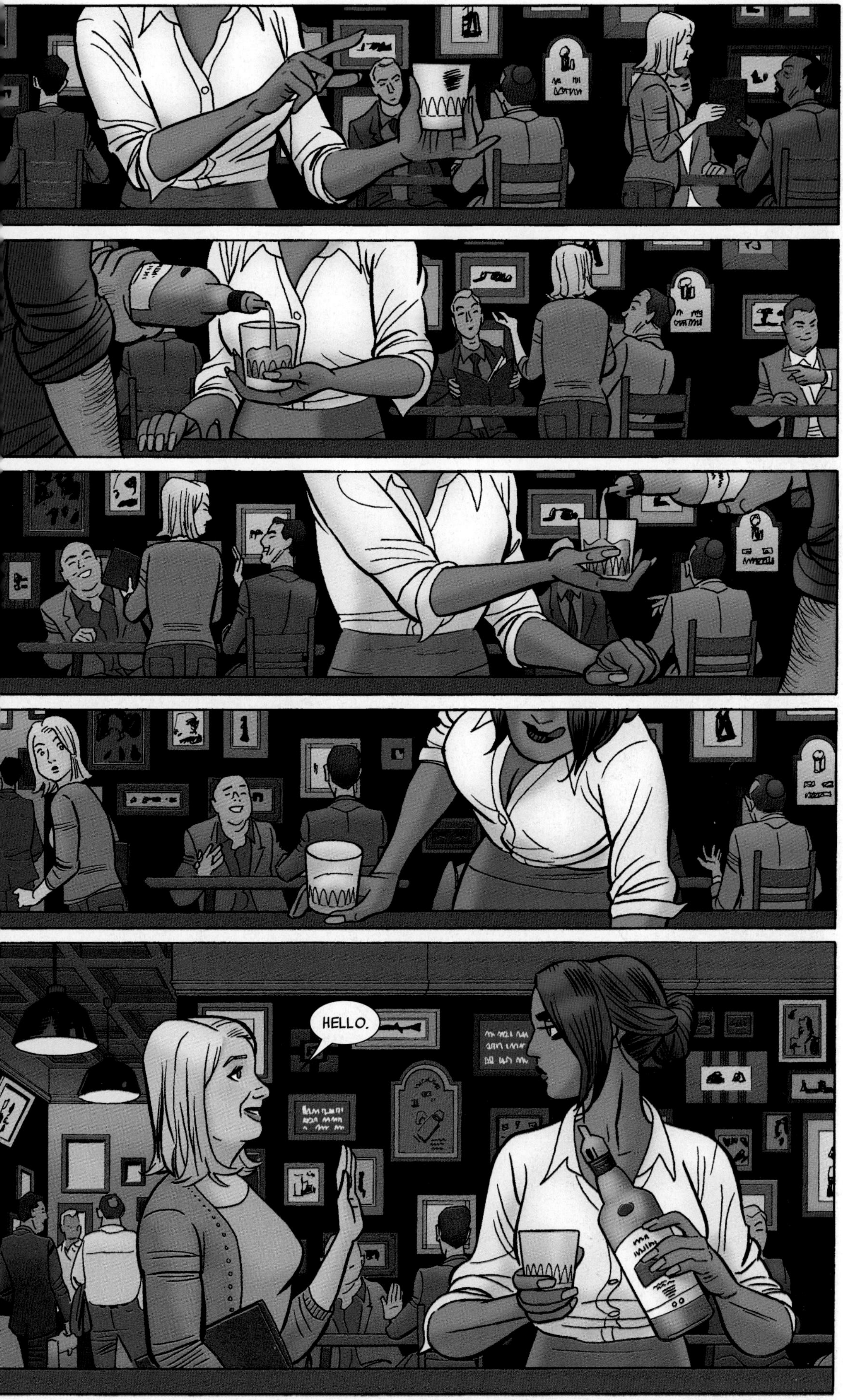
HELLO.

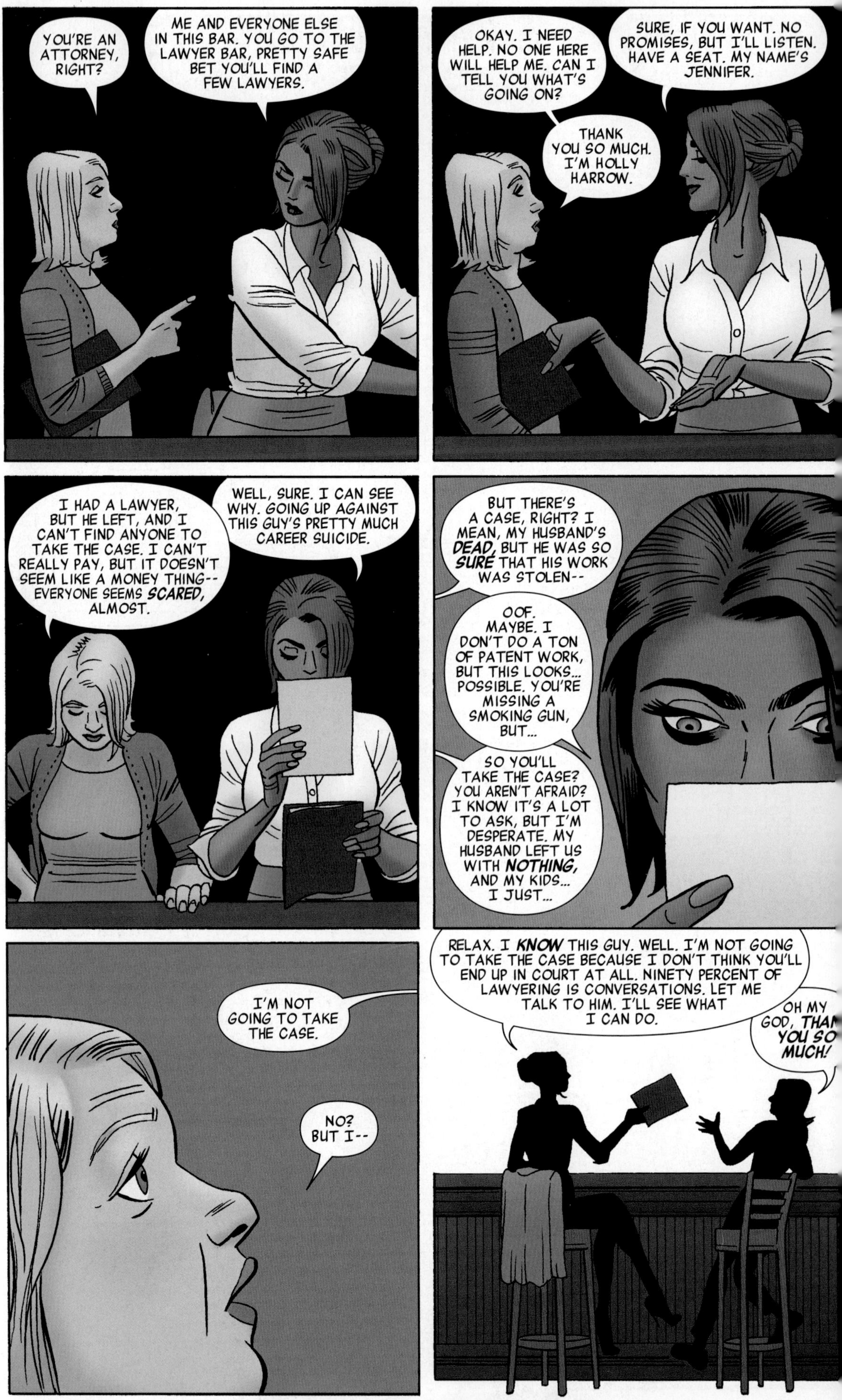
YOU'RE AN ATTORNEY, RIGHT?
ME AND EVERYONE ELSE IN THIS BAR. YOU GO TO THE LAWYER BAR, PRETTY SAFE BET YOU'LL FIND A FEW LAWYERS.
OKAY. I NEED HELP. NO ONE HERE WILL HELP ME. CAN I TELL YOU WHAT'S GOING ON?
SURE, IF YOU WANT. NO PROMISES, BUT I'LL LISTEN. HAVE A SEAT. MY NAME'S JENNIFER.
THANK YOU SO MUCH. I'M HOLLY HARROW.
I HAD A LAWYER, BUT HE LEFT, AND I CAN'T FIND ANYONE TO TAKE THE CASE. I CAN'T REALLY PAY, BUT IT DOESN'T SEEM LIKE A MONEY THING-- EVERYONE SEEMS SCARED, ALMOST.
WELL, SURE. I CAN SEE WHY. GOING UP AGAINST THIS GUY'S PRETTY MUCH CAREER SUICIDE.
BUT THERE'S A CASE, RIGHT? I MEAN, MY HUSBAND'S DEAD, BUT HE WAS SO SURE THAT HIS WORK WAS STOLEN--
OOF. MAYBE. I DON'T DO A TON OF PATENT WORK, BUT THIS LOOKS... POSSIBLE. YOU'RE MISSING A SMOKING GUN, BUT...
SO YOU'LL TAKE THE CASE? YOU AREN'T AFRAID? I KNOW IT'S A LOT TO ASK, BUT I'M DESPERATE. MY HUSBAND LEFT US WITH NOTHING, AND MY KIDS... I JUST...
I'M NOT GOING TO TAKE THE CASE.
NO? BUT I--
RELAX. I KNOW THIS GUY. WELL. I'M NOT GOING TO TAKE THE CASE BECAUSE I DON'T THINK YOU'LL END UP IN COURT AT ALL. NINETY PERCENT OF LAWYERING IS CONVERSATIONS. LET ME TALK TO HIM. I'LL SEE WHAT I CAN DO.
OH MY GOD, THA YOU SO MUCH!

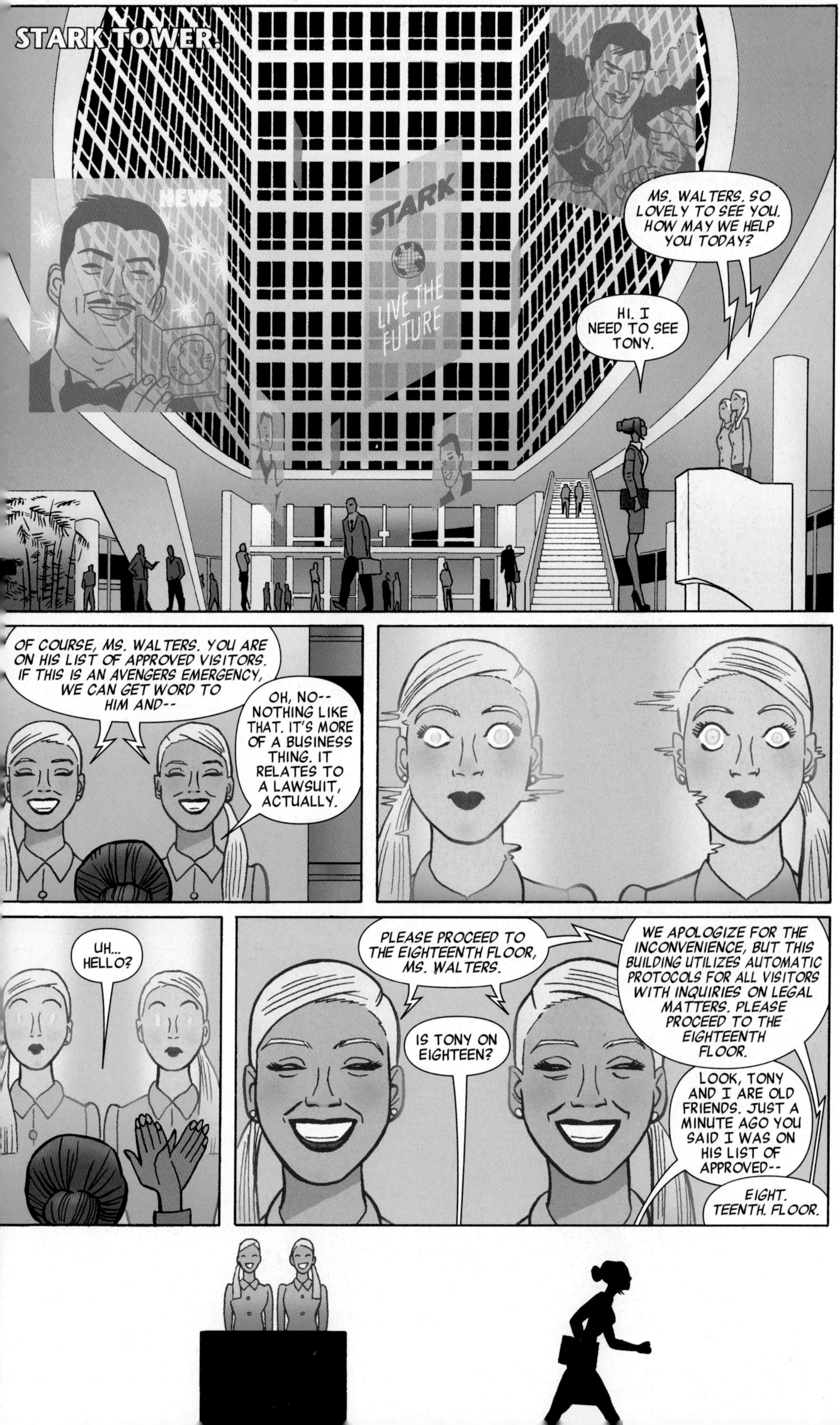
STARK TOWER.
NEWS
STARK
LIVE THE FUTURE
MS. WALTERS. SO LOVELY TO SEE YOU. HOW MAY WE HELP YOU TODAY?
HI. I NEED TO SEE TONY.
OF COURSE, MS. WALTERS. YOU ARE ON HIS LIST OF APPROVED VISITORS. IF THIS IS AN AVENGERS EMERGENCY, WE CAN GET WORD TO HIM AND--
OH, NO-- NOTHING LIKE THAT. IT'S MORE OF A BUSINESS THING. IT RELATES TO A LAWSUIT, ACTUALLY.
UH... HELLO?
PLEASE PROCEED TO THE EIGHTEENTH FLOOR, MS. WALTERS.
WE APOLOGIZE FOR THE INCONVENIENCE, BUT THIS BUILDING UTILIZES AUTOMATIC PROTOCOLS FOR ALL VISITORS WITH INQUIRIES ON LEGAL MATTERS. PLEASE PROCEED TO THE EIGHTEENTH FLOOR.
IS TONY ON EIGHTEEN?
LOOK, TONY AND I ARE OLD FRIENDS. JUST A MINUTE AGO YOU SAID I WAS ON HIS LIST OF APPROVED--
EIGHT. TEENTH. FLOOR.

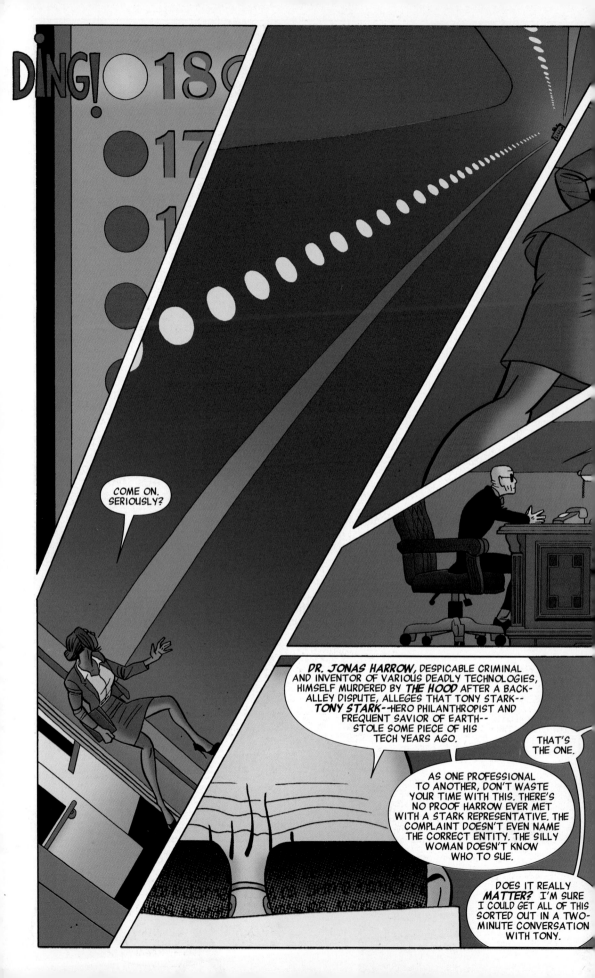

DING! ●18 ○17 ○1

COME ON. SERIOUSLY?

DR. JONAS HARROW, DESPICABLE CRIMINAL AND INVENTOR OF VARIOUS DEADLY TECHNOLOGIES, HIMSELF MURDERED BY *THE HOOD* AFTER A BACK-ALLEY DISPUTE, ALLEGES THAT TONY STARK-- *TONY STARK*--HERO PHILANTHROPIST AND FREQUENT SAVIOR OF EARTH-- STOLE SOME PIECE OF HIS TECH YEARS AGO.

THAT'S THE ONE.

AS ONE PROFESSIONAL TO ANOTHER, DON'T WASTE YOUR TIME WITH THIS. THERE'S NO PROOF HARROW EVER MET WITH A STARK REPRESENTATIVE. THE COMPLAINT DOESN'T EVEN NAME THE CORRECT ENTITY. THE SILLY WOMAN DOESN'T KNOW WHO TO SUE.

DOES IT REALLY *MATTER?* I'M SURE I COULD GET ALL OF THIS SORTED OUT IN A TWO-MINUTE CONVERSATION WITH TONY.

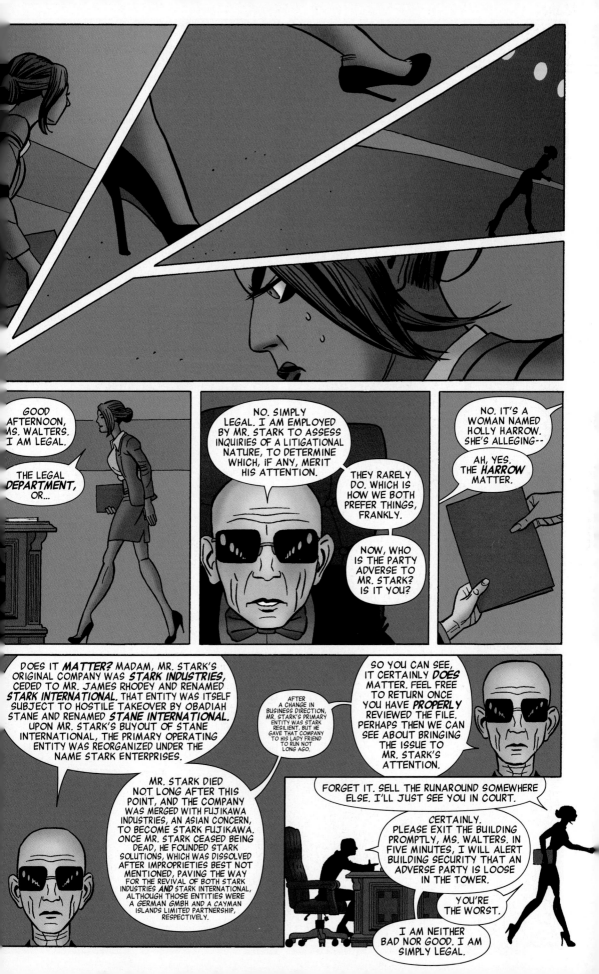

GOOD AFTERNOON, MS. WALTERS. I AM LEGAL.

THE LEGAL **DEPARTMENT,** OR...

NO. SIMPLY LEGAL. I AM EMPLOYED BY MR. STARK TO ASSESS INQUIRIES OF A LITIGATIONAL NATURE, TO DETERMINE WHICH, IF ANY, MERIT HIS ATTENTION.

THEY RARELY DO. WHICH IS HOW WE BOTH PREFER THINGS, FRANKLY.

NOW, WHO IS THE PARTY ADVERSE TO MR. STARK? IS IT YOU?

NO. IT'S A WOMAN NAMED HOLLY HARROW. SHE'S ALLEGING--

AH, YES. THE **HARROW** MATTER.

DOES IT **MATTER?** MADAM, MR. STARK'S ORIGINAL COMPANY WAS **STARK INDUSTRIES,** CEDED TO MR. JAMES RHODEY AND RENAMED **STARK INTERNATIONAL.** THAT ENTITY WAS ITSELF SUBJECT TO HOSTILE TAKEOVER BY OBADIAH STANE AND RENAMED **STANE INTERNATIONAL.** UPON MR. STARK'S BUYOUT OF STANE INTERNATIONAL, THE PRIMARY OPERATING ENTITY WAS REORGANIZED UNDER THE NAME STARK ENTERPRISES.

AFTER A CHANGE IN BUSINESS DIRECTION, MR. STARK'S PRIMARY ENTITY WAS STARK RESILIENT, BUT HE GAVE THAT COMPANY TO HIS LADY FRIEND TO RUN NOT LONG AGO.

MR. STARK DIED NOT LONG AFTER THIS POINT, AND THE COMPANY WAS MERGED WITH FUJIKAWA INDUSTRIES, AN ASIAN CONCERN, TO BECOME STARK FUJIKAWA. ONCE MR. STARK CEASED BEING DEAD, HE FOUNDED STARK SOLUTIONS, WHICH WAS DISSOLVED AFTER IMPROPRIETIES BEST NOT MENTIONED, PAVING THE WAY FOR THE REVIVAL OF BOTH STARK INDUSTRIES **AND** STARK INTERNATIONAL, ALTHOUGH THOSE ENTITIES WERE A GERMAN GMBH AND A CAYMAN ISLANDS LIMITED PARTNERSHIP, RESPECTIVELY.

SO YOU CAN SEE, IT CERTAINLY **DOES** MATTER. FEEL FREE TO RETURN ONCE YOU HAVE **PROPERLY** REVIEWED THE FILE. PERHAPS THEN WE CAN SEE ABOUT BRINGING THE ISSUE TO MR. STARK'S ATTENTION.

FORGET IT. SELL THE RUNAROUND SOMEWHERE ELSE. I'LL JUST SEE YOU IN COURT.

CERTAINLY. PLEASE EXIT THE BUILDING PROMPTLY, MS. WALTERS. IN FIVE MINUTES, I WILL ALERT BUILDING SECURITY THAT AN ADVERSE PARTY IS LOOSE IN THE TOWER.

YOU'RE THE WORST.

I AM NEITHER BAD NOR GOOD. I AM SIMPLY LEGAL.

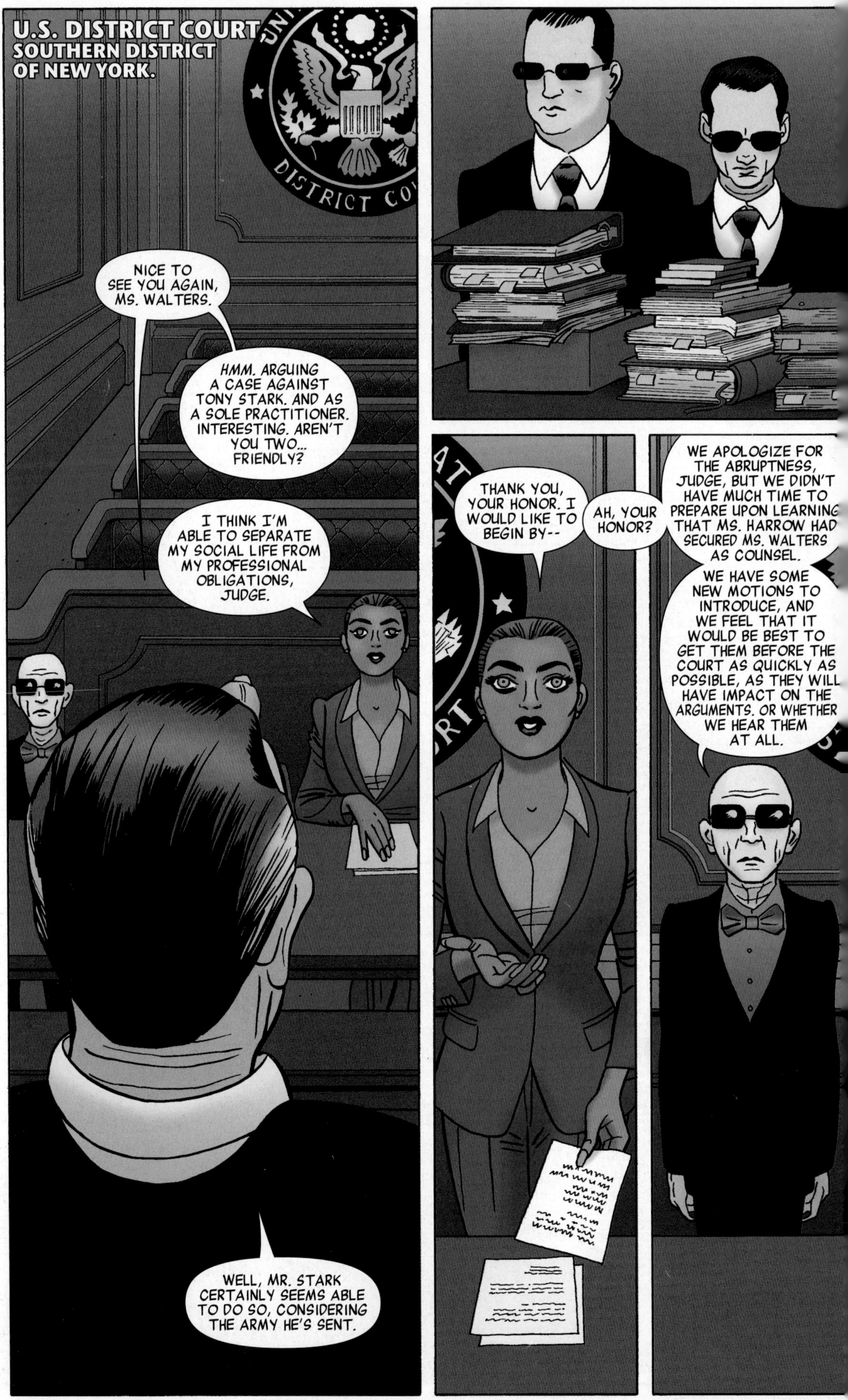
U.S. DISTRICT COURT SOUTHERN DISTRICT OF NEW YORK.
NICE TO SEE YOU AGAIN, MS. WALTERS.
HMM. ARGUING A CASE AGAINST TONY STARK. AND AS A SOLE PRACTITIONER. INTERESTING. AREN'T YOU TWO... FRIENDLY?
I THINK I'M ABLE TO SEPARATE MY SOCIAL LIFE FROM MY PROFESSIONAL OBLIGATIONS, JUDGE.
WELL, MR. STARK CERTAINLY SEEMS ABLE TO DO SO, CONSIDERING THE ARMY HE'S SENT.
THANK YOU, YOUR HONOR. I WOULD LIKE TO BEGIN BY--
AH, YOUR HONOR?
WE APOLOGIZE FOR THE ABRUPTNESS, JUDGE, BUT WE DIDN'T HAVE MUCH TIME TO PREPARE UPON LEARNING THAT MS. HARROW HAD SECURED MS. WALTERS AS COUNSEL.
WE HAVE SOME NEW MOTIONS TO INTRODUCE, AND WE FEEL THAT IT WOULD BE BEST TO GET THEM BEFORE THE COURT AS QUICKLY AS POSSIBLE, AS THEY WILL HAVE IMPACT ON THE ARGUMENTS. OR WHETHER WE HEAR THEM AT ALL.

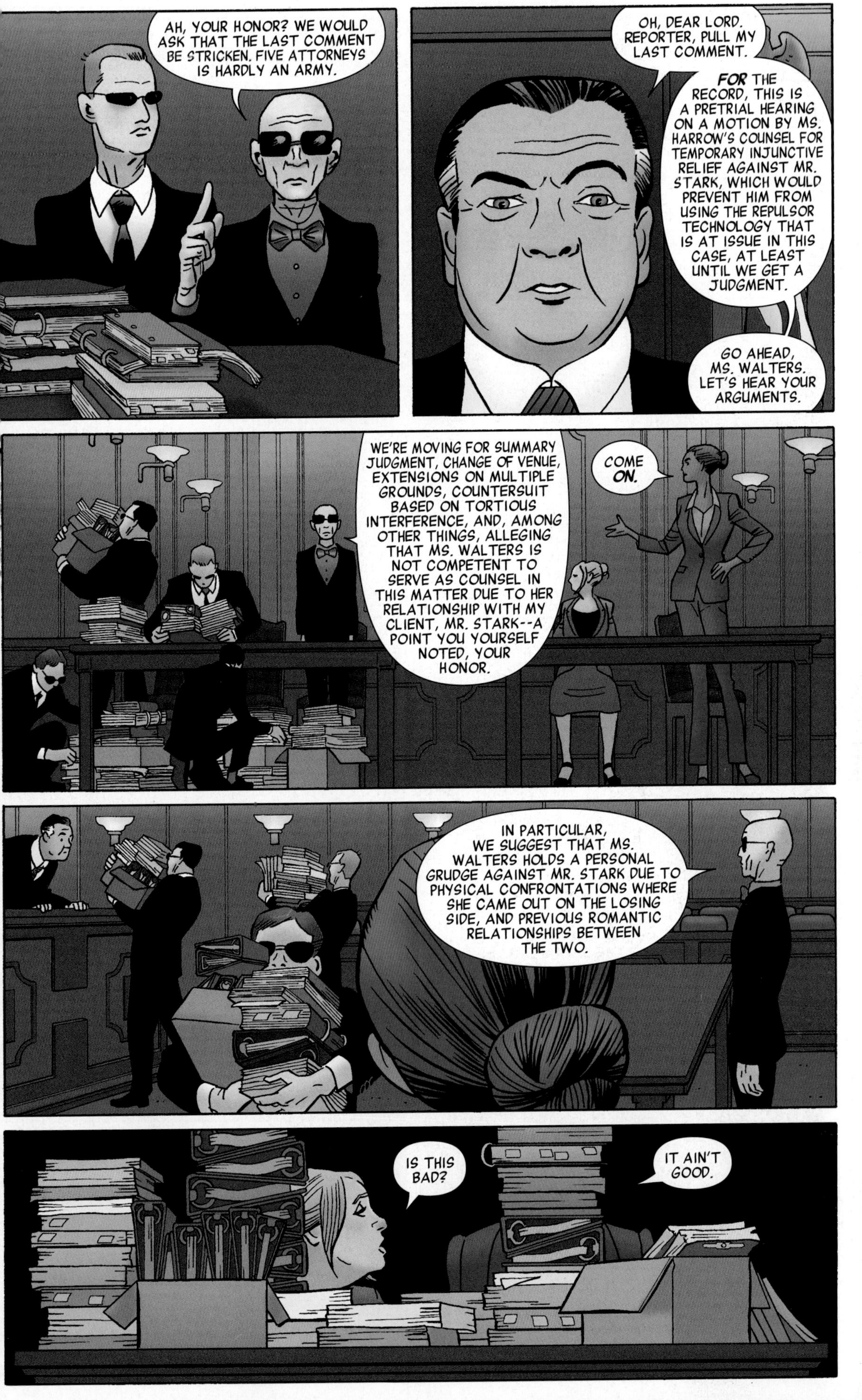
AH, YOUR HONOR? WE WOULD ASK THAT THE LAST COMMENT BE STRICKEN. FIVE ATTORNEYS IS HARDLY AN ARMY.
OH, DEAR LORD. REPORTER, PULL MY LAST COMMENT.
FOR THE RECORD, THIS IS A PRETRIAL HEARING ON A MOTION BY MS. HARROW'S COUNSEL FOR TEMPORARY INJUNCTIVE RELIEF AGAINST MR. STARK, WHICH WOULD PREVENT HIM FROM USING THE REPULSOR TECHNOLOGY THAT IS AT ISSUE IN THIS CASE, AT LEAST UNTIL WE GET A JUDGMENT.
GO AHEAD, MS. WALTERS. LET'S HEAR YOUR ARGUMENTS.
WE'RE MOVING FOR SUMMARY JUDGMENT, CHANGE OF VENUE, EXTENSIONS ON MULTIPLE GROUNDS, COUNTERSUIT BASED ON TORTIOUS INTERFERENCE, AND, AMONG OTHER THINGS, ALLEGING THAT MS. WALTERS IS NOT COMPETENT TO SERVE AS COUNSEL IN THIS MATTER DUE TO HER RELATIONSHIP WITH MY CLIENT, MR. STARK--A POINT YOU YOURSELF NOTED, YOUR HONOR.
COME ON.
IN PARTICULAR, WE SUGGEST THAT MS. WALTERS HOLDS A PERSONAL GRUDGE AGAINST MR. STARK DUE TO PHYSICAL CONFRONTATIONS WHERE SHE CAME OUT ON THE LOSING SIDE, AND PREVIOUS ROMANTIC RELATIONSHIPS BETWEEN THE TWO.
IS THIS BAD?
IT AIN'T GOOD.

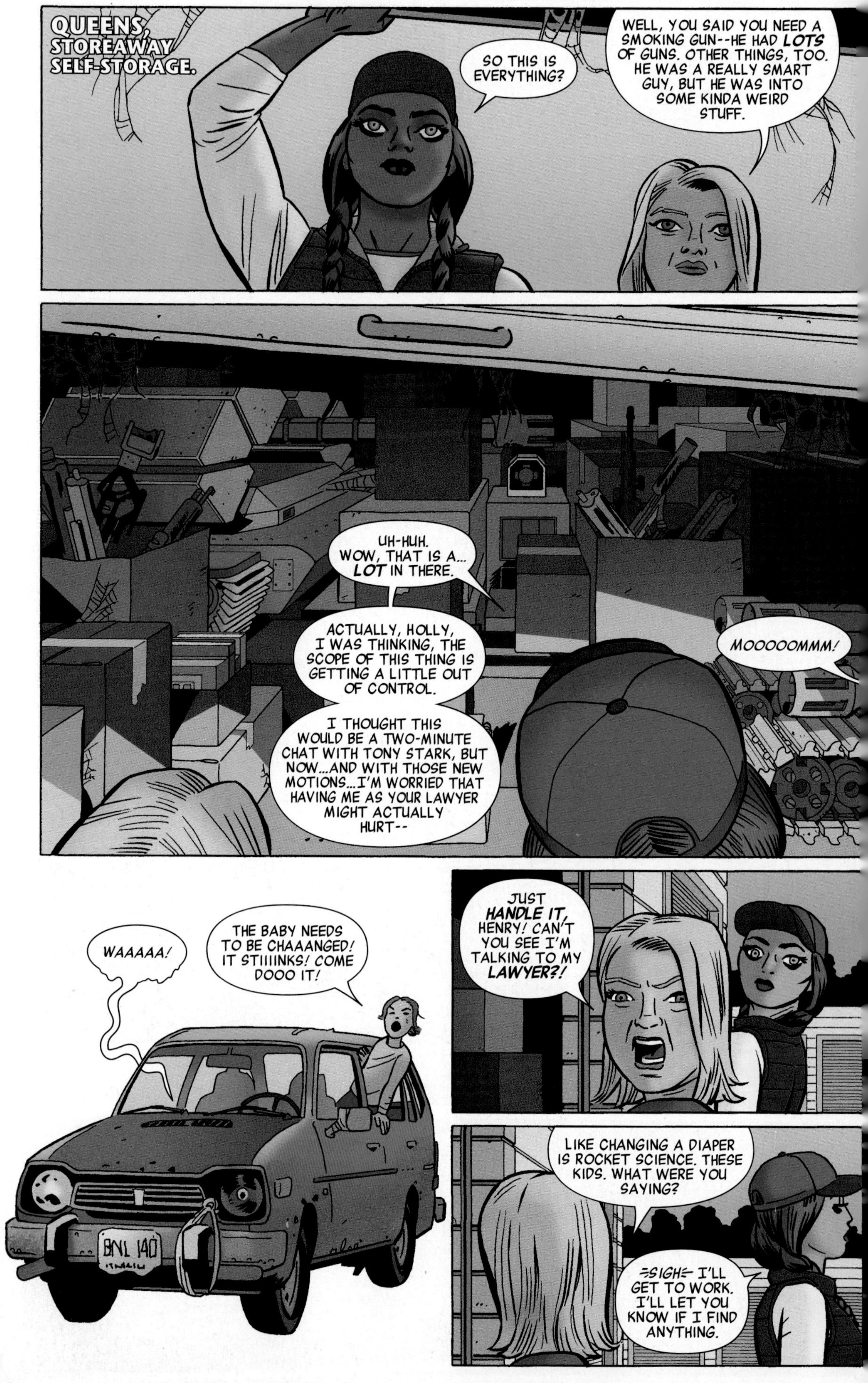
QUEENS, STOREAWAY SELF-STORAGE.
SO THIS IS EVERYTHING?
WELL, YOU SAID YOU NEED A SMOKING GUN--HE HAD LOTS OF GUNS. OTHER THINGS, TOO. HE WAS A REALLY SMART GUY, BUT HE WAS INTO SOME KINDA WEIRD STUFF.
UH-HUH. WOW, THAT IS A... LOT IN THERE.
ACTUALLY, HOLLY, I WAS THINKING, THE SCOPE OF THIS THING IS GETTING A LITTLE OUT OF CONTROL.
I THOUGHT THIS WOULD BE A TWO-MINUTE CHAT WITH TONY STARK, BUT NOW...AND WITH THOSE NEW MOTIONS...I'M WORRIED THAT HAVING ME AS YOUR LAWYER MIGHT ACTUALLY HURT--
MOOOOOMMM!
WAAAAA!
THE BABY NEEDS TO BE CHAAANGED! IT STIIIINKS! COME DOOO IT!
BNL 140
JUST HANDLE IT, HENRY! CAN'T YOU SEE I'M TALKING TO MY LAWYER?!
LIKE CHANGING A DIAPER IS ROCKET SCIENCE. THESE KIDS. WHAT WERE YOU SAYING?
=SIGH= I'LL GET TO WORK. I'LL LET YOU KNOW IF I FIND ANYTHING.

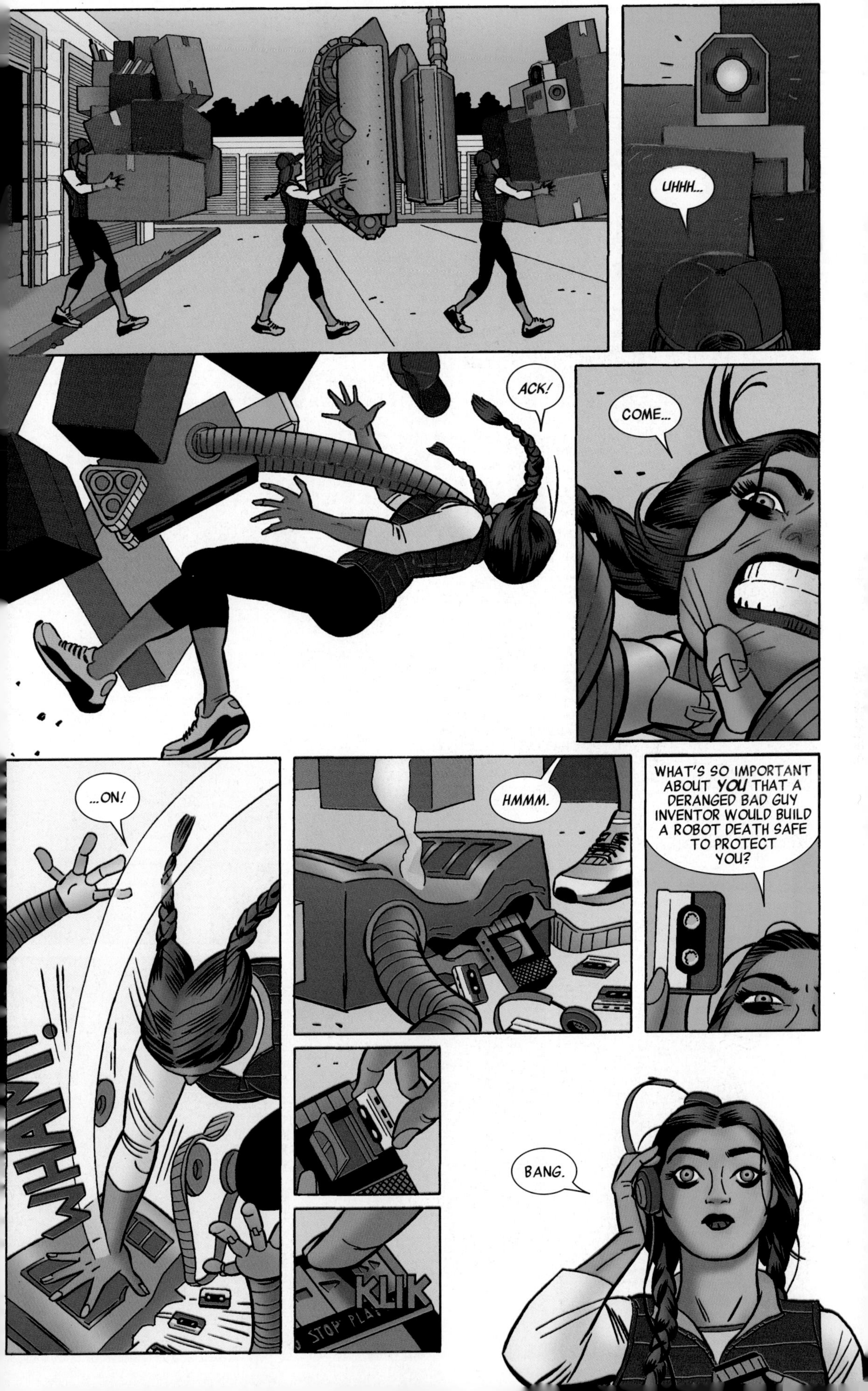
UHHH...
ACK!
COME...
...ON!
WHAM!
HMMM.
WHAT'S SO IMPORTANT ABOUT YOU THAT A DERANGED BAD GUY INVENTOR WOULD BUILD A ROBOT DEATH SAFE TO PROTECT YOU?
KLIK
STOP PLA
BANG.

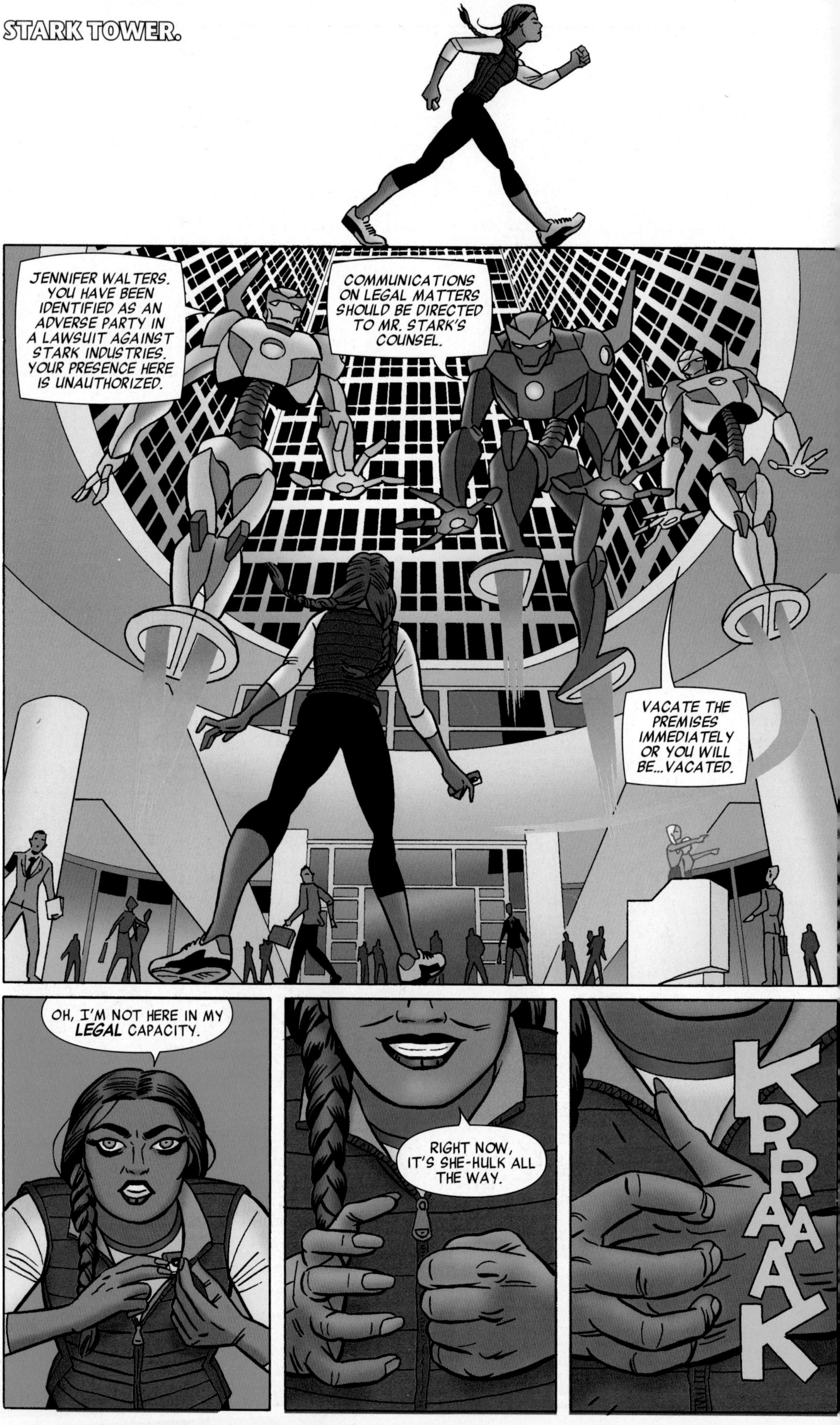

STARK TOWER.
JENNIFER WALTERS. YOU HAVE BEEN IDENTIFIED AS AN ADVERSE PARTY IN A LAWSUIT AGAINST STARK INDUSTRIES. YOUR PRESENCE HERE IS UNAUTHORIZED.
COMMUNICATIONS ON LEGAL MATTERS SHOULD BE DIRECTED TO MR. STARK'S COUNSEL.
VACATE THE PREMISES IMMEDIATELY OR YOU WILL BE...VACATED.
OH, I'M NOT HERE IN MY LEGAL CAPACITY.
RIGHT NOW, IT'S SHE-HULK ALL THE WAY.
KRRAAAAK

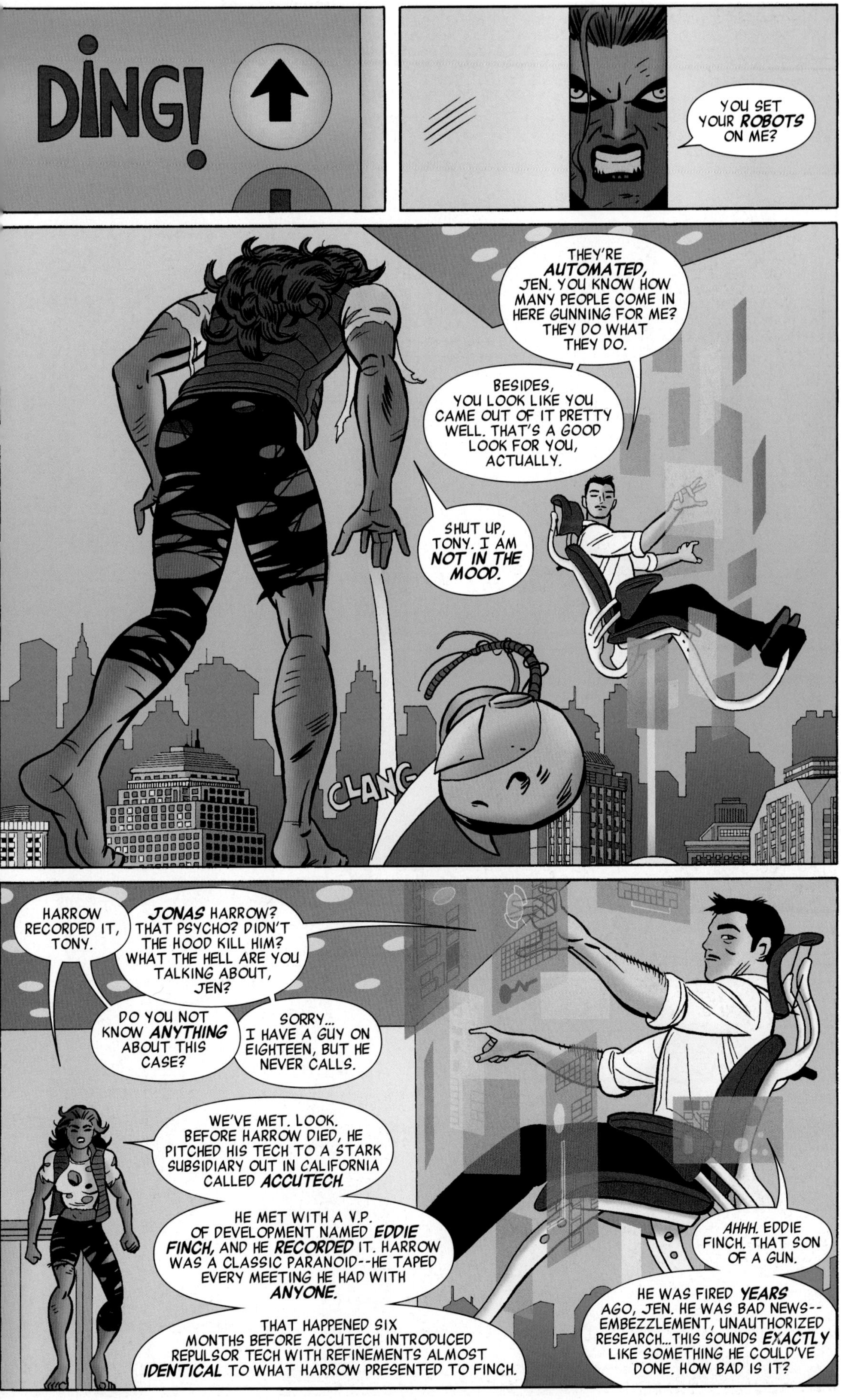
DING!
YOU SET YOUR ROBOTS ON ME?
THEY'RE AUTOMATED, JEN. YOU KNOW HOW MANY PEOPLE COME IN HERE GUNNING FOR ME? THEY DO WHAT THEY DO.
BESIDES, YOU LOOK LIKE YOU CAME OUT OF IT PRETTY WELL. THAT'S A GOOD LOOK FOR YOU, ACTUALLY.
SHUT UP, TONY. I AM NOT IN THE MOOD.
CLANG
HARROW RECORDED IT, TONY.
JONAS HARROW? THAT PSYCHO? DIDN'T THE HOOD KILL HIM? WHAT THE HELL ARE YOU TALKING ABOUT, JEN?
DO YOU NOT KNOW ANYTHING ABOUT THIS CASE?
SORRY... I HAVE A GUY ON EIGHTEEN, BUT HE NEVER CALLS.
WE'VE MET. LOOK. BEFORE HARROW DIED, HE PITCHED HIS TECH TO A STARK SUBSIDIARY OUT IN CALIFORNIA CALLED ACCUTECH.
HE MET WITH A V.P. OF DEVELOPMENT NAMED EDDIE FINCH, AND HE RECORDED IT. HARROW WAS A CLASSIC PARANOID--HE TAPED EVERY MEETING HE HAD WITH ANYONE.
THAT HAPPENED SIX MONTHS BEFORE ACCUTECH INTRODUCED REPULSOR TECH WITH REFINEMENTS ALMOST IDENTICAL TO WHAT HARROW PRESENTED TO FINCH.
AHHH. EDDIE FINCH. THAT SON OF A GUN.
HE WAS FIRED YEARS AGO, JEN. HE WAS BAD NEWS--EMBEZZLEMENT, UNAUTHORIZED RESEARCH...THIS SOUNDS EXACTLY LIKE SOMETHING HE COULD'VE DONE. HOW BAD IS IT?

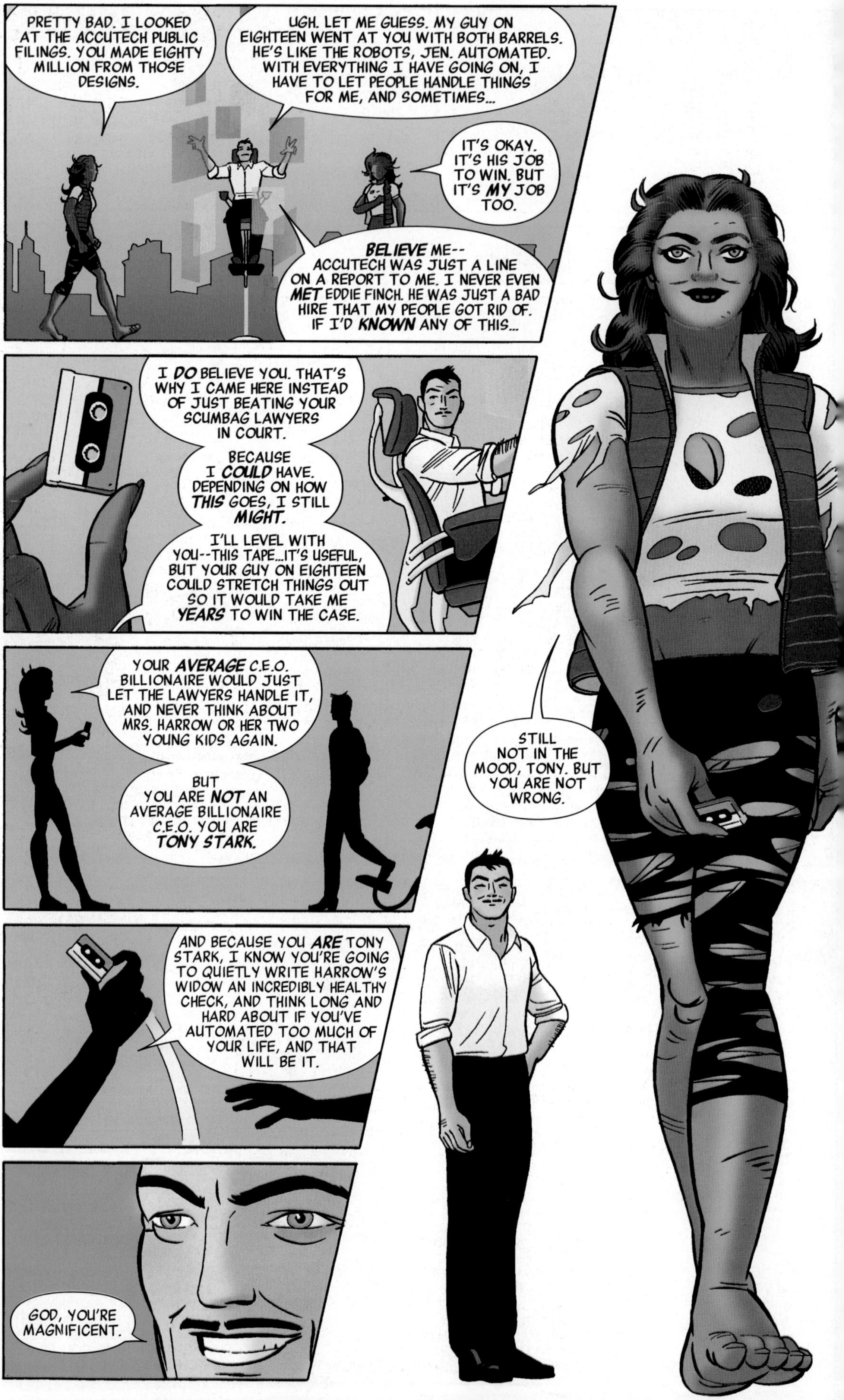
PRETTY BAD. I LOOKED AT THE ACCUTECH PUBLIC FILINGS. YOU MADE EIGHTY MILLION FROM THOSE DESIGNS.
UGH. LET ME GUESS. MY GUY ON EIGHTEEN WENT AT YOU WITH BOTH BARRELS. HE'S LIKE THE ROBOTS, JEN. AUTOMATED. WITH EVERYTHING I HAVE GOING ON, I HAVE TO LET PEOPLE HANDLE THINGS FOR ME, AND SOMETIMES...
IT'S OKAY. IT'S HIS JOB TO WIN. BUT IT'S MY JOB TOO.
BELIEVE ME-- ACCUTECH WAS JUST A LINE ON A REPORT TO ME. I NEVER EVEN MET EDDIE FINCH. HE WAS JUST A BAD HIRE THAT MY PEOPLE GOT RID OF. IF I'D KNOWN ANY OF THIS...
I DO BELIEVE YOU. THAT'S WHY I CAME HERE INSTEAD OF JUST BEATING YOUR SCUMBAG LAWYERS IN COURT.
BECAUSE I COULD HAVE. DEPENDING ON HOW THIS GOES, I STILL MIGHT.
I'LL LEVEL WITH YOU--THIS TAPE...IT'S USEFUL, BUT YOUR GUY ON EIGHTEEN COULD STRETCH THINGS OUT SO IT WOULD TAKE ME YEARS TO WIN THE CASE.
YOUR AVERAGE C.E.O. BILLIONAIRE WOULD JUST LET THE LAWYERS HANDLE IT, AND NEVER THINK ABOUT MRS. HARROW OR HER TWO YOUNG KIDS AGAIN.
BUT YOU ARE NOT AN AVERAGE BILLIONAIRE C.E.O. YOU ARE TONY STARK.
STILL NOT IN THE MOOD, TONY. BUT YOU ARE NOT WRONG.
AND BECAUSE YOU ARE TONY STARK, I KNOW YOU'RE GOING TO QUIETLY WRITE HARROW'S WIDOW AN INCREDIBLY HEALTHY CHECK, AND THINK LONG AND HARD ABOUT IF YOU'VE AUTOMATED TOO MUCH OF YOUR LIFE, AND THAT WILL BE IT.
GOD, YOU'RE MAGNIFICENT.

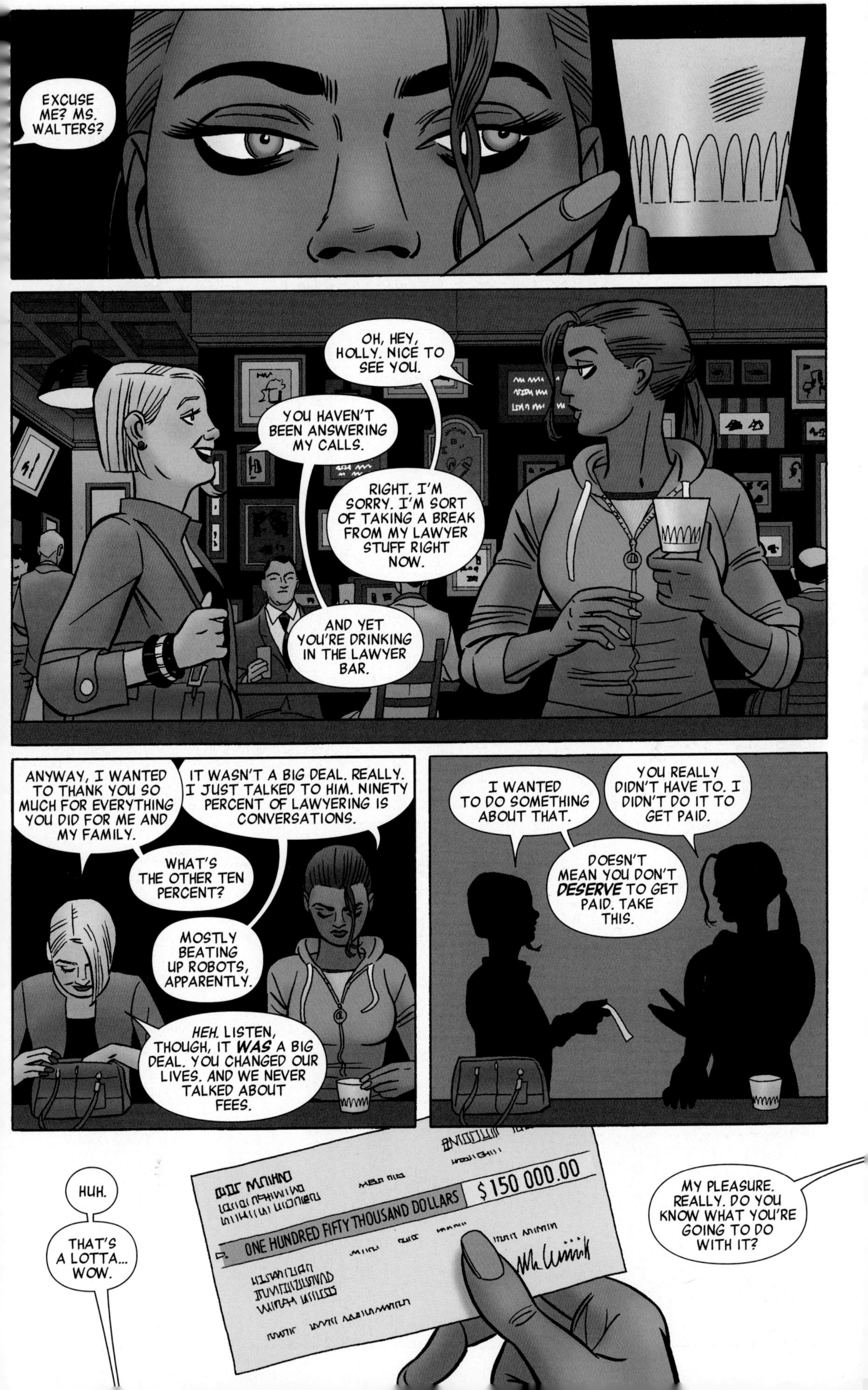
EXCUSE ME? MS. WALTERS?
OH, HEY, HOLLY. NICE TO SEE YOU.
YOU HAVEN'T BEEN ANSWERING MY CALLS.
RIGHT. I'M SORRY. I'M SORT OF TAKING A BREAK FROM MY LAWYER STUFF RIGHT NOW.
AND YET YOU'RE DRINKING IN THE LAWYER BAR.
ANYWAY, I WANTED TO THANK YOU SO MUCH FOR EVERYTHING YOU DID FOR ME AND MY FAMILY.
IT WASN'T A BIG DEAL. REALLY. I JUST TALKED TO HIM. NINETY PERCENT OF LAWYERING IS CONVERSATIONS.
WHAT'S THE OTHER TEN PERCENT?
MOSTLY BEATING UP ROBOTS, APPARENTLY.
HEH. LISTEN, THOUGH, IT WAS A BIG DEAL. YOU CHANGED OUR LIVES. AND WE NEVER TALKED ABOUT FEES.
I WANTED TO DO SOMETHING ABOUT THAT.
YOU REALLY DIDN'T HAVE TO. I DIDN'T DO IT TO GET PAID.
DOESN'T MEAN YOU DON'T DESERVE TO GET PAID. TAKE THIS.
HUH.
THAT'S A LOTTA... WOW.
$150 000.00
ONE HUNDRED FIFTY THOUSAND DOLLARS
MY PLEASURE. REALLY. DO YOU KNOW WHAT YOU'RE GOING TO DO WITH IT?

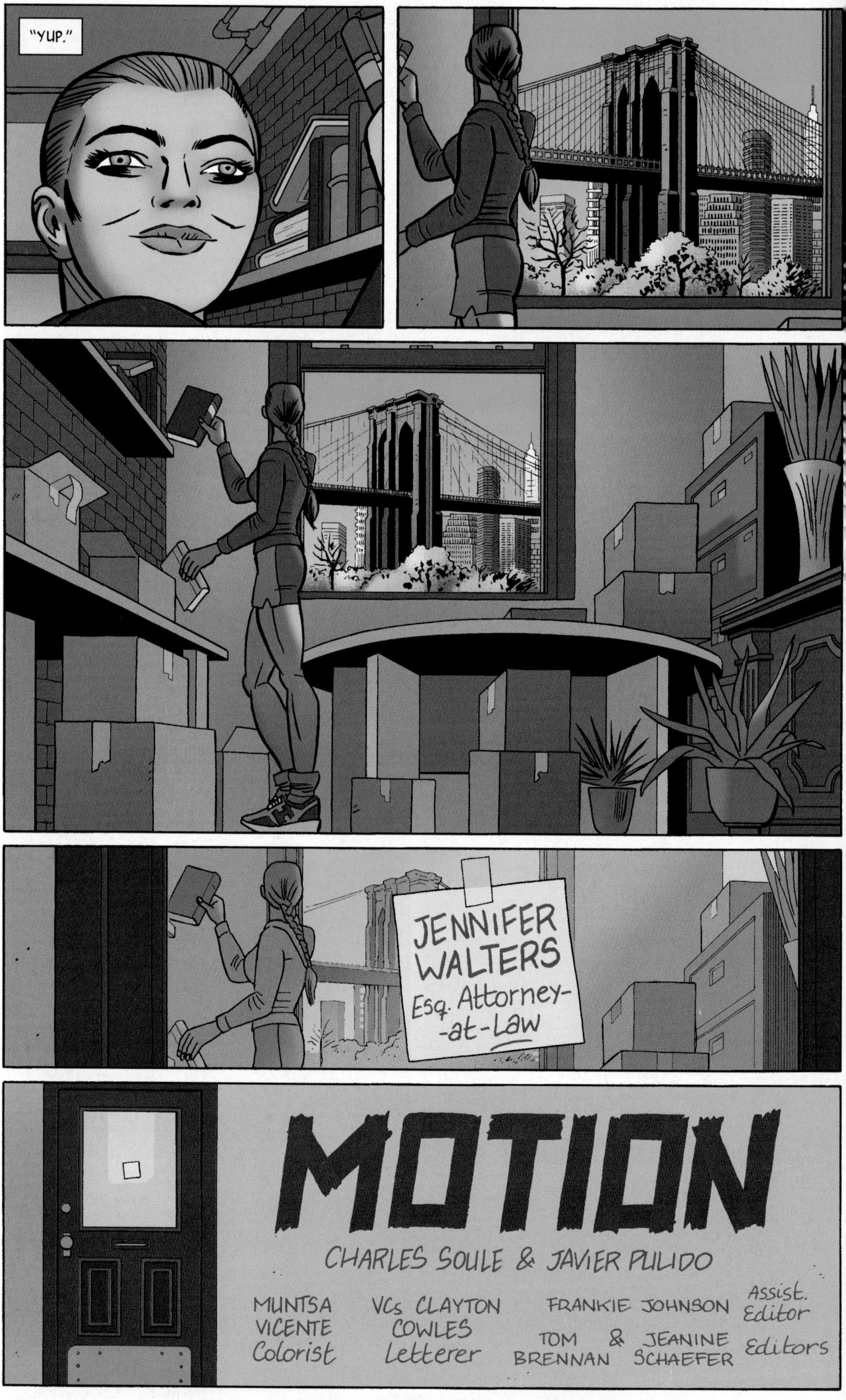
"YUP."
JENNIFER WALTERS Esq. Attorney-at-Law
MOTION
CHARLES SOULE & JAVIER PULIDO
MUNTSA VICENTE Colorist
VCs CLAYTON COWLES Letterer
FRANKIE JOHNSON Assist. Editor
TOM BRENNAN & JEANINE SCHAEFER Editors

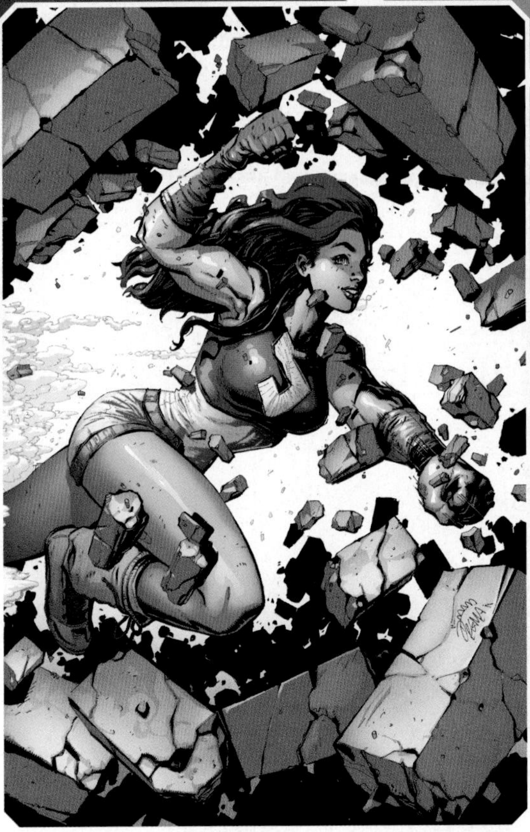

SHE-HULK #1
Variant by Ryan Stegman & Edgar Delgado

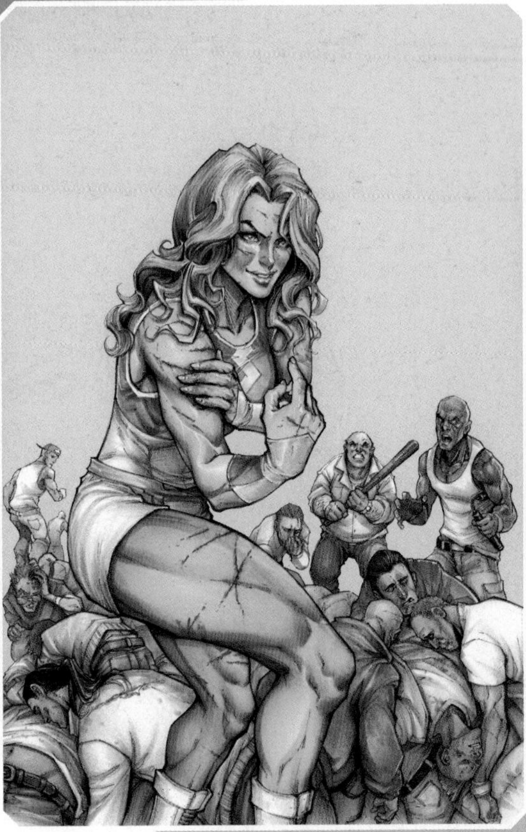

SHE-HULK #1
Variant by Siya Oum

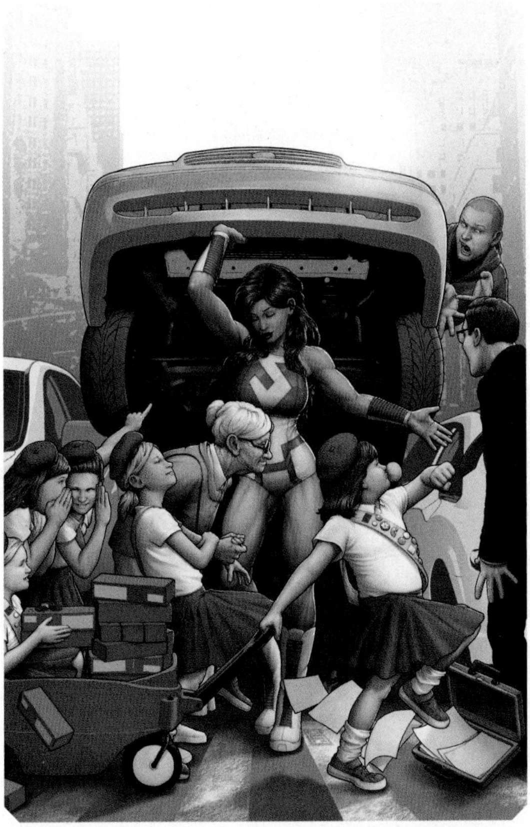

SHE-HULK #1
Variant by John Tyler Christopher

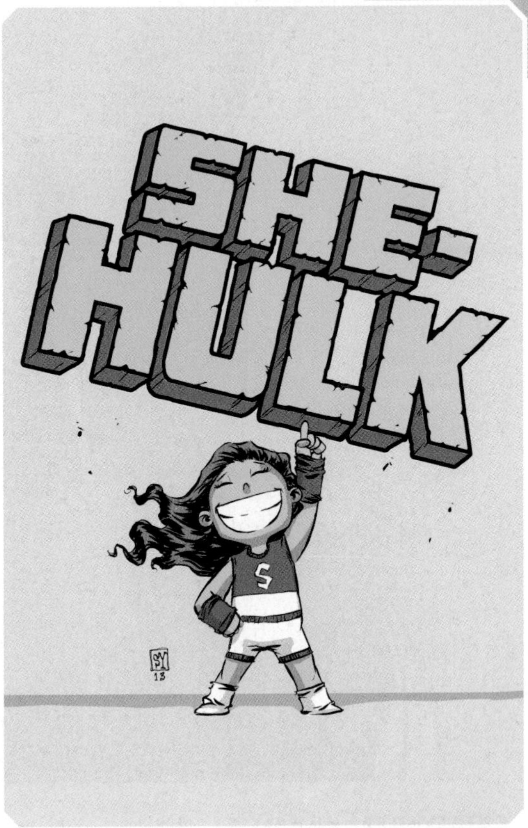
SHE-
HULK

SHE-HULK #1
Variant by Skottie Young

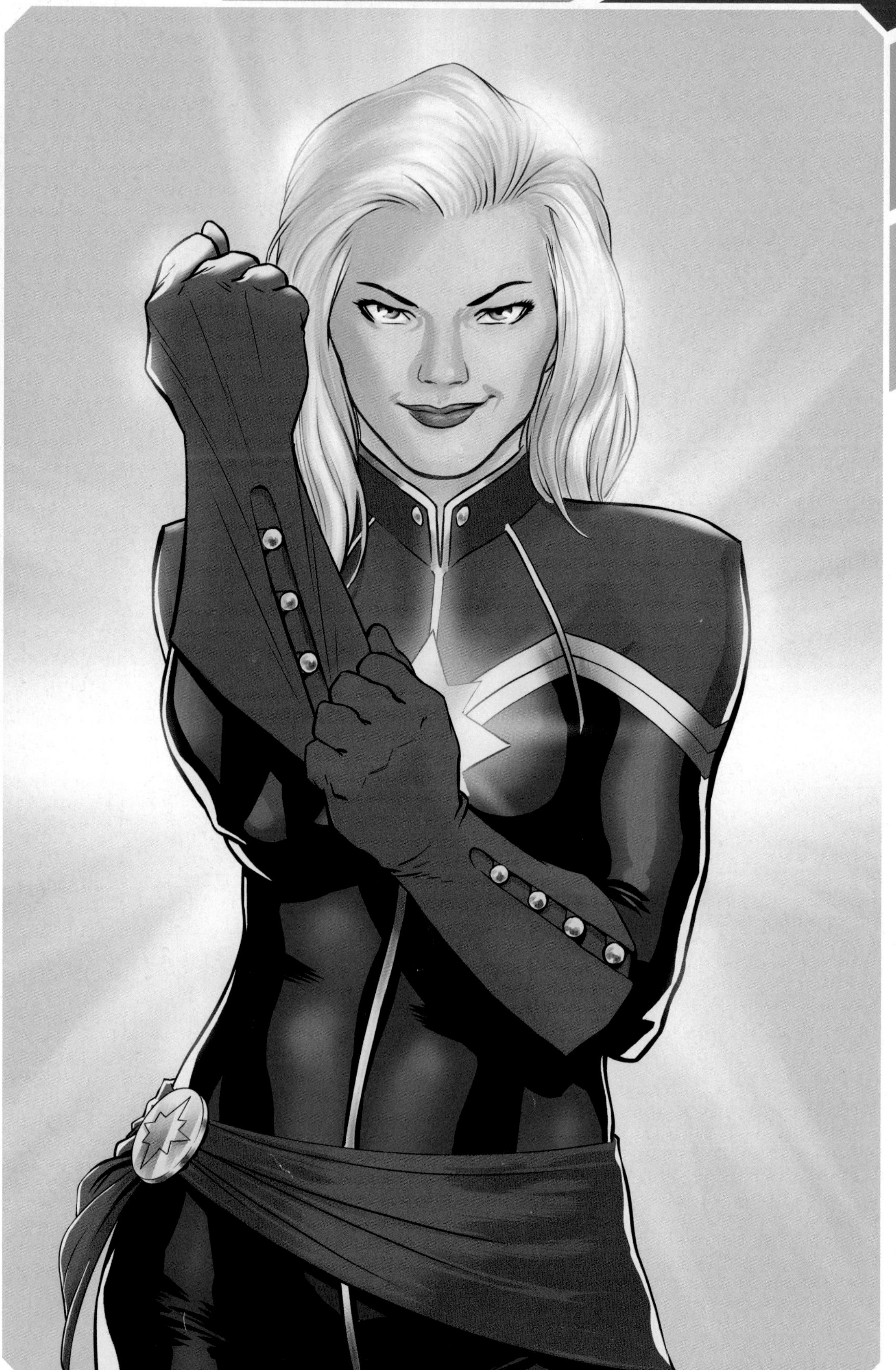

CAPTAIN MARVEL #1

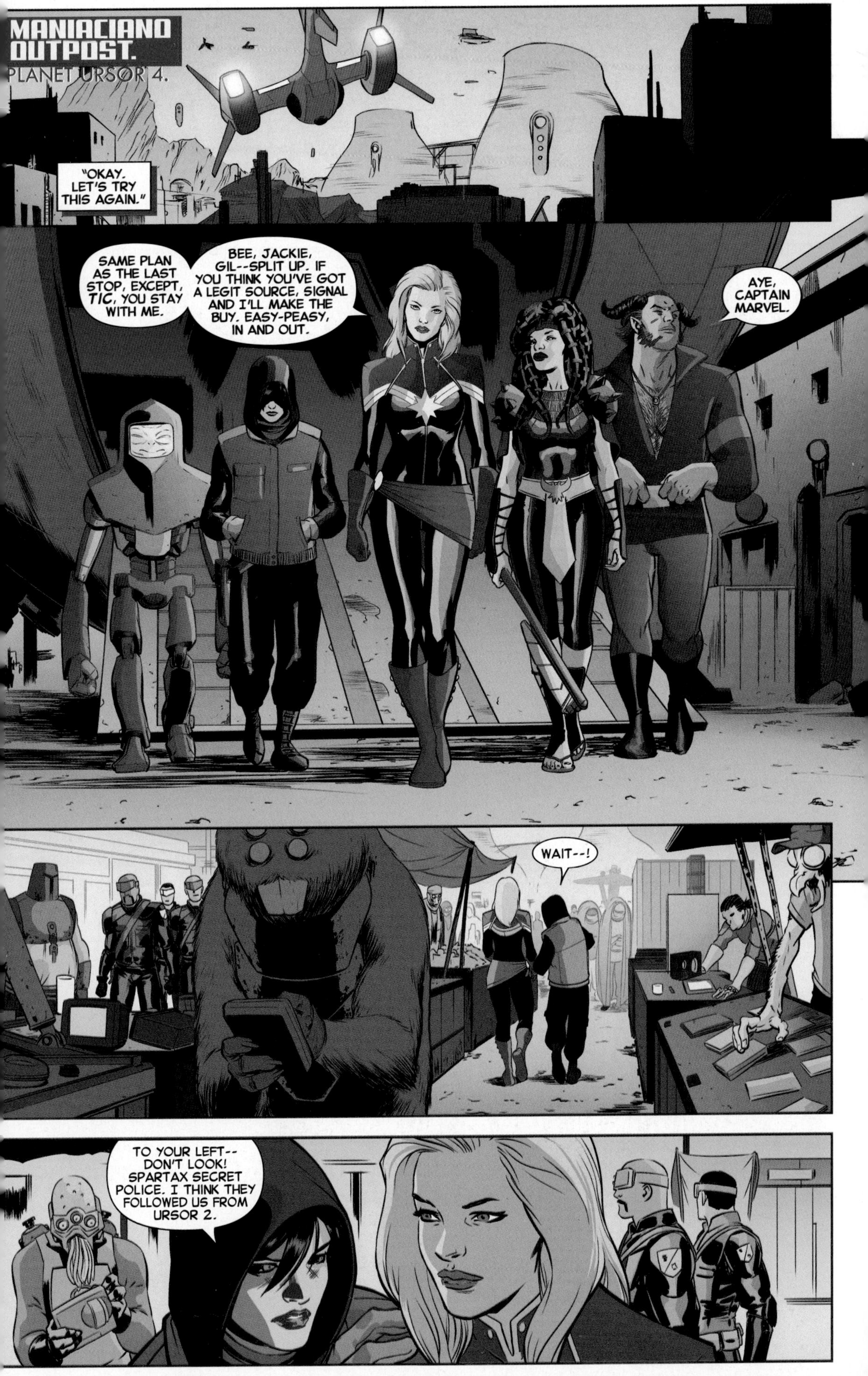
MANIACIANO OUTPOST.
PLANET URSOR 4.
"OKAY. LET'S TRY THIS AGAIN."
SAME PLAN AS THE LAST STOP, EXCEPT, TIC, YOU STAY WITH ME.
BEE, JACKIE, GIL--SPLIT UP. IF YOU THINK YOU'VE GOT A LEGIT SOURCE, SIGNAL AND I'LL MAKE THE BUY. EASY-PEASY, IN AND OUT.
AYE, CAPTAIN MARVEL.
WAIT--!
TO YOUR LEFT-- DON'T LOOK! SPARTAX SECRET POLICE. I THINK THEY FOLLOWED US FROM URSOR 2.

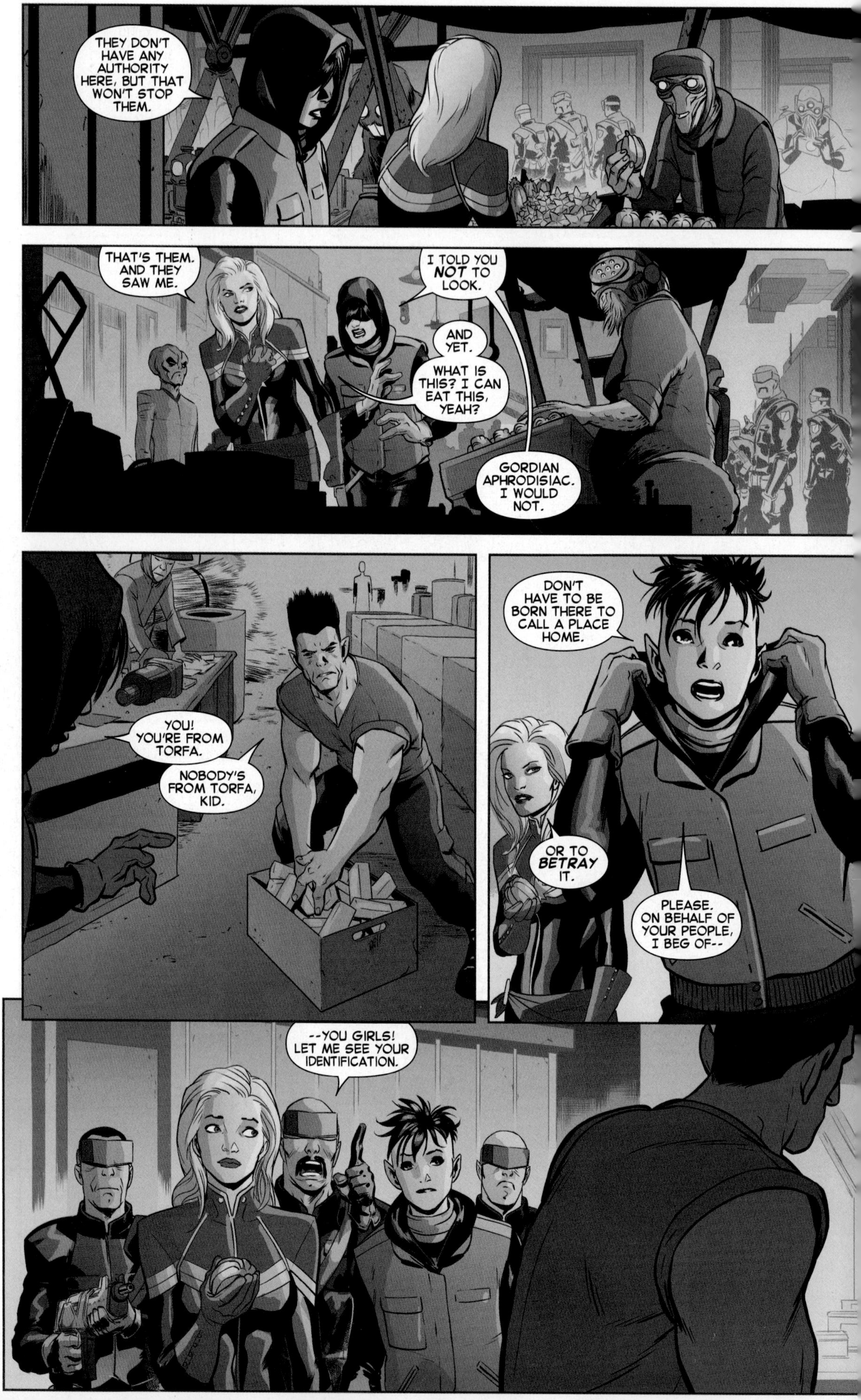
THEY DON'T HAVE ANY AUTHORITY HERE, BUT THAT WON'T STOP THEM.
THAT'S THEM. AND THEY SAW ME.
I TOLD YOU NOT TO LOOK.
AND YET.
WHAT IS THIS? I CAN EAT THIS, YEAH?
GORDIAN APHRODISIAC. I WOULD NOT.
YOU! YOU'RE FROM TORFA.
NOBODY'S FROM TORFA, KID.
DON'T HAVE TO BE BORN THERE TO CALL A PLACE HOME.
OR TO BETRAY IT.
PLEASE. ON BEHALF OF YOUR PEOPLE, I BEG OF--
--YOU GIRLS! LET ME SEE YOUR IDENTIFICATION.

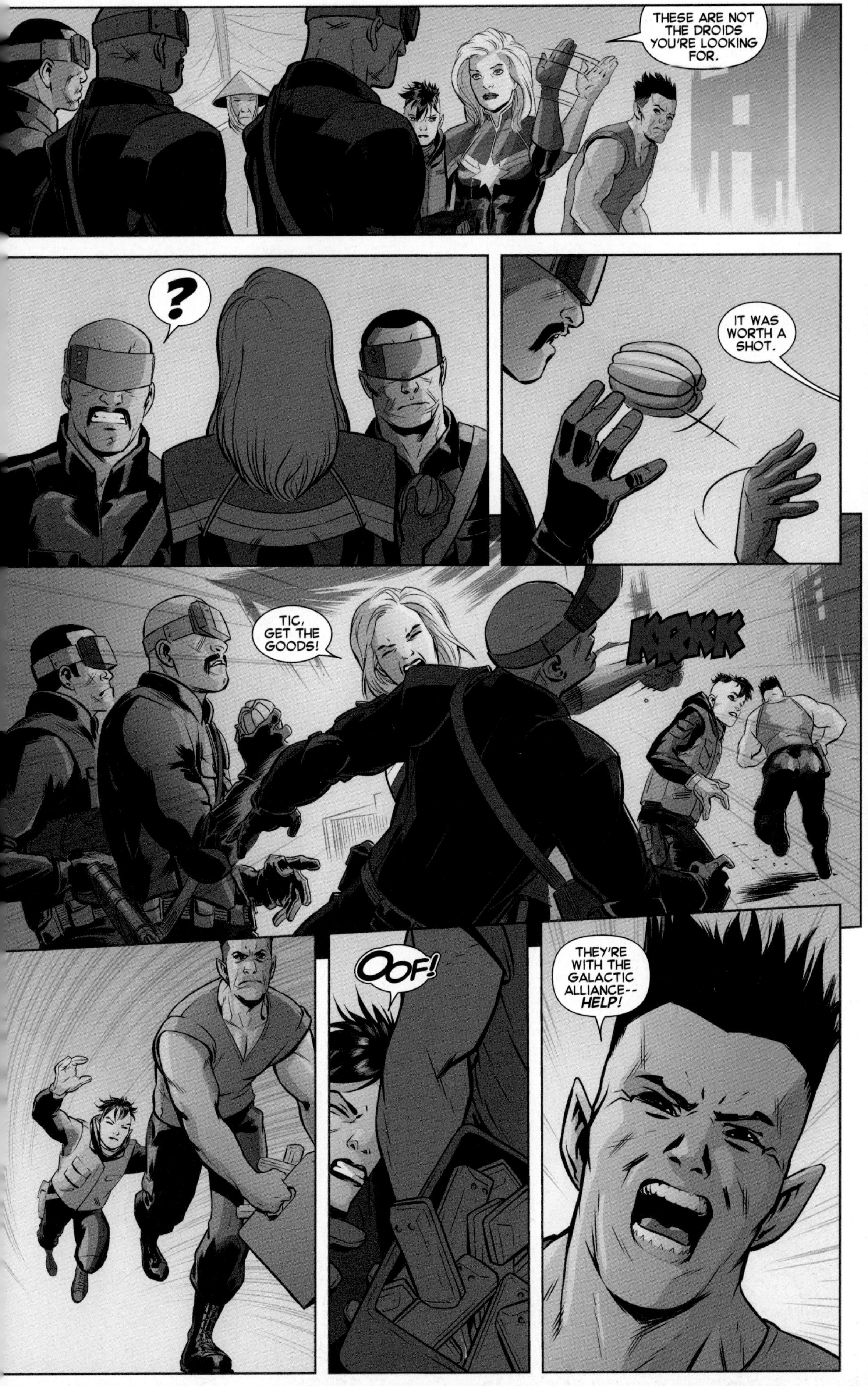

THESE ARE NOT THE DROIDS YOU'RE LOOKING FOR.
?
IT WAS WORTH A SHOT.
TIC, GET THE GOODS!
KRKK
OOF!
THEY'RE WITH THE GALACTIC ALLIANCE-- HELP!

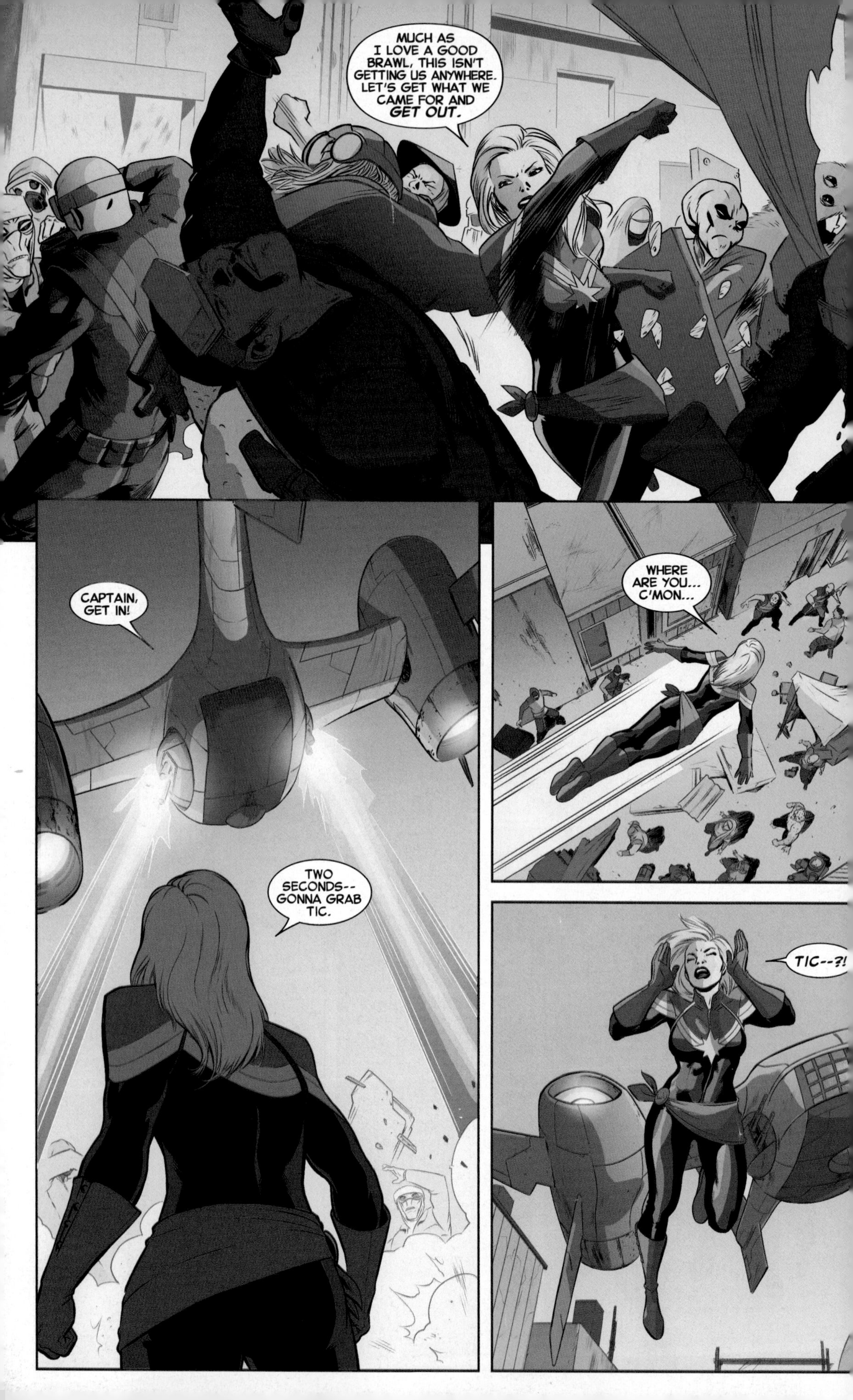
MUCH AS I LOVE A GOOD BRAWL, THIS ISN'T GETTING US ANYWHERE. LET'S GET WHAT WE CAME FOR AND GET OUT.
CAPTAIN, GET IN!
TWO SECONDS-- GONNA GRAB TIC.
WHERE ARE YOU... C'MON...
TIC--?!

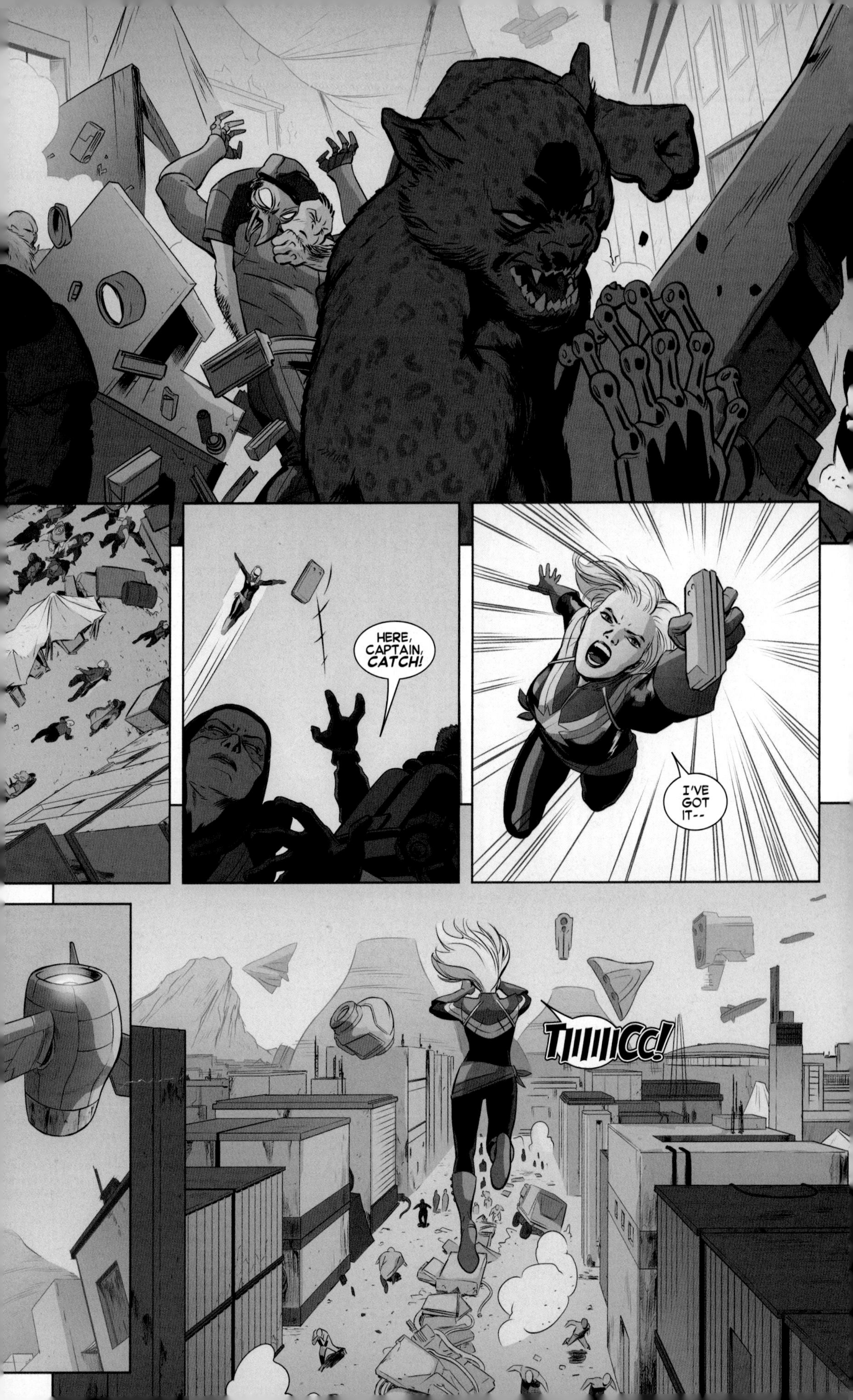
HERE, CAPTAIN, CATCH!
I'VE GOT IT--
TIIIIICC!

CAPTAIN MARVEL

HIGHER, FURTHER, FASTER, MORE.
PART ONE

KELLY SUE DeCONNICK
WRITER

DAVID LOPEZ
ART

LEE LOUGHRIDGE
COLOR ART

VC'S JOE CARAMAGNA
LETTERER

DAVID LOPEZ
COVER ARTIST

JOHN CASSADAY & LAURA MARTIN; LEINIL YU & SUNNY GHO; DAVID LOPEZ; SKOTTIE YOUNG
VARIANT COVER ARTISTS

DEVIN LEWIS
ASSISTANT EDITOR

SANA AMANAT
EDITOR

STEPHEN WACKER & NICK LOWE
SENIOR EDITORS

AXEL ALONSO
EDITOR IN CHIEF

JOE QUESADA
CHIEF CREATIVE OFFICER

DAN BUCKLEY
PUBLISHER

ALAN FINE
EXEC. PRODUCER

FOR AERIS

SIX
WEEKS
AGO.

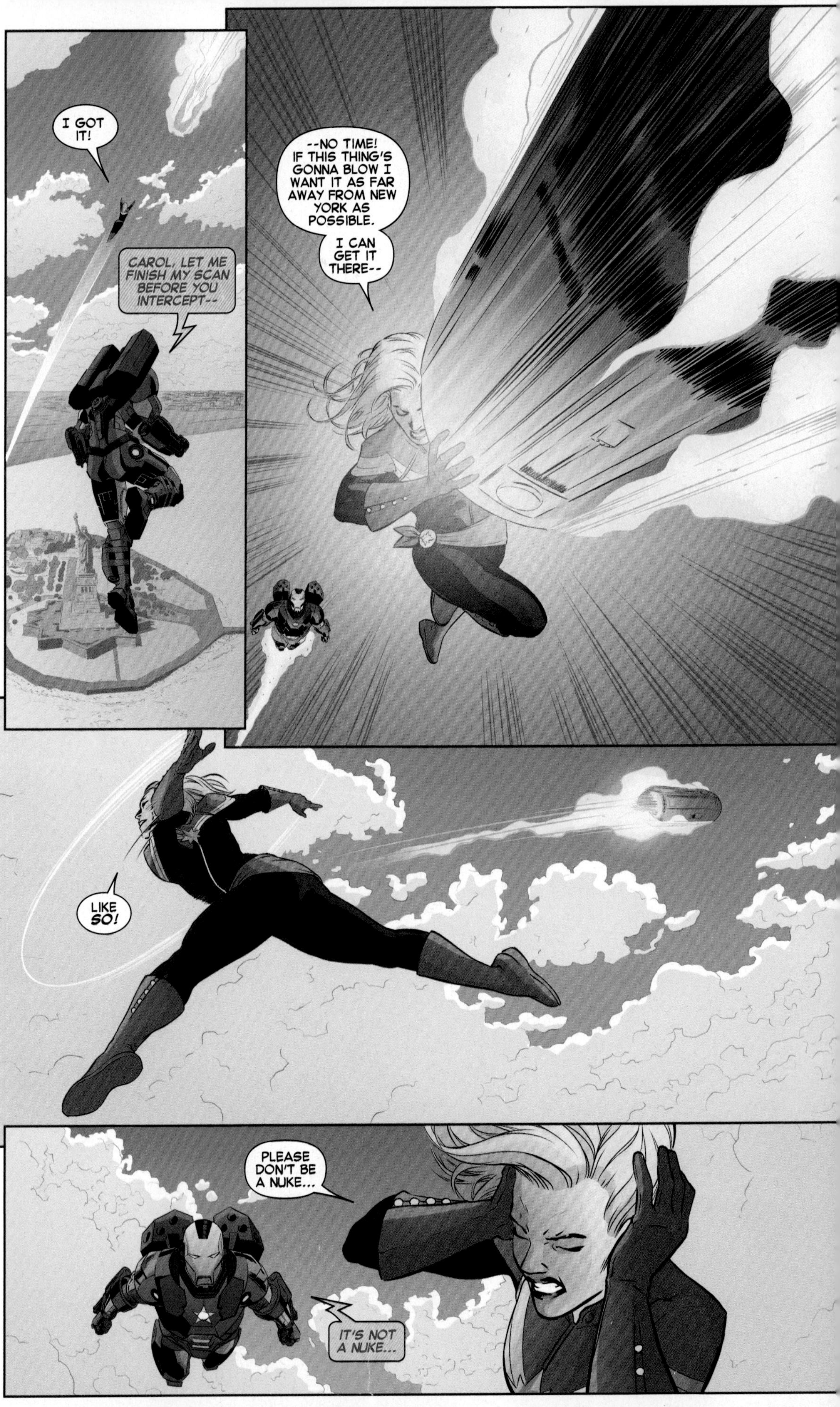
I GOT IT!
CAROL, LET ME FINISH MY SCAN BEFORE YOU INTERCEPT--
--NO TIME! IF THIS THING'S GONNA BLOW I WANT IT AS FAR AWAY FROM NEW YORK AS POSSIBLE.
I CAN GET IT THERE--
LIKE SO!
PLEASE DON'T BE A NUKE...
IT'S NOT A NUKE...

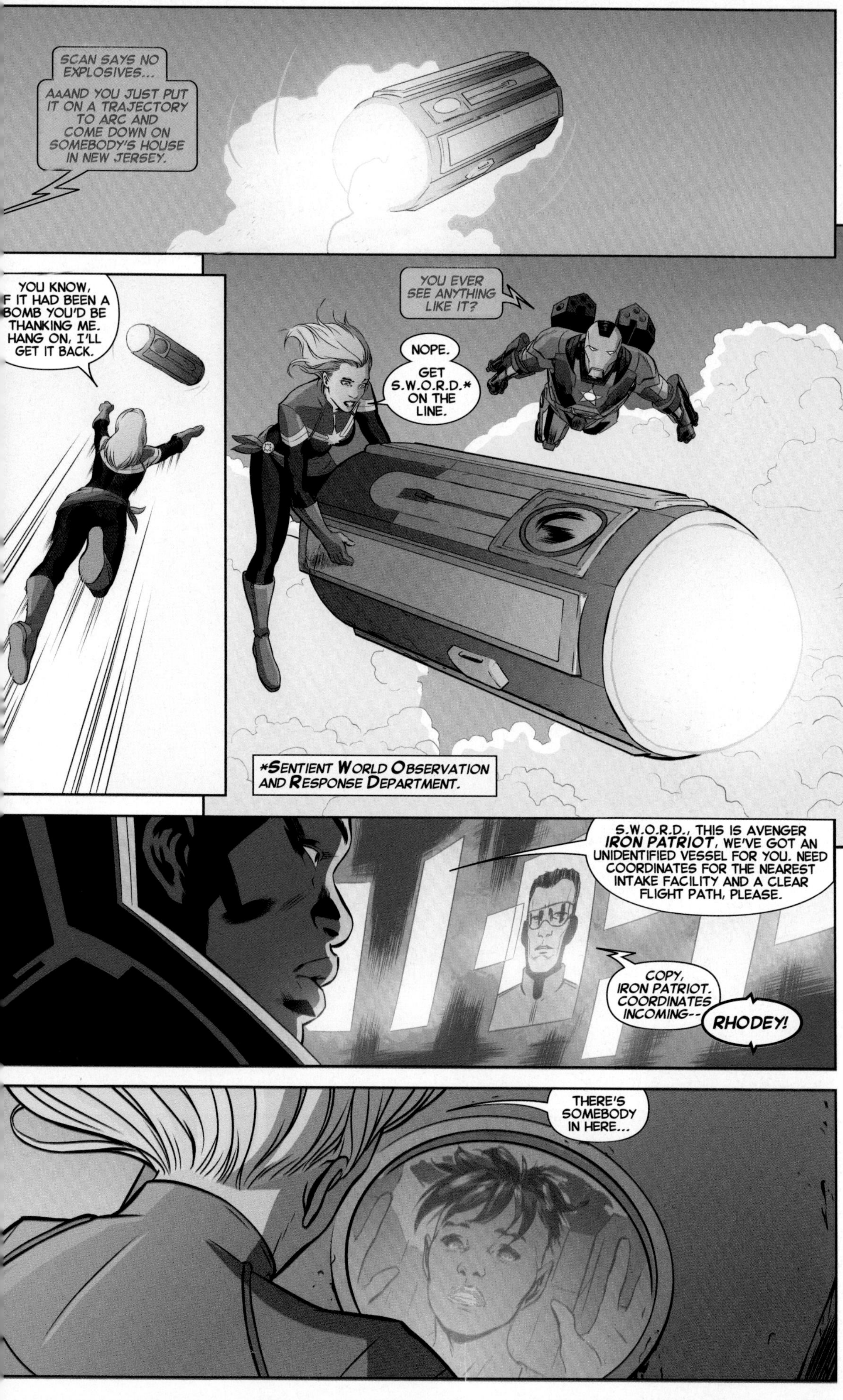
SCAN SAYS NO EXPLOSIVES...
AAAND YOU JUST PUT IT ON A TRAJECTORY TO ARC AND COME DOWN ON SOMEBODY'S HOUSE IN NEW JERSEY.
YOU KNOW, IF IT HAD BEEN A BOMB YOU'D BE THANKING ME. HANG ON, I'LL GET IT BACK.
YOU EVER SEE ANYTHING LIKE IT?
NOPE. GET S.W.O.R.D.* ON THE LINE.
*SENTIENT WORLD OBSERVATION AND RESPONSE DEPARTMENT.
S.W.O.R.D., THIS IS AVENGER IRON PATRIOT, WE'VE GOT AN UNIDENTIFIED VESSEL FOR YOU. NEED COORDINATES FOR THE NEAREST INTAKE FACILITY AND A CLEAR FLIGHT PATH, PLEASE.
COPY, IRON PATRIOT. COORDINATES INCOMING--
RHODEY!
THERE'S SOMEBODY IN HERE...

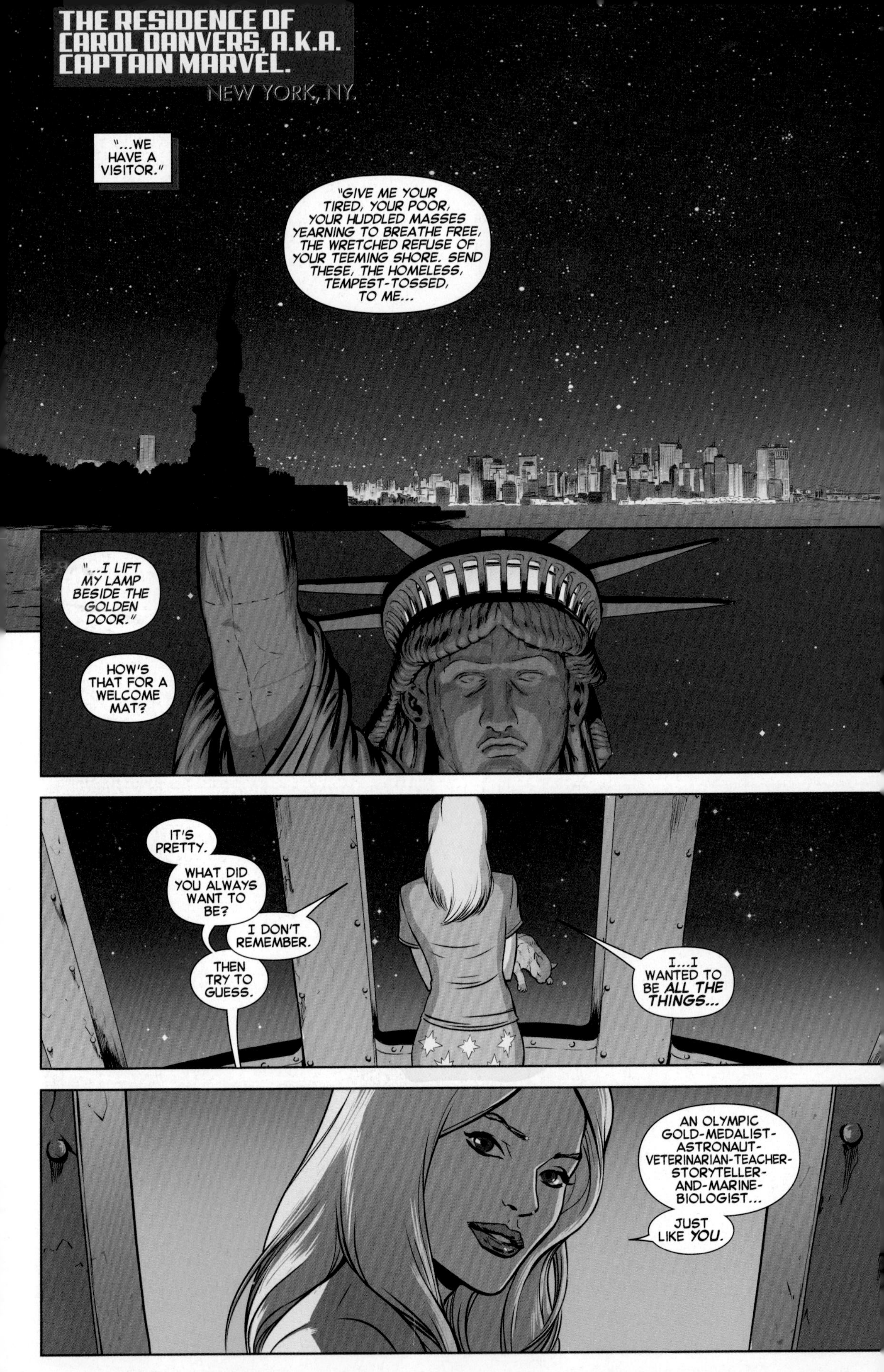
THE RESIDENCE OF CAROL DANVERS, A.K.A. CAPTAIN MARVEL.
NEW YORK, NY.
"...WE HAVE A VISITOR."
"GIVE ME YOUR TIRED, YOUR POOR, YOUR HUDDLED MASSES YEARNING TO BREATHE FREE, THE WRETCHED REFUSE OF YOUR TEEMING SHORE. SEND THESE, THE HOMELESS, TEMPEST-TOSSED, TO ME...
"...I LIFT MY LAMP BESIDE THE GOLDEN DOOR."
HOW'S THAT FOR A WELCOME MAT?
IT'S PRETTY.
WHAT DID YOU ALWAYS WANT TO BE?
I DON'T REMEMBER.
THEN TRY TO GUESS.
I...I WANTED TO BE ALL THE THINGS...
AN OLYMPIC GOLD-MEDALIST-ASTRONAUT-VETERINARIAN-TEACHER-STORYTELLER-AND-MARINE-BIOLOGIST...
JUST LIKE YOU.

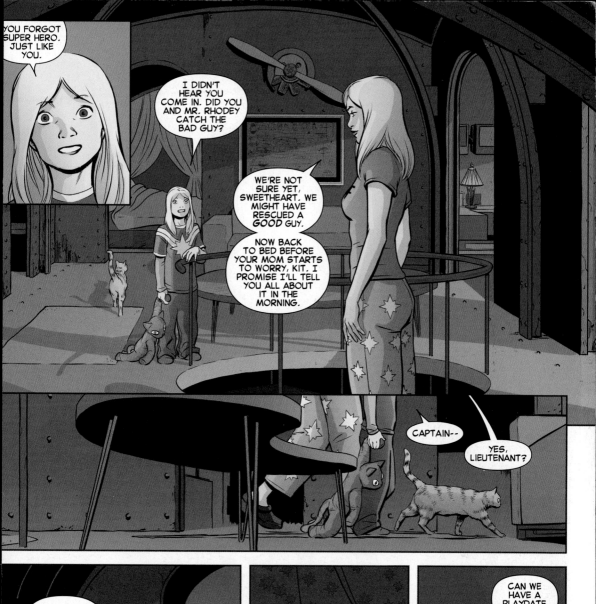

YOU FORGOT SUPER HERO. JUST LIKE YOU.

I DIDN'T HEAR YOU COME IN. DID YOU AND MR. RHODEY CATCH THE BAD GUY?

WE'RE NOT SURE YET, SWEETHEART. WE MIGHT HAVE RESCUED A GOOD GUY.

NOW BACK TO BED BEFORE YOUR MOM STARTS TO WORRY, KIT. I PROMISE I'LL TELL YOU ALL ABOUT IT IN THE MORNING.

CAPTAIN--

YES, LIEUTENANT?

THANK YOU FOR LETTING US STAY WITH YOU WHILE MOM GETS HER JOB STUFF WORKED OUT.

IT'S MY PLEASURE, LT.

CAPTAIN--

SHH!

ONE MORE QUESTION.

ONE MORE.

CAN WE HAVE A PLAYDATE WITH HIM?

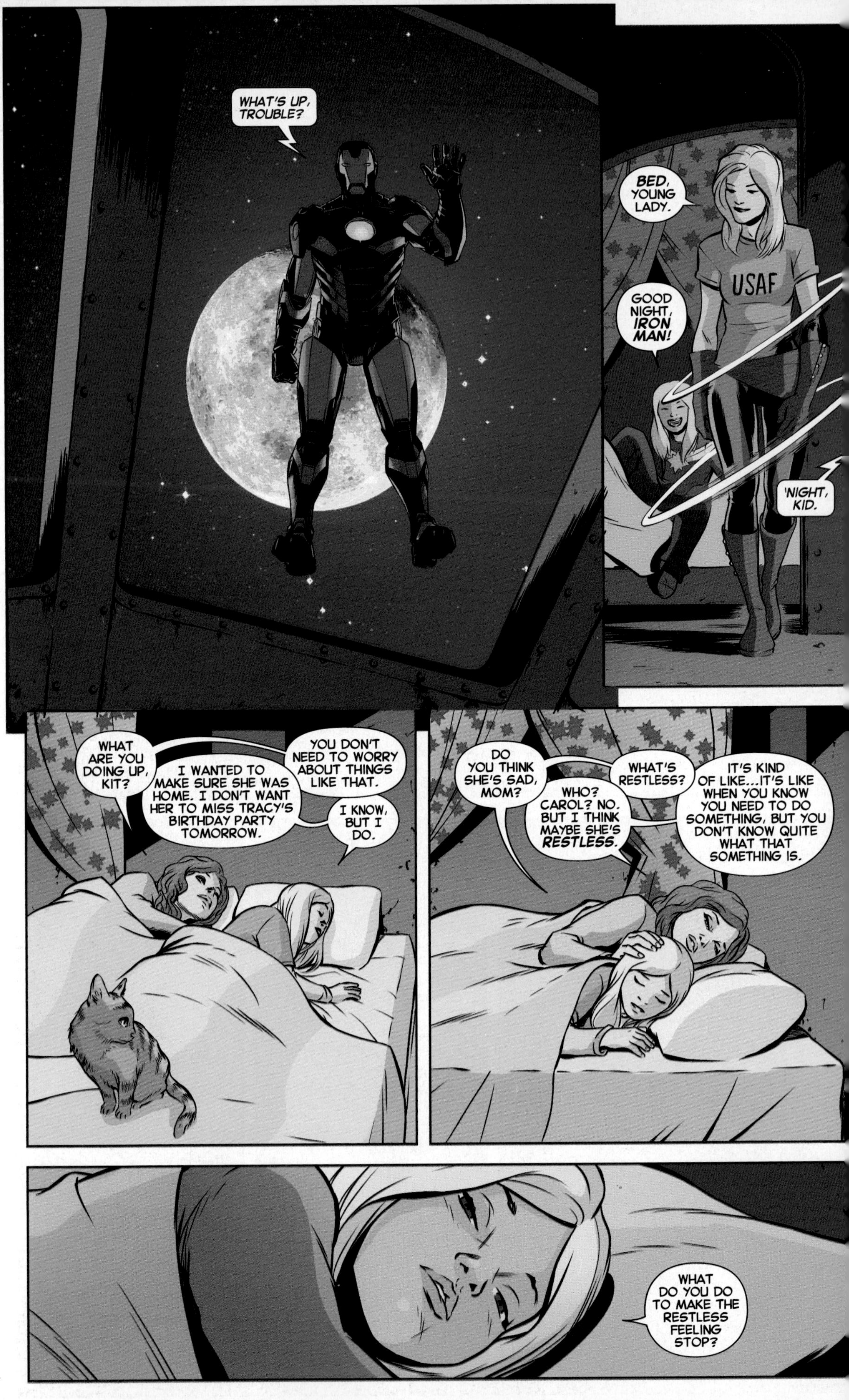
WHAT'S UP, TROUBLE?
BED, YOUNG LADY.
GOOD NIGHT, IRON MAN!
'NIGHT, KID.
WHAT ARE YOU DOING UP, KIT?
I WANTED TO MAKE SURE SHE WAS HOME. I DON'T WANT HER TO MISS TRACY'S BIRTHDAY PARTY TOMORROW.
YOU DON'T NEED TO WORRY ABOUT THINGS LIKE THAT.
I KNOW, BUT I DO.
DO YOU THINK SHE'S SAD, MOM?
WHO? CAROL? NO. BUT I THINK MAYBE SHE'S RESTLESS.
WHAT'S RESTLESS?
IT'S KIND OF LIKE...IT'S LIKE WHEN YOU KNOW YOU NEED TO DO SOMETHING, BUT YOU DON'T KNOW QUITE WHAT THAT SOMETHING IS.
WHAT DO YOU DO TO MAKE THE RESTLESS FEELING STOP?

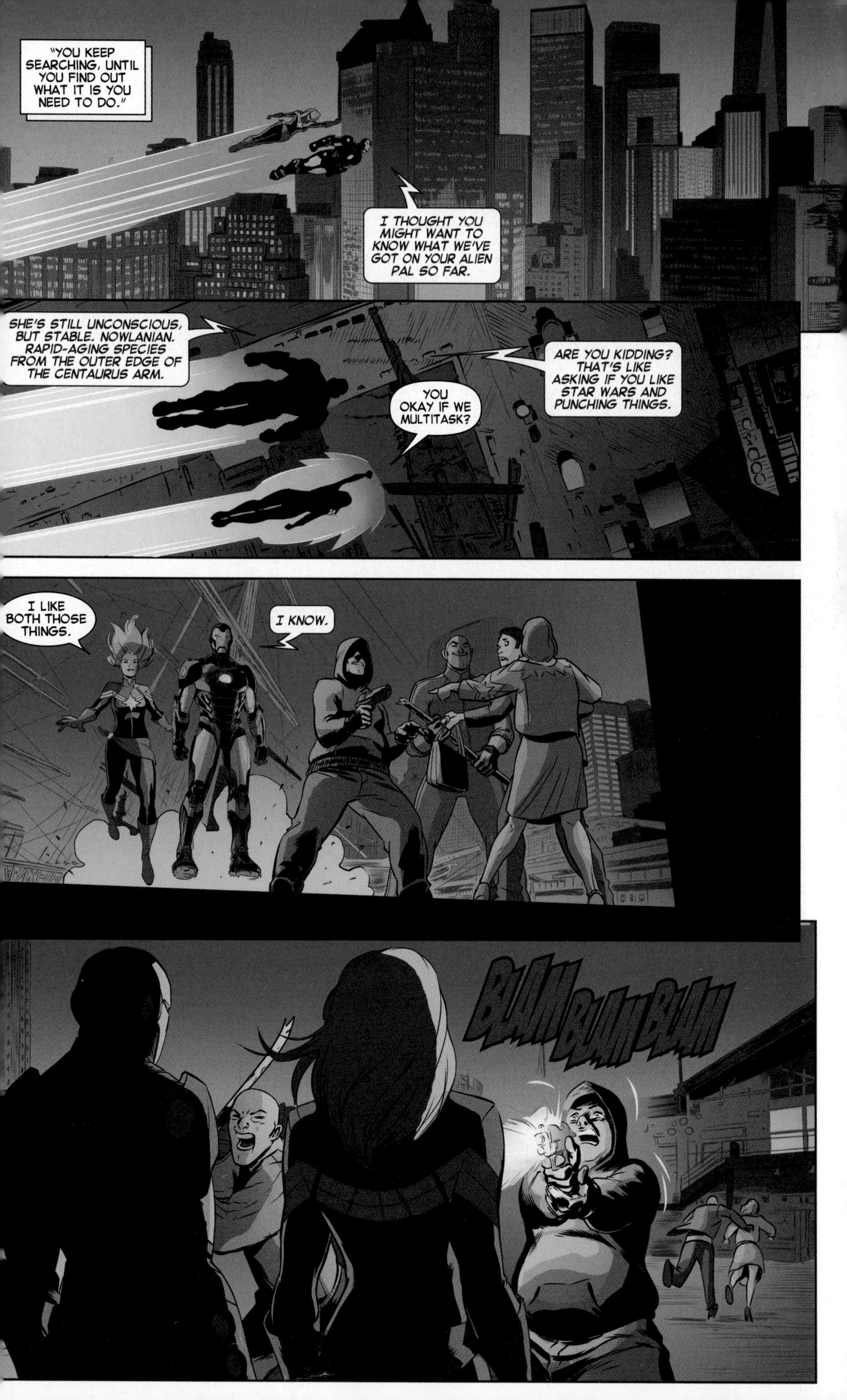
"YOU KEEP SEARCHING, UNTIL YOU FIND OUT WHAT IT IS YOU NEED TO DO."
I THOUGHT YOU MIGHT WANT TO KNOW WHAT WE'VE GOT ON YOUR ALIEN PAL SO FAR.
SHE'S STILL UNCONSCIOUS, BUT STABLE. NOWLANIAN. RAPID-AGING SPECIES FROM THE OUTER EDGE OF THE CENTAURUS ARM.
YOU OKAY IF WE MULTITASK?
ARE YOU KIDDING? THAT'S LIKE ASKING IF YOU LIKE STAR WARS AND PUNCHING THINGS.
I LIKE BOTH THOSE THINGS.
I KNOW.
BLAM BLAM BLAM

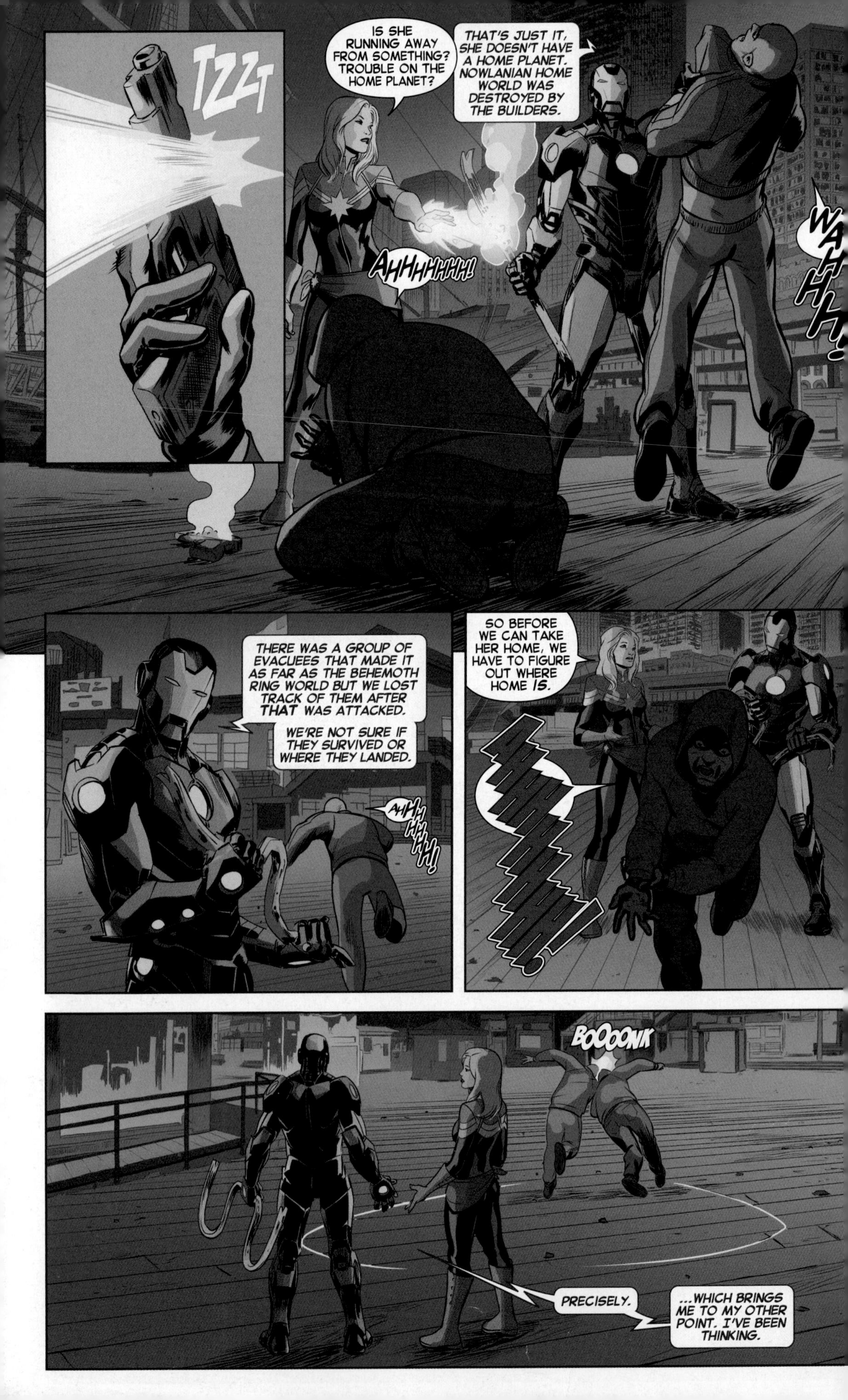
TZZT
IS SHE RUNNING AWAY FROM SOMETHING? TROUBLE ON THE HOME PLANET?
THAT'S JUST IT, SHE DOESN'T HAVE A HOME PLANET. NOWLANIAN HOME WORLD WAS DESTROYED BY THE BUILDERS.
AHHHHHHH!
WAHHHH!
THERE WAS A GROUP OF EVACUEES THAT MADE IT AS FAR AS THE BEHEMOTH RING WORLD BUT WE LOST TRACK OF THEM AFTER THAT WAS ATTACKED.
WE'RE NOT SURE IF THEY SURVIVED OR WHERE THEY LANDED.
AHHHHHH!
SO BEFORE WE CAN TAKE HER HOME, WE HAVE TO FIGURE OUT WHERE HOME IS.
BOOOONK
PRECISELY.
...WHICH BRINGS ME TO MY OTHER POINT. I'VE BEEN THINKING.

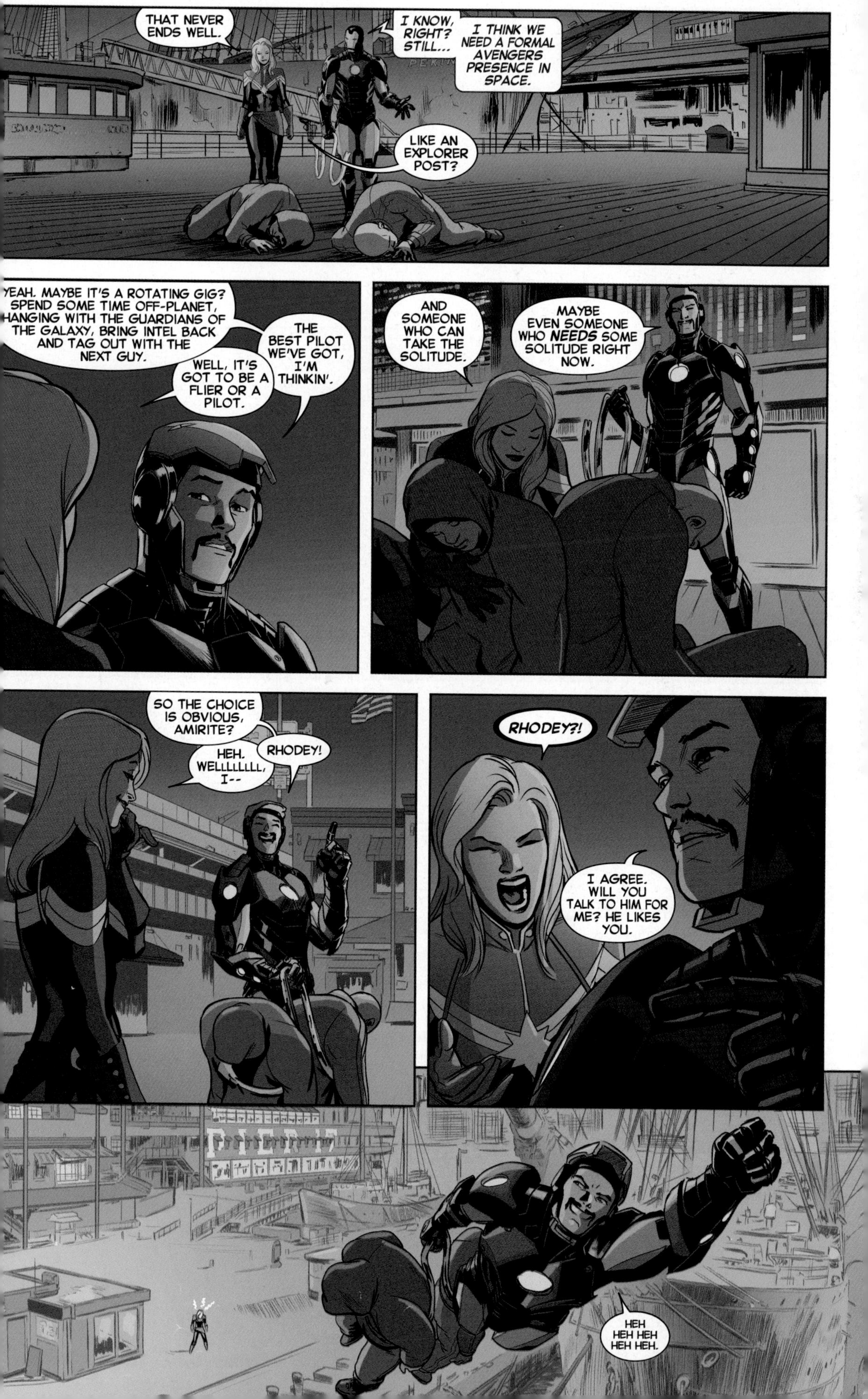
THAT NEVER ENDS WELL.
I KNOW, RIGHT? STILL...
I THINK WE NEED A FORMAL AVENGERS PRESENCE IN SPACE.
LIKE AN EXPLORER POST?
YEAH. MAYBE IT'S A ROTATING GIG? SPEND SOME TIME OFF-PLANET, HANGING WITH THE GUARDIANS OF THE GALAXY, BRING INTEL BACK AND TAG OUT WITH THE NEXT GUY.
WELL, IT'S GOT TO BE A FLIER OR A PILOT.
THE BEST PILOT WE'VE GOT, I'M THINKIN'.
AND SOMEONE WHO CAN TAKE THE SOLITUDE.
MAYBE EVEN SOMEONE WHO NEEDS SOME SOLITUDE RIGHT NOW.
SO THE CHOICE IS OBVIOUS, AMIRITE?
HEH. WELLLLLLLL, I--
RHODEY!
RHODEY?!
I AGREE. WILL YOU TALK TO HIM FOR ME? HE LIKES YOU.
PIER 17
HEH HEH HEH HEH HEH.

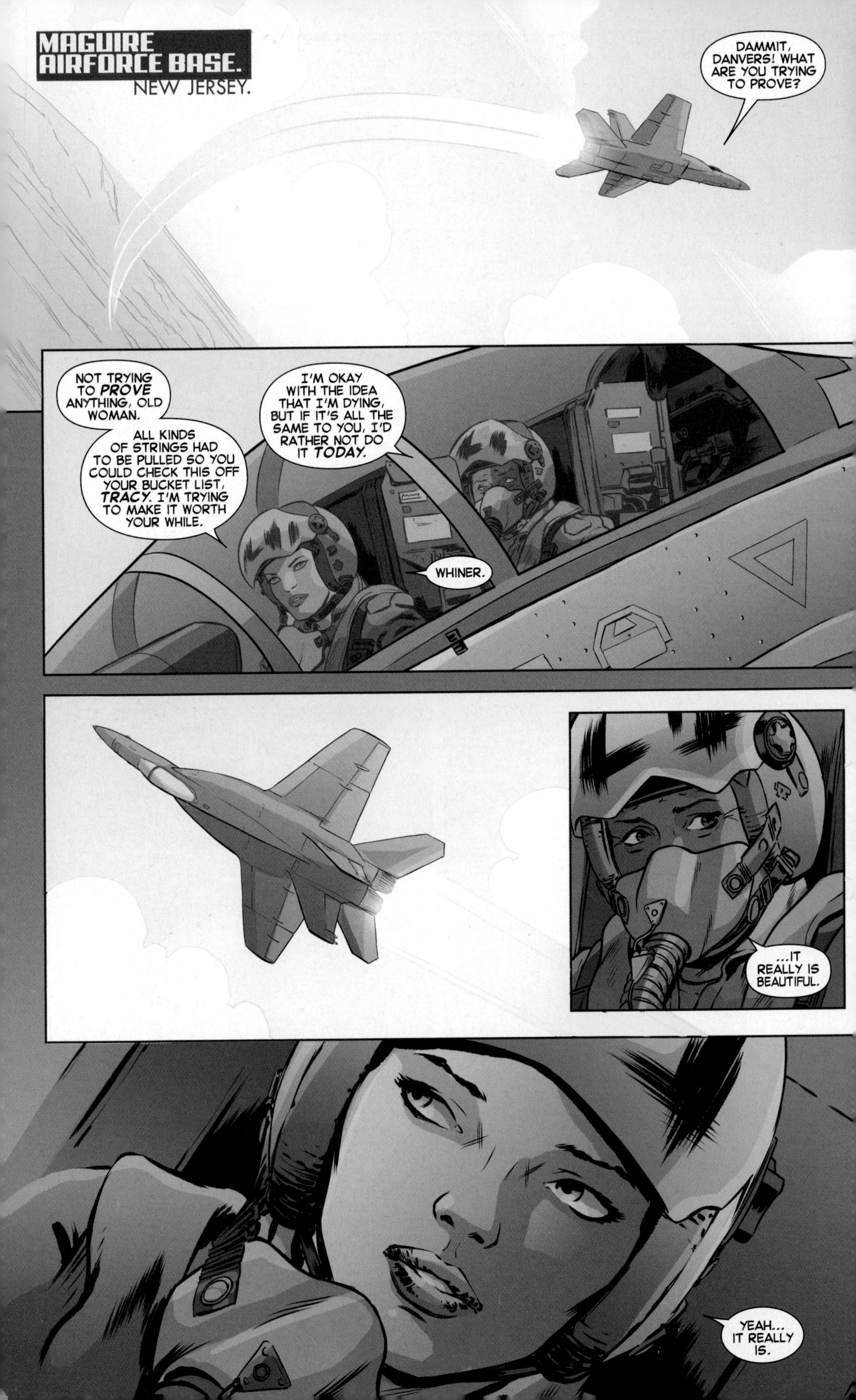
MAGUIRE AIRFORCE BASE.
NEW JERSEY.
DAMMIT, DANVERS! WHAT ARE YOU TRYING TO PROVE?
NOT TRYING TO PROVE ANYTHING, OLD WOMAN.
ALL KINDS OF STRINGS HAD TO BE PULLED SO YOU COULD CHECK THIS OFF YOUR BUCKET LIST, TRACY. I'M TRYING TO MAKE IT WORTH YOUR WHILE.
I'M OKAY WITH THE IDEA THAT I'M DYING, BUT IF IT'S ALL THE SAME TO YOU, I'D RATHER NOT DO IT TODAY.
WHINER.
...IT REALLY IS BEAUTIFUL.
YEAH... IT REALLY IS.

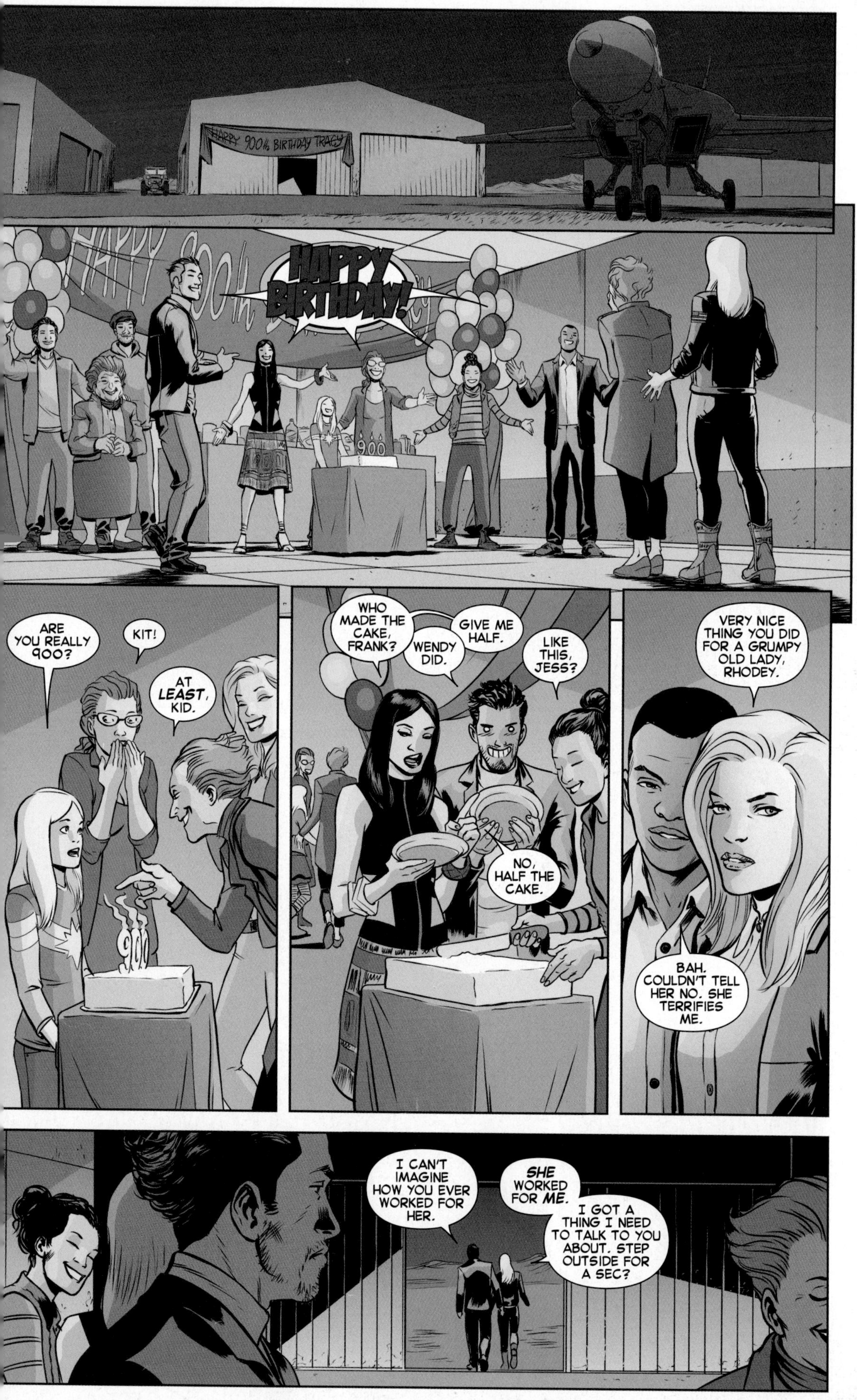

HAPPY 900th BIRTHDAY TRACY
HAPPY BIRTHDAY!
ARE YOU REALLY 900?
KIT!
AT LEAST, KID.
WHO MADE THE CAKE, FRANK?
GIVE ME HALF.
WENDY DID.
LIKE THIS, JESS?
NO, HALF THE CAKE.
VERY NICE THING YOU DID FOR A GRUMPY OLD LADY, RHODEY.
BAH. COULDN'T TELL HER NO. SHE TERRIFIES ME.
I CAN'T IMAGINE HOW YOU EVER WORKED FOR HER.
SHE WORKED FOR ME.
I GOT A THING I NEED TO TALK TO YOU ABOUT. STEP OUTSIDE FOR A SEC?

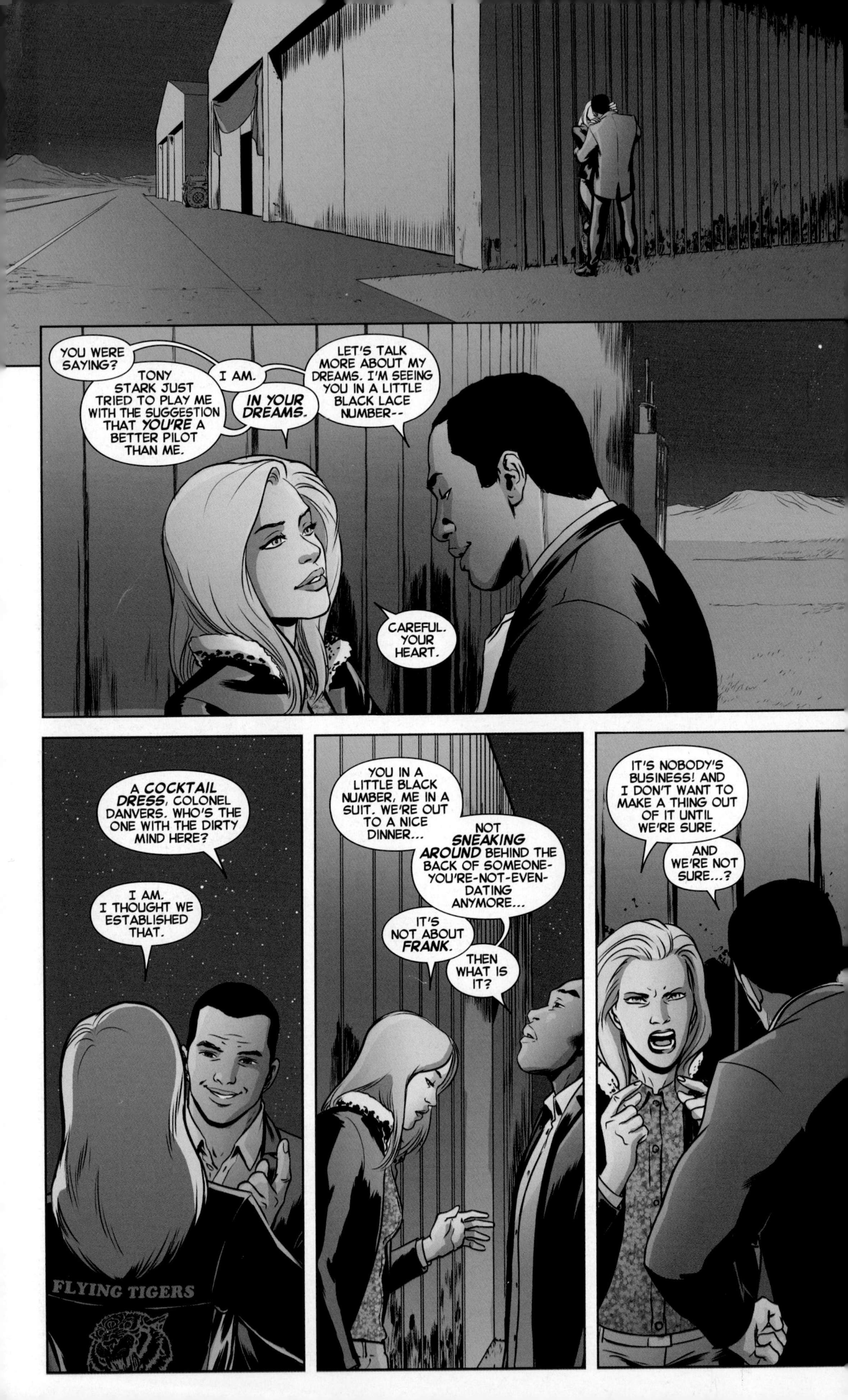
YOU WERE SAYING?
TONY STARK JUST TRIED TO PLAY ME WITH THE SUGGESTION THAT YOU'RE A BETTER PILOT THAN ME.
I AM.
IN YOUR DREAMS.
LET'S TALK MORE ABOUT MY DREAMS. I'M SEEING YOU IN A LITTLE BLACK LACE NUMBER--
CAREFUL. YOUR HEART.
A COCKTAIL DRESS, COLONEL DANVERS. WHO'S THE ONE WITH THE DIRTY MIND HERE?
I AM. I THOUGHT WE ESTABLISHED THAT.
FLYING TIGERS
YOU IN A LITTLE BLACK NUMBER, ME IN A SUIT. WE'RE OUT TO A NICE DINNER...
NOT SNEAKING AROUND BEHIND THE BACK OF SOMEONE-YOU'RE-NOT-EVEN-DATING ANYMORE...
IT'S NOT ABOUT FRANK.
THEN WHAT IS IT?
IT'S NOBODY'S BUSINESS! AND I DON'T WANT TO MAKE A THING OUT OF IT UNTIL WE'RE SURE.
AND WE'RE NOT SURE...?

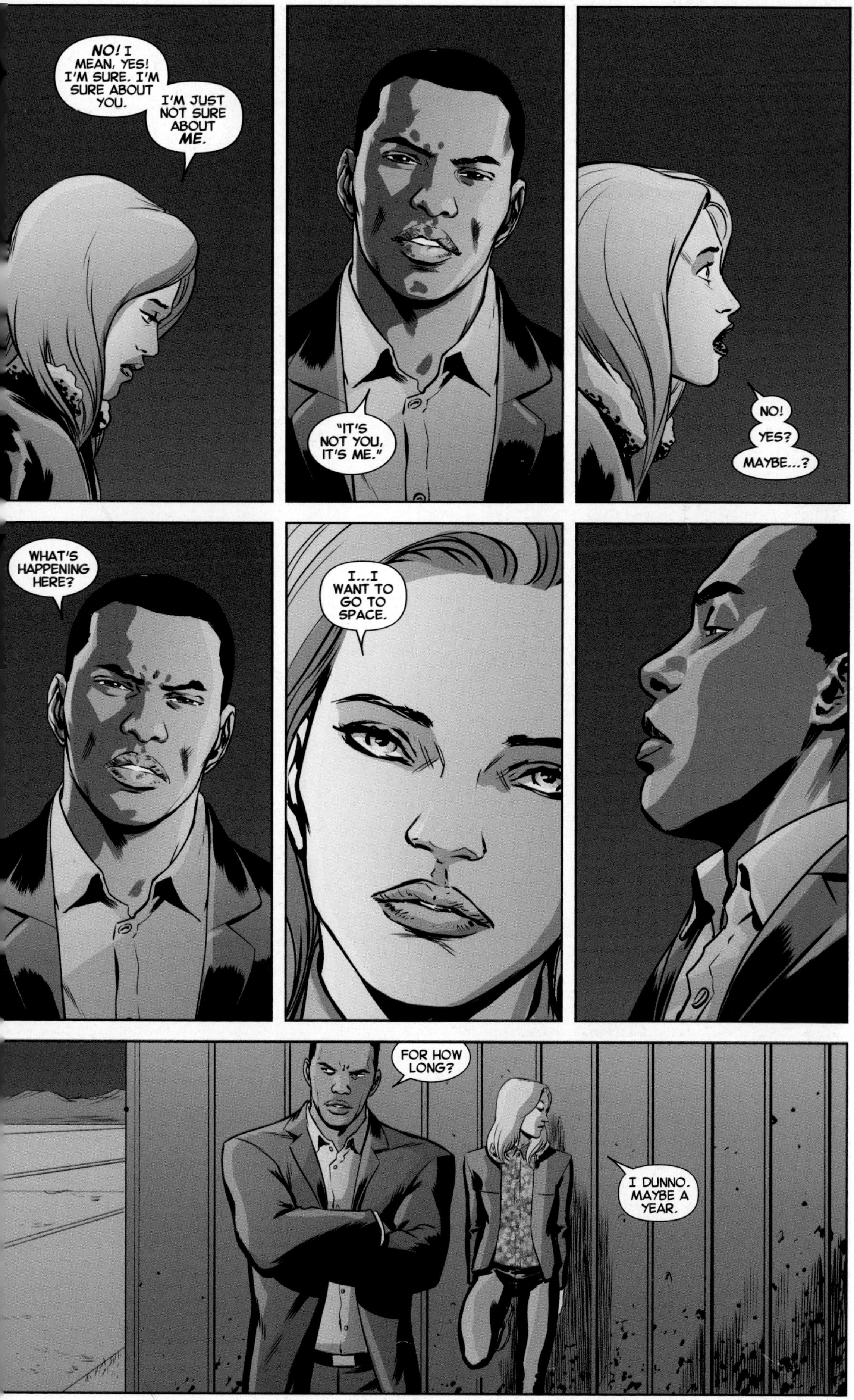
NO! I MEAN, YES! I'M SURE. I'M SURE ABOUT YOU.
I'M JUST NOT SURE ABOUT ME.
"IT'S NOT YOU, IT'S ME."
NO!
YES?
MAYBE...?
WHAT'S HAPPENING HERE?
I...I WANT TO GO TO SPACE.
FOR HOW LONG?
I DUNNO. MAYBE A YEAR.

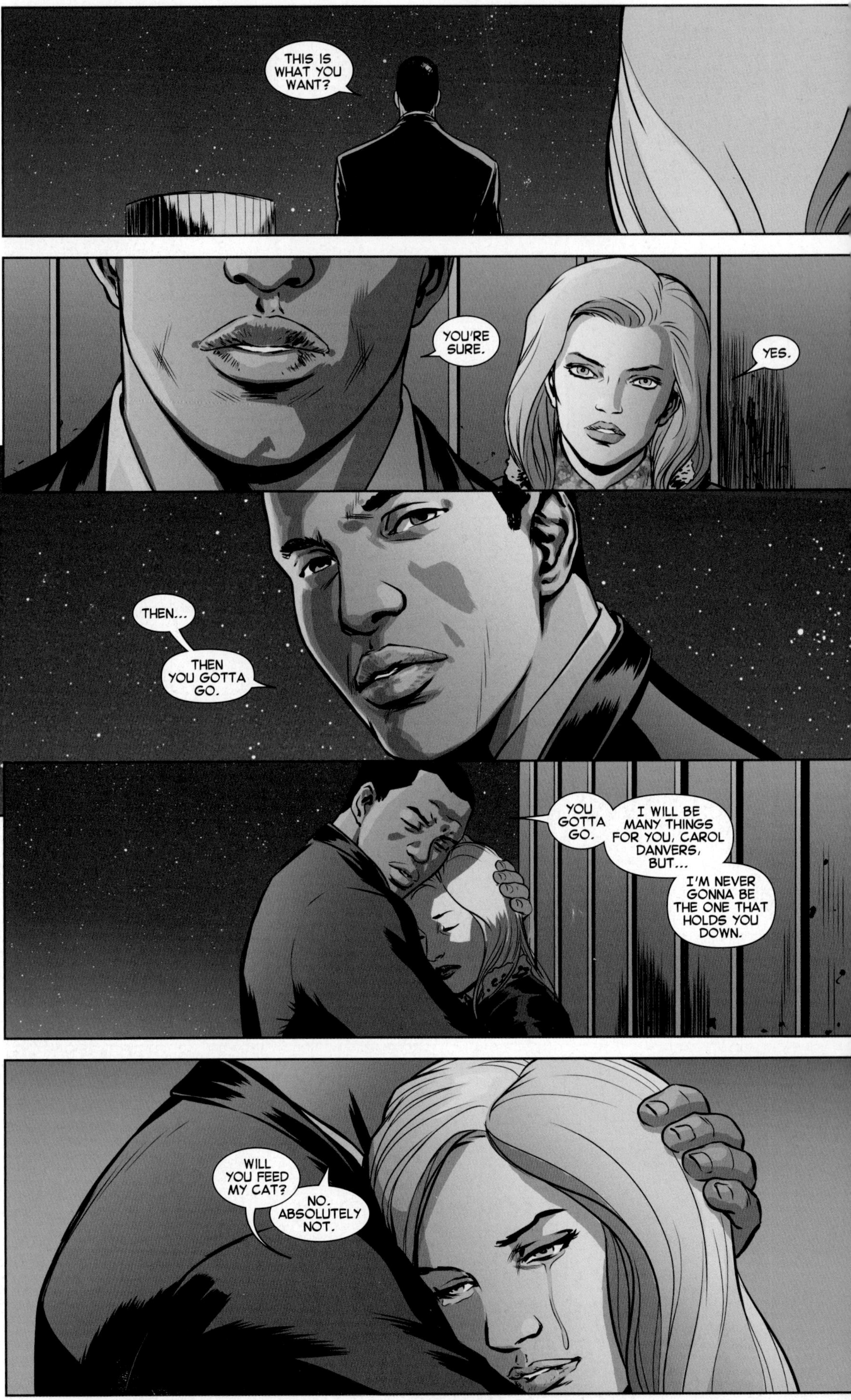
THIS IS WHAT YOU WANT?
YOU'RE SURE.
YES.
THEN...
THEN YOU GOTTA GO.
YOU GOTTA GO.
I WILL BE MANY THINGS FOR YOU, CAROL DANVERS, BUT...
I'M NEVER GONNA BE THE ONE THAT HOLDS YOU DOWN.
WILL YOU FEED MY CAT?
NO. ABSOLUTELY NOT.

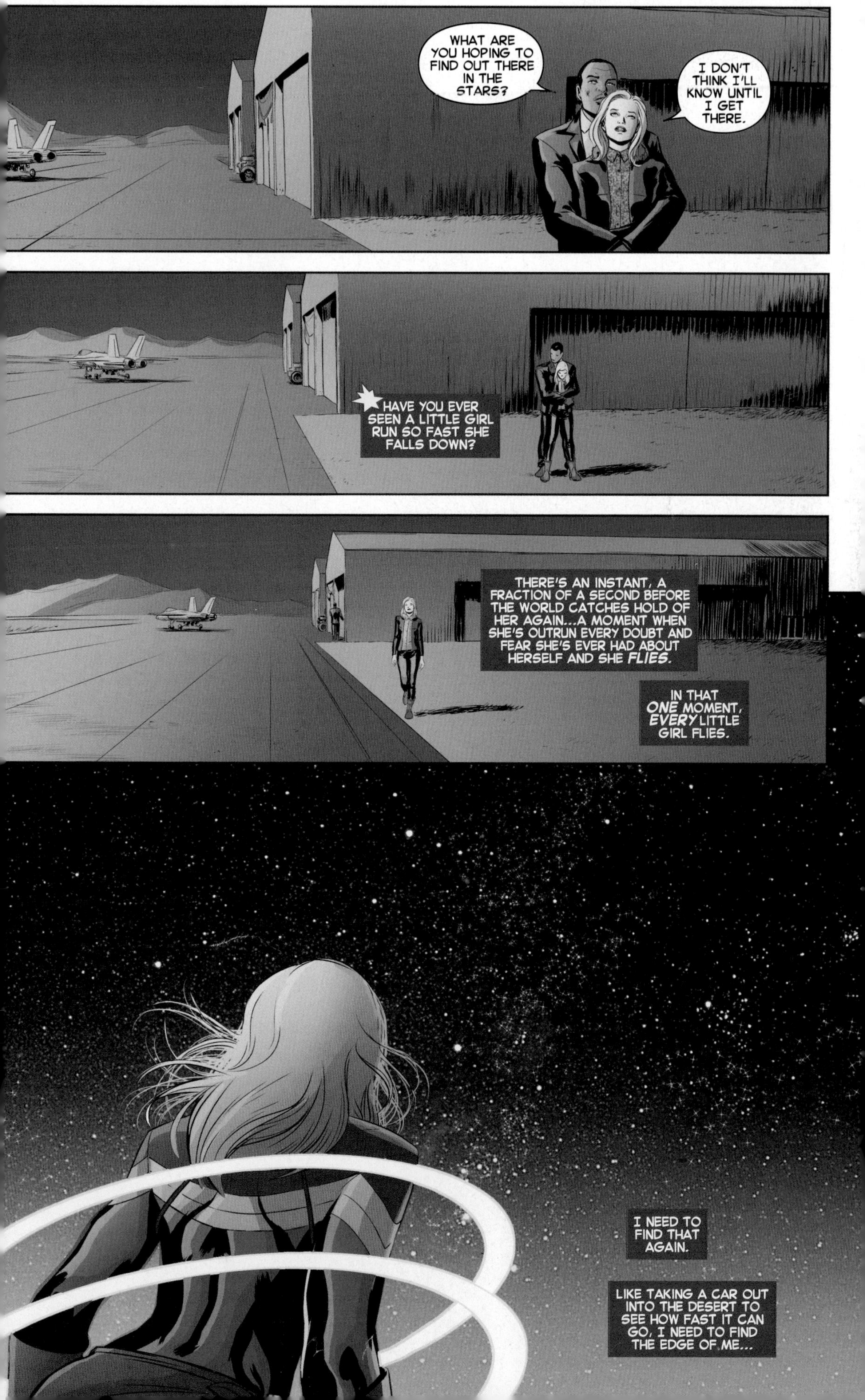

WHAT ARE YOU HOPING TO FIND OUT THERE IN THE STARS?
I DON'T THINK I'LL KNOW UNTIL I GET THERE.
HAVE YOU EVER SEEN A LITTLE GIRL RUN SO FAST SHE FALLS DOWN?
THERE'S AN INSTANT, A FRACTION OF A SECOND BEFORE THE WORLD CATCHES HOLD OF HER AGAIN...A MOMENT WHEN SHE'S OUTRUN EVERY DOUBT AND FEAR SHE'S EVER HAD ABOUT HERSELF AND SHE *FLIES.*
IN THAT *ONE* MOMENT, *EVERY* LITTLE GIRL FLIES.
I NEED TO FIND THAT AGAIN.
LIKE TAKING A CAR OUT INTO THE DESERT TO SEE HOW FAST IT CAN GO, I NEED TO FIND THE EDGE OF ME...

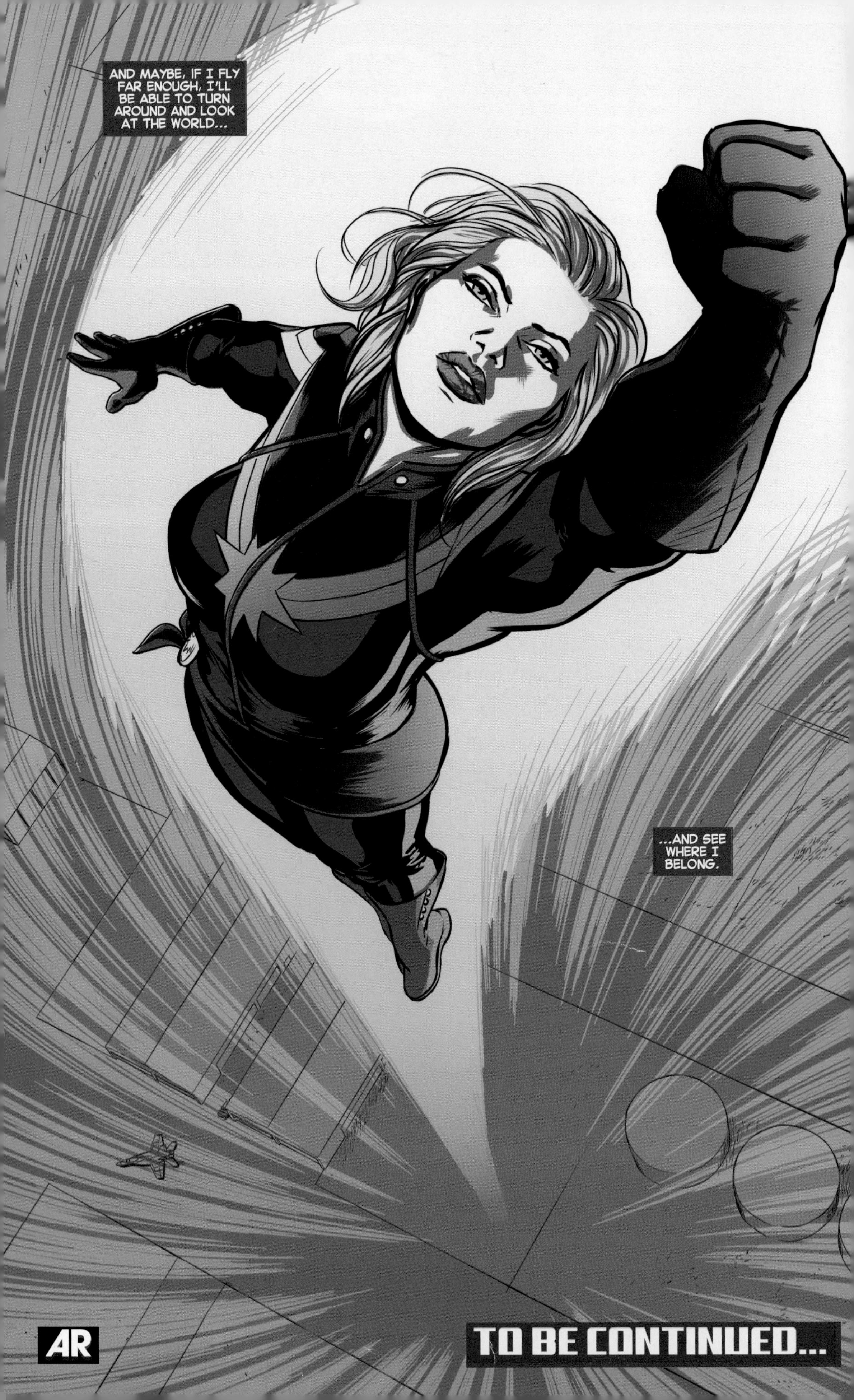
AND MAYBE, IF I FLY FAR ENOUGH, I'LL BE ABLE TO TURN AROUND AND LOOK AT THE WORLD...
...AND SEE WHERE I BELONG.
TO BE CONTINUED...

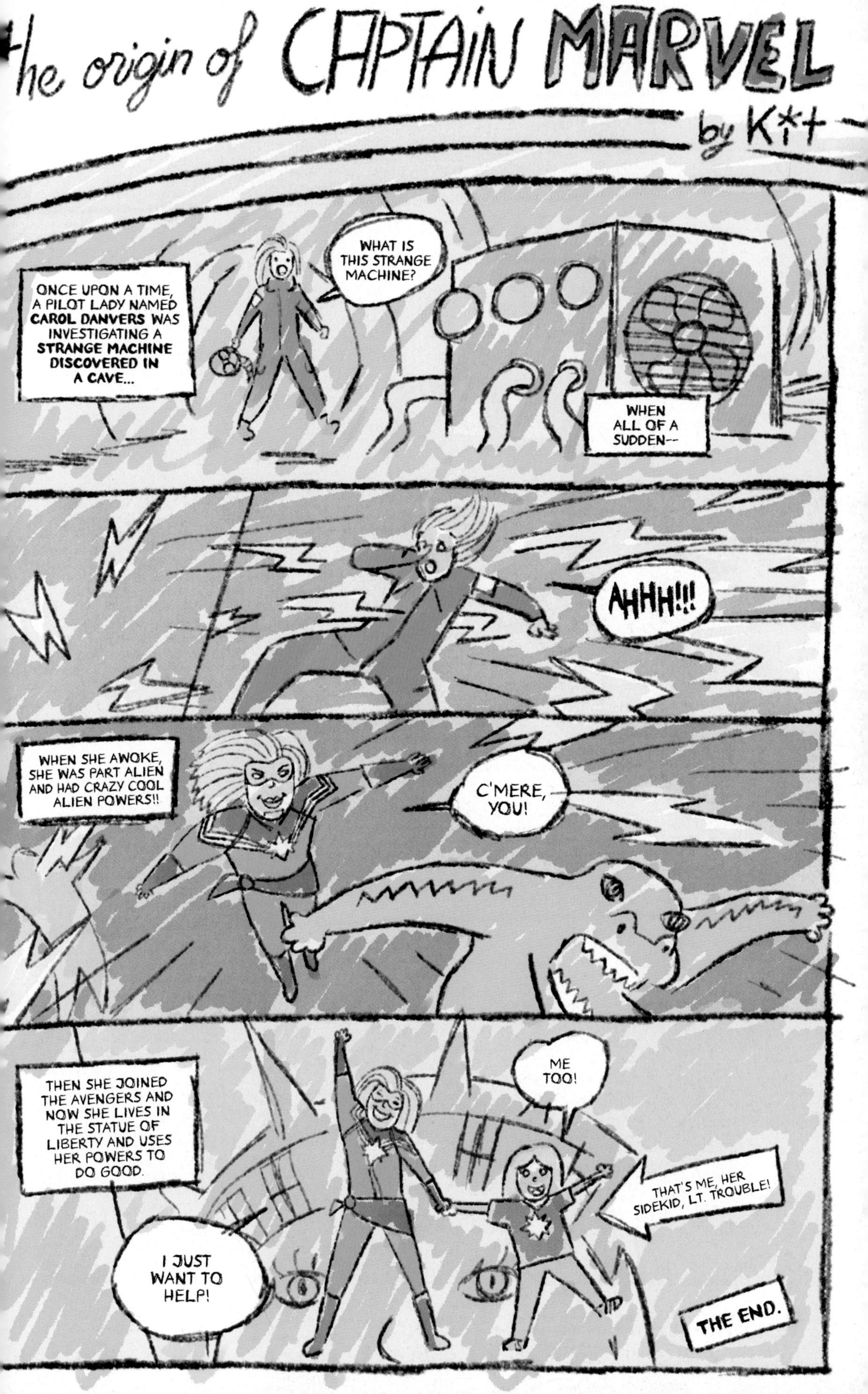
the origin of CAPTAIN MARVEL
by K*t
ONCE UPON A TIME, A PILOT LADY NAMED CAROL DANVERS WAS INVESTIGATING A STRANGE MACHINE DISCOVERED IN A CAVE...
WHAT IS THIS STRANGE MACHINE?
WHEN ALL OF A SUDDEN--
AHHH!!!
WHEN SHE AWOKE, SHE WAS PART ALIEN AND HAD CRAZY COOL ALIEN POWERS!!
C'MERE, YOU!
THEN SHE JOINED THE AVENGERS AND NOW SHE LIVES IN THE STATUE OF LIBERTY AND USES HER POWERS TO DO GOOD.
ME TOO!
THAT'S ME, HER SIDEKID, LT. TROUBLE!
I JUST WANT TO HELP!
THE END.

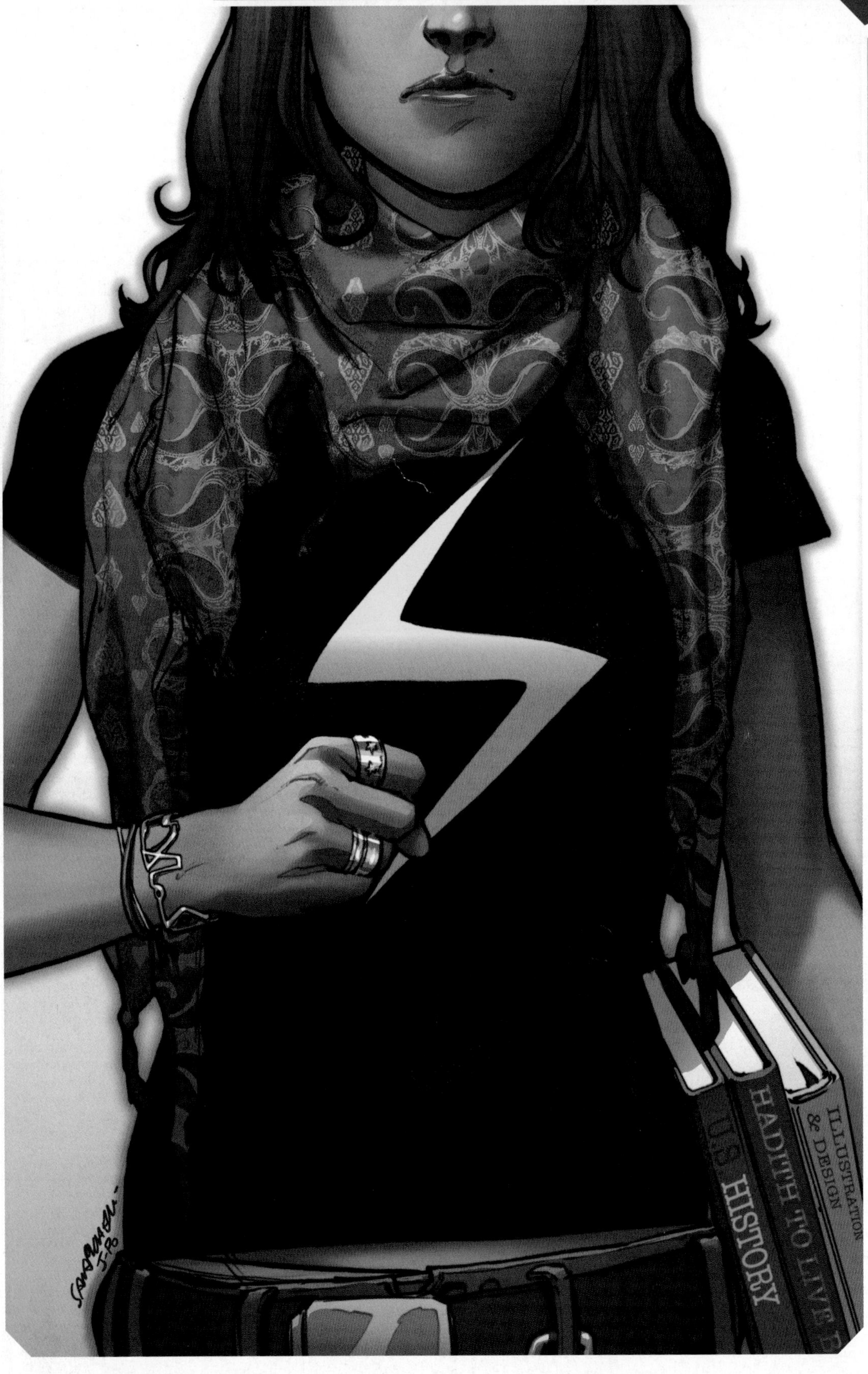
U.S. HISTORY
HADITH TO LIVE
ILLUSTRATION & DESIGN

MS. MARVEL #1

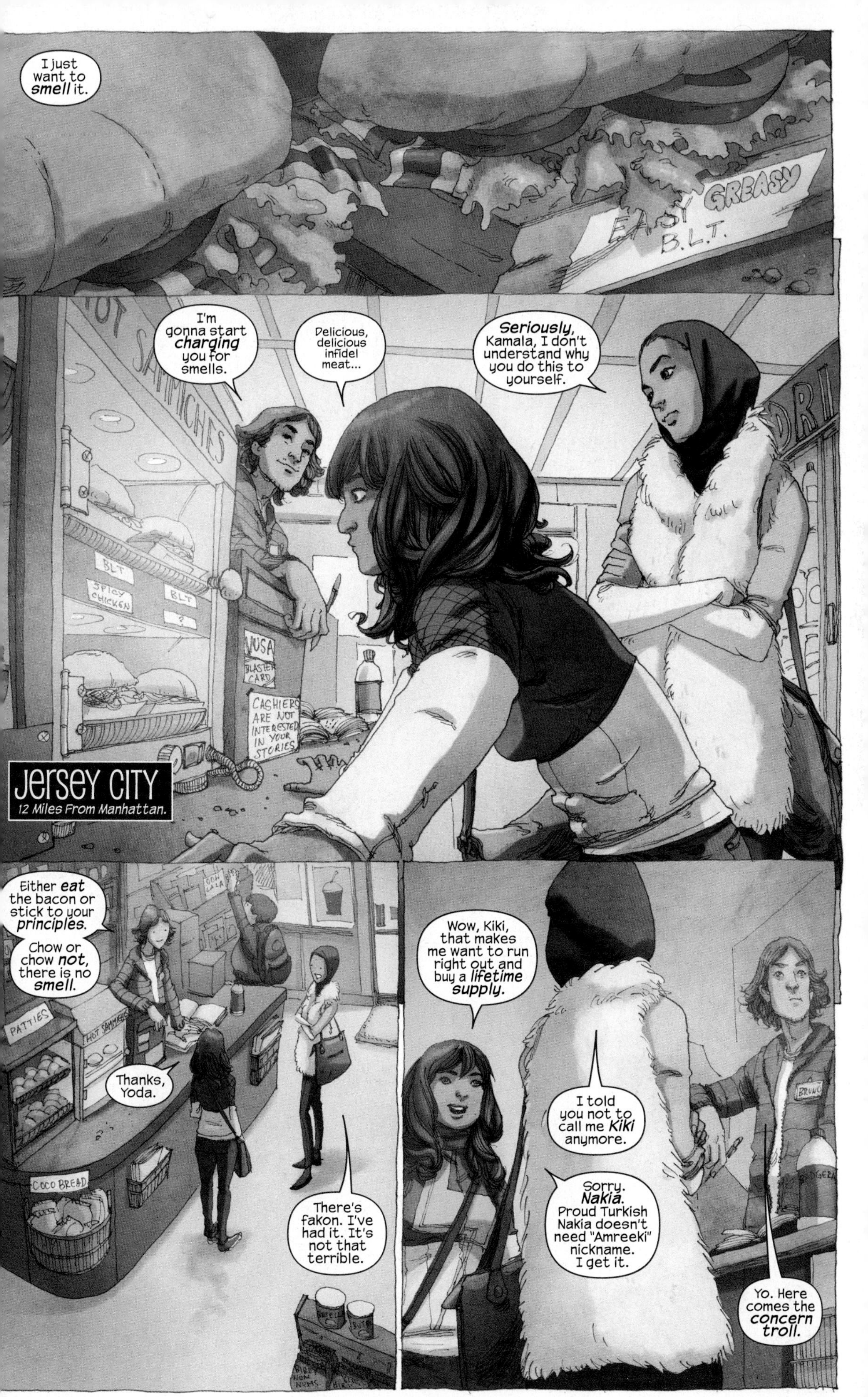
I just want to smell it.
EASY GREASY B.L.T.
I'm gonna start charging you for smells.
Delicious, delicious infidel meat...
Seriously, Kamala, I don't understand why you do this to yourself.
HOT SAMMICHES
BLT
SPICY CHICKEN
BLT
VISA BLASTER CARD
CASHIERS ARE NOT INTERESTED IN YOUR STORIES
JERSEY CITY
12 Miles From Manhattan.
Either eat the bacon or stick to your principles.
Chow or chow not, there is no smell.
PATTIES
HOT SAMMICHES
Thanks, Yoda.
COCO BREAD
There's fakon. I've had it. It's not that terrible.
Wow, Kiki, that makes me want to run right out and buy a lifetime supply.
I told you not to call me Kiki anymore.
Sorry. Nakia. Proud Turkish Nakia doesn't need "Amreeki" nickname. I get it.
BRUNO
Yo. Here comes the concern troll.

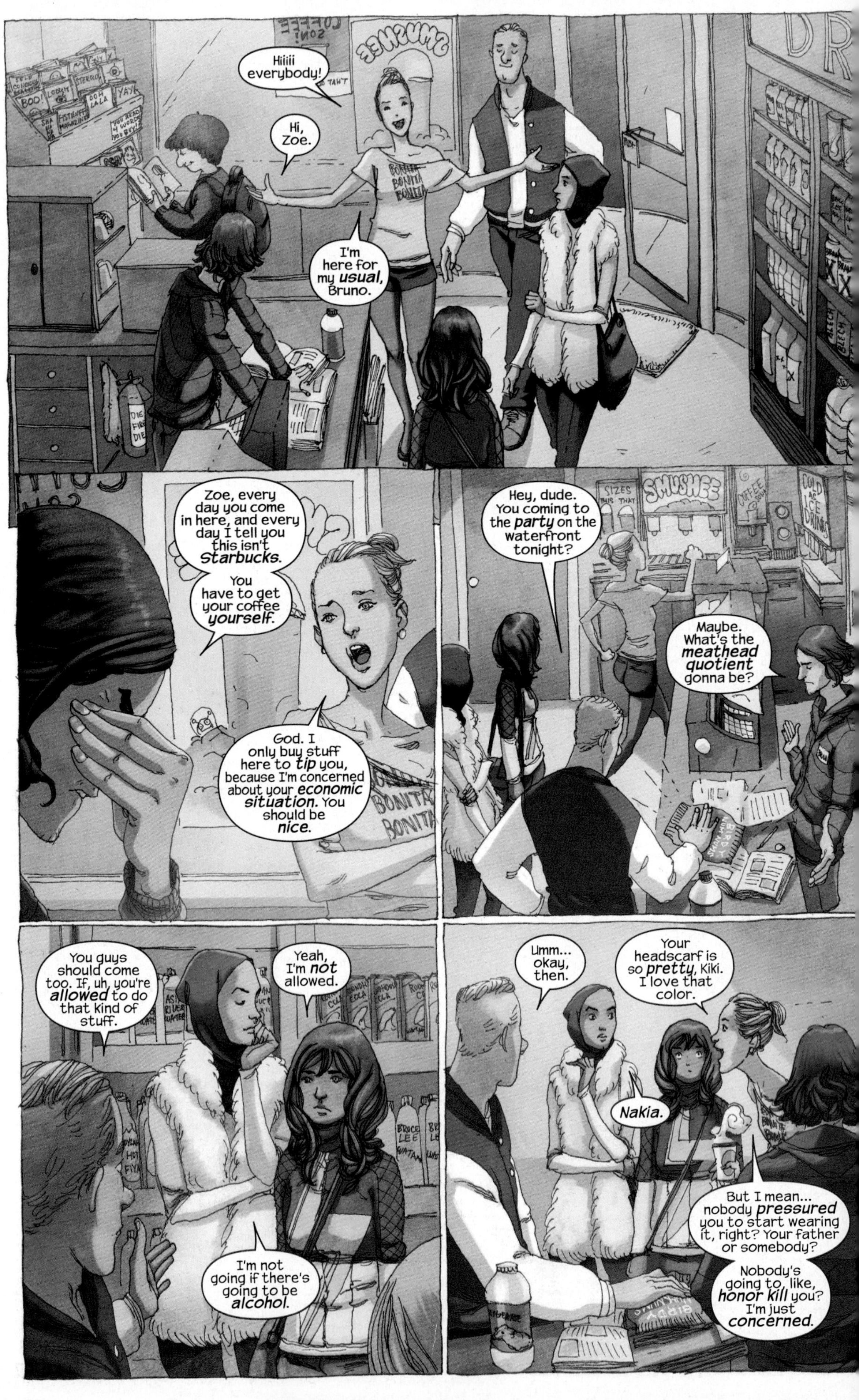
Hiiiii everybody!
Hi, Zoe.
I'm here for my *usual,* Bruno.
Zoe, every day you come in here, and every day I tell you this isn't **Starbucks.**
You have to get your coffee ***yourself.***
God. I only buy stuff here to *tip* you, because I'm concerned about your ***economic situation.*** You should be ***nice.***
Hey, dude. You coming to the *party* on the waterfront tonight?
Maybe. What's the ***meathead quotient*** gonna be?
You guys should come too. If, uh, you're ***allowed*** to do that kind of stuff.
Yeah, I'm ***not*** allowed.
I'm not going if there's going to be ***alcohol.***
Umm... okay, then.
Your headscarf is so ***pretty,*** Kiki. I love that color.
Nakia.
But I mean... nobody ***pressured*** you to start wearing it, right? Your father or somebody?
Nobody's going to, like, ***honor kill*** you? I'm just ***concerned.***

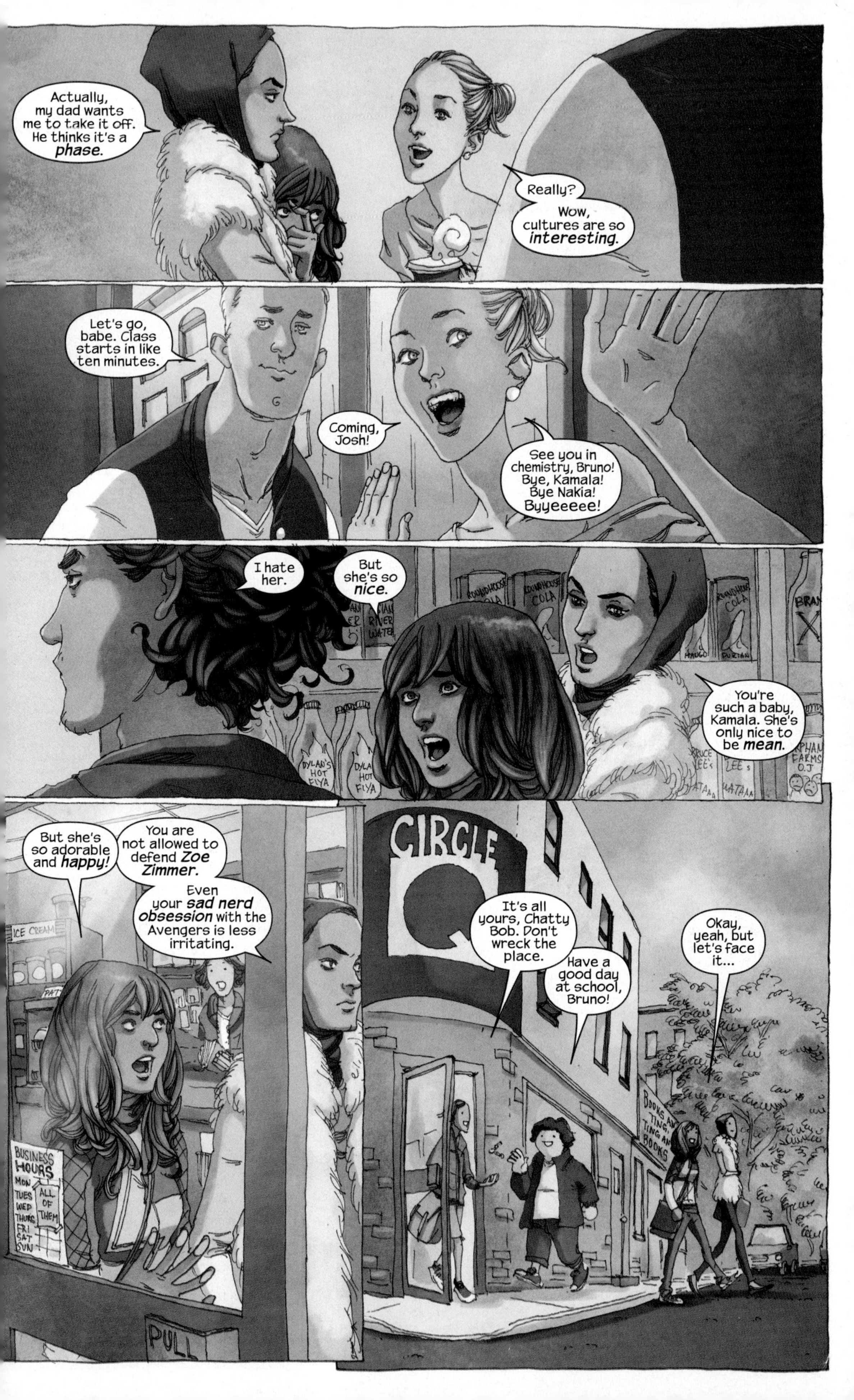
Actually, my dad wants me to take it off. He thinks it's a *phase*.
Really?
Wow, cultures are so *interesting*.
Let's go, babe. Class starts in like ten minutes.
Coming, Josh!
See you in chemistry, Bruno! Bye, Kamala! Bye Nakia! Byyeeeee!
I hate her.
But she's so *nice*.
You're such a baby, Kamala. She's only nice to be *mean*.
But she's so adorable and *happy*!
You are not allowed to defend *Zoe Zimmer*.
Even your *sad nerd obsession* with the Avengers is less irritating.
It's all yours, Chatty Bob. Don't wreck the place.
Have a good day at school, Bruno!
Okay, yeah, but let's face it...
CIRCLE Q
ICE CREAM
BUSINESS HOURS
MON TUES WED THURS FRI SAT SUN
ALL OF THEM
BOOKS AN' TING, TING AN' BOOKS
PULL

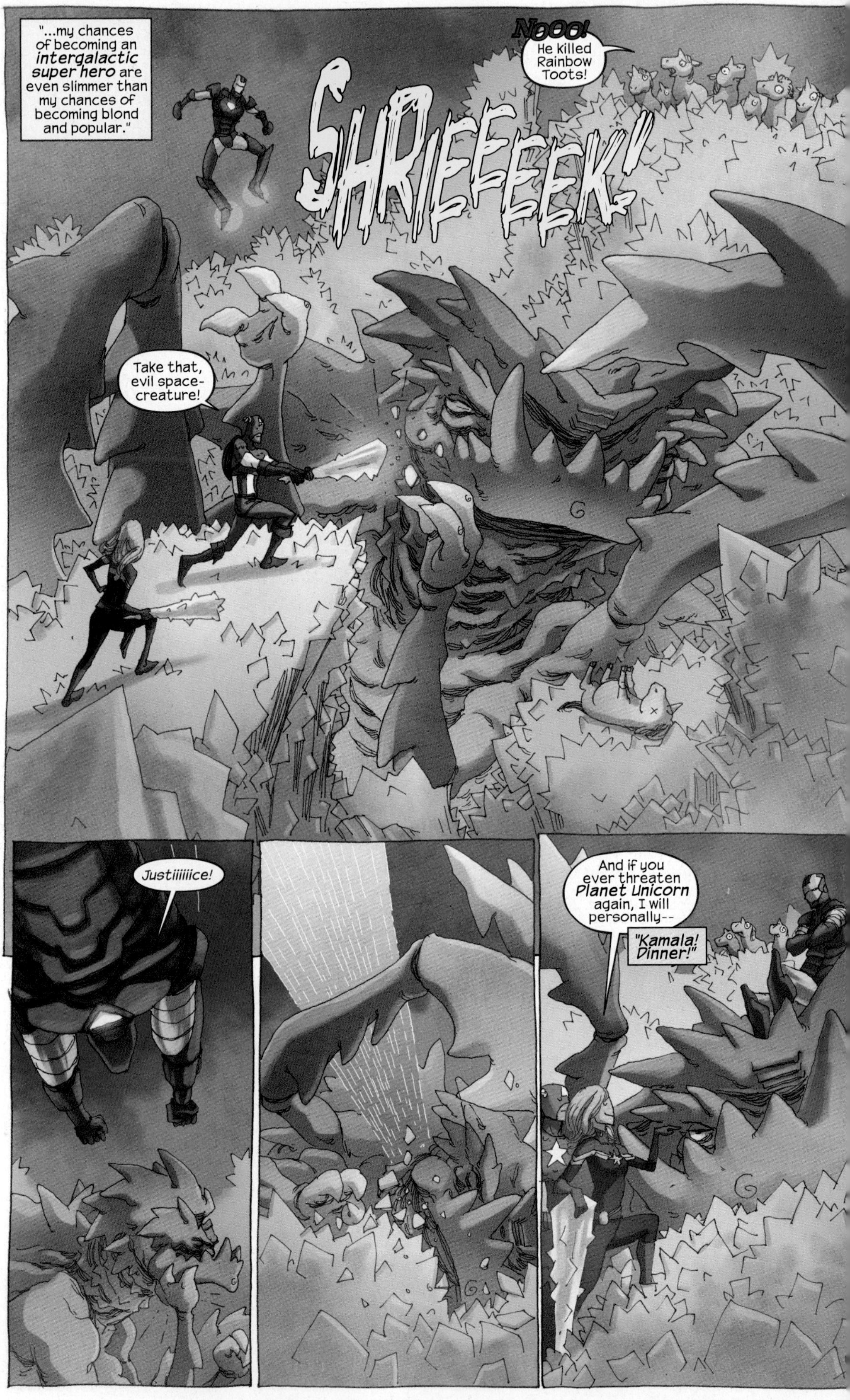
"...my chances of becoming an *intergalactic super hero* are even slimmer than my chances of becoming blond and popular."
SHRIEEEEK!
NOOOO!
He killed Rainbow Toots!
Take that, evil space-creature!
Justiiiiiice!
And if you ever threaten *Planet Unicorn* again, I will personally--
"Kamala! Dinner!"

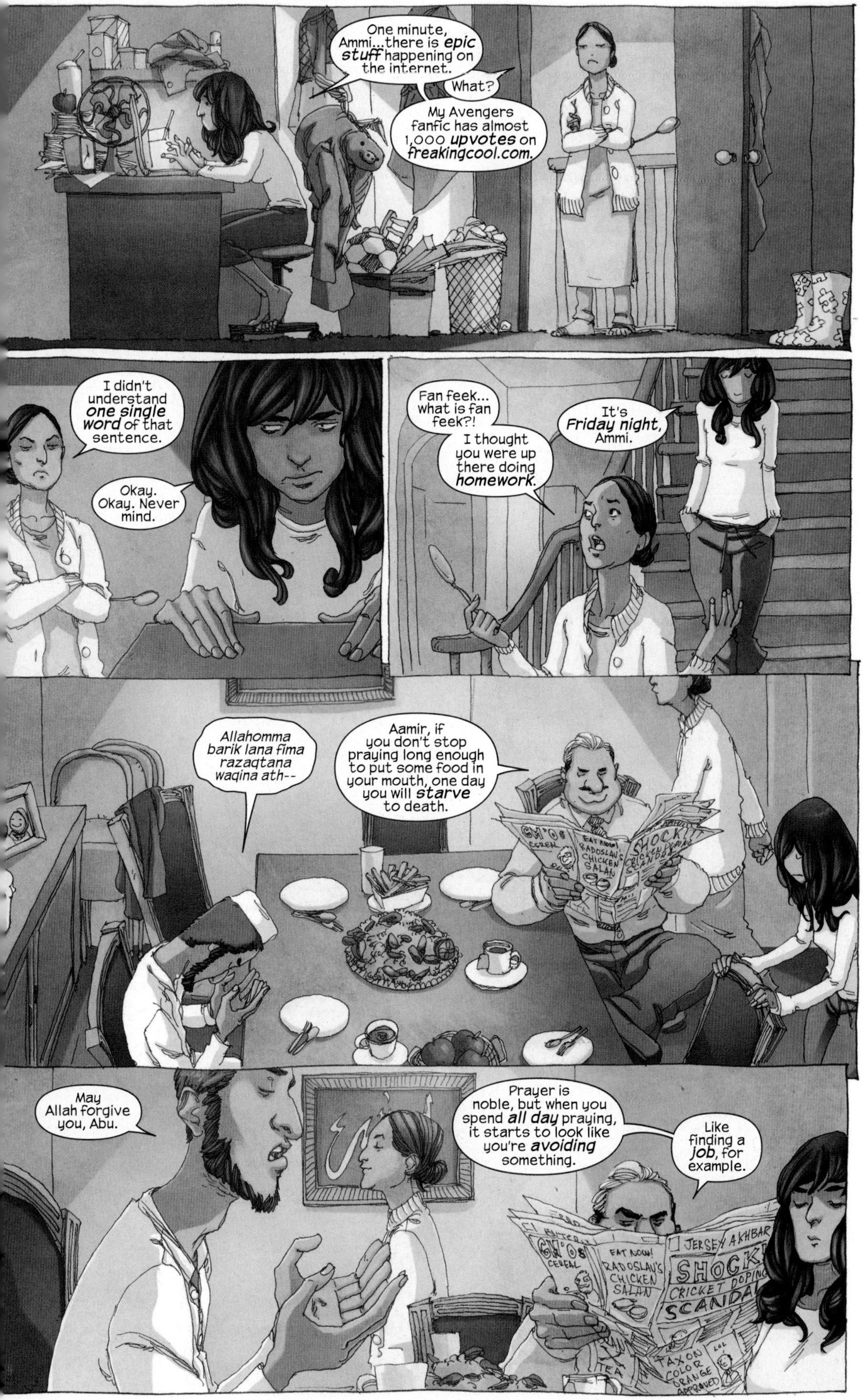
One minute, Ammi...there is epic stuff happening on the internet.
What?
My Avengers fanfic has almost 1,000 upvotes on freakingcool.com.
I didn't understand one single word of that sentence.
Okay. Okay. Never mind.
Fan feek... what is fan feek?!
I thought you were up there doing homework.
It's Friday night, Ammi.
Allahomma barik lana fima razaqtana waqina ath--
Aamir, if you don't stop praying long enough to put some food in your mouth, one day you will starve to death.
May Allah forgive you, Abu.
Prayer is noble, but when you spend all day praying, it starts to look like you're avoiding something.
Like finding a job, for example.
JERSEY AKHBAR
EAT NOW!
RADOSLAV'S CHICKEN SALAN

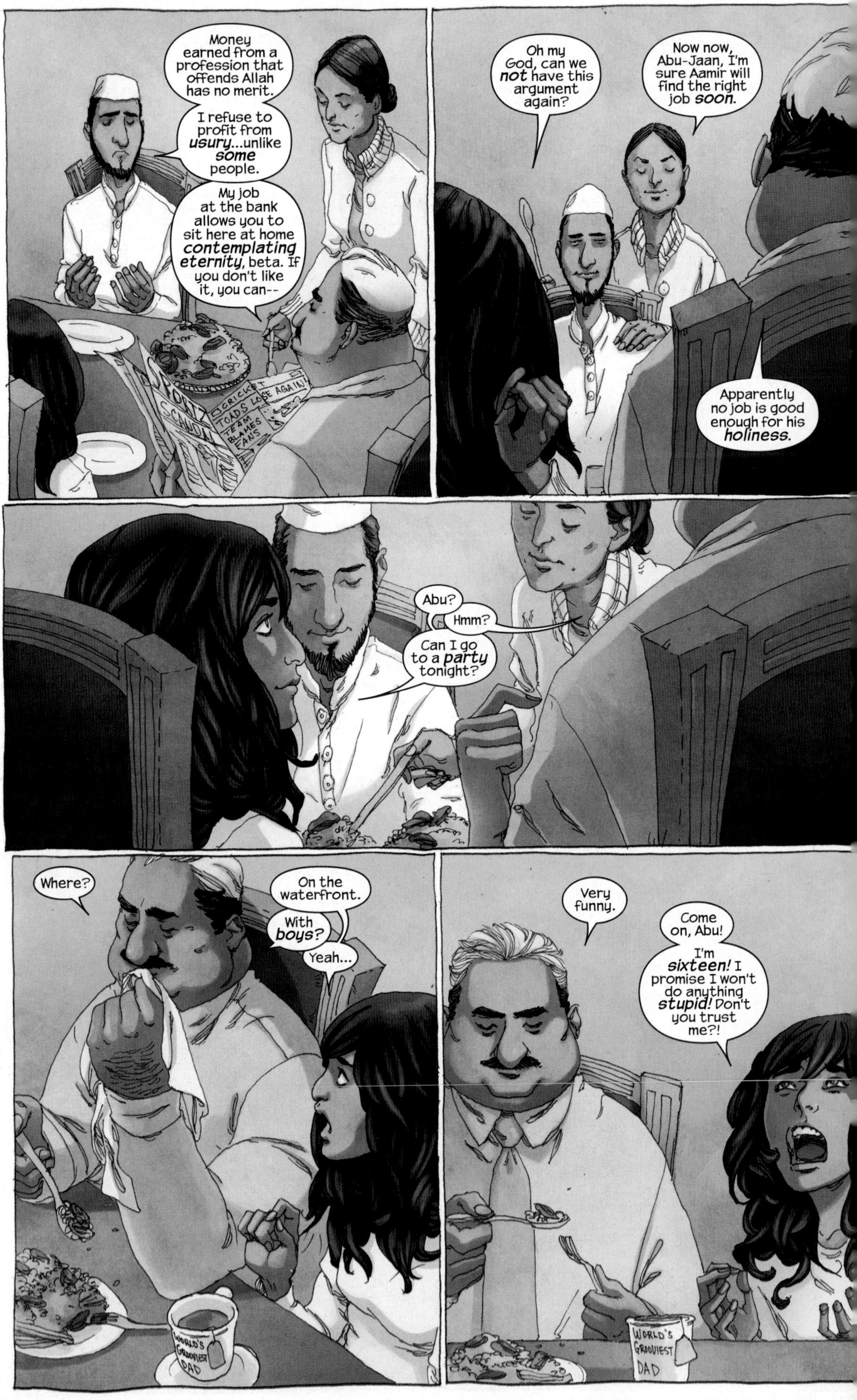
Money earned from a profession that offends Allah has no merit.
I refuse to profit from usury...unlike some people.
My job at the bank allows you to sit here at home contemplating eternity, beta. If you don't like it, you can--
SPORTZ
SCANDAL
CRICKET
TOADS LOSE AGAIN!
TEAM BLAMES FANS
Oh my God, can we not have this argument again?
Now now, Abu-Jaan, I'm sure Aamir will find the right job soon.
Apparently no job is good enough for his holiness.
Abu?
Hmm?
Can I go to a party tonight?
Where?
On the waterfront.
With boys?
Yeah...
WORLD'S GROOVIEST DAD
Very funny.
Come on, Abu!
I'm sixteen! I promise I won't do anything stupid! Don't you trust me?!
WORLD'S GROOVIEST DAD

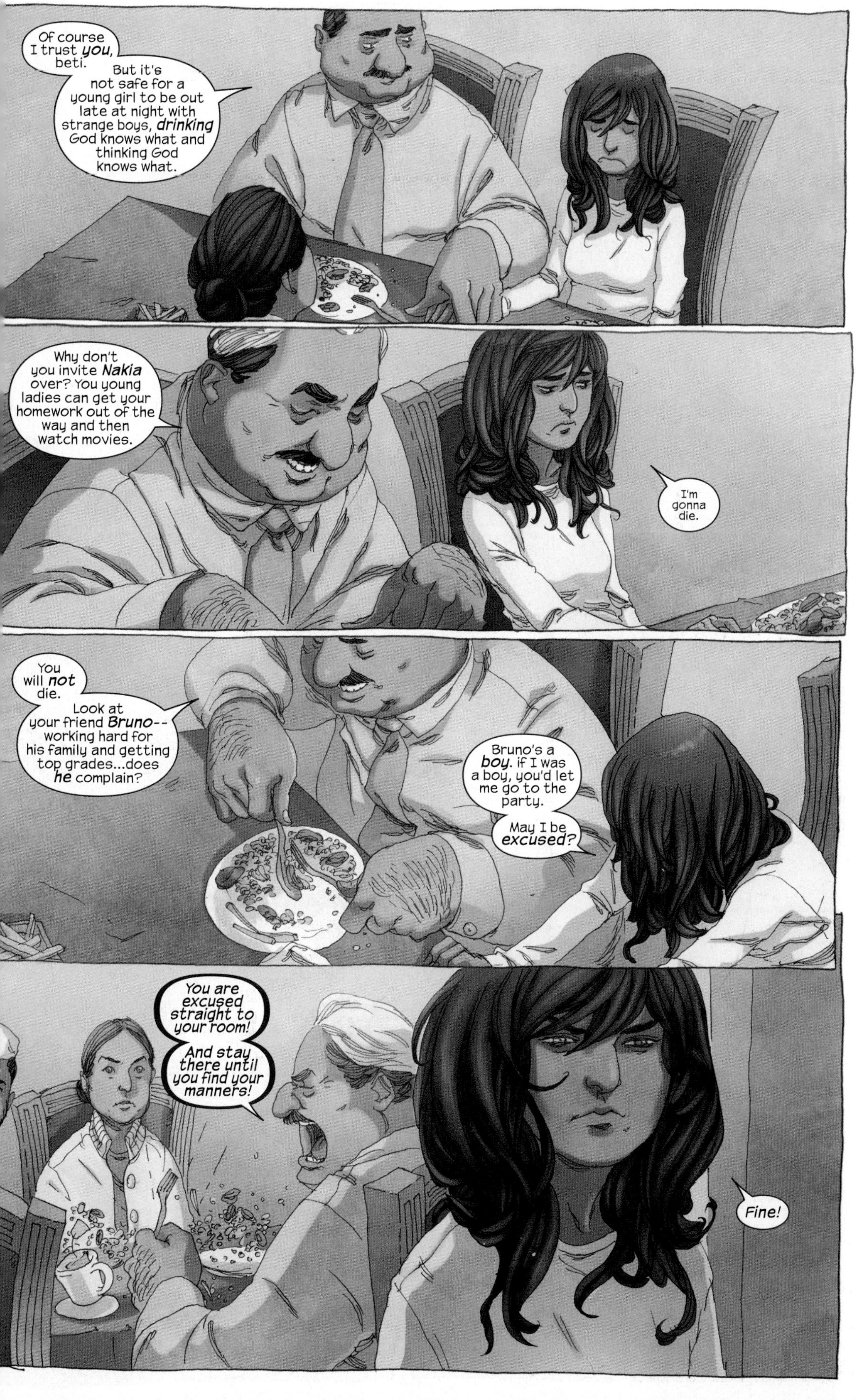

Of course I trust you, beti.
But it's not safe for a young girl to be out late at night with strange boys, drinking God knows what and thinking God knows what.
Why don't you invite Nakia over? You young ladies can get your homework out of the way and then watch movies.
I'm gonna die.
You will not die.
Look at your friend Bruno-- working hard for his family and getting top grades...does he complain?
Bruno's a boy. If I was a boy, you'd let me go to the party.
May I be excused?
You are excused straight to your room!
And stay there until you find your manners!
Fine!

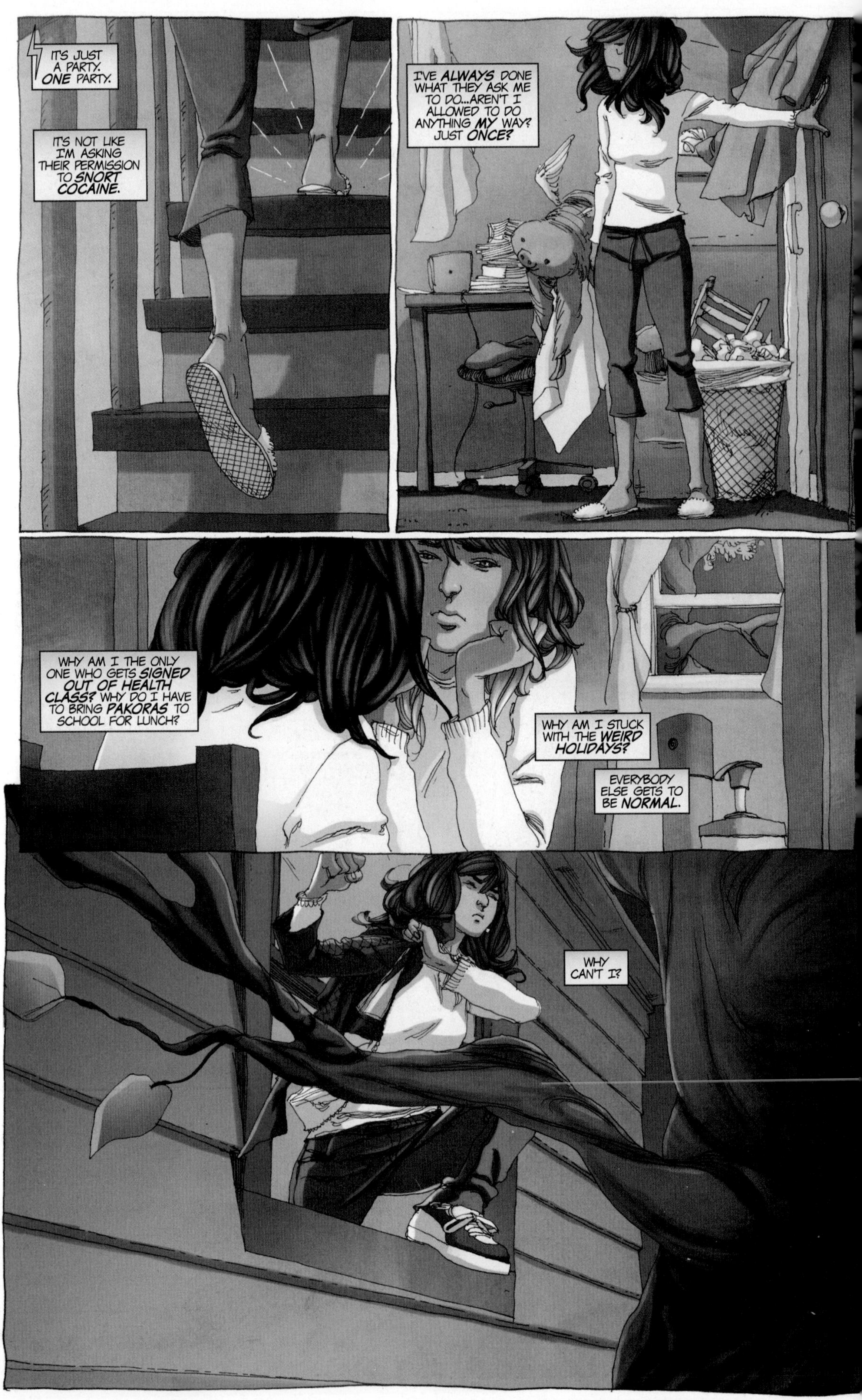
IT'S JUST A PARTY. ONE PARTY.
IT'S NOT LIKE I'M ASKING THEIR PERMISSION TO SNORT COCAINE.
I'VE ALWAYS DONE WHAT THEY ASK ME TO DO...AREN'T I ALLOWED TO DO ANYTHING MY WAY? JUST ONCE?
WHY AM I THE ONLY ONE WHO GETS SIGNED OUT OF HEALTH CLASS? WHY DO I HAVE TO BRING PAKORAS TO SCHOOL FOR LUNCH?
WHY AM I STUCK WITH THE WEIRD HOLIDAYS?
EVERYBODY ELSE GETS TO BE NORMAL.
WHY CAN'T I?

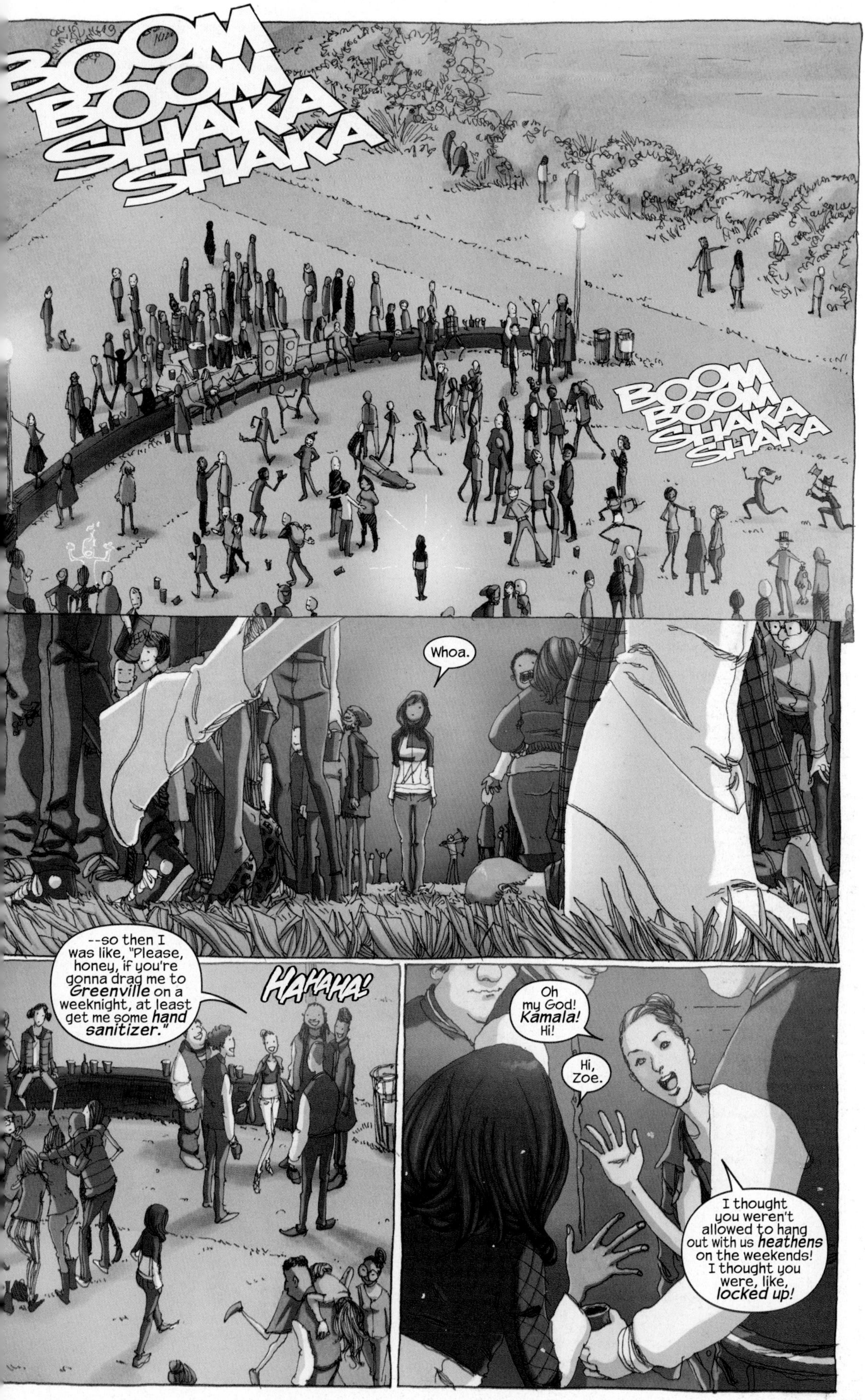
BOOM BOOM SHAKA SHAKA
BOOM BOOM SHAKA SHAKA
Whoa.
--so then I was like, "Please, honey, if you're gonna drag me to Greenville on a weeknight, at least get me some hand sanitizer."
HAHAHA!
Oh my God! Kamala! Hi!
Hi, Zoe.
I thought you weren't allowed to hang out with us heathens on the weekends! I thought you were, like, locked up!

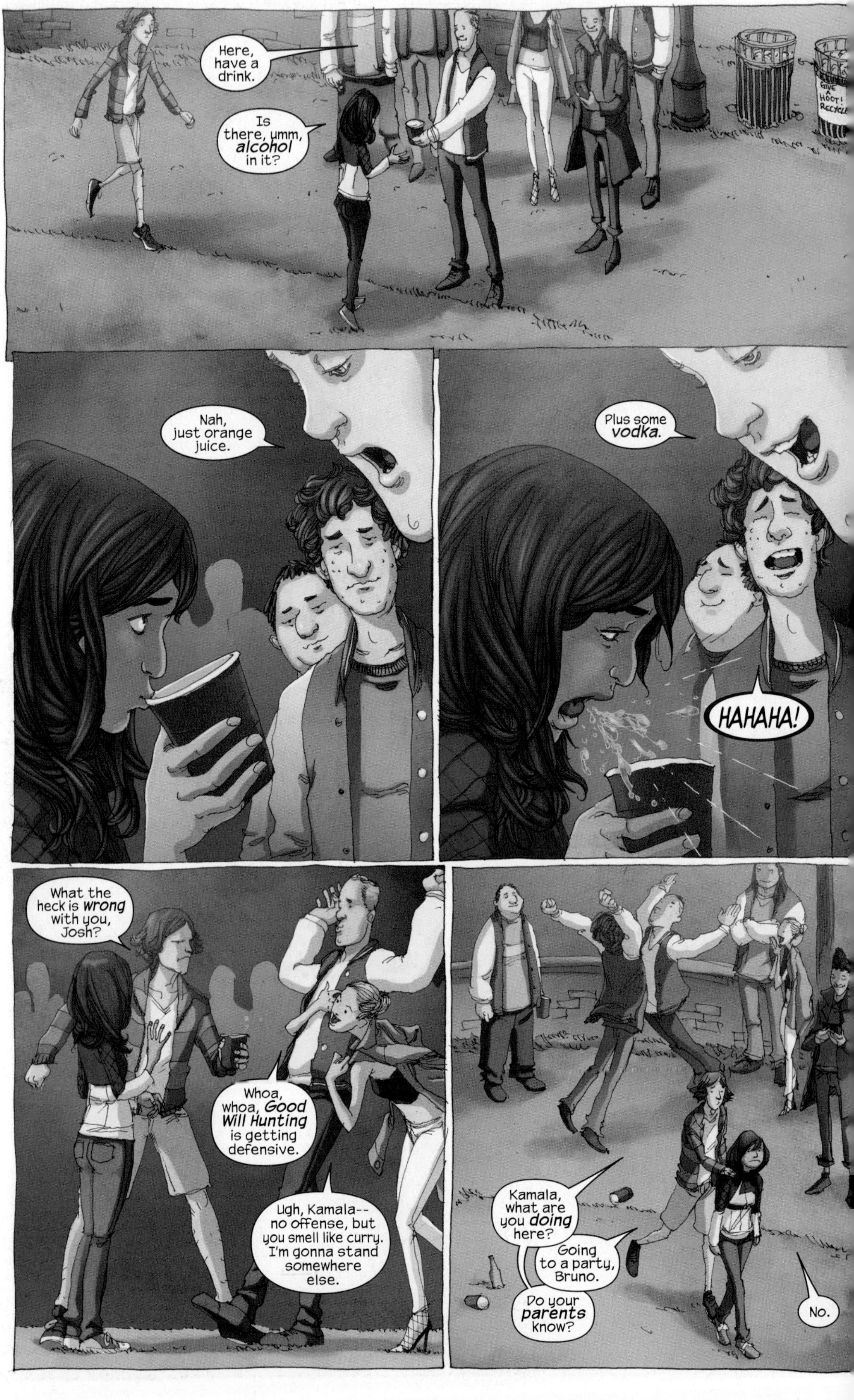
Here, have a drink.
Is there, umm, alcohol in it?
Nah, just orange juice.
Plus some vodka.
HAHAHA!
What the heck is wrong with you, Josh?
Whoa, whoa, Good Will Hunting is getting defensive.
Ugh, Kamala-- no offense, but you smell like curry. I'm gonna stand somewhere else.
GIVE A HOOT! RECYCLE
Kamala, what are you doing here?
Going to a party, Bruno.
Do your parents know?
No.

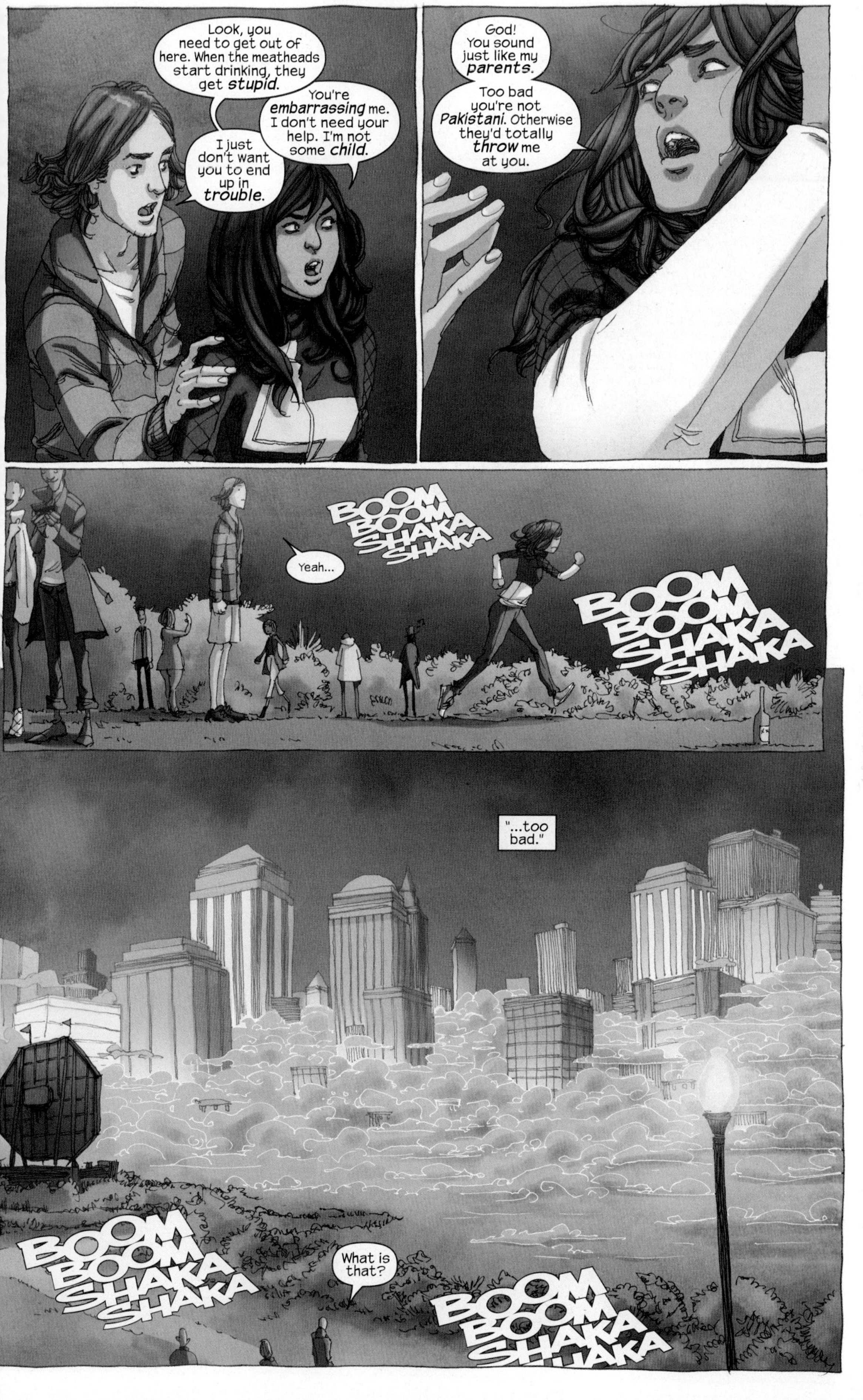
Look, you need to get out of here. When the meatheads start drinking, they get *stupid*.
I just don't want you to end up in *trouble*.
You're *embarrassing* me. I don't need your help. I'm not some *child*.
God! You sound just like my *parents*.
Too bad you're not *Pakistani*. Otherwise they'd totally *throw* me at you.
BOOM BOOM SHAKA SHAKA
Yeah...
BOOM BOOM SHAKA SHAKA
"...too bad."
BOOM BOOM SHAKA SHAKA
What is that?
BOOM BOOM SHAKA SHAKA

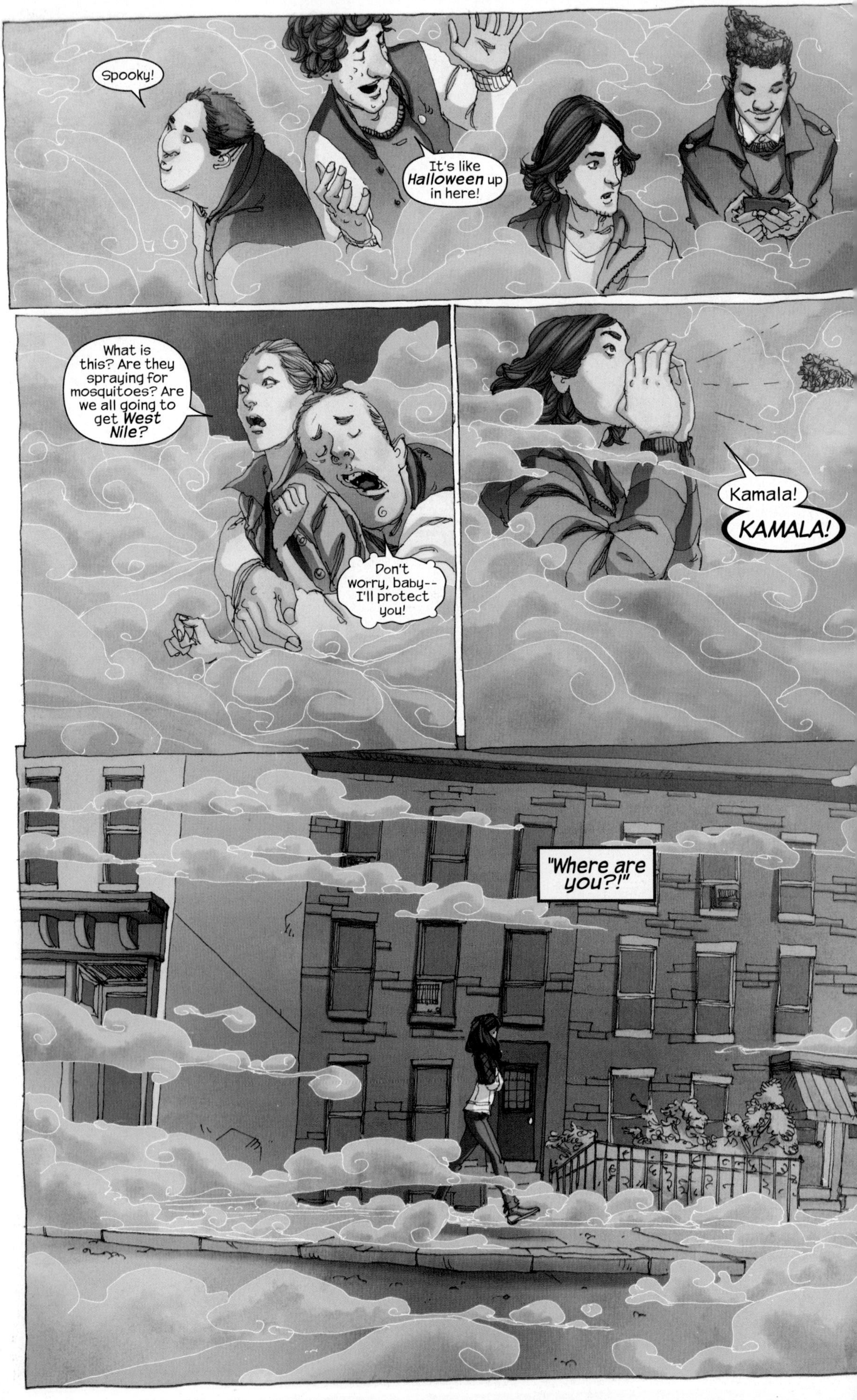
Spooky!
It's like *Halloween* up in here!
What is this? Are they spraying for mosquitoes? Are we all going to get *West Nile*?
Don't worry, baby--I'll protect you!
Kamala!
KAMALA!
"Where are you?!"

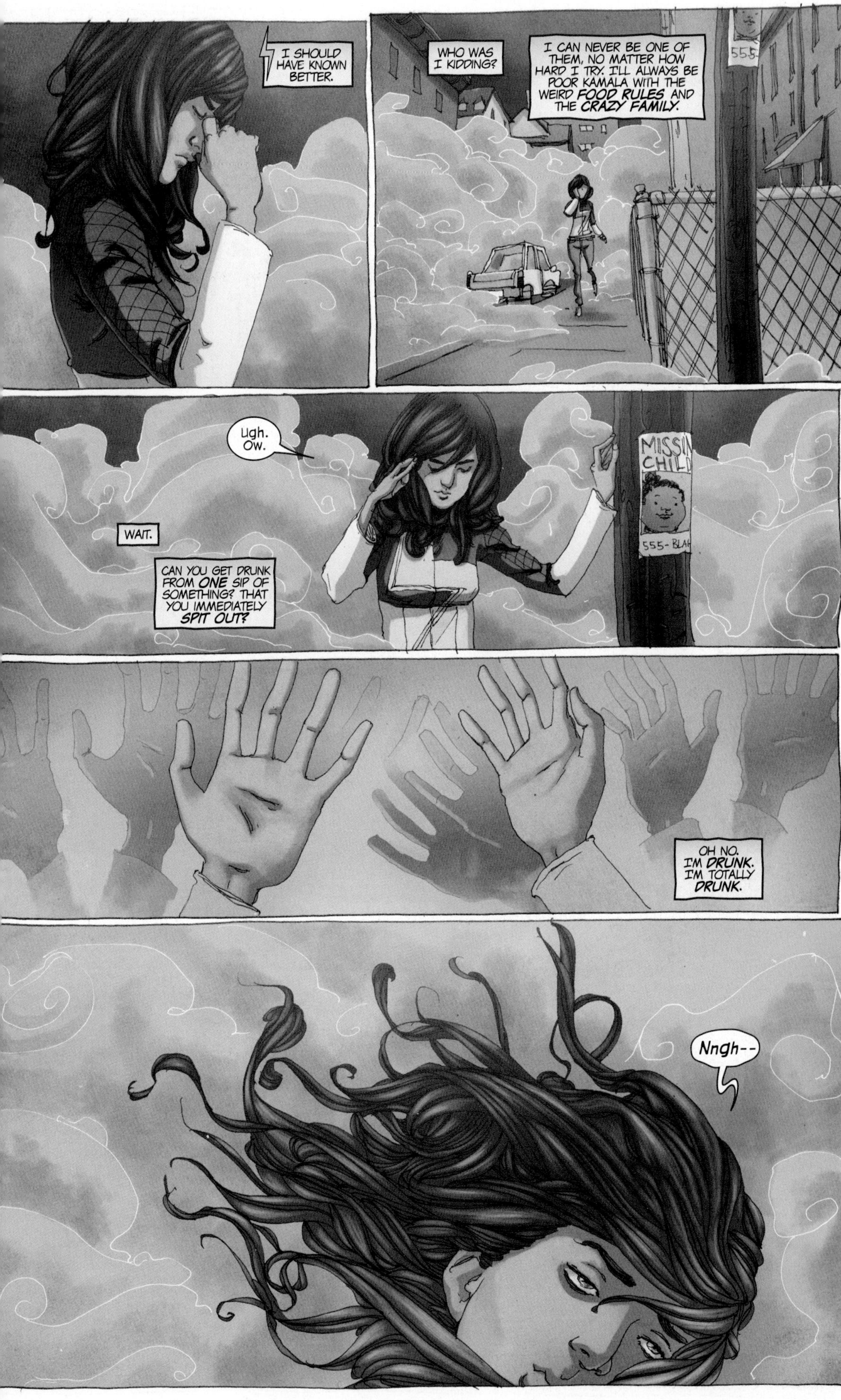
I SHOULD HAVE KNOWN BETTER.
WHO WAS I KIDDING?
I CAN NEVER BE ONE OF THEM, NO MATTER HOW HARD I TRY. I'LL ALWAYS BE POOR KAMALA WITH THE WEIRD FOOD RULES AND THE CRAZY FAMILY.
555-
Ugh. Ow.
MISSIN CHILD
555-BLAH
WAIT.
CAN YOU GET DRUNK FROM ONE SIP OF SOMETHING? THAT YOU IMMEDIATELY SPIT OUT?
OH NO. I'M DRUNK. I'M TOTALLY DRUNK.
Nngh--

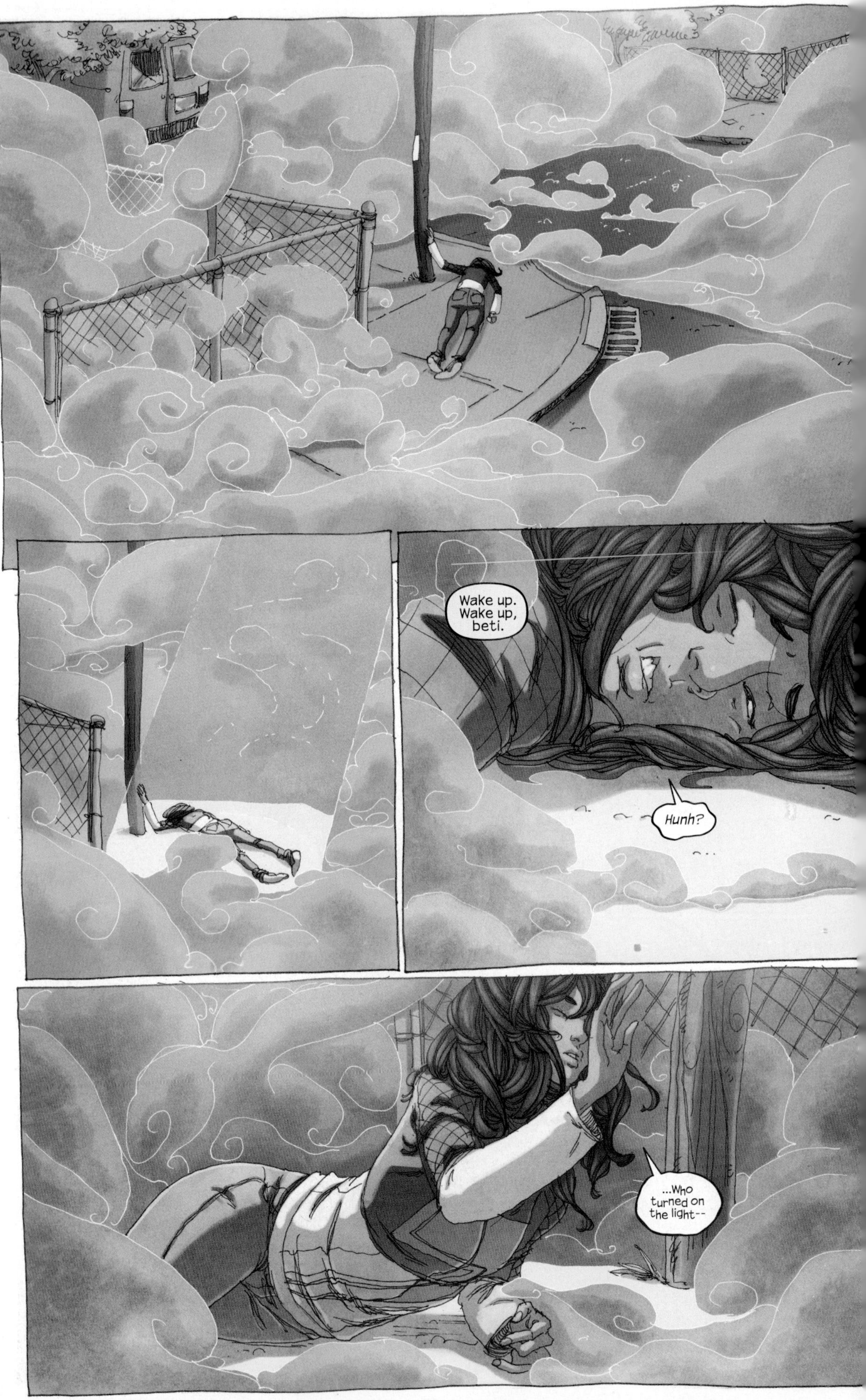
Wake up. Wake up, beti.
Hunh?
...Who turned on the light--

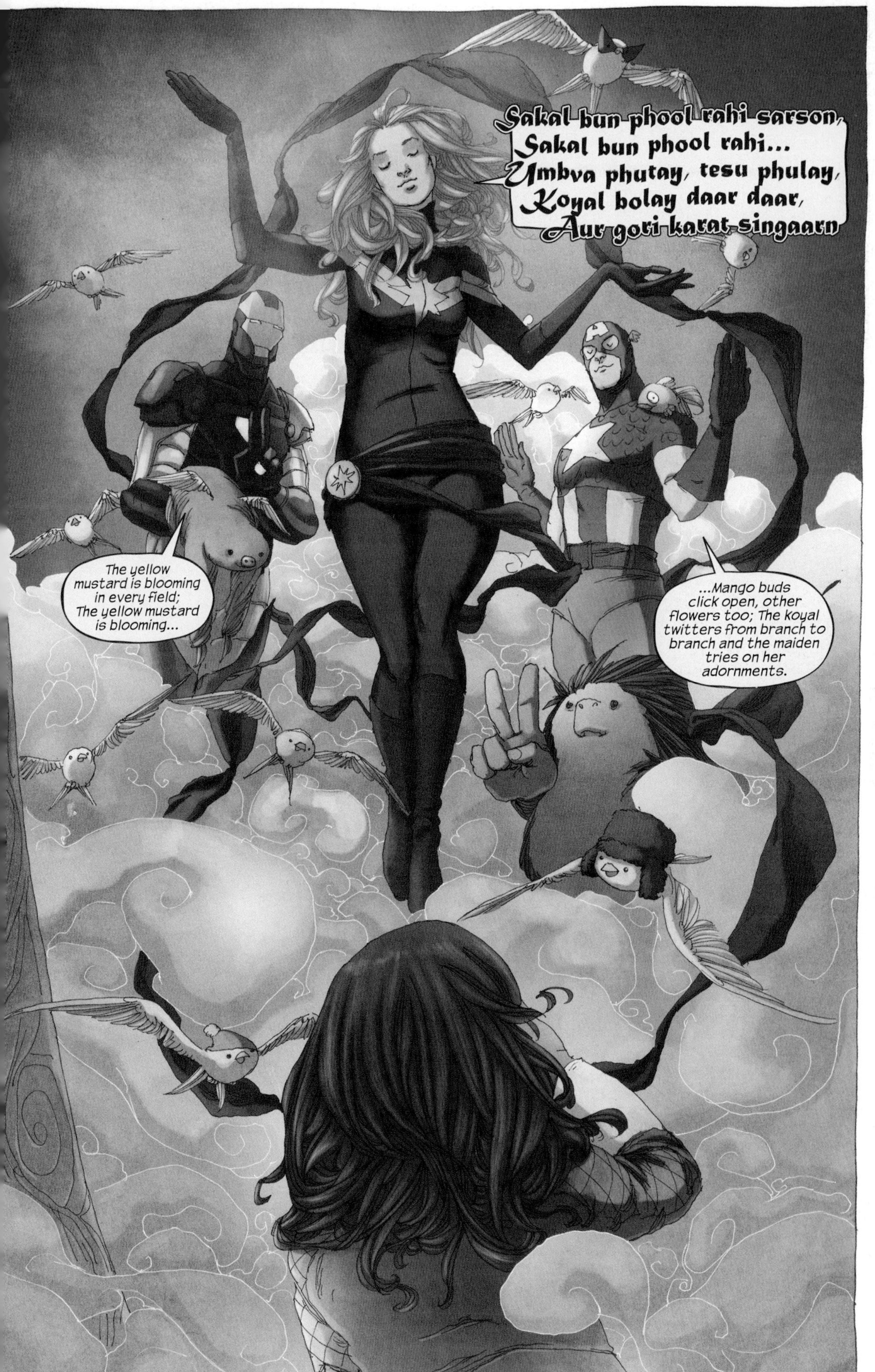

Sakal bun phool rahi sarson, Sakal bun phool rahi... Umbva phutay, tesu phulay, Koyal bolay daar daar, Aur gori karat singaarn
The yellow mustard is blooming in every field; The yellow mustard is blooming...
...Mango buds click open, other flowers too; The koyal twitters from branch to branch and the maiden tries on her adornments.

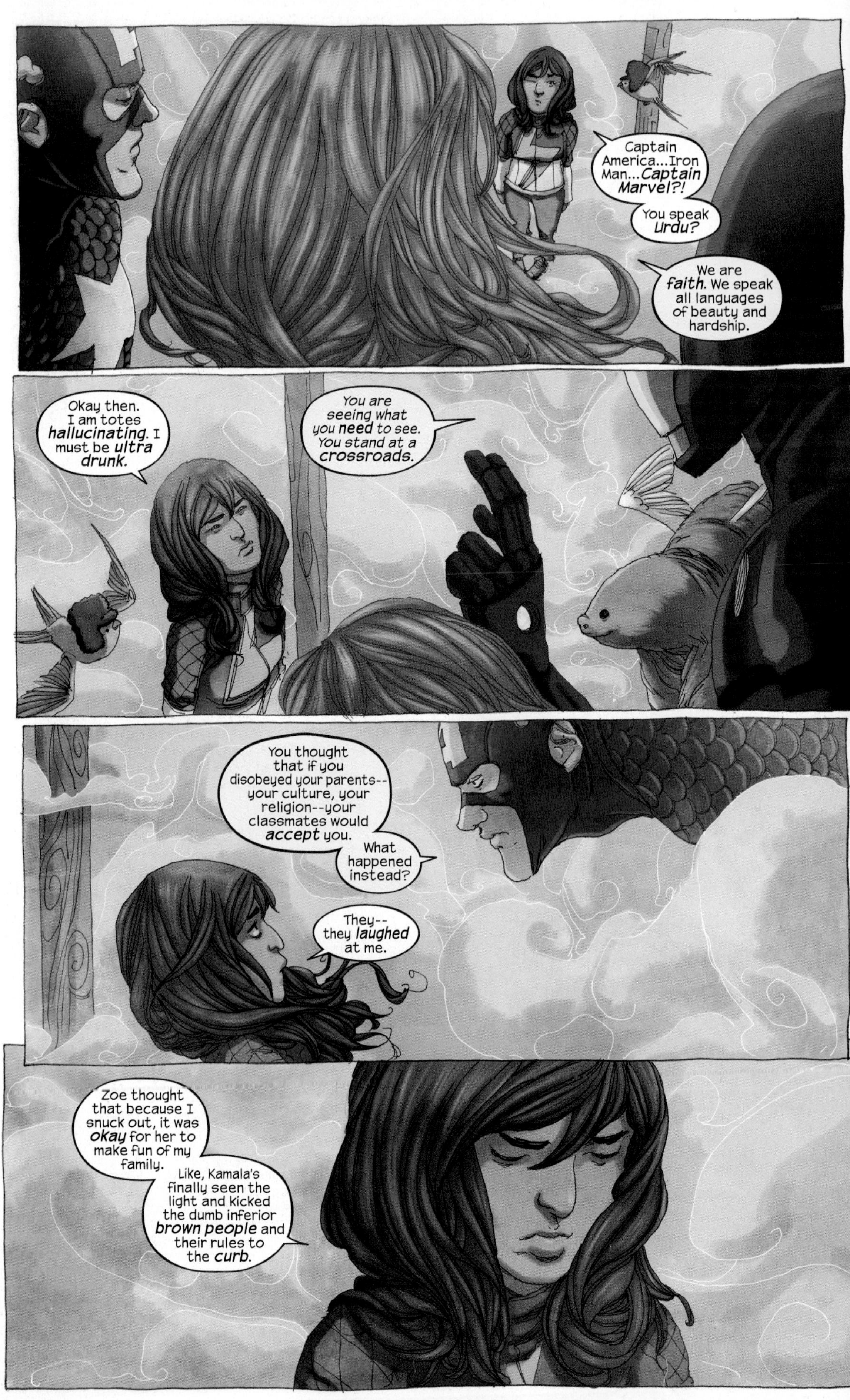
Captain America...Iron Man...Captain Marvel?!
You speak Urdu?
We are faith. We speak all languages of beauty and hardship.
Okay then. I am totes hallucinating. I must be ultra drunk.
You are seeing what you need to see. You stand at a crossroads.
You thought that if you disobeyed your parents--your culture, your religion--your classmates would accept you.
What happened instead?
They--they laughed at me.
Zoe thought that because I snuck out, it was okay for her to make fun of my family.
Like, Kamala's finally seen the light and kicked the dumb inferior brown people and their rules to the curb.

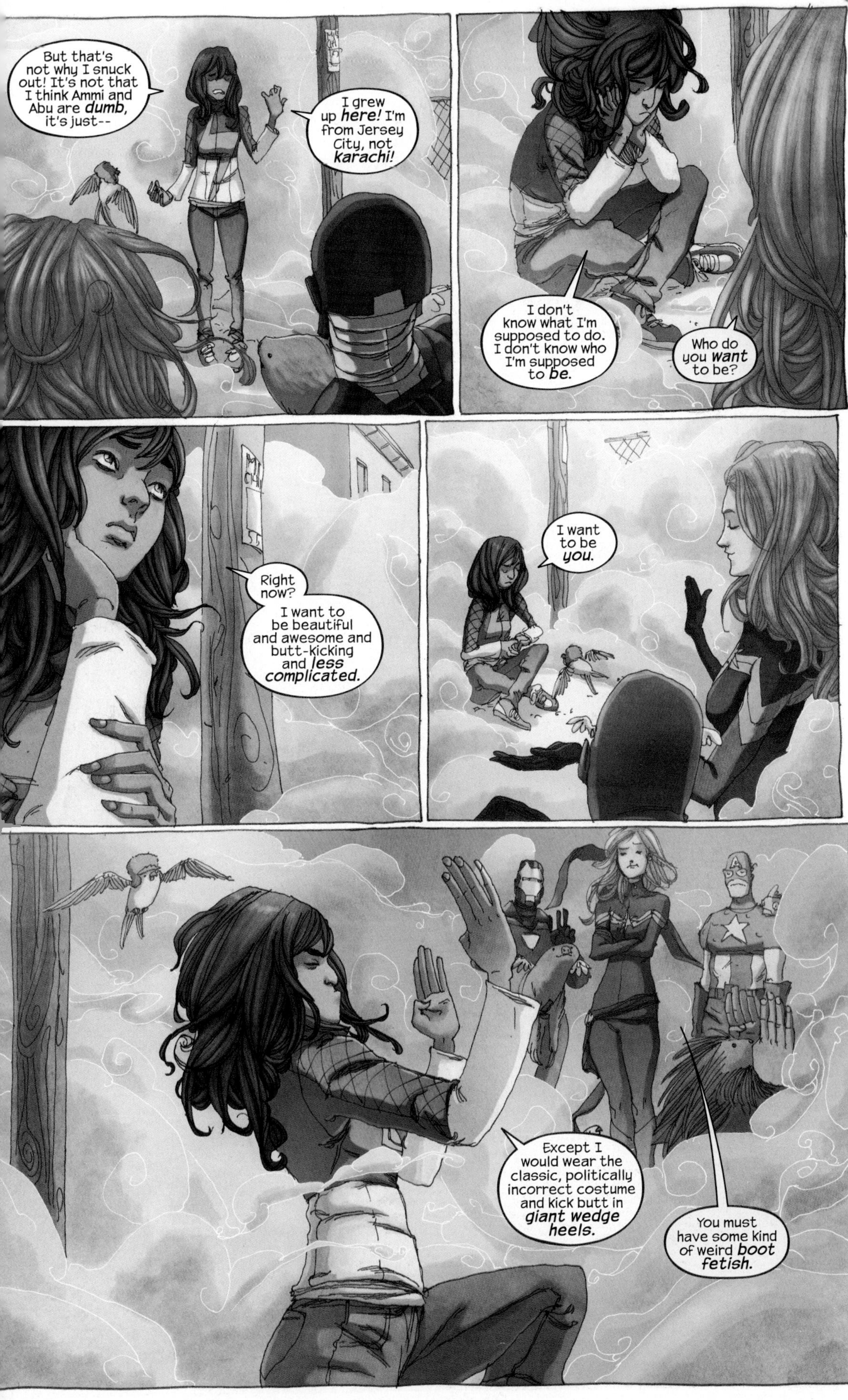

But that's not why I snuck out! It's not that I think Ammi and Abu are *dumb*, it's just--
I grew up *here!* I'm from Jersey City, not *karachi!*
I don't know what I'm supposed to do. I don't know who I'm supposed to *be*.
Who do you *want* to be?
Right now?
I want to be beautiful and awesome and butt-kicking and *less complicated.*
I want to be *you*.
Except I would wear the classic, politically incorrect costume and kick butt in *giant wedge heels*.
You must have some kind of weird *boot fetish*.

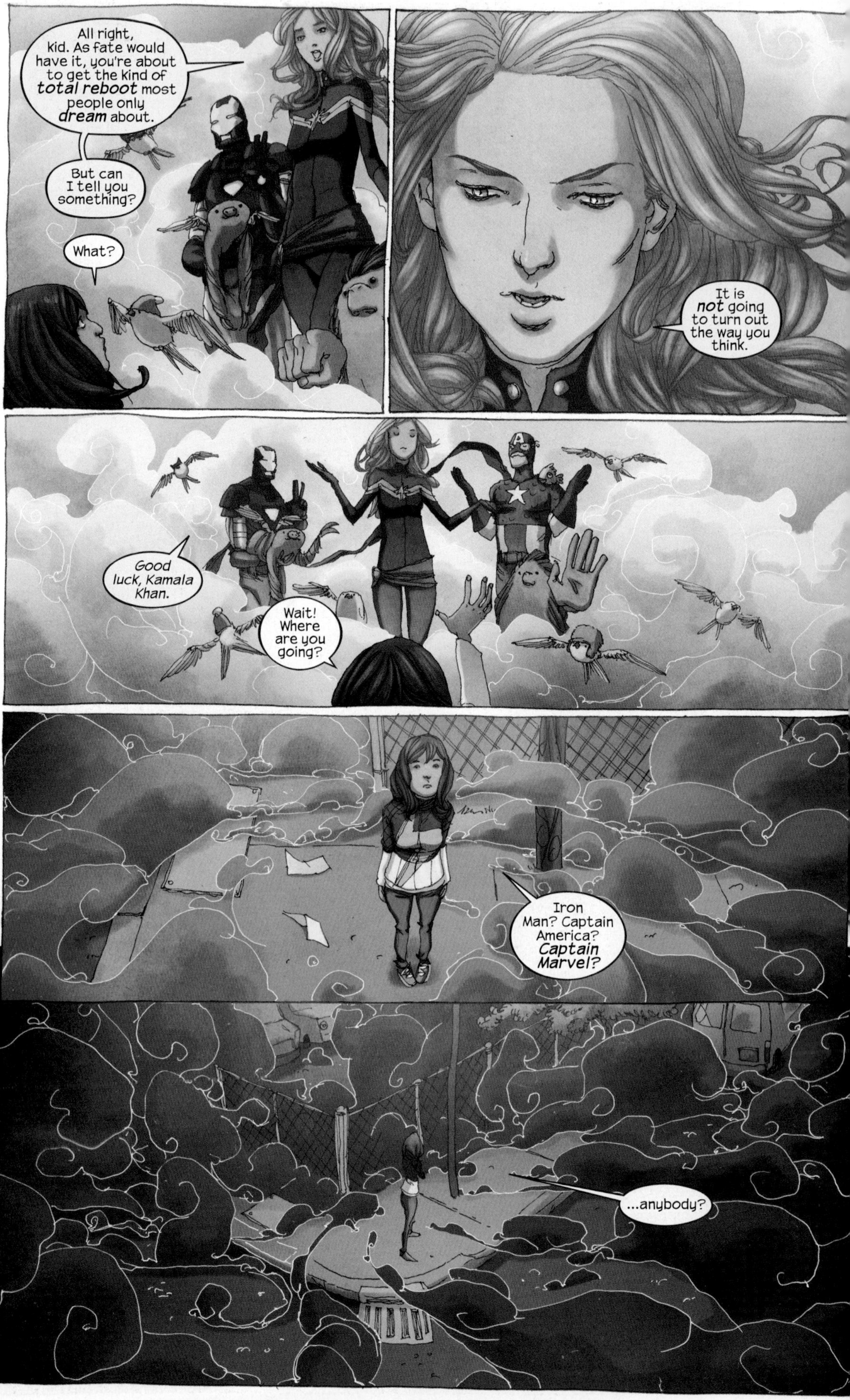
All right, kid. As fate would have it, you're about to get the kind of total reboot most people only dream about.
But can I tell you something?
What?
It is not going to turn out the way you think.
Good luck, Kamala Khan.
Wait! Where are you going?
Iron Man? Captain America? Captain Marvel?
...anybody?

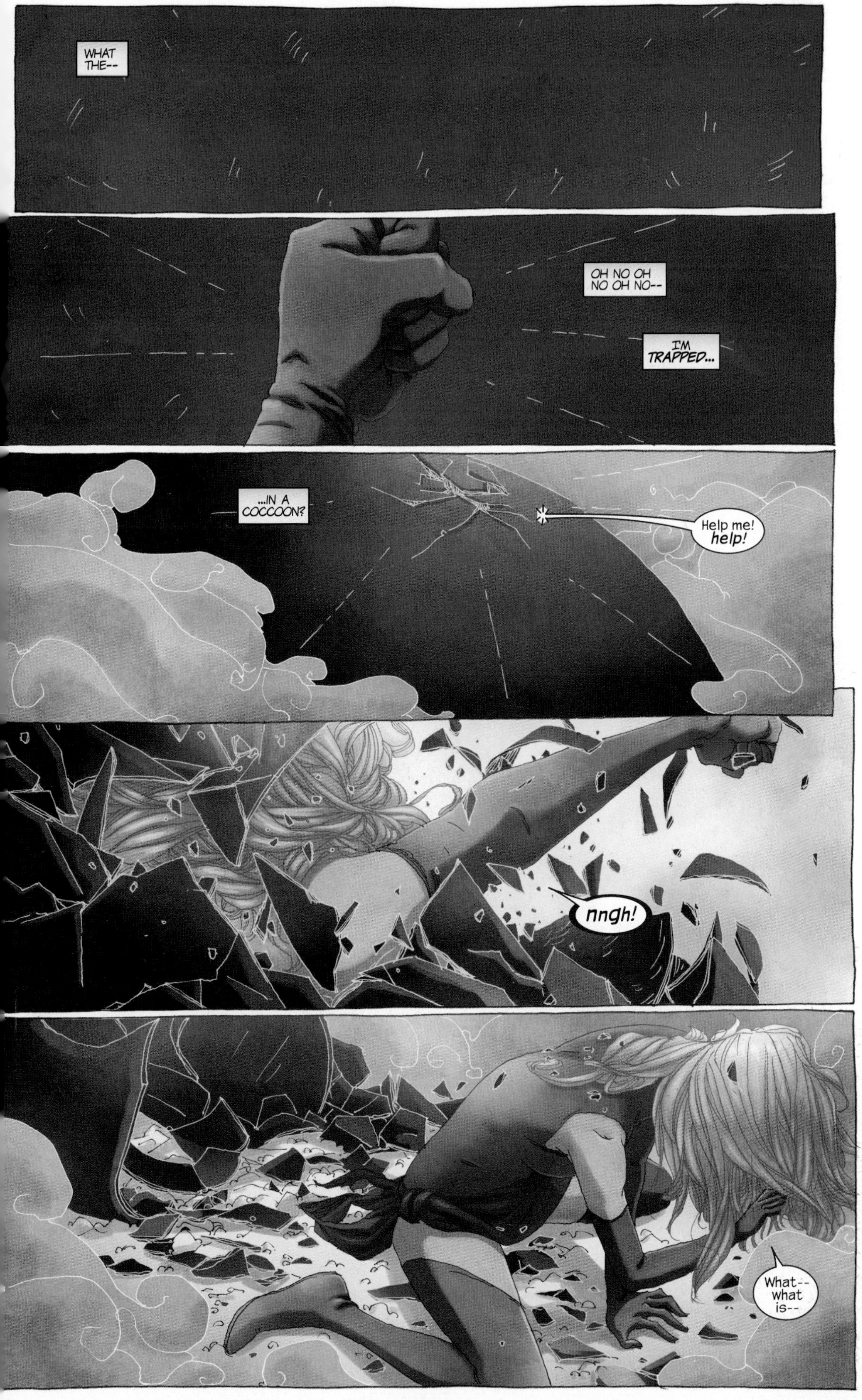
WHAT THE--
OH NO OH NO OH NO--
I'M TRAPPED...
...IN A COCCOON?
Help me! help!
nngh!
What--what is--

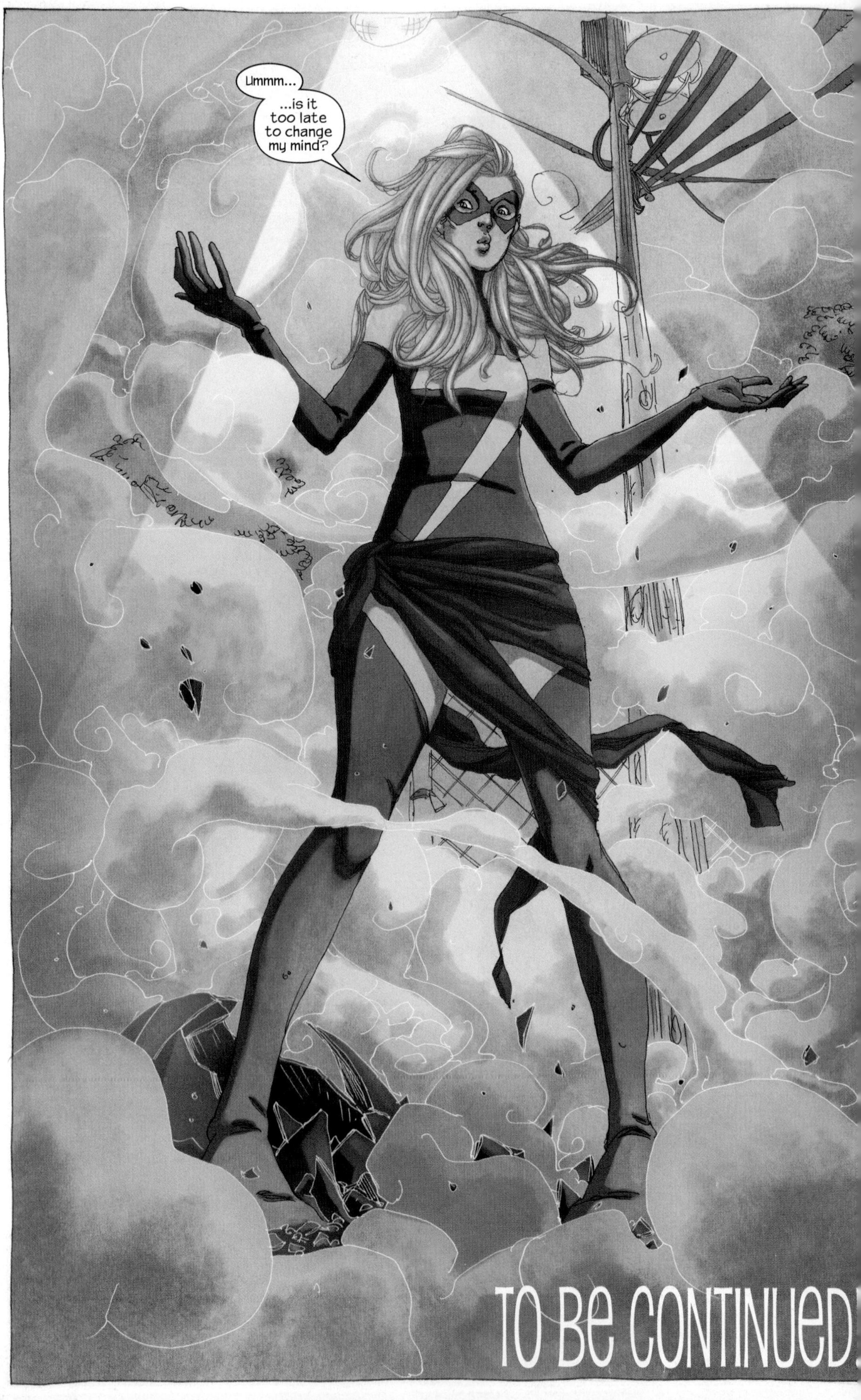
Ummm...
...is it too late to change my mind?
TO BE CONTINUED!

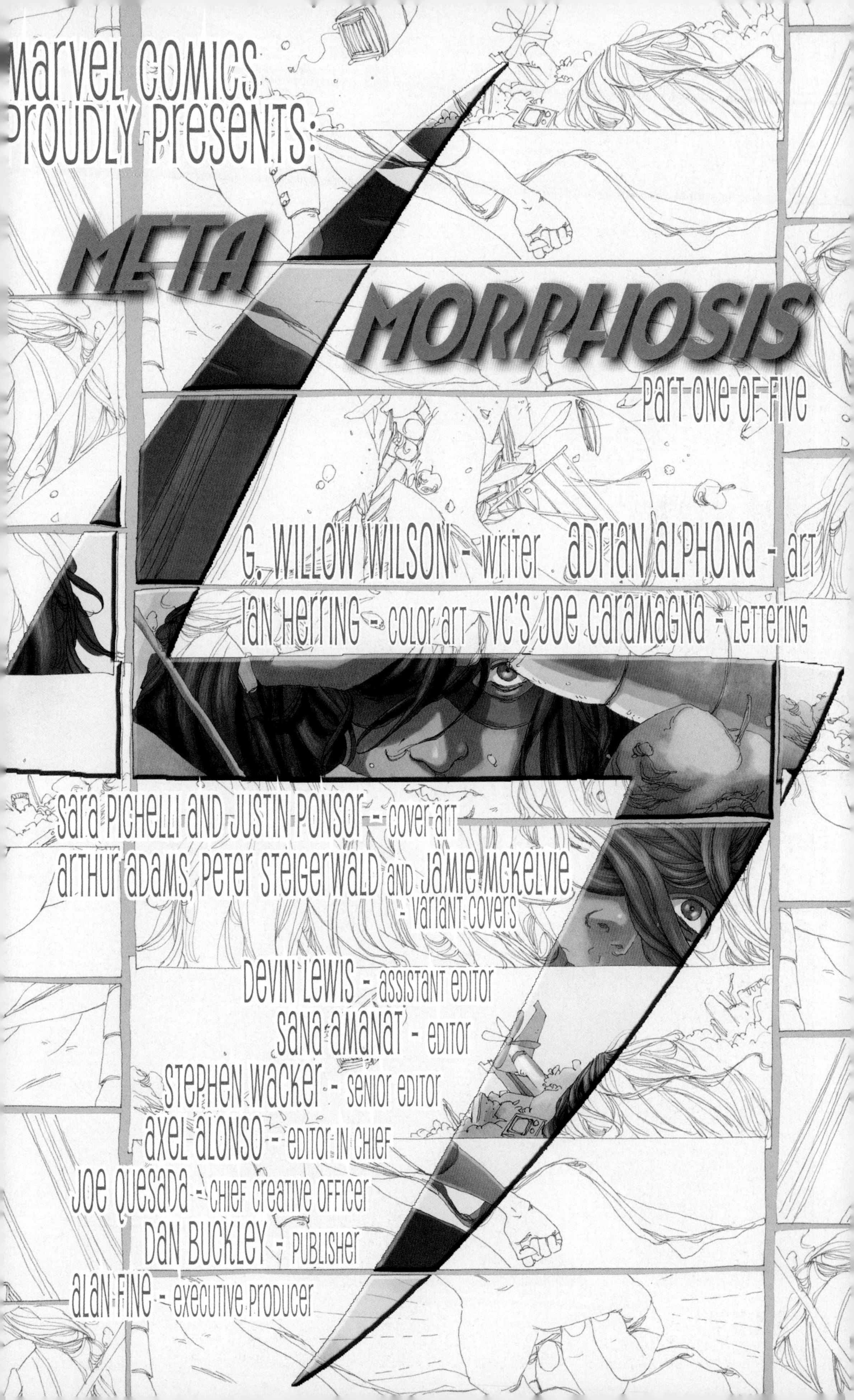
Marvel Comics
Proudly Presents:
META
MORPHIOSIS
Part One of Five
G. Willow Wilson - writer
Adrian Alphona - art
Ian Herring - color art
VC's Joe Caramagna - lettering
Sara Pichelli and Justin Ponsor - cover art
Arthur Adams, Peter Steigerwald and Jamie McKelvie
- variant covers
Devin Lewis - assistant editor
Sana Amanat - editor
Stephen Wacker - senior editor
Axel Alonso - editor in chief
Joe Quesada - chief creative officer
Dan Buckley - publisher
Alan Fine - executive producer

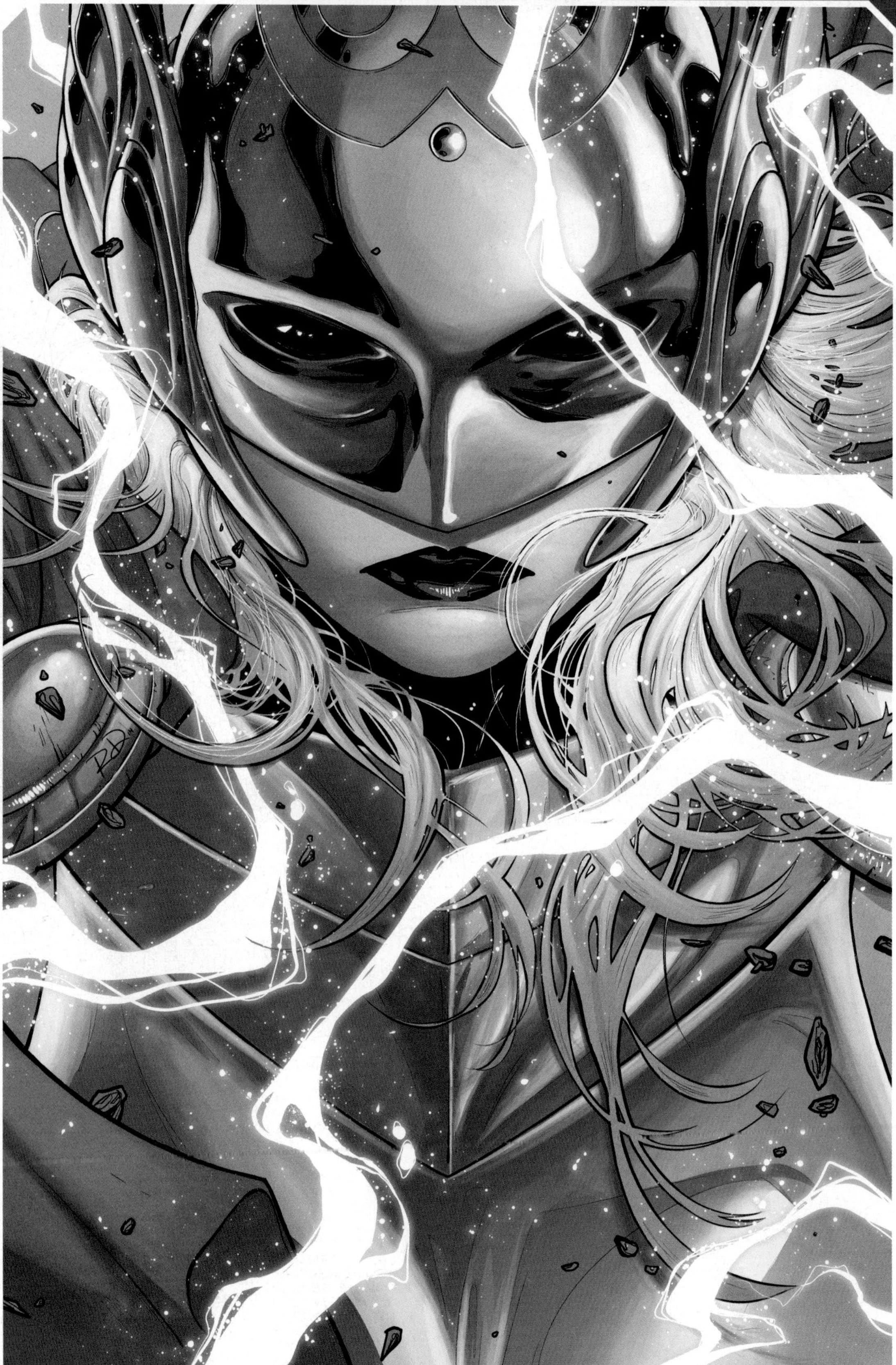

THOR #1

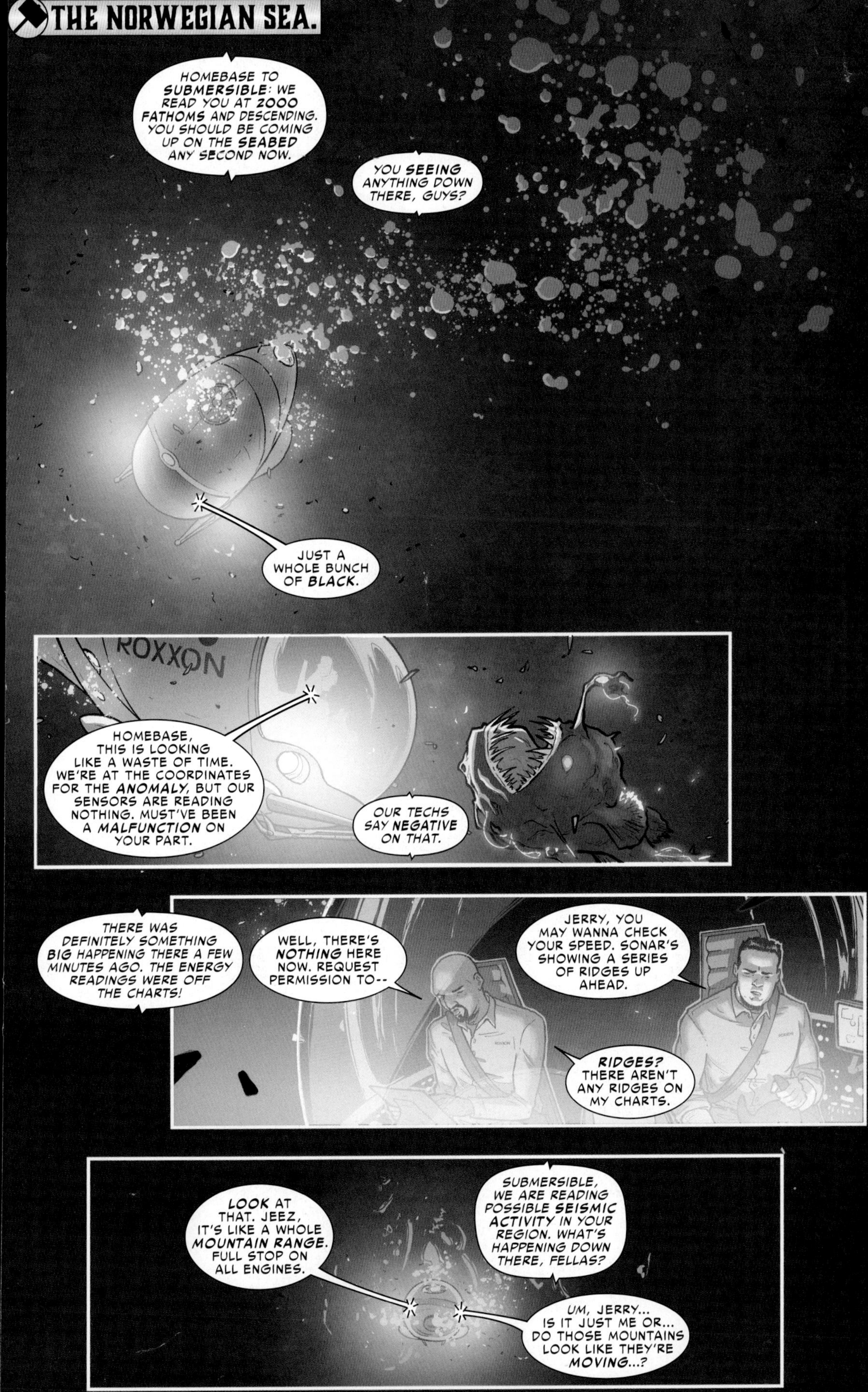
THE NORWEGIAN SEA.
HOMEBASE TO SUBMERSIBLE: WE READ YOU AT 2000 FATHOMS AND DESCENDING. YOU SHOULD BE COMING UP ON THE SEABED ANY SECOND NOW.
YOU SEEING ANYTHING DOWN THERE, GUYS?
JUST A WHOLE BUNCH OF BLACK.
ROXXON
HOMEBASE, THIS IS LOOKING LIKE A WASTE OF TIME. WE'RE AT THE COORDINATES FOR THE ANOMALY, BUT OUR SENSORS ARE READING NOTHING. MUST'VE BEEN A MALFUNCTION ON YOUR PART.
OUR TECHS SAY NEGATIVE ON THAT.
THERE WAS DEFINITELY SOMETHING BIG HAPPENING THERE A FEW MINUTES AGO. THE ENERGY READINGS WERE OFF THE CHARTS!
WELL, THERE'S NOTHING HERE NOW. REQUEST PERMISSION TO--
JERRY, YOU MAY WANNA CHECK YOUR SPEED. SONAR'S SHOWING A SERIES OF RIDGES UP AHEAD.
RIDGES? THERE AREN'T ANY RIDGES ON MY CHARTS.
LOOK AT THAT. JEEZ, IT'S LIKE A WHOLE MOUNTAIN RANGE. FULL STOP ON ALL ENGINES.
SUBMERSIBLE, WE ARE READING POSSIBLE SEISMIC ACTIVITY IN YOUR REGION. WHAT'S HAPPENING DOWN THERE, FELLAS?
UM, JERRY... IS IT JUST ME OR... DO THOSE MOUNTAINS LOOK LIKE THEY'RE MOVING...?

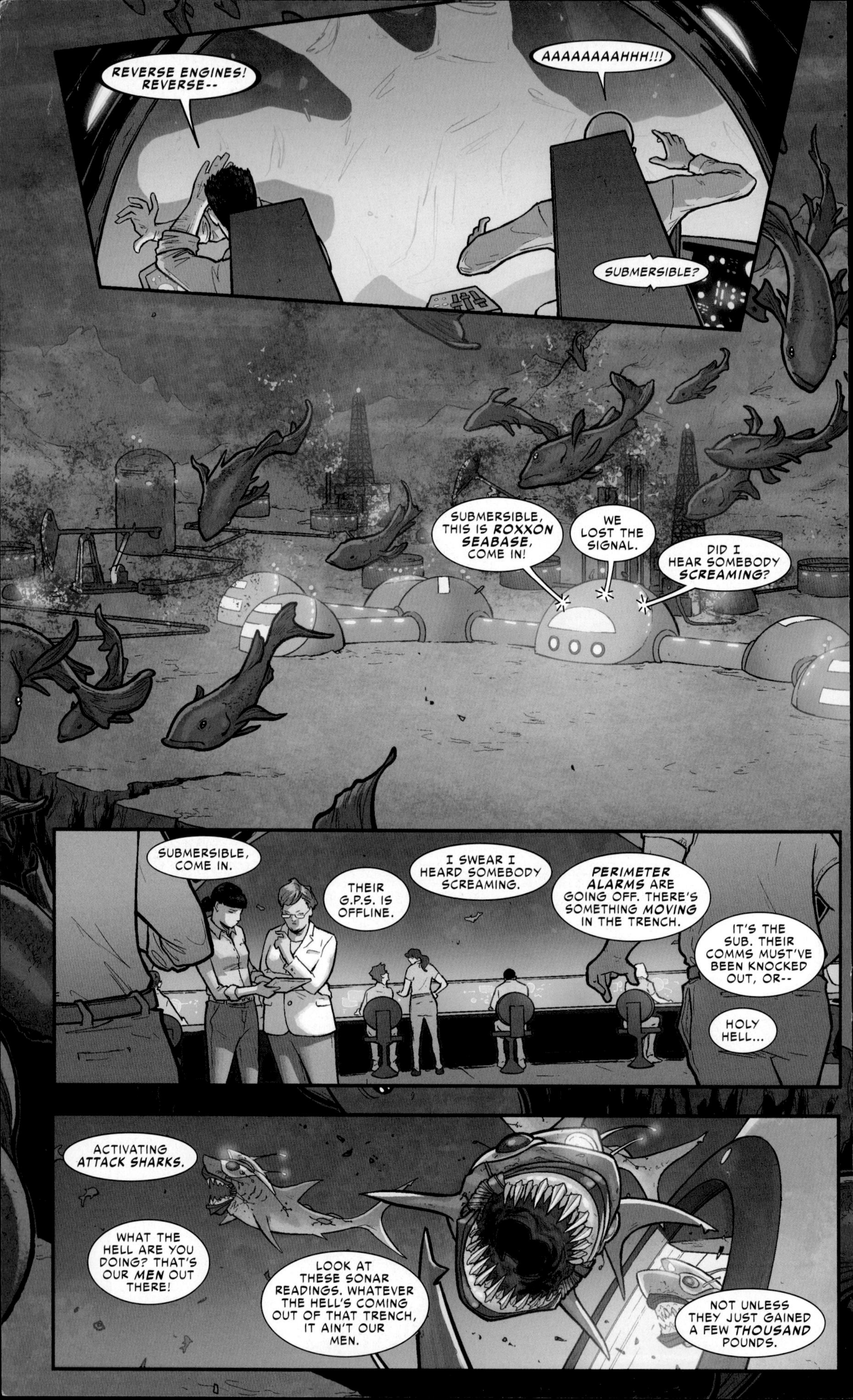
REVERSE ENGINES! REVERSE--
AAAAAAAAHHH!!!
SUBMERSIBLE?
SUBMERSIBLE, THIS IS ROXXON SEABASE, COME IN!
WE LOST THE SIGNAL.
DID I HEAR SOMEBODY SCREAMING?
SUBMERSIBLE, COME IN.
THEIR G.P.S. IS OFFLINE.
I SWEAR I HEARD SOMEBODY SCREAMING.
PERIMETER ALARMS ARE GOING OFF. THERE'S SOMETHING MOVING IN THE TRENCH.
IT'S THE SUB. THEIR COMMS MUST'VE BEEN KNOCKED OUT, OR--
HOLY HELL...
ACTIVATING ATTACK SHARKS.
WHAT THE HELL ARE YOU DOING? THAT'S OUR MEN OUT THERE!
LOOK AT THESE SONAR READINGS. WHATEVER THE HELL'S COMING OUT OF THAT TRENCH, IT AIN'T OUR MEN.
NOT UNLESS THEY JUST GAINED A FEW THOUSAND POUNDS.

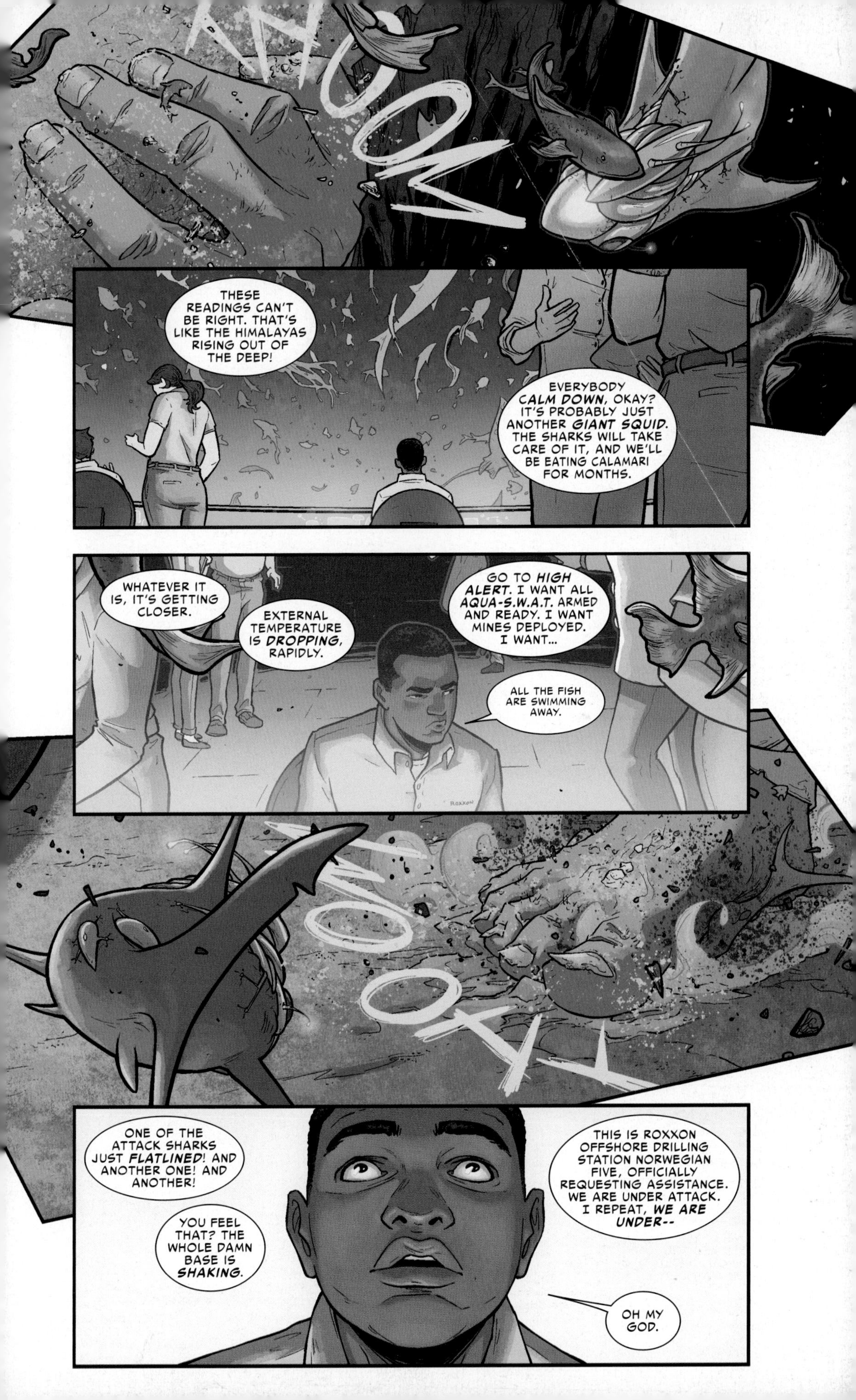

KRAKA-
THOOM
THESE READINGS CAN'T BE RIGHT. THAT'S LIKE THE HIMALAYAS RISING OUT OF THE DEEP!
EVERYBODY CALM DOWN, OKAY? IT'S PROBABLY JUST ANOTHER GIANT SQUID. THE SHARKS WILL TAKE CARE OF IT, AND WE'LL BE EATING CALAMARI FOR MONTHS.
WHATEVER IT IS, IT'S GETTING CLOSER.
EXTERNAL TEMPERATURE IS DROPPING, RAPIDLY.
GO TO HIGH ALERT. I WANT ALL AQUA-S.W.A.T. ARMED AND READY. I WANT MINES DEPLOYED. I WANT...
ALL THE FISH ARE SWIMMING AWAY.
ROXXON
KTOOOOOM
ONE OF THE ATTACK SHARKS JUST FLATLINED! AND ANOTHER ONE! AND ANOTHER!
YOU FEEL THAT? THE WHOLE DAMN BASE IS SHAKING.
THIS IS ROXXON OFFSHORE DRILLING STATION NORWEGIAN FIVE, OFFICIALLY REQUESTING ASSISTANCE. WE ARE UNDER ATTACK. I REPEAT, WE ARE UNDER--
OH MY GOD.

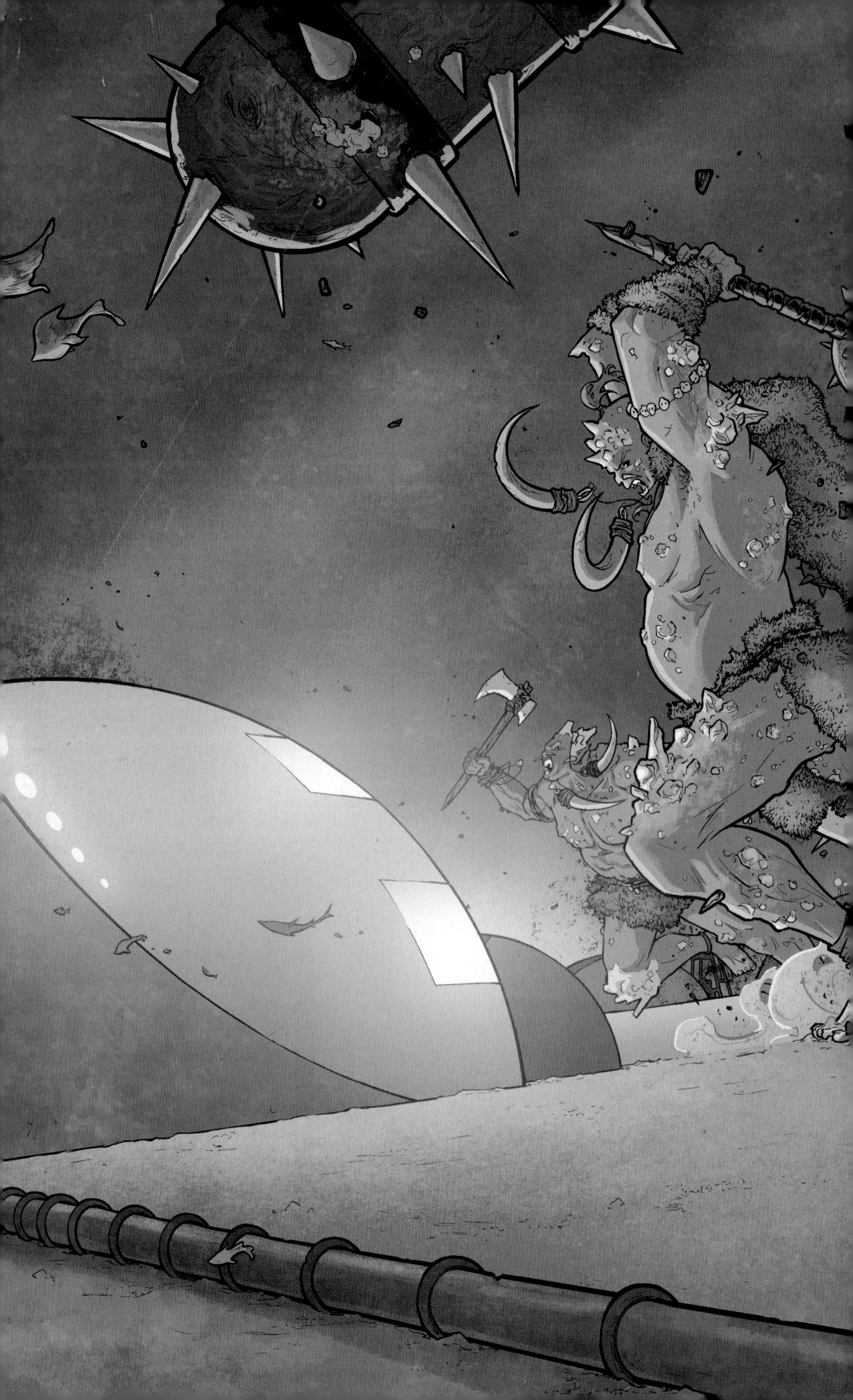

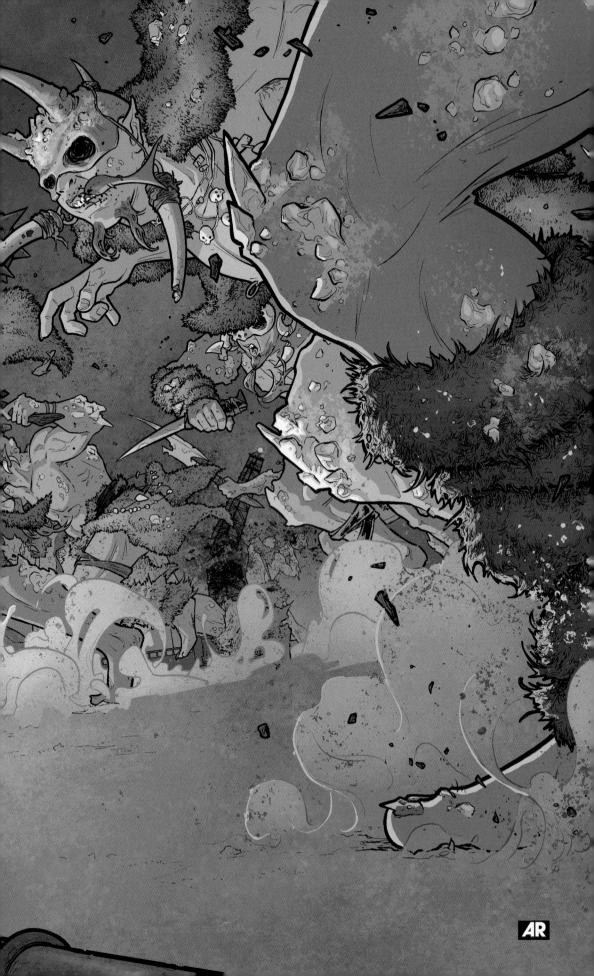

CHANGE HAS COME TO ASGARD.

AFTER A SELF-IMPOSED EXILE, ODIN THE ALL-FATHER HAS RETURNED TO HIS FORME KINGDOM (NOW CALLED ASGARDIA). BUT HIS WIFE FREYJA, WHO HAD BEEN RULIN ASGARDIA IN HIS STEAD AS THE ALL-MOTHER, HAS NO INTENTION OF LETTING THING GO BACK TO THE WAY THEY WERE BEFORE ODIN LEFT.

THE BIGGEST CHANGE, THOUGH, IS THAT THEIR SON THOR, THE GOD OF THUNDE NOW FINDS HIMSELF NO LONGER WORTHY OF WIELDING MJOLNIR, HIS ENCHANTE HAMMER. IN A RECENT BATTLE ON THE MOON, SUPERSPY NICK FURY--EMPOWERE WITH SECRETS HE STOLE FROM THE WATCHER--WHISPERED SOMETHING THAT CAUSE THOR TO DROP MJOLNIR TO THE MOON'S SURFACE, WHERE IT HAS REMAINED EVE SINCE. NO MATTER HOW HARD HE TRIES, THOR CANNOT LIFT IT.

WITH THE LEADERSHIP OF ASGARDIA UNCERTAIN AND THOR NOW IN A SEVEREL WEAKENED STATE, IT IS ONLY A MATTER OF TIME BEFORE THE ENEMIES OF ASGAR STRIKE, BRINGING DOOM TO BOTH THE FABLED REALM AND EARTH ITSELF.

IF HE BE WORTHY

JASON AARON
WRITER

RUSSELL DAUTERMAN
ARTIST

MATTHEW WILSON
COLOR ARTIST

VC's JOE SABINO
LETTERER & PRODUCTION

RUSSELL DAUTERMAN & FRANK MARTIN
COVER ARTISTS

SARA PICHELLI & LAURA MARTIN; ESAD RIBIC; ANDREW ROBINSON; ALEX ROSS; FIONA STAPLES; SKOTTIE YOUNG
VARIANT COVER ARTISTS

JON MOISAN
ASSISTANT EDITOR

WIL MOSS
EDITOR

AXEL ALONSO
EDITOR IN CHIEF

JOE QUESADA
CHIEF CREATIVE OFFICER

DAN BUCKLEY
PUBLISHER

ALAN FINE
EXECUTIVE PRODUCER

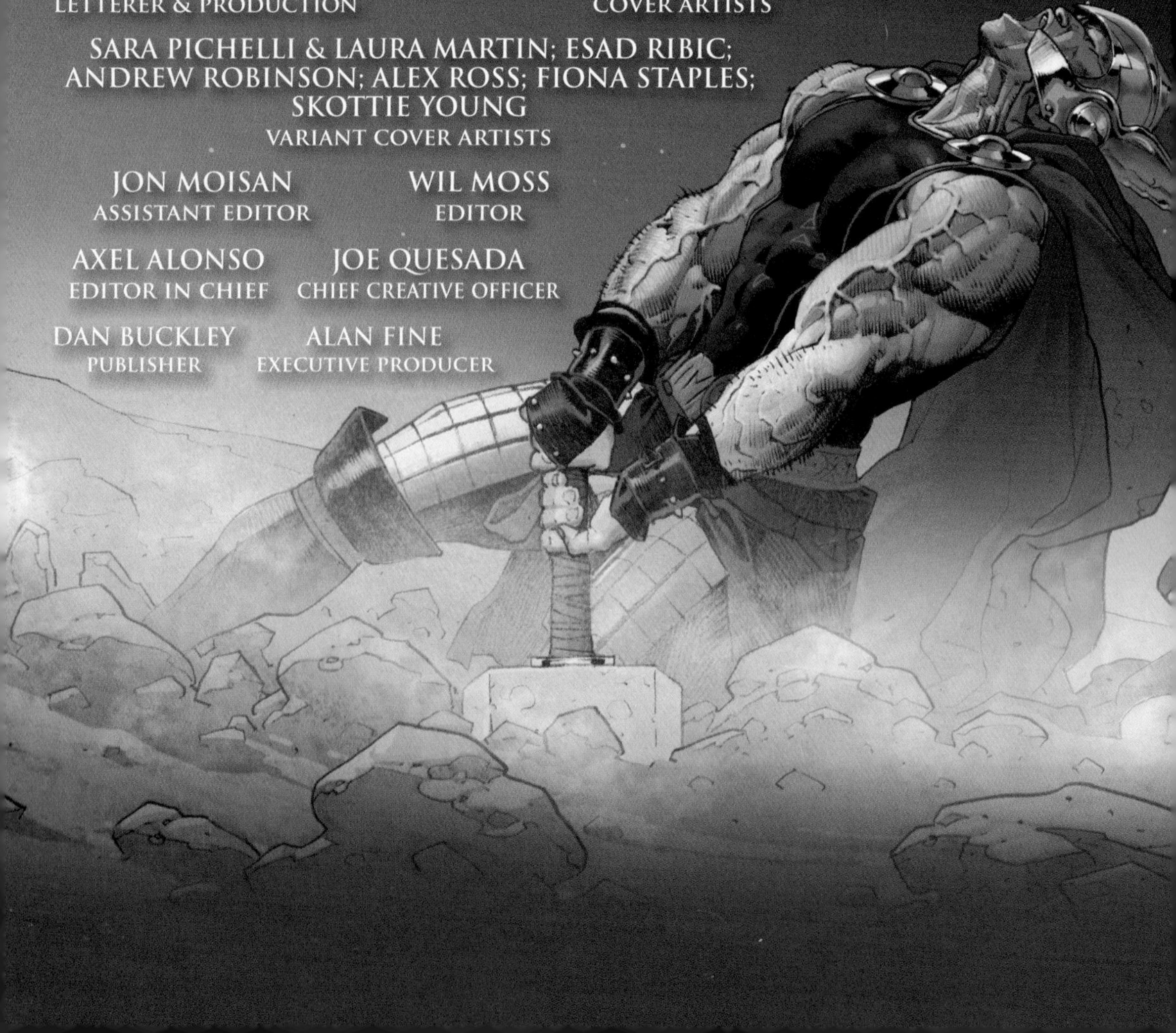

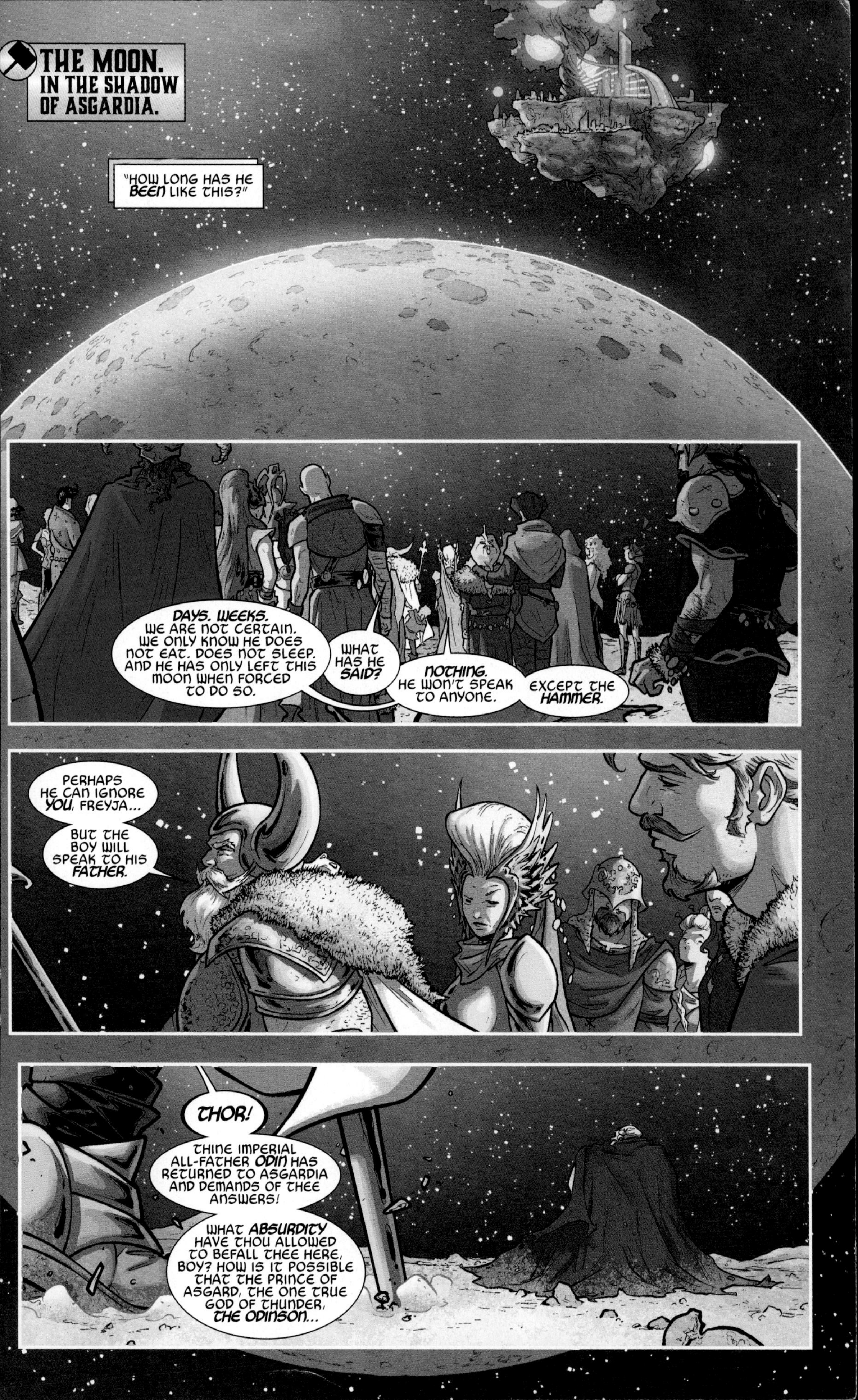
THE MOON. IN THE SHADOW OF ASGARDIA.
"HOW LONG HAS HE BEEN LIKE THIS?"
DAYS. WEEKS. WE ARE NOT CERTAIN. WE ONLY KNOW HE DOES NOT EAT. DOES NOT SLEEP. AND HE HAS ONLY LEFT THIS MOON WHEN FORCED TO DO SO.
WHAT HAS HE SAID?
NOTHING. HE WON'T SPEAK TO ANYONE.
EXCEPT THE HAMMER.
PERHAPS HE CAN IGNORE YOU, FREYJA...
BUT THE BOY WILL SPEAK TO HIS FATHER.
THOR!
THINE IMPERIAL ALL-FATHER ODIN HAS RETURNED TO ASGARDIA AND DEMANDS OF THEE ANSWERS!
WHAT ABSURDITY HAVE THOU ALLOWED TO BEFALL THEE HERE, BOY? HOW IS IT POSSIBLE THAT THE PRINCE OF ASGARD, THE ONE TRUE GOD OF THUNDER, THE ODINSON...

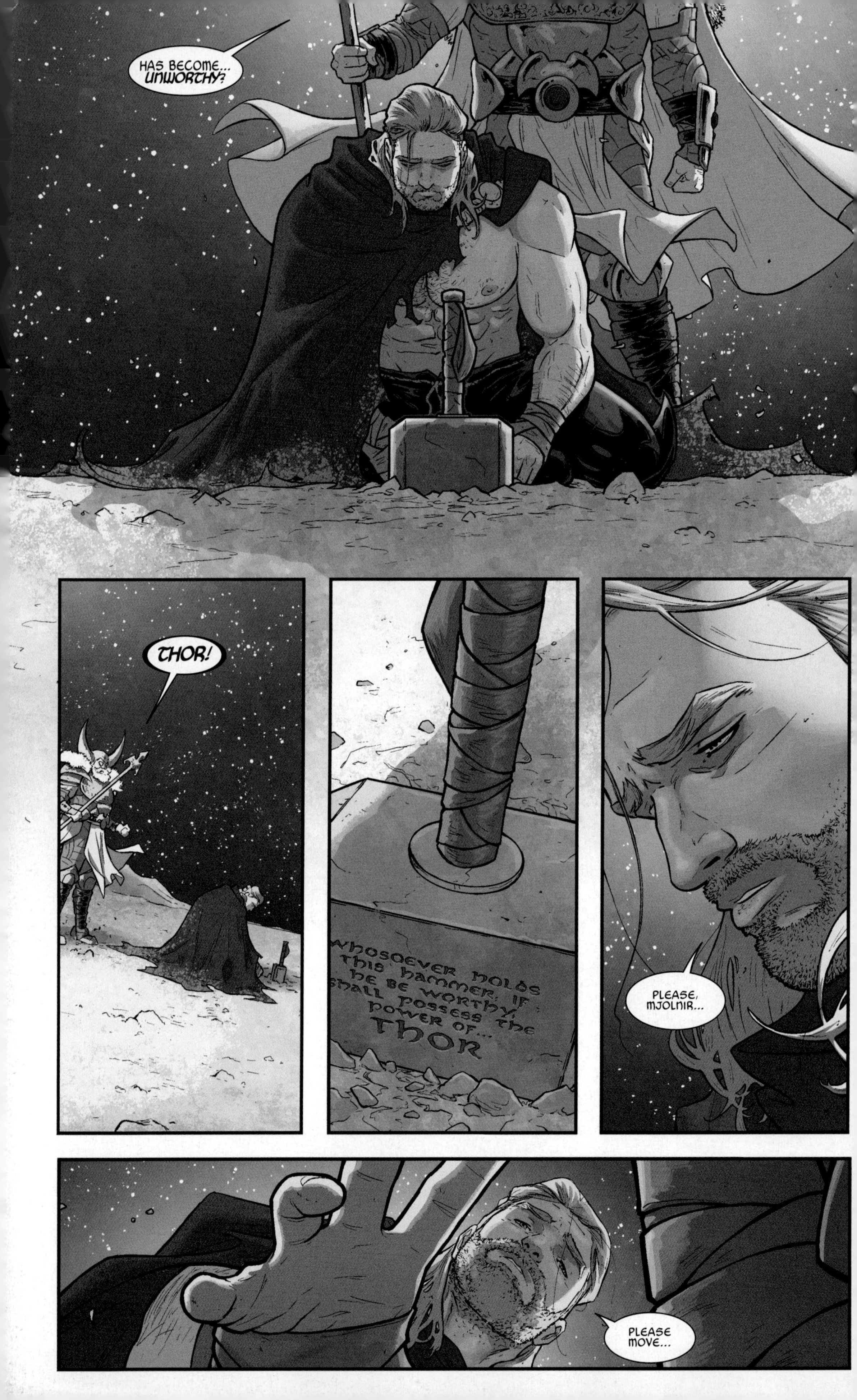
HAS BECOME... UNWORTHY?
THOR!
WHOSOEVER HOLDS THIS HAMMER, IF HE BE WORTHY, SHALL POSSESS THE POWER OF... THOR
PLEASE, MJOLNIR...
PLEASE MOVE...

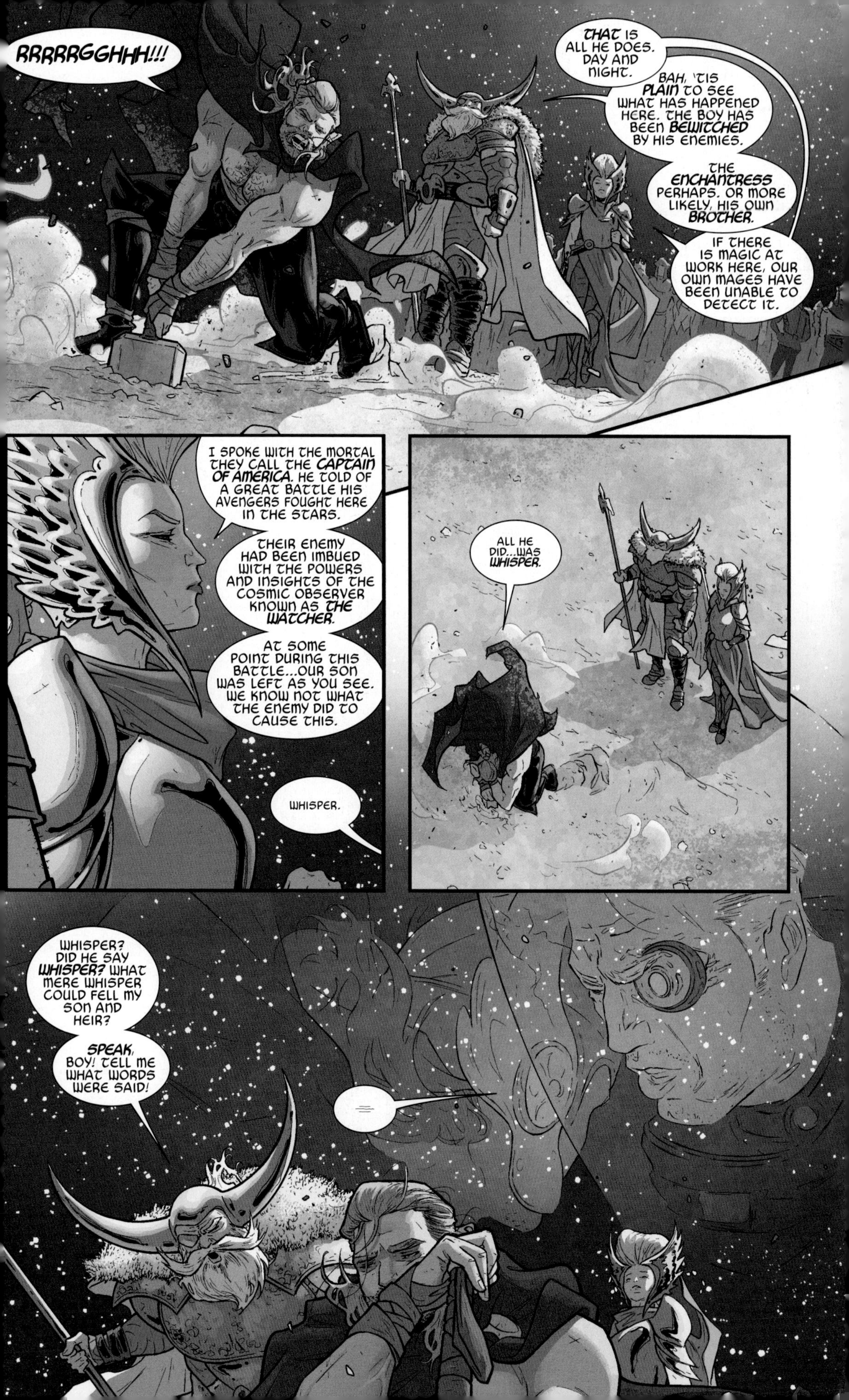
RRRRRGGHHH!!!
THAT IS ALL HE DOES. DAY AND NIGHT.
BAH, 'TIS PLAIN TO SEE WHAT HAS HAPPENED HERE. THE BOY HAS BEEN BEWITCHED BY HIS ENEMIES.
THE ENCHANTRESS PERHAPS. OR MORE LIKELY, HIS OWN BROTHER.
IF THERE IS MAGIC AT WORK HERE, OUR OWN MAGES HAVE BEEN UNABLE TO DETECT IT.
I SPOKE WITH THE MORTAL THEY CALL THE CAPTAIN OF AMERICA. HE TOLD OF A GREAT BATTLE HIS AVENGERS FOUGHT HERE IN THE STARS.
THEIR ENEMY HAD BEEN IMBUED WITH THE POWERS AND INSIGHTS OF THE COSMIC OBSERVER KNOWN AS THE WATCHER.
AT SOME POINT DURING THIS BATTLE...OUR SON WAS LEFT AS YOU SEE. WE KNOW NOT WHAT THE ENEMY DID TO CAUSE THIS.
WHISPER.
ALL HE DID...WAS WHISPER.
WHISPER? DID HE SAY WHISPER? WHAT MERE WHISPER COULD FELL MY SON AND HEIR?
SPEAK, BOY! TELL ME WHAT WORDS WERE SAID!

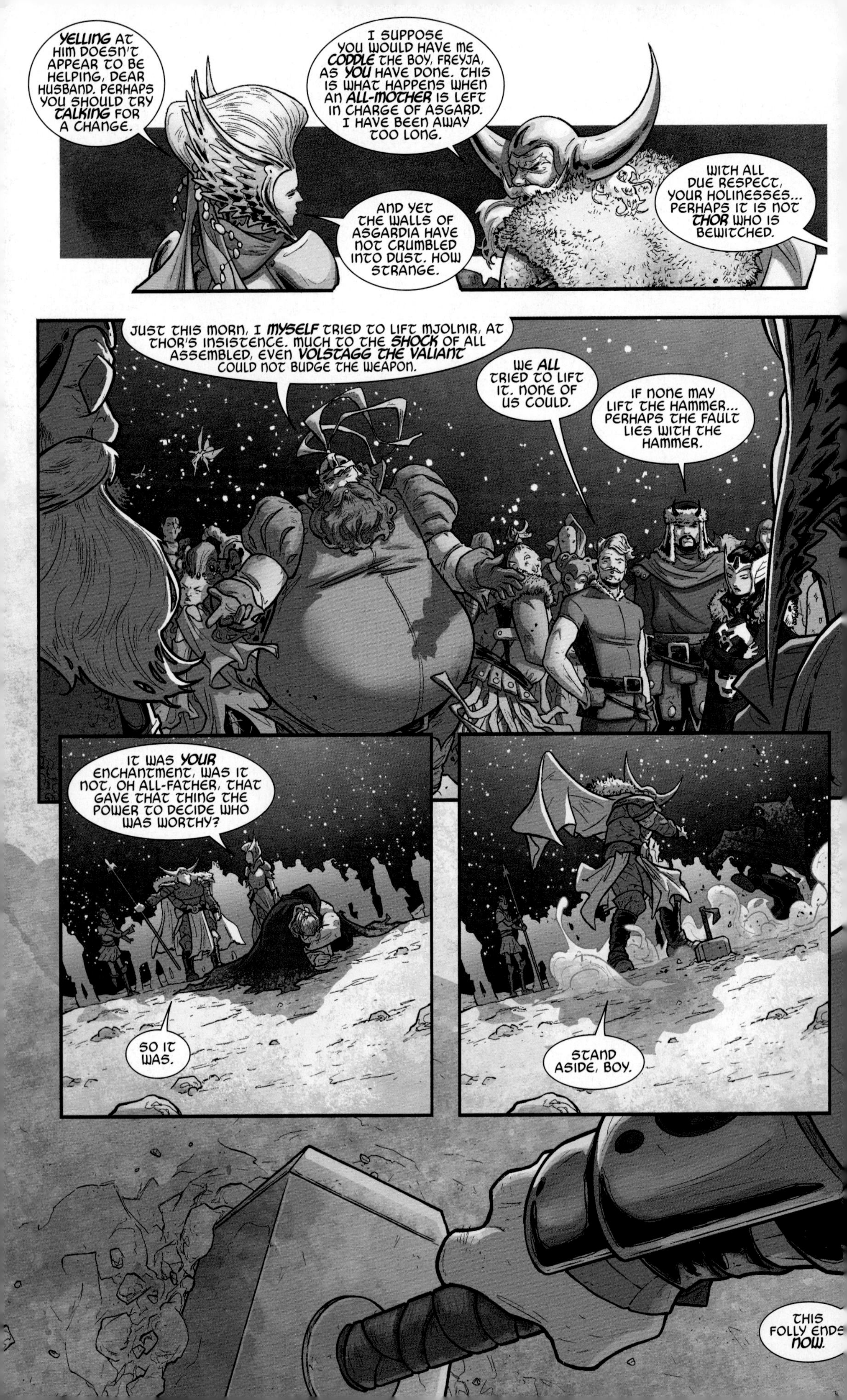
YELLING AT HIM DOESN'T APPEAR TO BE HELPING, DEAR HUSBAND. PERHAPS YOU SHOULD TRY TALKING FOR A CHANGE.
I SUPPOSE YOU WOULD HAVE ME CODDLE THE BOY, FREYJA, AS YOU HAVE DONE. THIS IS WHAT HAPPENS WHEN AN ALL-MOTHER IS LEFT IN CHARGE OF ASGARD. I HAVE BEEN AWAY TOO LONG.
AND YET THE WALLS OF ASGARDIA HAVE NOT CRUMBLED INTO DUST. HOW STRANGE.
WITH ALL DUE RESPECT, YOUR HOLINESSES... PERHAPS IT IS NOT THOR WHO IS BEWITCHED.
JUST THIS MORN, I MYSELF TRIED TO LIFT MJOLNIR, AT THOR'S INSISTENCE. MUCH TO THE SHOCK OF ALL ASSEMBLED, EVEN VOLSTAGG THE VALIANT COULD NOT BUDGE THE WEAPON.
WE ALL TRIED TO LIFT IT. NONE OF US COULD.
IF NONE MAY LIFT THE HAMMER... PERHAPS THE FAULT LIES WITH THE HAMMER.
IT WAS YOUR ENCHANTMENT, WAS IT NOT, OH ALL-FATHER, THAT GAVE THAT THING THE POWER TO DECIDE WHO WAS WORTHY?
SO IT WAS.
STAND ASIDE, BOY.
THIS FOLLY ENDS NOW.

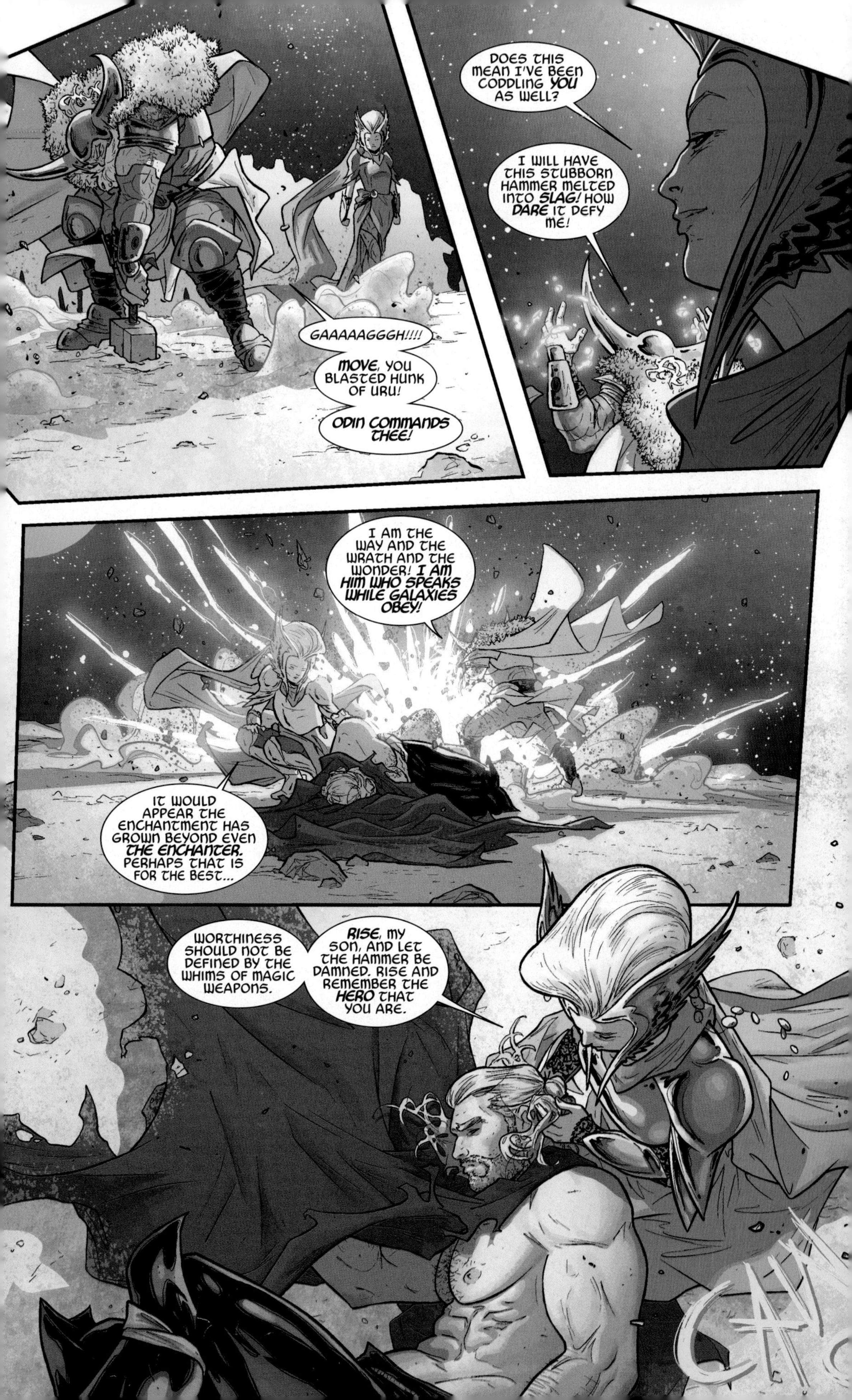
GAAAAAGGGH!!!!
MOVE, YOU BLASTED HUNK OF URU!
ODIN COMMANDS THEE!
DOES THIS MEAN I'VE BEEN CODDLING YOU AS WELL?
I WILL HAVE THIS STUBBORN HAMMER MELTED INTO SLAG! HOW DARE IT DEFY ME!
I AM THE WAY AND THE WRATH AND THE WONDER! I AM HIM WHO SPEAKS WHILE GALAXIES OBEY!
IT WOULD APPEAR THE ENCHANTMENT HAS GROWN BEYOND EVEN THE ENCHANTER. PERHAPS THAT IS FOR THE BEST...
WORTHINESS SHOULD NOT BE DEFINED BY THE WHIMS OF MAGIC WEAPONS.
RISE, MY SON, AND LET THE HAMMER BE DAMNED. RISE AND REMEMBER THE HERO THAT YOU ARE.

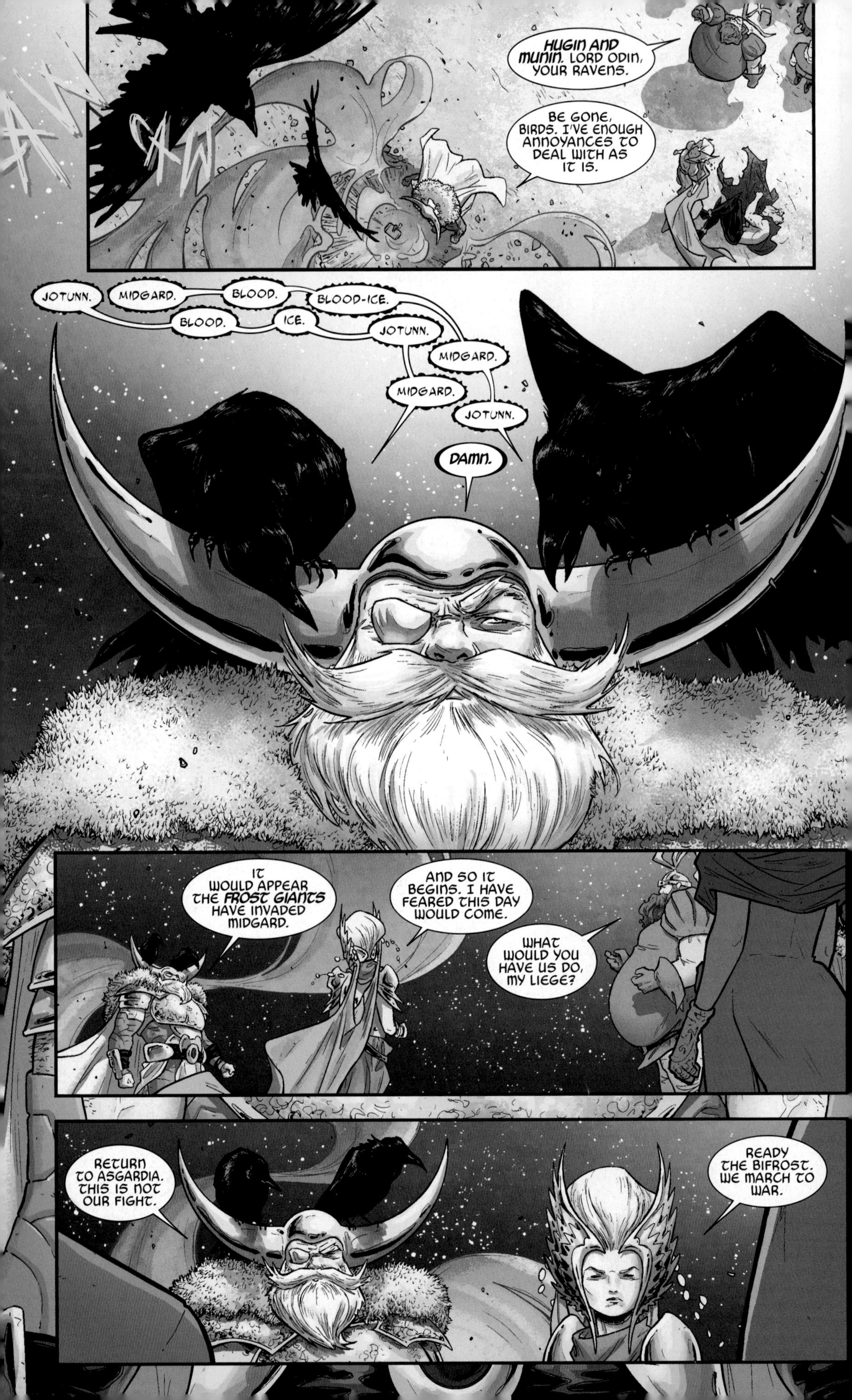

HUGIN AND MUNIN. LORD ODIN, YOUR RAVENS.
BE GONE, BIRDS. I'VE ENOUGH ANNOYANCES TO DEAL WITH AS IT IS.
JOTUNN.
MIDGARD.
BLOOD.
BLOOD-ICE.
BLOOD.
ICE.
JOTUNN.
MIDGARD.
MIDGARD.
JOTUNN.
DAMN.
IT WOULD APPEAR THE FROST GIANTS HAVE INVADED MIDGARD.
AND SO IT BEGINS. I HAVE FEARED THIS DAY WOULD COME.
WHAT WOULD YOU HAVE US DO, MY LIEGE?
RETURN TO ASGARDIA. THIS IS NOT OUR FIGHT.
READY THE BIFROST. WE MARCH TO WAR.

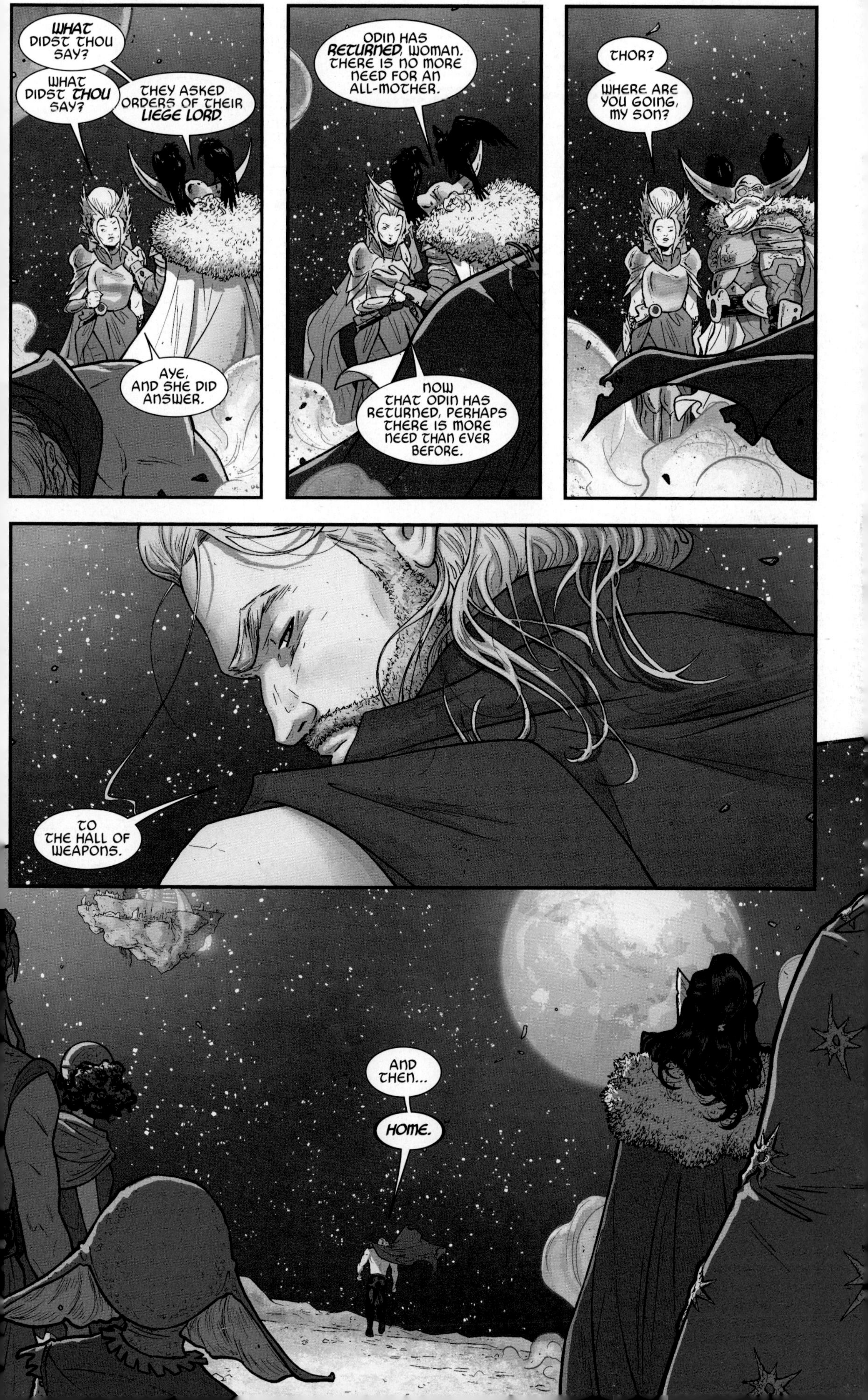
WHAT DIDST THOU SAY?
WHAT DIDST THOU SAY?
THEY ASKED ORDERS OF THEIR LIEGE LORD.
AYE, AND SHE DID ANSWER.
ODIN HAS RETURNED, WOMAN. THERE IS NO MORE NEED FOR AN ALL-MOTHER.
NOW THAT ODIN HAS RETURNED, PERHAPS THERE IS MORE NEED THAN EVER BEFORE.
THOR?
WHERE ARE YOU GOING, MY SON?
TO THE HALL OF WEAPONS.
AND THEN...
HOME.

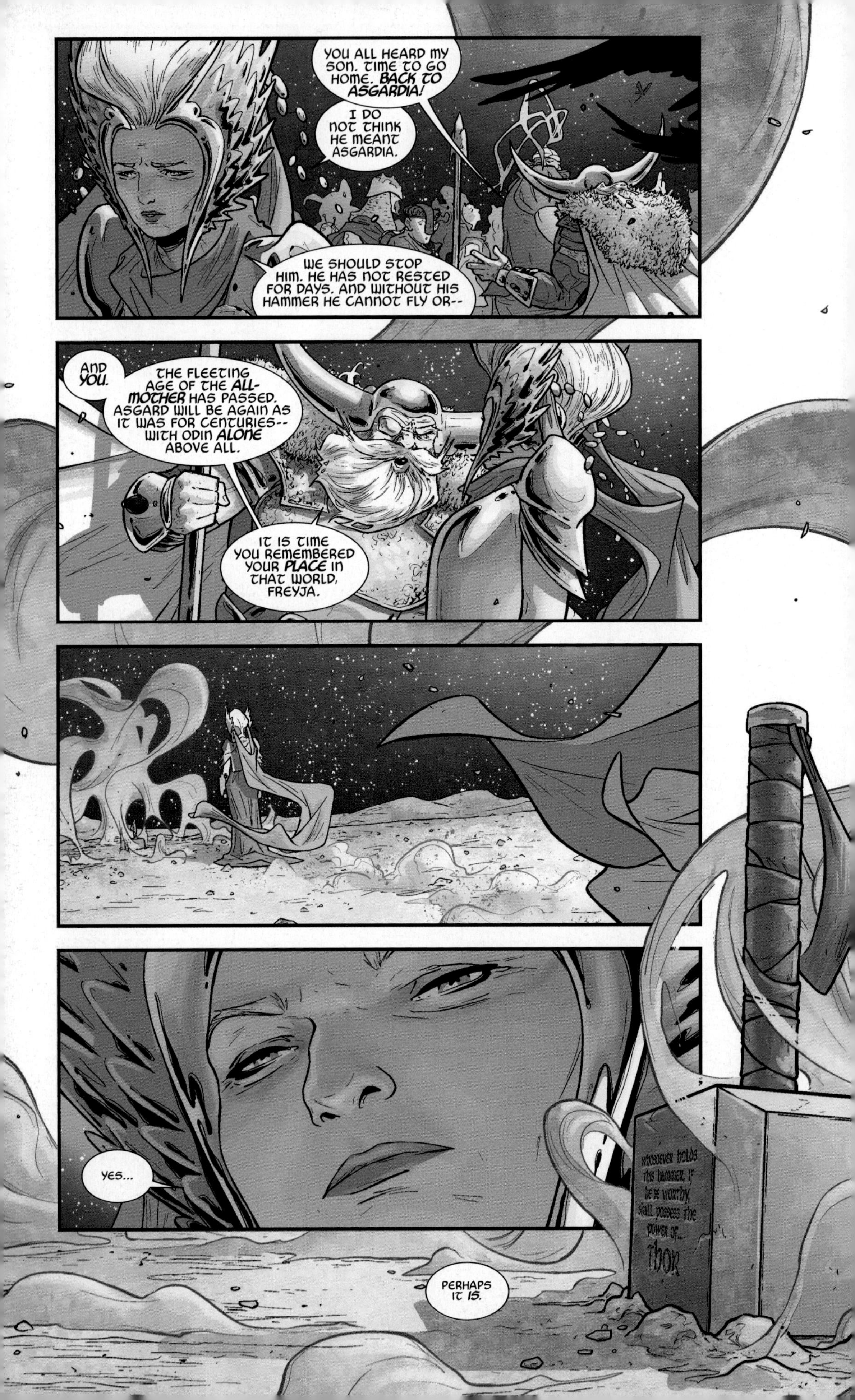
YOU ALL HEARD MY SON. TIME TO GO HOME. BACK TO ASGARDIA!
I DO NOT THINK HE MEANT ASGARDIA.
WE SHOULD STOP HIM. HE HAS NOT RESTED FOR DAYS. AND WITHOUT HIS HAMMER HE CANNOT FLY OR--
AND YOU.
THE FLEETING AGE OF THE ALL-MOTHER HAS PASSED. ASGARD WILL BE AGAIN AS IT WAS FOR CENTURIES-- WITH ODIN ALONE ABOVE ALL.
IT IS TIME YOU REMEMBERED YOUR PLACE IN THAT WORLD, FREYJA.
YES...
Whosoever holds this hammer, if he be worthy, shall possess the power of... THOR
PERHAPS IT IS.

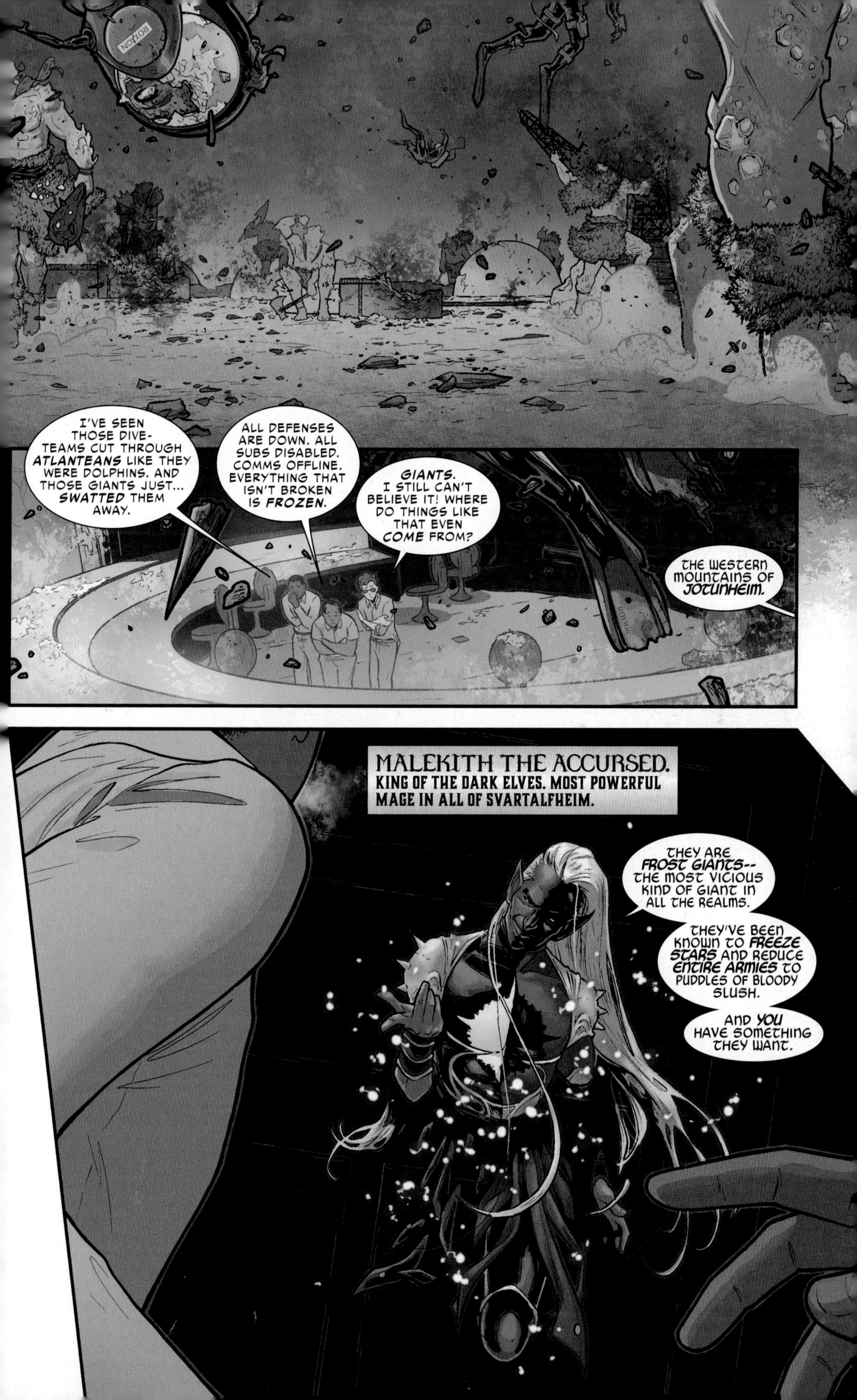
ROXXON
I'VE SEEN THOSE DIVE-TEAMS CUT THROUGH ATLANTEANS LIKE THEY WERE DOLPHINS. AND THOSE GIANTS JUST... SWATTED THEM AWAY.
ALL DEFENSES ARE DOWN. ALL SUBS DISABLED. COMMS OFFLINE. EVERYTHING THAT ISN'T BROKEN IS FROZEN.
GIANTS. I STILL CAN'T BELIEVE IT! WHERE DO THINGS LIKE THAT EVEN COME FROM?
THE WESTERN MOUNTAINS OF JOTUNHEIM.
MALEKITH THE ACCURSED.
KING OF THE DARK ELVES. MOST POWERFUL MAGE IN ALL OF SVARTALFHEIM.
THEY ARE FROST GIANTS-- THE MOST VICIOUS KIND OF GIANT IN ALL THE REALMS.
THEY'VE BEEN KNOWN TO FREEZE STARS AND REDUCE ENTIRE ARMIES TO PUDDLES OF BLOODY SLUSH.
AND YOU HAVE SOMETHING THEY WANT.

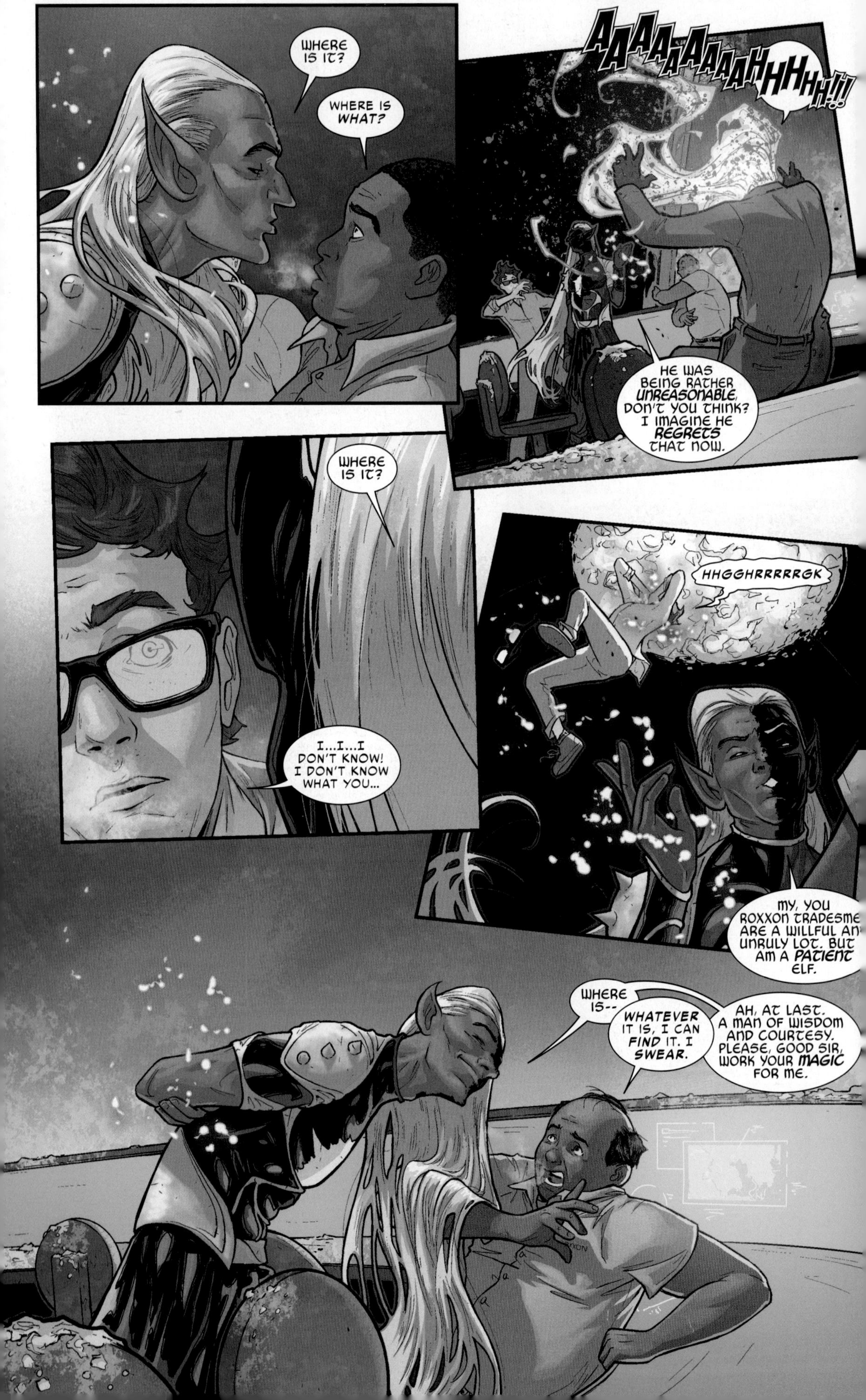
WHERE IS IT?
WHERE IS WHAT?
AAAAAAAAAAAHHHHH!!!
HE WAS BEING RATHER UNREASONABLE, DON'T YOU THINK? I IMAGINE HE REGRETS THAT NOW.
WHERE IS IT?
I...I...I DON'T KNOW! I DON'T KNOW WHAT YOU...
HHGGHRRRRRGK
MY, YOU ROXXON TRADESME ARE A WILLFUL AN UNRULY LOT. BUT AM A PATIENT ELF.
WHERE IS--
WHATEVER IT IS, I CAN FIND IT. I SWEAR.
AH, AT LAST. A MAN OF WISDOM AND COURTESY. PLEASE, GOOD SIR, WORK YOUR MAGIC FOR ME.

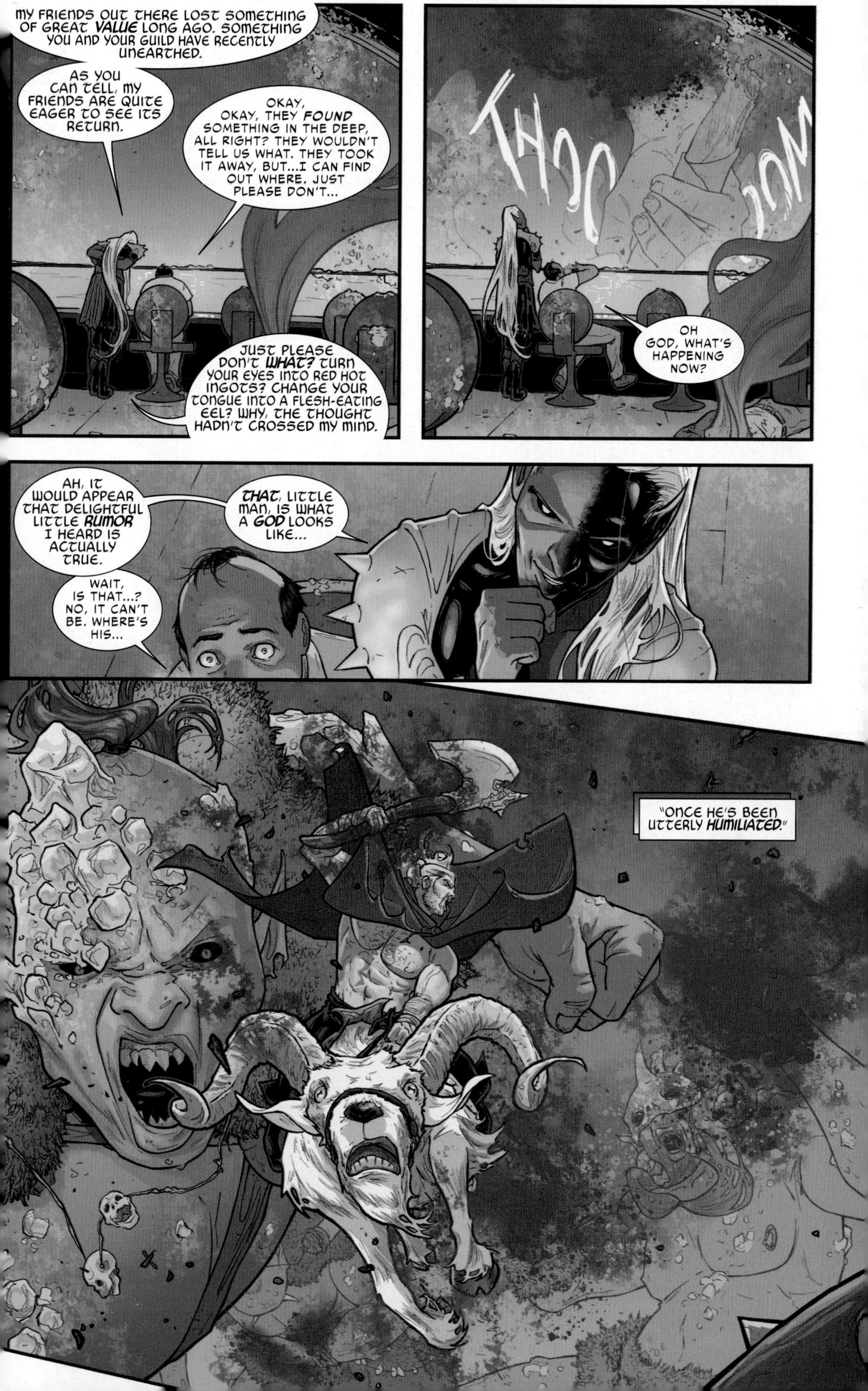

MY FRIENDS OUT THERE LOST SOMETHING OF GREAT VALUE LONG AGO. SOMETHING YOU AND YOUR GUILD HAVE RECENTLY UNEARTHED.
AS YOU CAN TELL, MY FRIENDS ARE QUITE EAGER TO SEE ITS RETURN.
OKAY, OKAY, THEY FOUND SOMETHING IN THE DEEP, ALL RIGHT? THEY WOULDN'T TELL US WHAT. THEY TOOK IT AWAY, BUT...I CAN FIND OUT WHERE. JUST PLEASE DON'T...
JUST PLEASE DON'T WHAT? TURN YOUR EYES INTO RED HOT INGOTS? CHANGE YOUR TONGUE INTO A FLESH-EATING EEL? WHY, THE THOUGHT HADN'T CROSSED MY MIND.
THOOM
OH GOD, WHAT'S HAPPENING NOW?
AH, IT WOULD APPEAR THAT DELIGHTFUL LITTLE RUMOR I HEARD IS ACTUALLY TRUE.
THAT, LITTLE MAN, IS WHAT A GOD LOOKS LIKE...
WAIT, IS THAT...? NO, IT CAN'T BE. WHERE'S HIS...
"ONCE HE'S BEEN UTTERLY HUMILIATED."

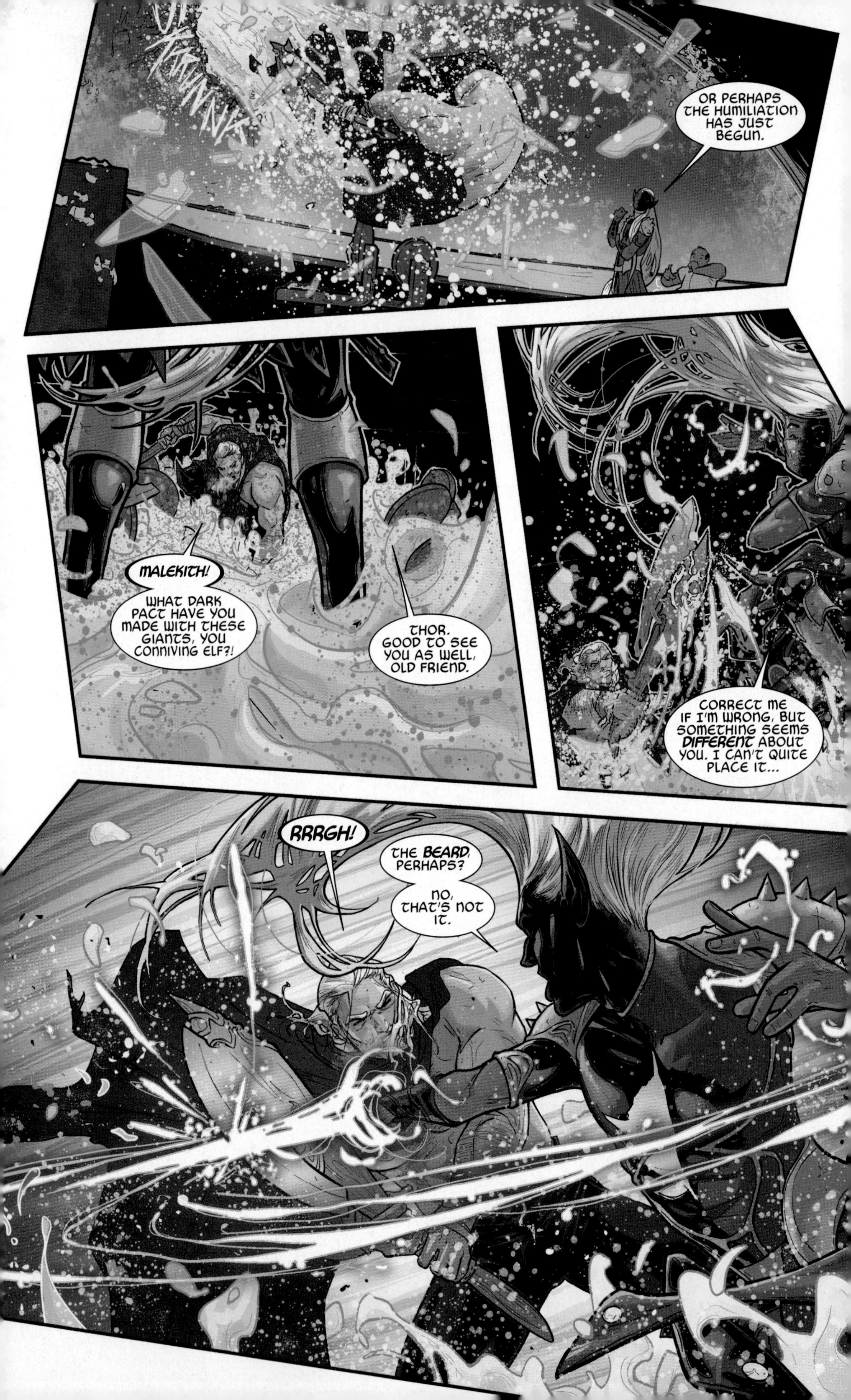
KRAKKA-KRUNNK
OR PERHAPS THE HUMILIATION HAS JUST BEGUN.
MALEKITH!
WHAT DARK PACT HAVE YOU MADE WITH THESE GIANTS, YOU CONNIVING ELF?!
THOR. GOOD TO SEE YOU AS WELL, OLD FRIEND.
CORRECT ME IF I'M WRONG, BUT SOMETHING SEEMS DIFFERENT ABOUT YOU. I CAN'T QUITE PLACE IT...
RRRGH!
THE BEARD, PERHAPS?
NO, THAT'S NOT IT.

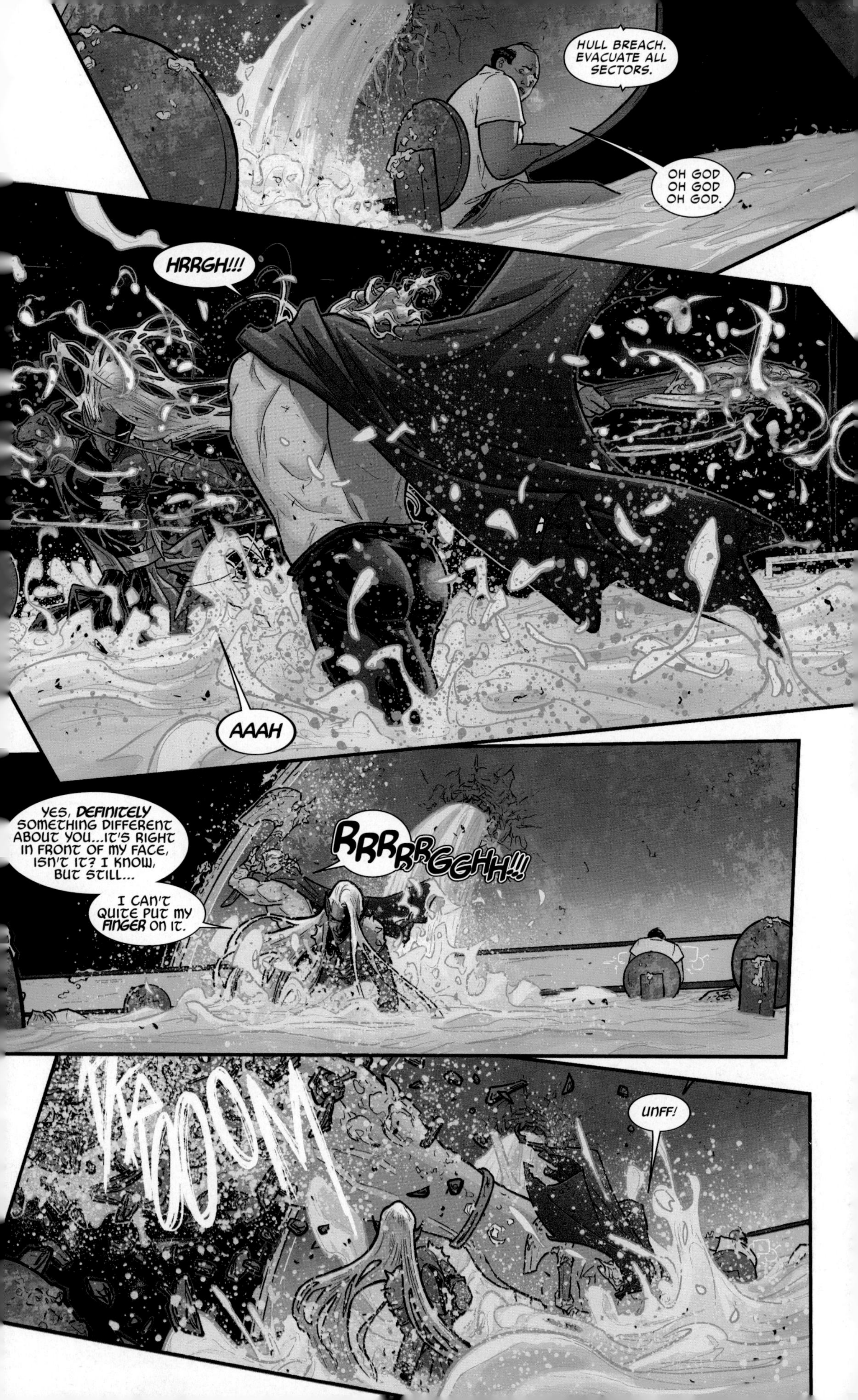
HULL BREACH. EVACUATE ALL SECTORS.
OH GOD OH GOD OH GOD.
HRRGH!!!
AAAH
YES, DEFINITELY SOMETHING DIFFERENT ABOUT YOU...IT'S RIGHT IN FRONT OF MY FACE, ISN'T IT? I KNOW, BUT STILL...
I CAN'T QUITE PUT MY FINGER ON IT.
RRRRRGGHH!!!
KKAOOOM
UNFF!

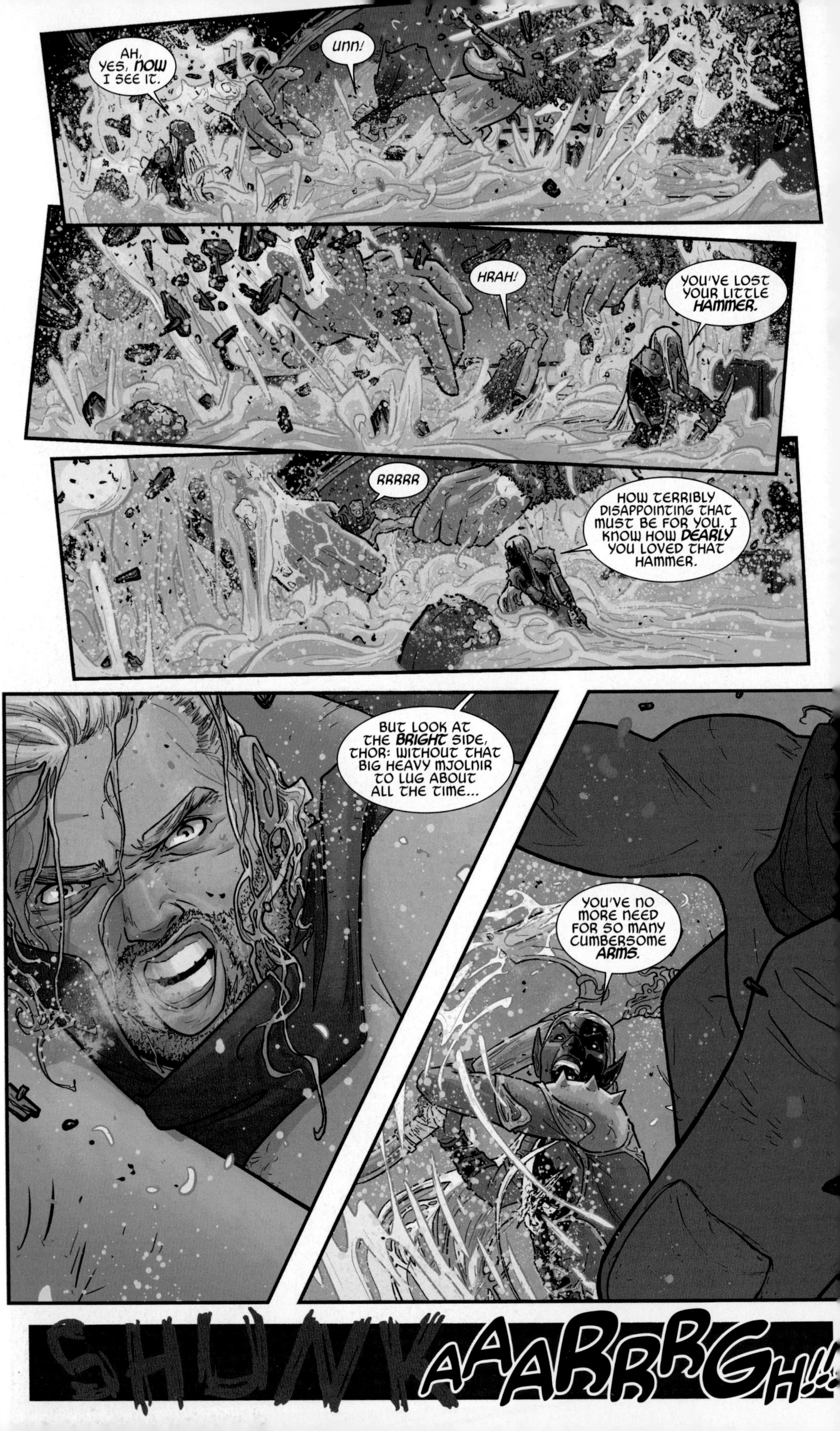

AH, YES, NOW I SEE IT.
UNN!
HRAH!
YOU'VE LOST YOUR LITTLE HAMMER.
BRRRR
HOW TERRIBLY DISAPPOINTING THAT MUST BE FOR YOU. I KNOW HOW DEARLY YOU LOVED THAT HAMMER.
BUT LOOK AT THE BRIGHT SIDE, THOR: WITHOUT THAT BIG HEAVY MJOLNIR TO LUG ABOUT ALL THE TIME...
YOU'VE NO MORE NEED FOR SO MANY CUMBERSOME ARMS.
SHUNK
AAARRRGH!!

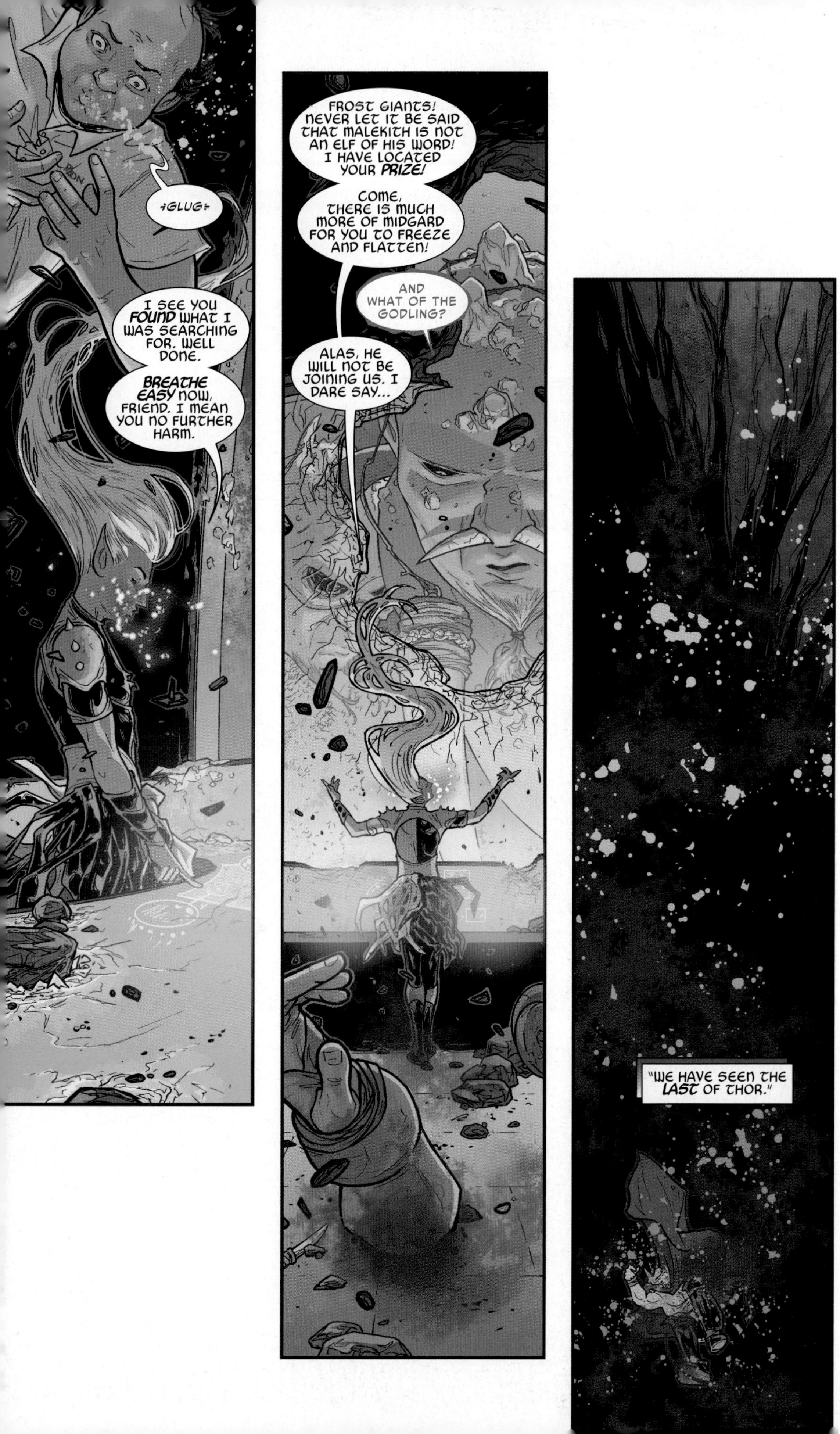

-GLUG-
I SEE YOU FOUND WHAT I WAS SEARCHING FOR. WELL DONE.
BREATHE EASY NOW, FRIEND. I MEAN YOU NO FURTHER HARM.
FROST GIANTS! NEVER LET IT BE SAID THAT MALEKITH IS NOT AN ELF OF HIS WORD! I HAVE LOCATED YOUR PRIZE!
COME, THERE IS MUCH MORE OF MIDGARD FOR YOU TO FREEZE AND FLATTEN!
AND WHAT OF THE GODLING?
ALAS, HE WILL NOT BE JOINING US. I DARE SAY...
"WE HAVE SEEN THE LAST OF THOR."

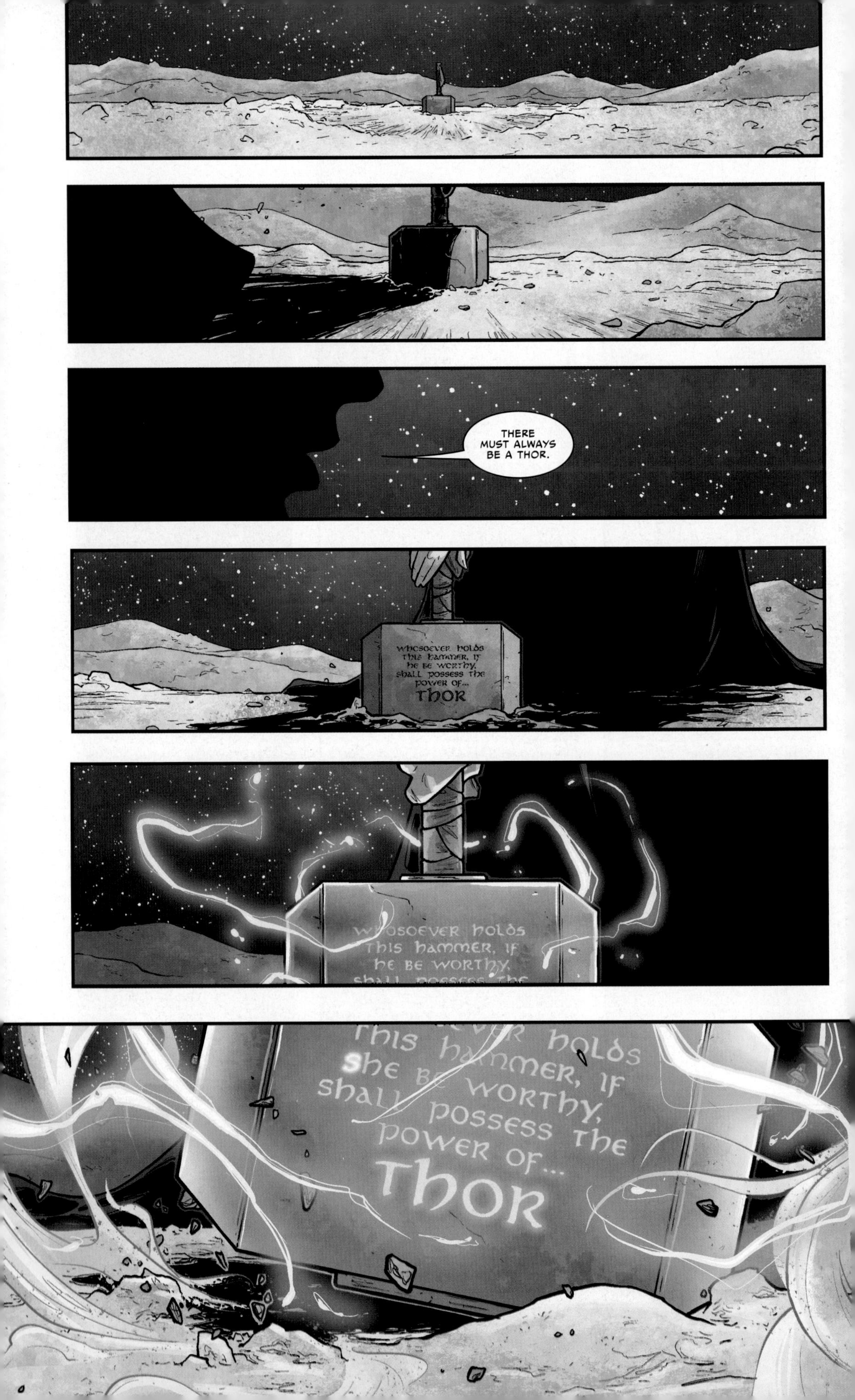
THERE MUST ALWAYS BE A THOR.
WHOSOEVER HOLDS THIS HAMMER, IF HE BE WORTHY, SHALL POSSESS THE POWER OF... THOR
WHOSOEVER HOLDS THIS HAMMER, IF HE BE WORTHY,
THIS HAMMER, IF SHE BE WORTHY, POSSESS THE POWER OF... THOR

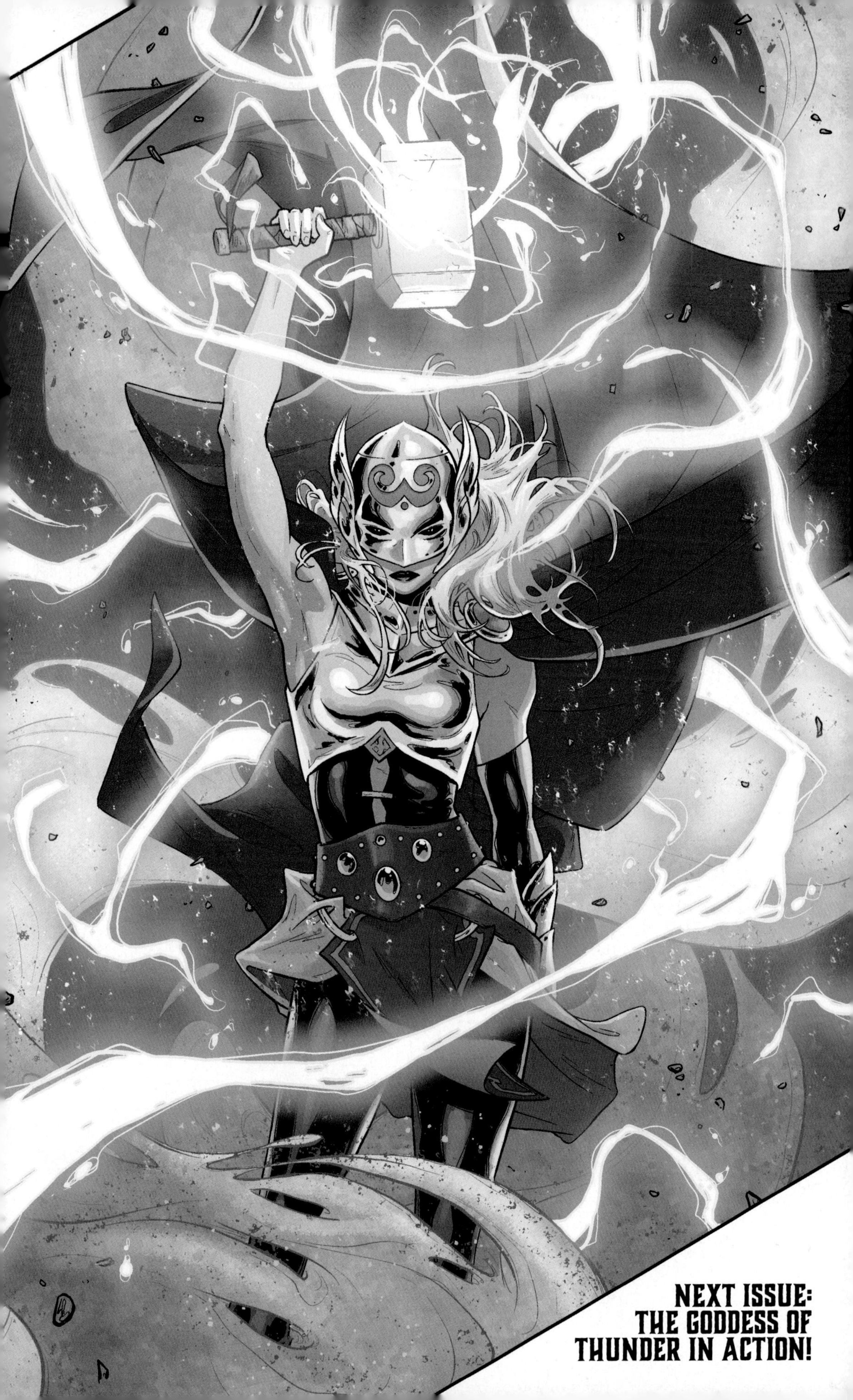
NEXT ISSUE:
THE GODDESS OF
THUNDER IN ACTION!

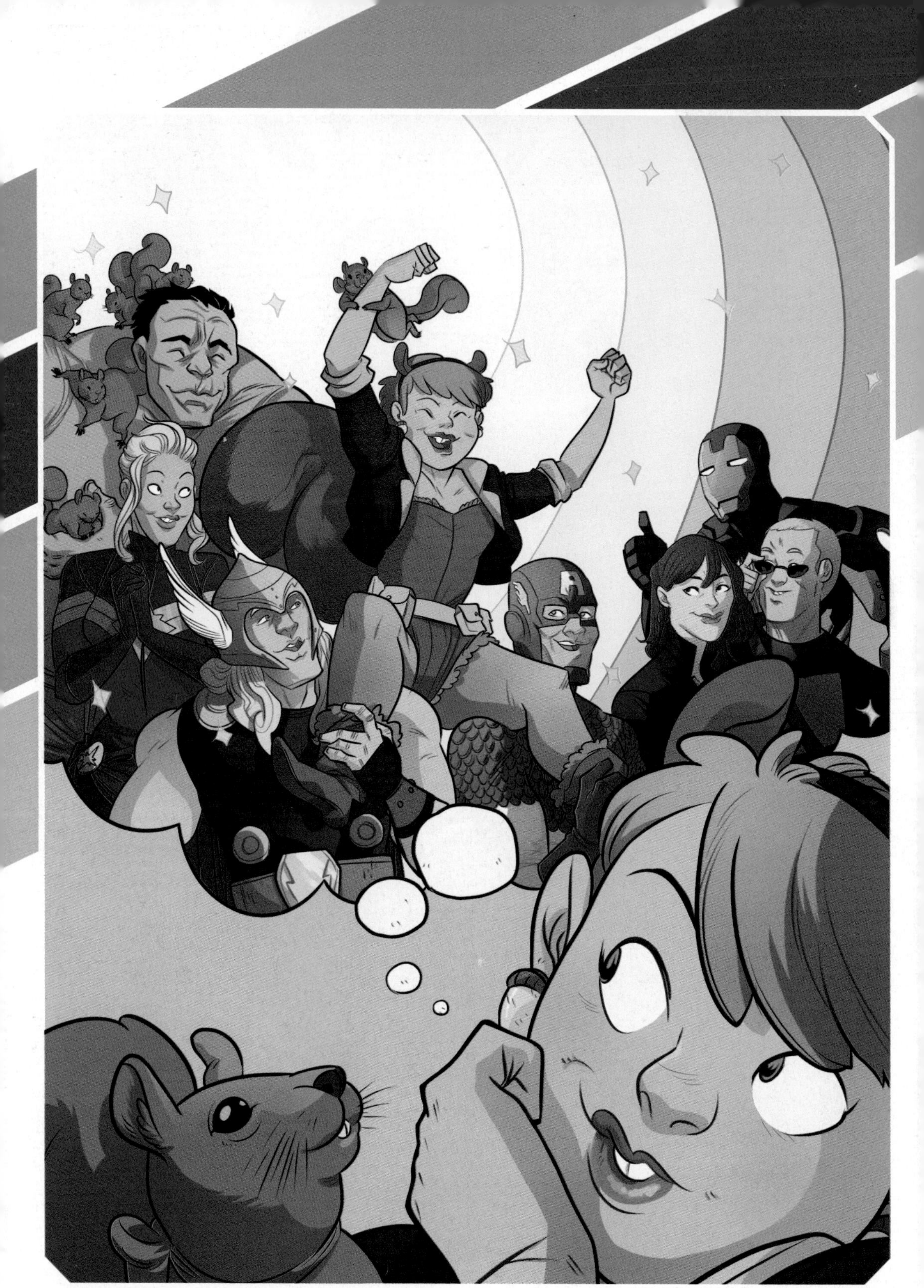

THE UNBEATABLE SQUIRREL GIRL #1

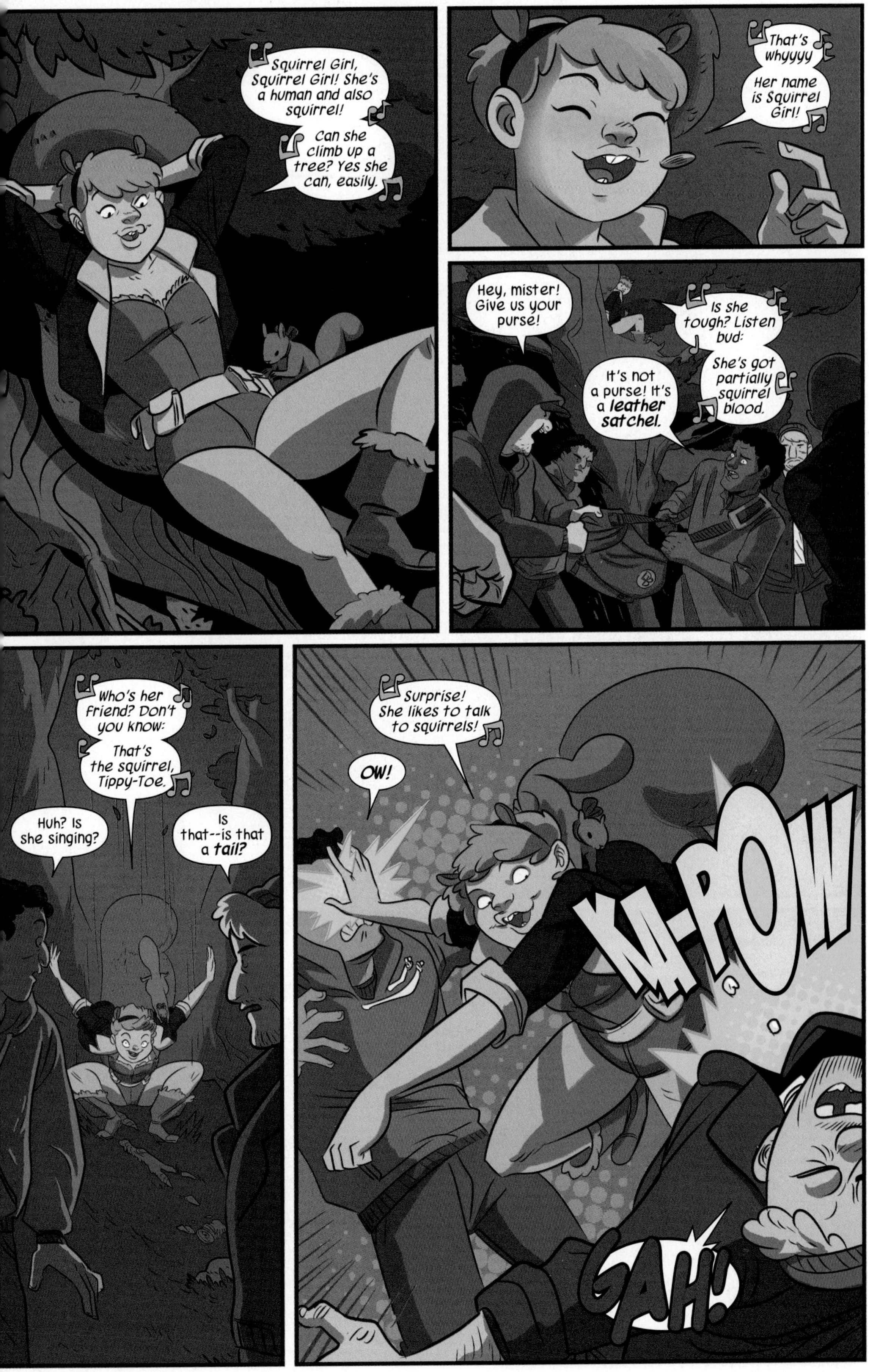
Squirrel Girl, Squirrel Girl! She's a human and also squirrel!
Can she climb up a tree? Yes she can, easily.
That's whyyyy
Her name is Squirrel Girl!
Hey, mister! Give us your purse!
Is she tough? Listen bud:
She's got partially squirrel blood.
It's not a purse! It's a **leather satchel.**
Who's her friend? Don't you know:
That's the squirrel, Tippy-Toe.
Huh? Is she singing?
Is that--is that a ***tail?***
Surprise! She likes to talk to squirrels!
OW!
KA-POW
GAH!

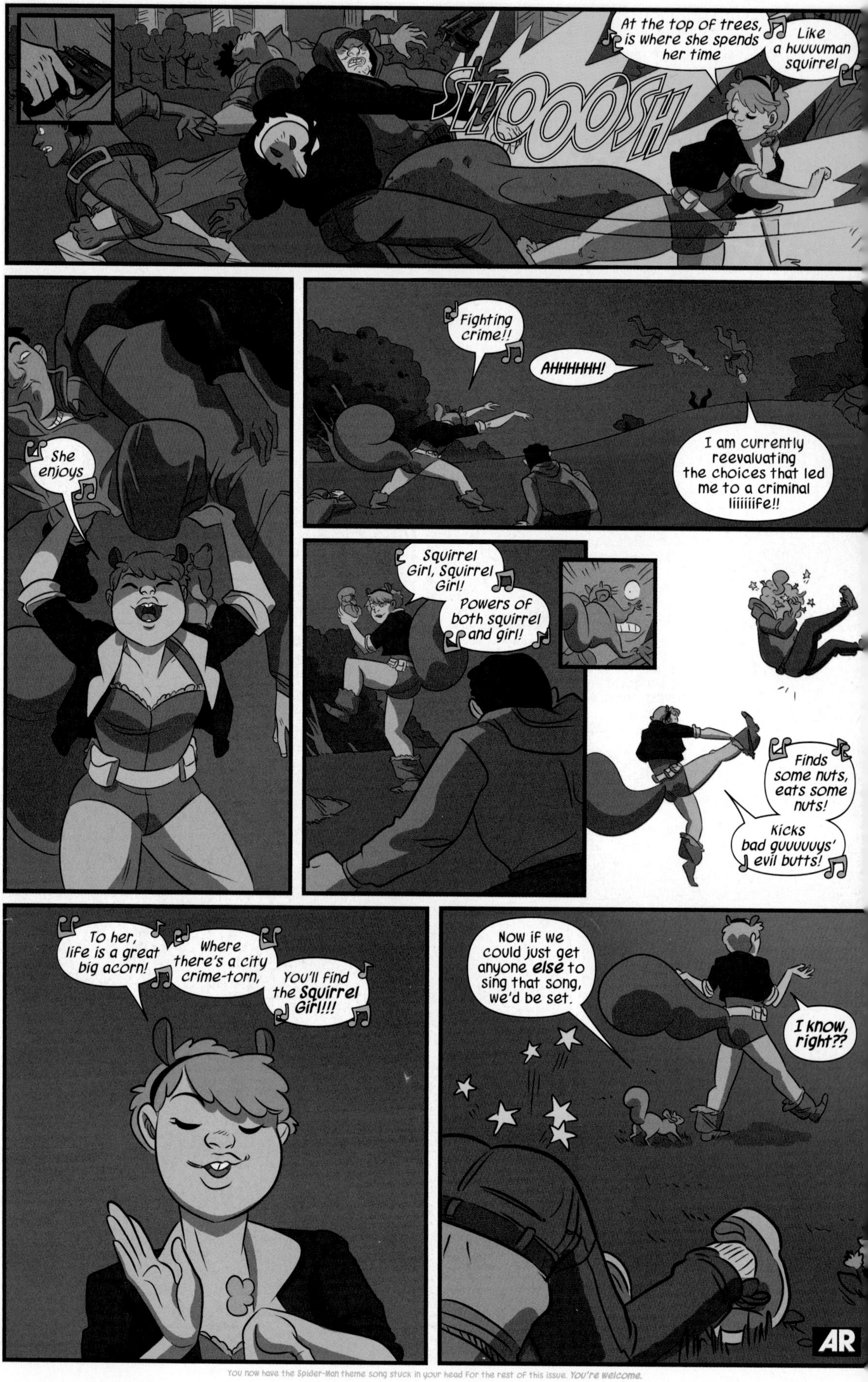
SWOOOSH
At the top of trees, is where she spends her time
Like a huuuuman squirrel
She enjoys
Fighting crime!!
AHHHHHH!
I am currently reevaluating the choices that led me to a criminal liiiiiife!!
Squirrel Girl, Squirrel Girl!
Powers of both squirrel and girl!
Finds some nuts, eats some nuts!
Kicks bad guuuuuys' evil butts!
To her, life is a great big acorn!
Where there's a city crime-torn,
You'll find the Squirrel Girl!!!
Now if we could just get anyone else to sing that song, we'd be set.
I know, right??
AR

You now have the Spider-Man theme song stuck in your head for the rest of this issue. *You're welcome.*

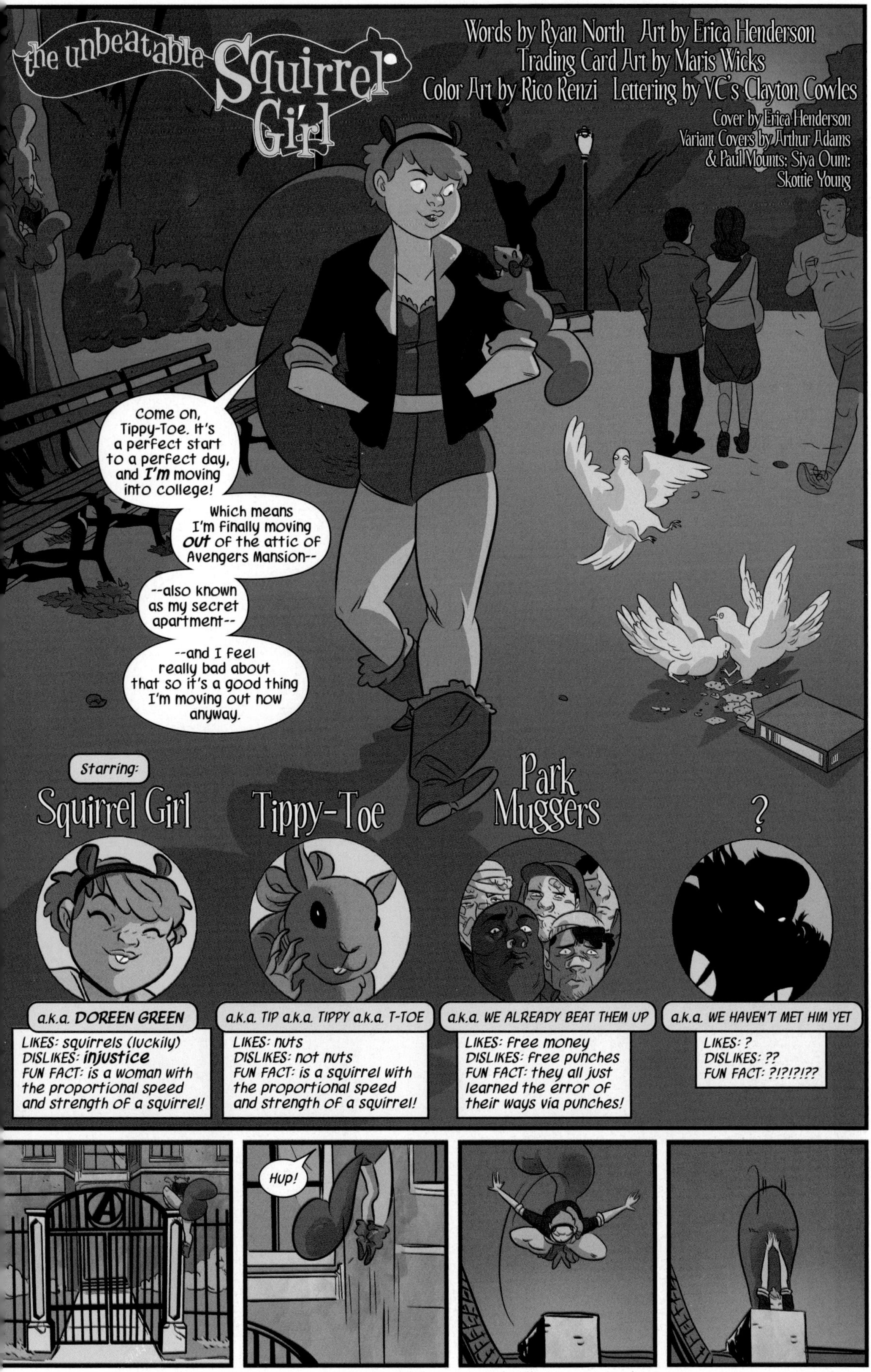
the unbeatable Squirrel Girl
Words by Ryan North Art by Erica Henderson
Trading Card Art by Maris Wicks
Color Art by Rico Renzi Lettering by VC's Clayton Cowles
Cover by Erica Henderson
Variant Covers by Arthur Adams & Paul Mounts; Siya Oum; Skottie Young
Come on, Tippy-Toe. It's a perfect start to a perfect day, and *I'm* moving into college!
Which means I'm finally moving ***out*** of the attic of Avengers Mansion--
--also known as my secret apartment--
--and I feel really bad about that so it's a good thing I'm moving out now anyway.
Starring:
Squirrel Girl
a.k.a. DOREEN GREEN
LIKES: squirrels (luckily)
DISLIKES: **injustice**
FUN FACT: is a woman with the proportional speed and strength of a squirrel!
Tippy-Toe
a.k.a. TIP a.k.a. TIPPY a.k.a. T-TOE
LIKES: nuts
DISLIKES: not nuts
FUN FACT: is a squirrel with the proportional speed and strength of a squirrel!
Park Muggers
a.k.a. WE ALREADY BEAT THEM UP
LIKES: free money
DISLIKES: free punches
FUN FACT: they all just learned the error of their ways via punches!
?
a.k.a. WE HAVEN'T MET HIM YET
LIKES: ?
DISLIKES: ??
FUN FACT: ?!?!?!??
Hup!

Wait, did I say the Spider-Man theme song? *Obviously* I meant the *Squirrel Girl* theme song. Who even *is* Spider-Man?

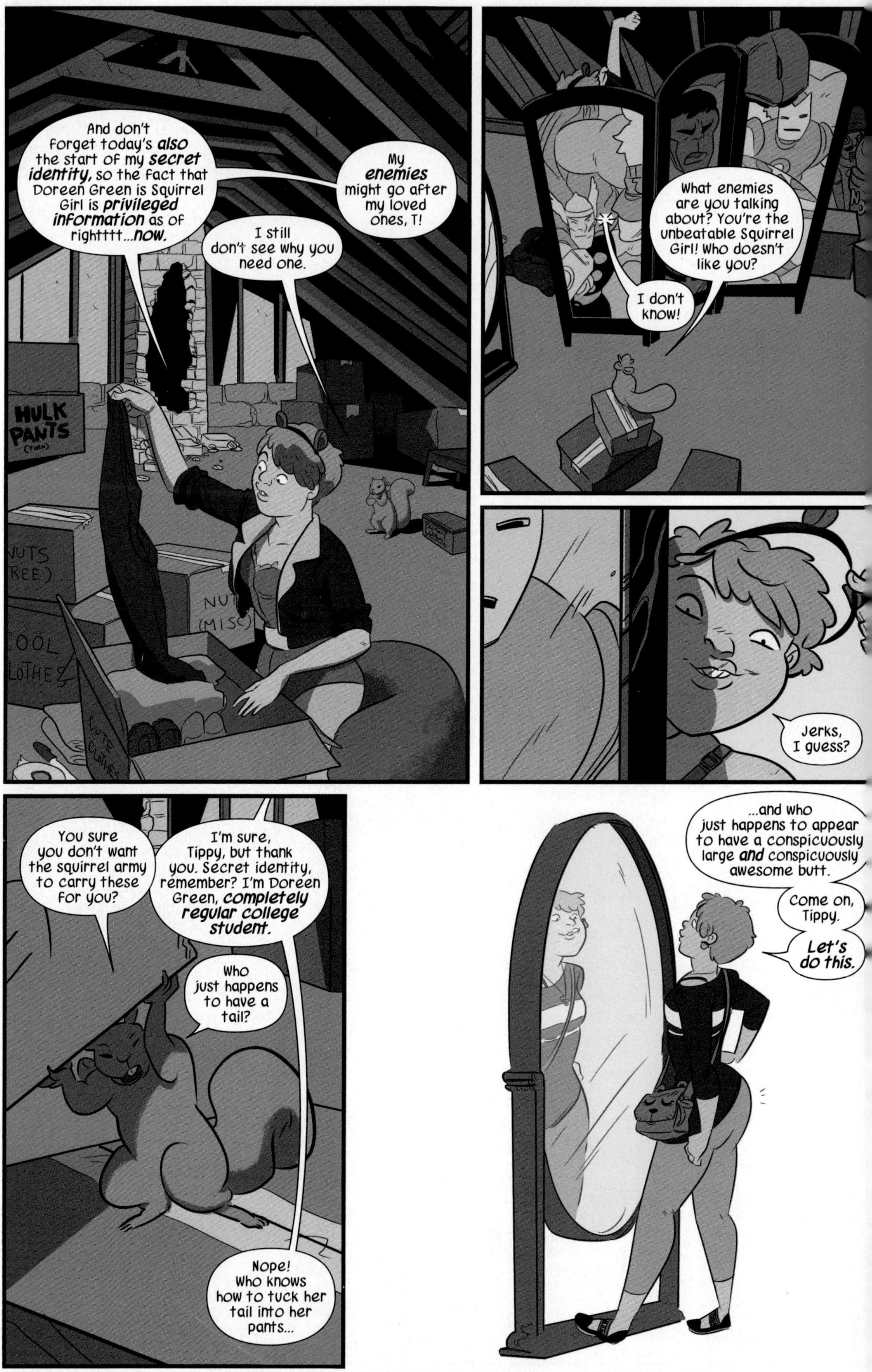
And don't forget today's *also* the start of my *secret identity,* so the fact that Doreen Green is Squirrel Girl is *privileged information* as of righttttt...*now.*
My *enemies* might go after my loved ones, T!
I still don't see why you need one.
HULK PANTS (TORN)
NUTS (TREE)
NUTS (MISC)
COOL CLOTHES
CUTE CLOTHES
What enemies are you talking about? You're the unbeatable Squirrel Girl! Who doesn't like you?
I don't know!
Jerks, I guess?
You sure you don't want the squirrel army to carry these for you?
I'm sure, Tippy, but thank you. Secret identity, remember? I'm Doreen Green, *completely regular college student.*
Who just happens to have a tail?
Nope! Who knows how to tuck her tail into her pants...
...and who just happens to appear to have a conspicuously large *and* conspicuously awesome butt.
Come on, Tippy.
Let's do this.

NOT PICTURED: Other tiny boxes labelled "Ant-Man's Tiny Vans," "Ant-Man's Aunt's Flans," and "Ant-Man's Rejected Costumes (OFF-Brand)"

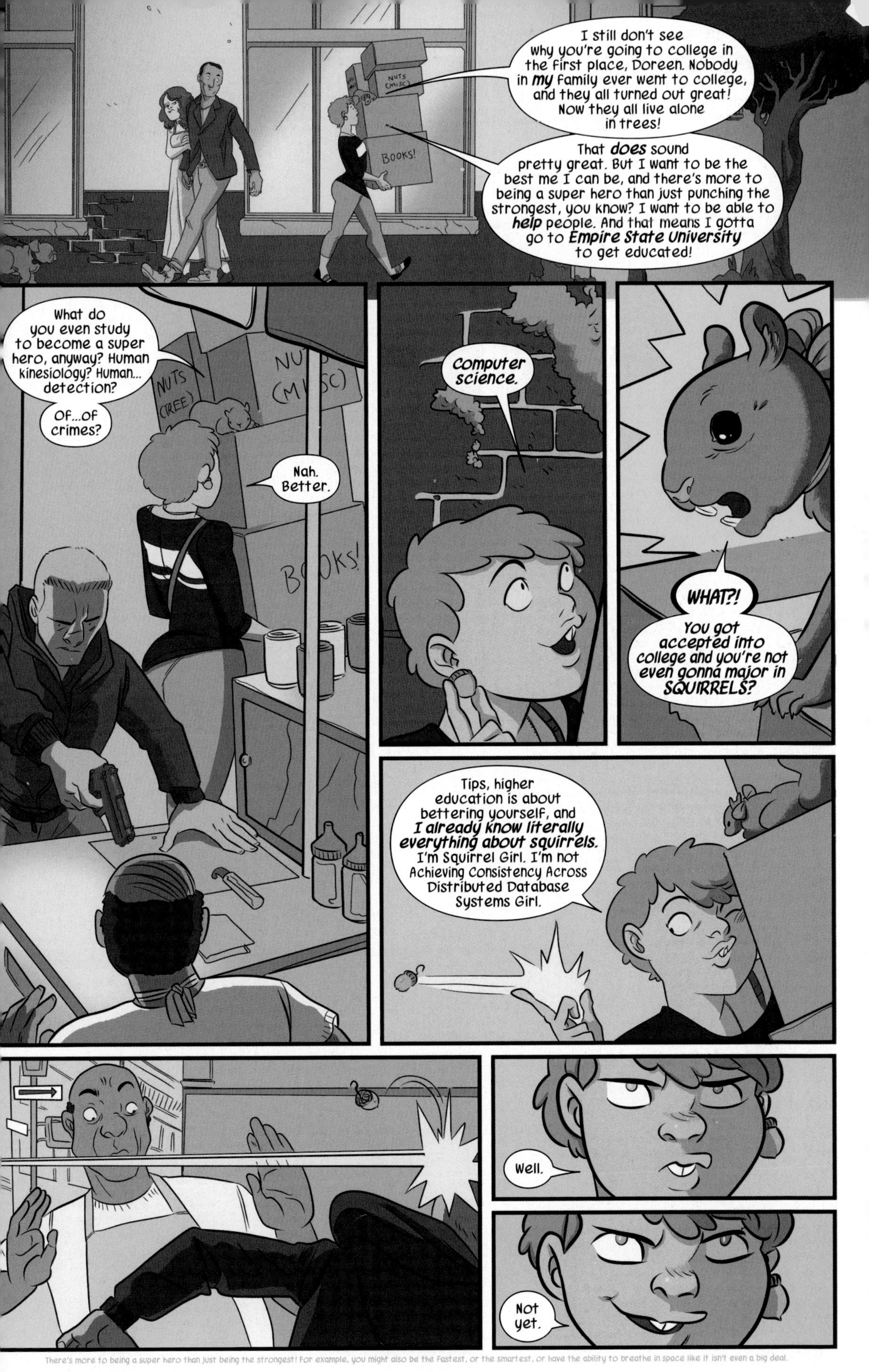
NUTS (MISC)
BOOKS!
I still don't see why you're going to college in the first place, Doreen. Nobody in *my* family ever went to college, and they all turned out great! Now they all live alone in trees!
That *does* sound pretty great. But I want to be the best me I can be, and there's more to being a super hero than just punching the strongest, you know? I want to be able to *help* people. And that means I gotta go to *Empire State University* to get educated!
What do you even study to become a super hero, anyway? Human kinesiology? Human... detection?
Of...of crimes?
NUTS (TREE)
NUTS (MISC)
Nah. Better.
BOOKS!
Computer science.
WHAT?!
You got accepted into college and you're not even gonna major in SQUIRRELS?
Tips, higher education is about bettering yourself, and *I already know literally everything about squirrels.* I'm Squirrel Girl. I'm not Achieving Consistency Across Distributed Database Systems Girl.
Well.
Not yet.

There's more to being a super hero than just being the strongest! For example, you might also be the fastest, or the smartest, or have the ability to breathe in space like it isn't even a big deal.

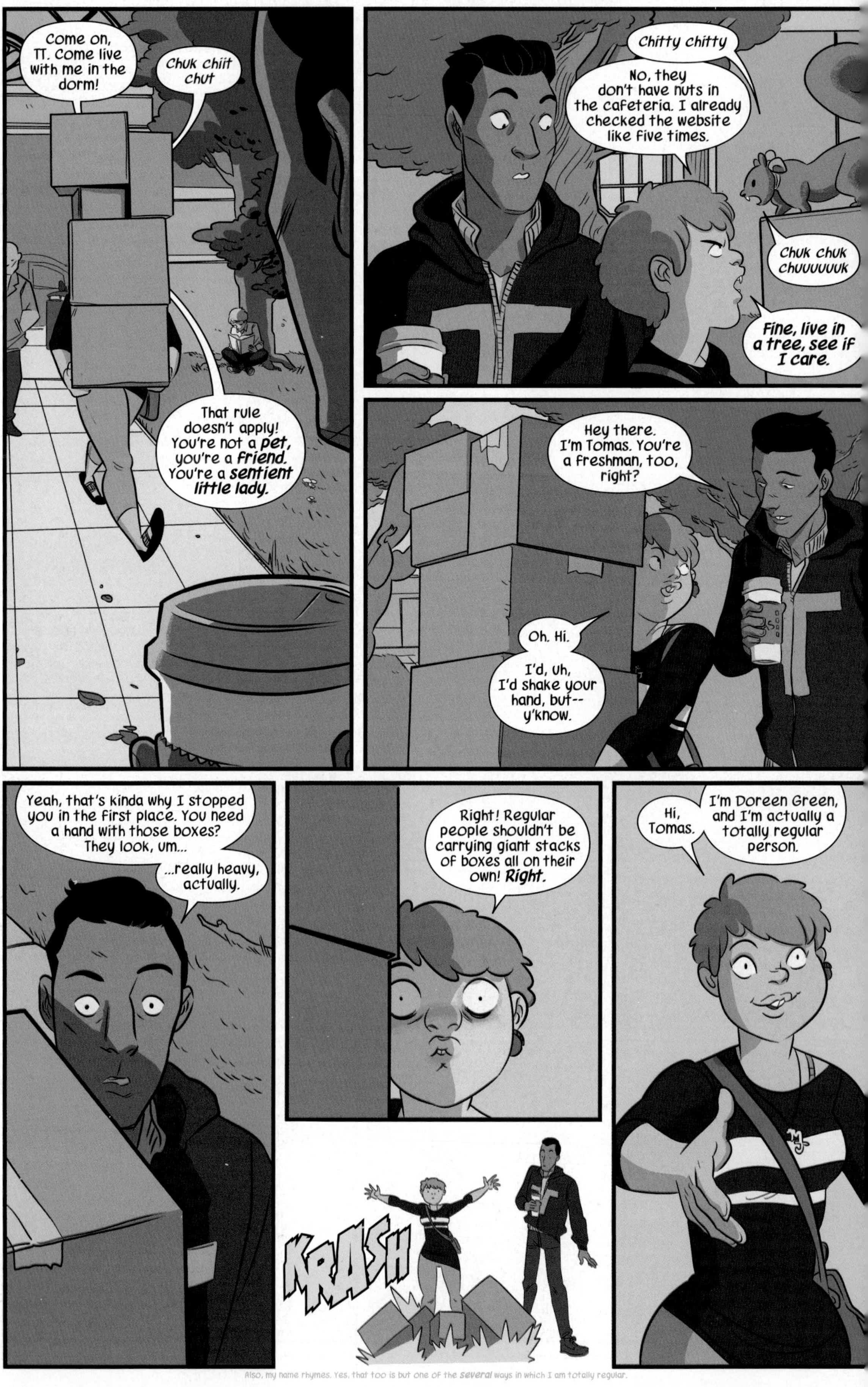
Come on, TT. Come live with me in the dorm!
Chuk chiit chut
That rule doesn't apply! You're not a pet, you're a friend. You're a sentient little lady.
Chitty chitty
No, they don't have nuts in the cafeteria. I already checked the website like five times.
Chuk chuk chuuuuuuk
Fine, live in a tree, see if I care.
Hey there. I'm Tomas. You're a freshman, too, right?
Oh. Hi.
I'd, uh, I'd shake your hand, but-- y'know.
Yeah, that's kinda why I stopped you in the first place. You need a hand with those boxes? They look, um...
...really heavy, actually.
Right! Regular people shouldn't be carrying giant stacks of boxes all on their own! Right.
KRASH
Hi, Tomas.
I'm Doreen Green, and I'm actually a totally regular person.

Also, my name rhymes. Yes, that too is but one of the *several* ways in which I am totally regular.

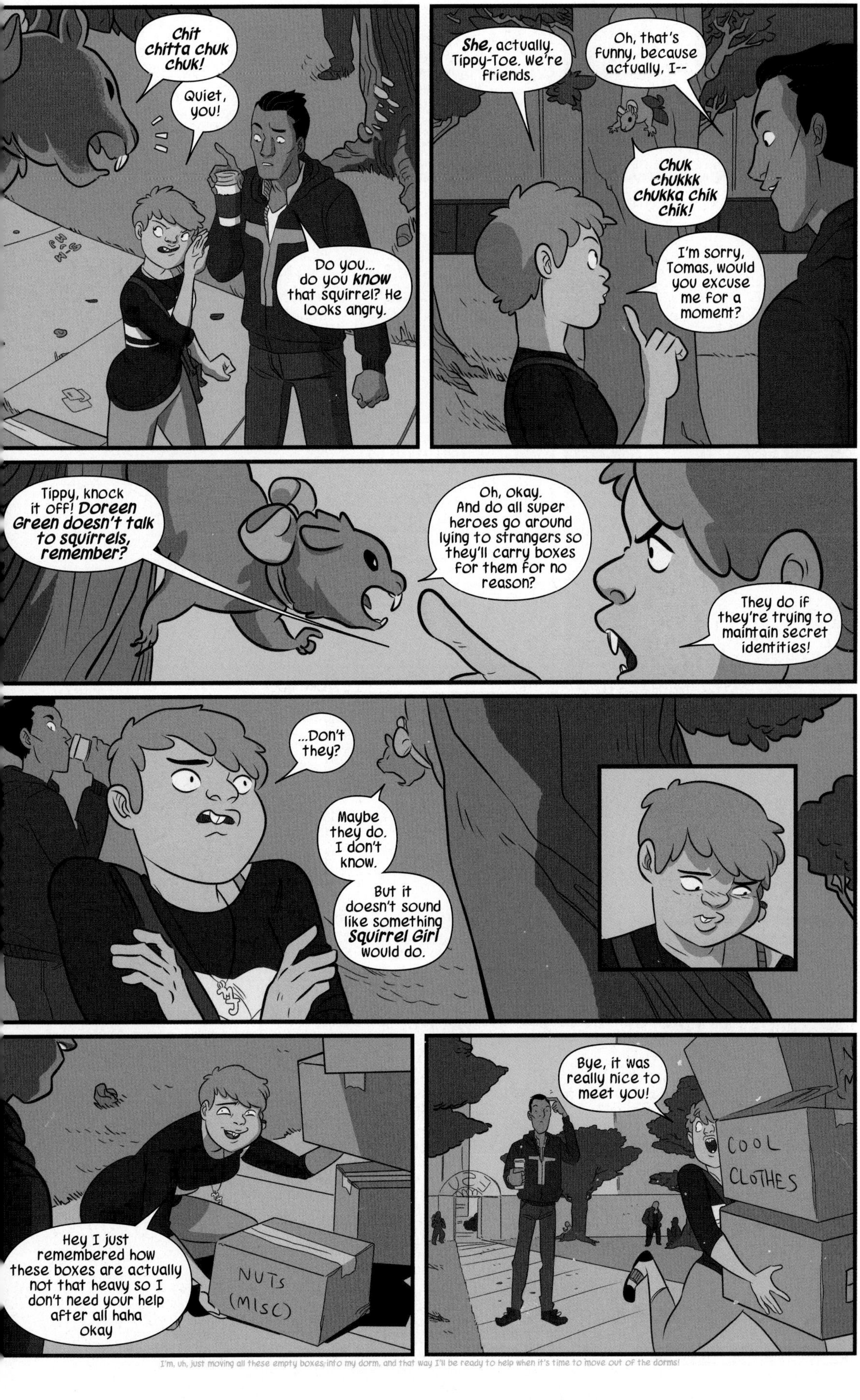

Chit chitta chuk chuk!
Quiet, you!
Do you... do you know that squirrel? He looks angry.
She, actually. Tippy-Toe. We're friends.
Oh, that's funny, because actually, I--
Chuk chukkk chukka chik chik!
I'm sorry, Tomas, would you excuse me for a moment?
Tippy, knock it off! Doreen Green doesn't talk to squirrels, remember?
Oh, okay. And do all super heroes go around lying to strangers so they'll carry boxes for them for no reason?
They do if they're trying to maintain secret identities!
...Don't they?
Maybe they do. I don't know.
But it doesn't sound like something Squirrel Girl would do.
Hey I just remembered how these boxes are actually not that heavy so I don't need your help after all haha okay
NUTS (MISC)
Bye, it was really nice to meet you!
COOL CLOTHES

I'm, uh, just moving all these empty boxes into my dorm, and that way I'll be ready to help when it's time to move out of the dorms!

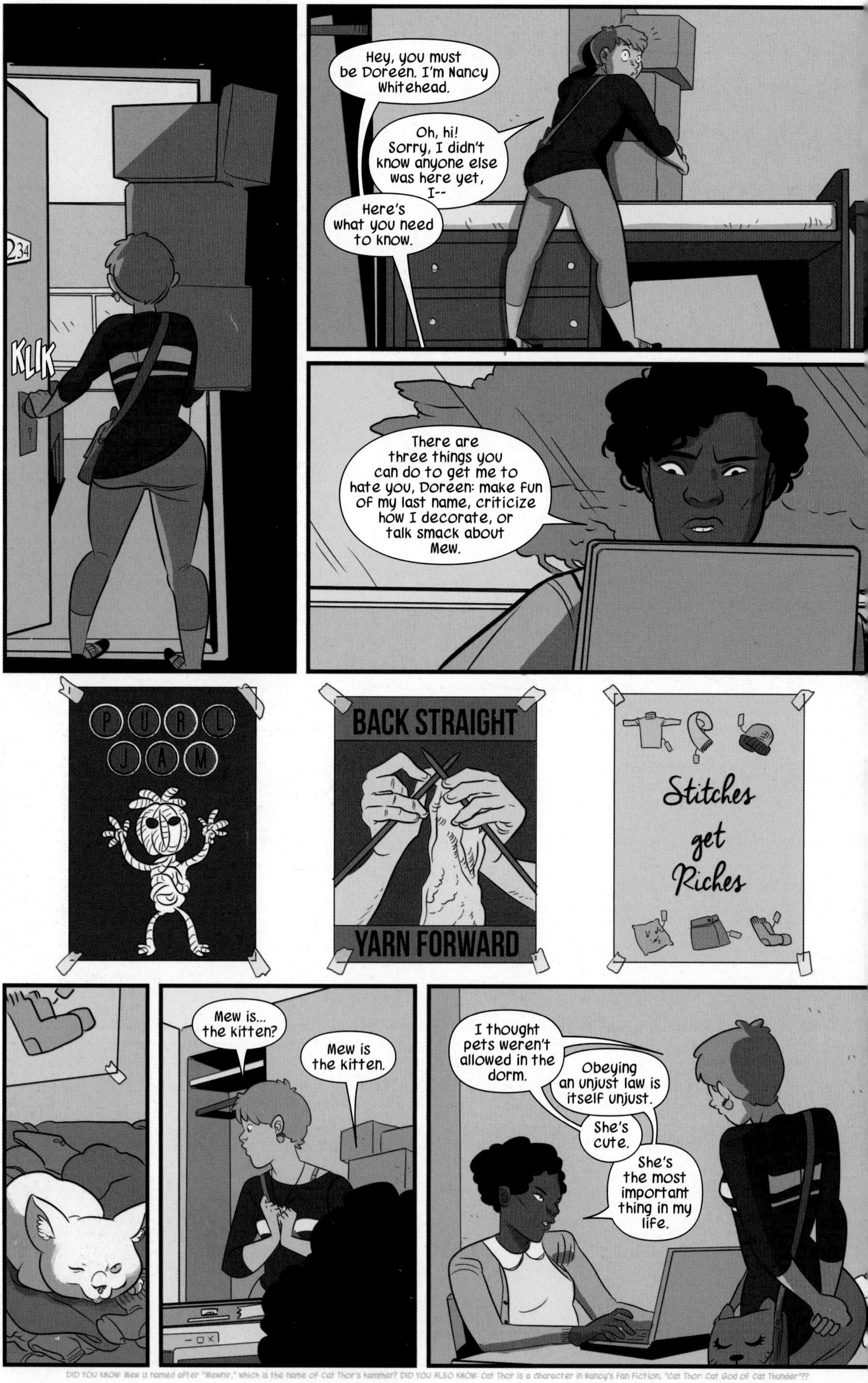
KLIK
Hey, you must be Doreen. I'm Nancy Whitehead.
Oh, hi! Sorry, I didn't know anyone else was here yet, I--
Here's what you need to know.
There are three things you can do to get me to hate you, Doreen: make fun of my last name, criticize how I decorate, or talk smack about Mew.
PURL JAM
BACK STRAIGHT
YARN FORWARD
Stitches get Riches
Mew is... the kitten?
Mew is the kitten.
I thought pets weren't allowed in the dorm.
Obeying an unjust law is itself unjust.
She's cute.
She's the most important thing in my life.

DID YOU KNOW: Mew is named after "Mewnir," which is the name of Cat Thor's hammer? DID YOU ALSO KNOW: Cat Thor is a character in Nancy's Fan Fiction, "Cat Thor: Cat God of Cat Thunder"??

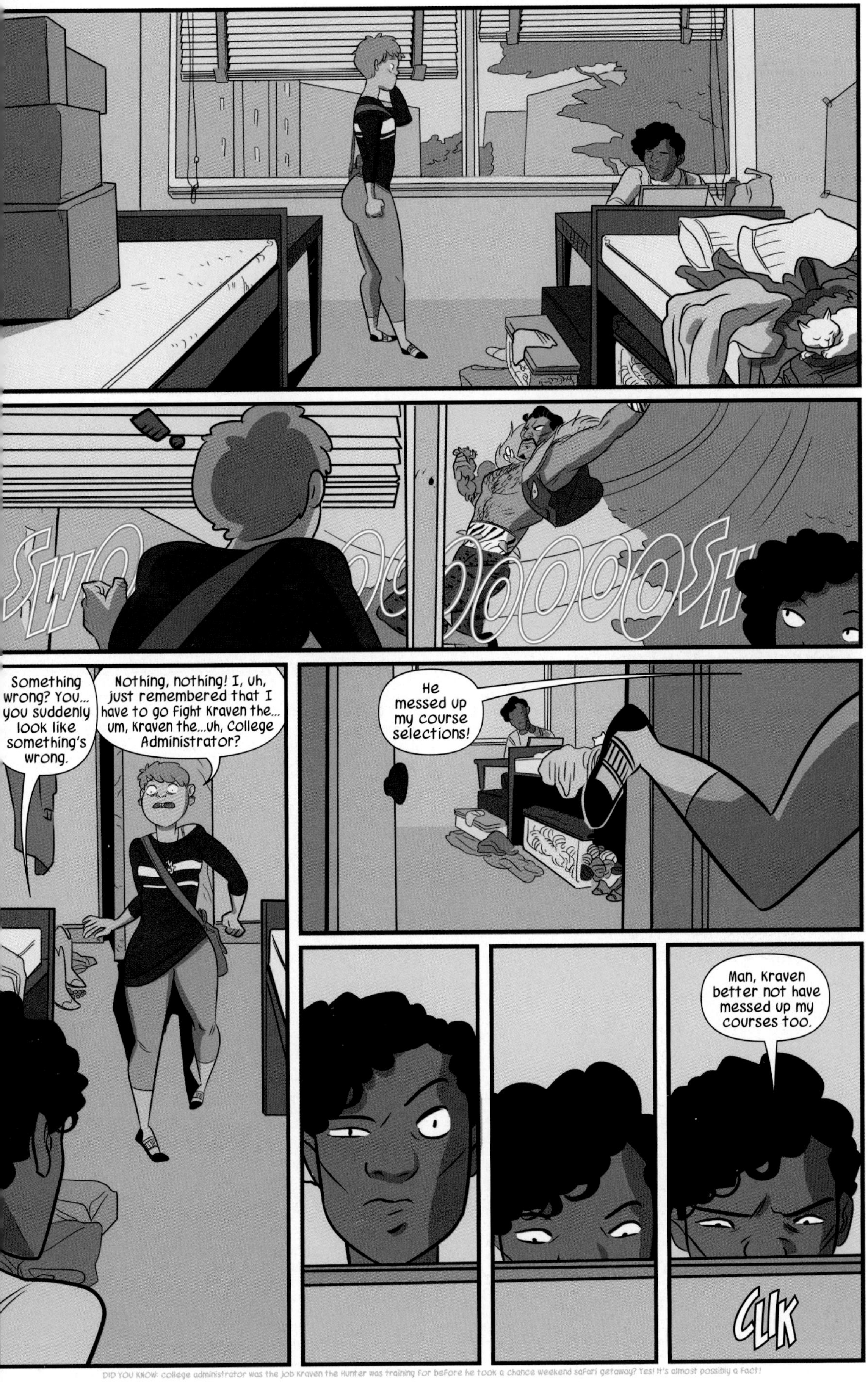
SWOOOOOOOOSH
Something wrong? You... you suddenly look like something's wrong.
Nothing, nothing! I, uh, just remembered that I have to go fight Kraven the... um, Kraven the...uh, College Administrator?
He messed up my course selections!
Man, Kraven better not have messed up my courses too.
CLIK

DID YOU KNOW: college administrator was the job Kraven the Hunter was training for before he took a chance weekend safari getaway? Yes! It's almost possibly a fact!

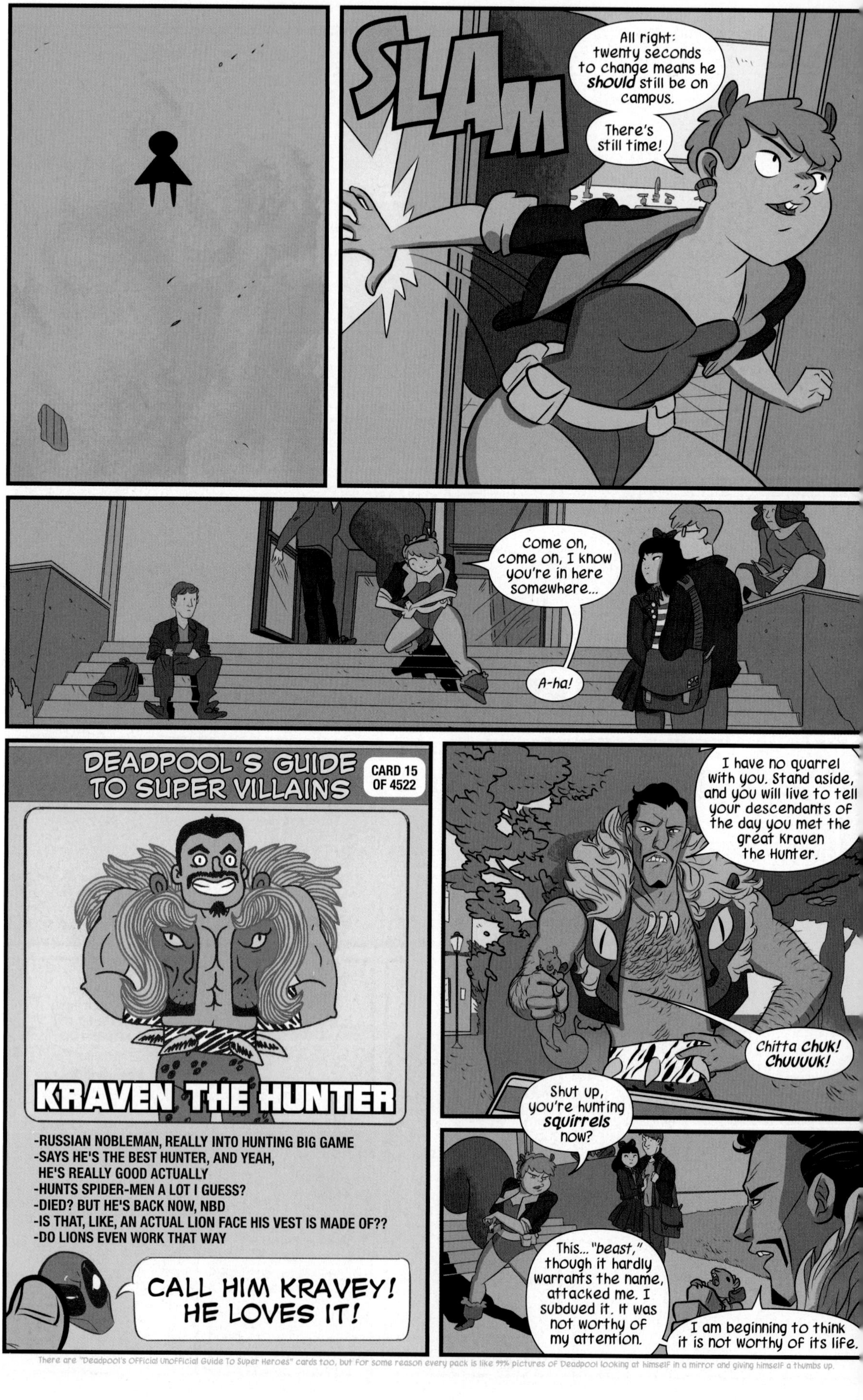
SLAM
All right: twenty seconds to change means he *should* still be on campus.
There's still time!
Come on, come on, I know you're in here somewhere...
A-ha!
DEADPOOL'S GUIDE TO SUPER VILLAINS
CARD 15 OF 4522
KRAVEN THE HUNTER
-RUSSIAN NOBLEMAN, REALLY INTO HUNTING BIG GAME
-SAYS HE'S THE BEST HUNTER, AND YEAH, HE'S REALLY GOOD ACTUALLY
-HUNTS SPIDER-MEN A LOT I GUESS?
-DIED? BUT HE'S BACK NOW, NBD
-IS THAT, LIKE, AN ACTUAL LION FACE HIS VEST IS MADE OF??
-DO LIONS EVEN WORK THAT WAY
CALL HIM KRAVEY! HE LOVES IT!
I have no quarrel with you. Stand aside, and you will live to tell your descendants of the day you met the great Kraven the Hunter.
Chitta *CHUK!* *CHUUUUK!*
Shut up, you're hunting *squirrels* now?
This... "*beast*," though it hardly warrants the name, attacked me. I subdued it. It was not worthy of my attention.
I am beginning to think it is not worthy of its life.

There are "Deadpool's Official Unofficial Guide To Super Heroes" cards too, but for some reason every pack is like 99% pictures of Deadpool looking at himself in a mirror and giving himself a thumbs up.

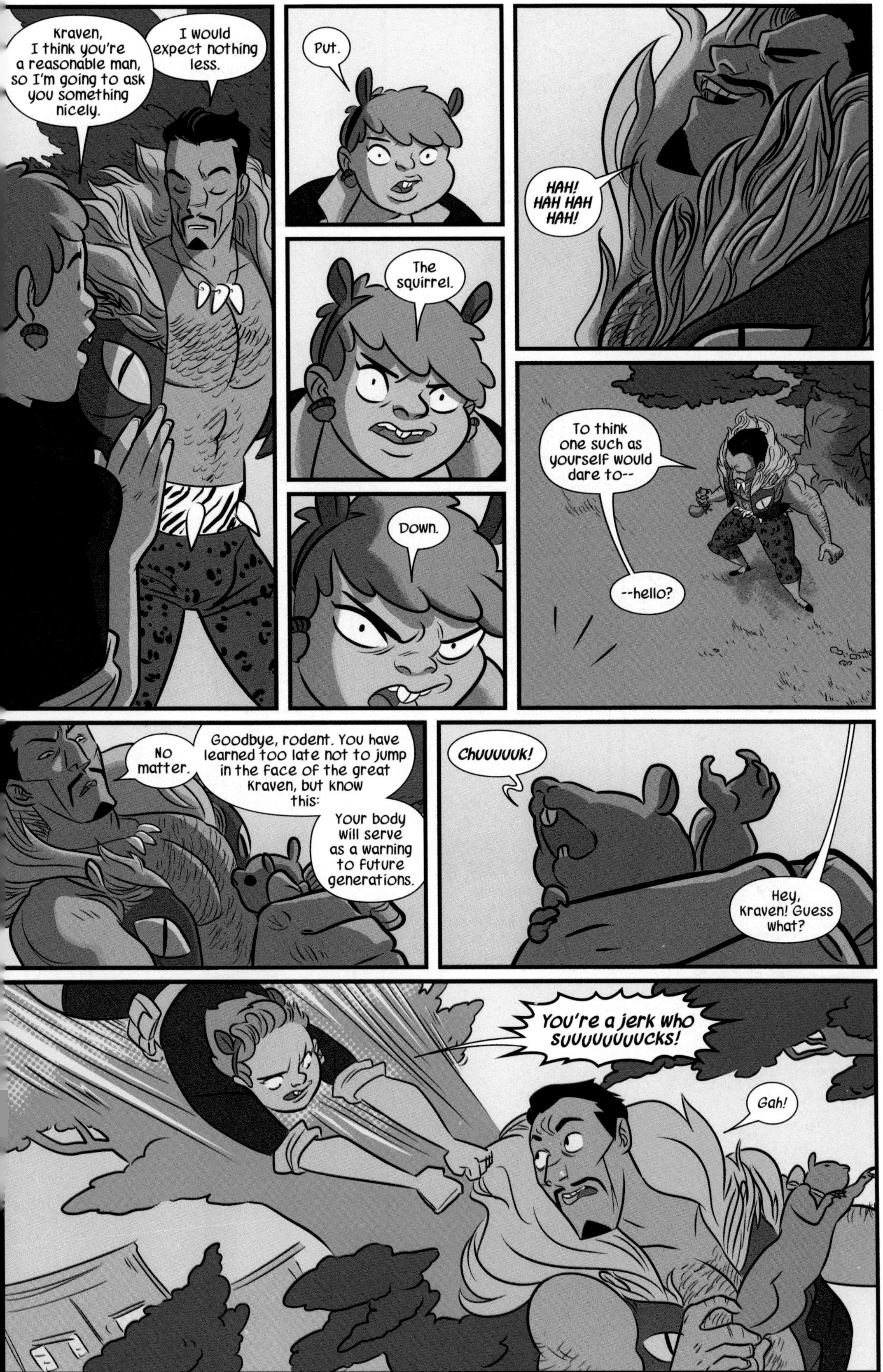
Kraven, I think you're a reasonable man, so I'm going to ask you something nicely.
I would expect nothing less.
Put.
HAH! HAH HAH HAH!
The squirrel.
Down.
To think one such as yourself would dare to--
--hello?
No matter.
Goodbye, rodent. You have learned too late not to jump in the face of the great Kraven, but know this:
Your body will serve as a warning to future generations.
Chuuuuuk!
Hey, Kraven! Guess what?
You're a jerk who SUUUUUUUCKS!
Gah!

Listen, all I have are these "Deadpool Super Villain" cards, not "Deadpool Great One-Liners For Heroes To Use On Super Villain" cards. I'm not made of money over here.

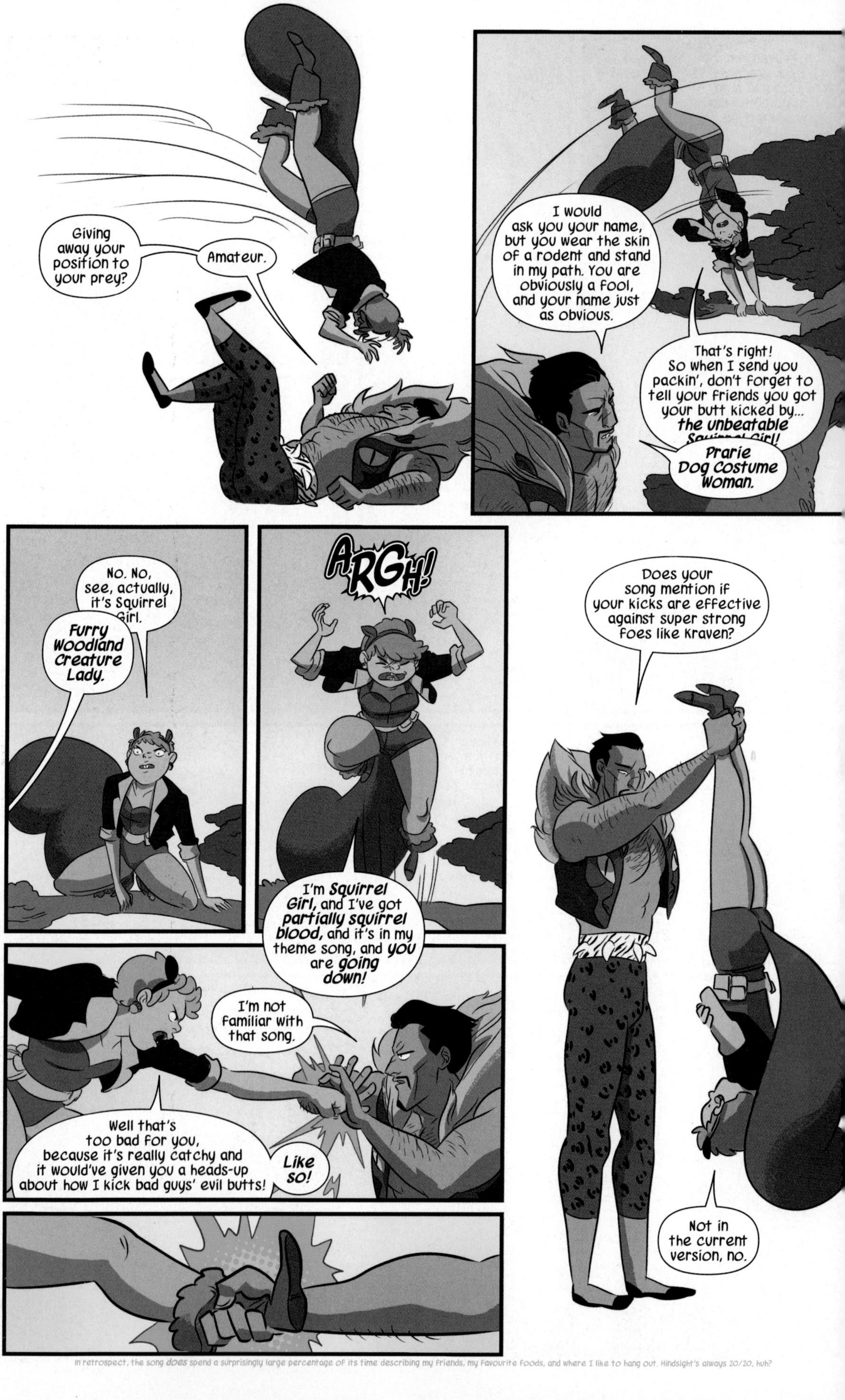
Giving away your position to your prey?
Amateur.
I would ask you your name, but you wear the skin of a rodent and stand in my path. You are obviously a fool, and your name just as obvious.
That's right! So when I send you packin', don't forget to tell your friends you got your butt kicked by... *the unbeatable*
Prarie Dog Costume Woman.
No. No, see, actually, it's Squirrel
Furry Woodland Creature Lady.
ARGH!
I'm *Squirrel Girl,* and I've got *partially squirrel blood,* and it's in my theme song, and *you* are *going down!*
I'm not familiar with that song.
Well that's too bad for you, because it's really catchy and it would've given you a heads-up about how I kick bad guys' evil butts!
Like so!
Does your song mention if your kicks are effective against super strong foes like Kraven?
Not in the current version, no.

In retrospect, the song *does* spend a surprisingly large percentage of its time describing my friends, my favourite foods, and where I like to hang out. Hindsight's always 20/20, huh?

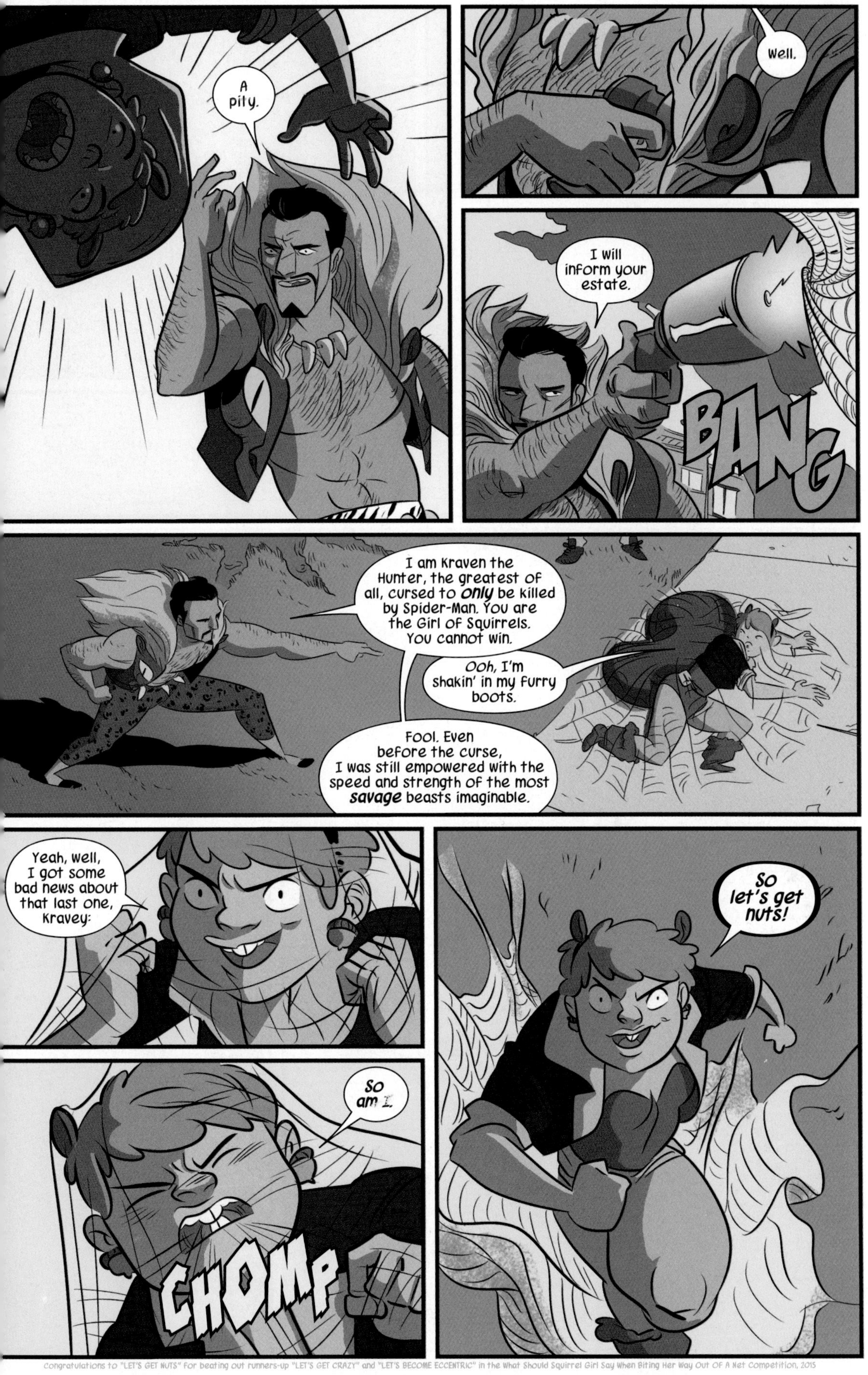
A pity.
Well.
I will inform your estate.
BANG
I am Kraven the Hunter, the greatest of all, cursed to *only* be killed by Spider-Man. You are the Girl of Squirrels. You cannot win.
Ooh, I'm shakin' in my furry boots.
Fool. Even before the curse, I was still empowered with the speed and strength of the most *savage* beasts imaginable.
Yeah, well, I got some bad news about that last one, Kravey:
So am I.
CHOMP
So let's get nuts!

Congratulations to "LET'S GET NUTS" for beating out runners-up "LET'S GET CRAZY" and "LET'S BECOME ECCENTRIC" in the What Should Squirrel Girl Say When Biting Her Way Out Of A Net Competition, 2015

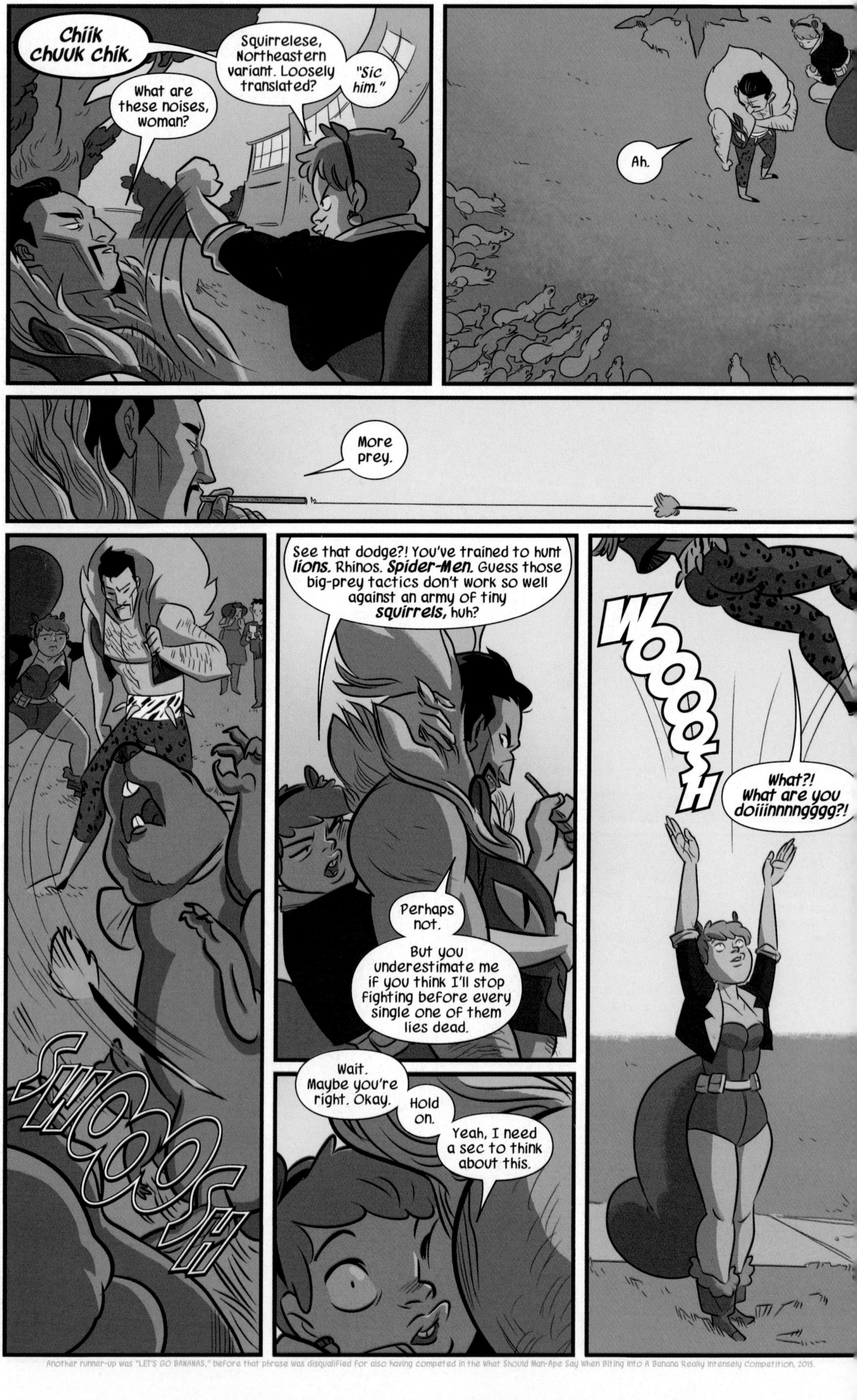
Chiik chuuk chik.
What are these noises, woman?
Squirrelese, Northeastern variant. Loosely translated?
"Sic him."
Ah.
More prey.
See that dodge?! You've trained to hunt lions. Rhinos. Spider-Men. Guess those big-prey tactics don't work so well against an army of tiny squirrels, huh?
Perhaps not.
But you underestimate me if you think I'll stop fighting before every single one of them lies dead.
SHOOOOSH
Wait. Maybe you're right. Okay.
Hold on.
Yeah, I need a sec to think about this.
WOOOOOSH
What?! What are you doiiinnnngggg?!

Another runner-up was "LET'S GO BANANAS," before that phrase was disqualified for also having competed in the What Should Man-Ape Say When Biting Into A Banana Really Intensely Competition, 2015.

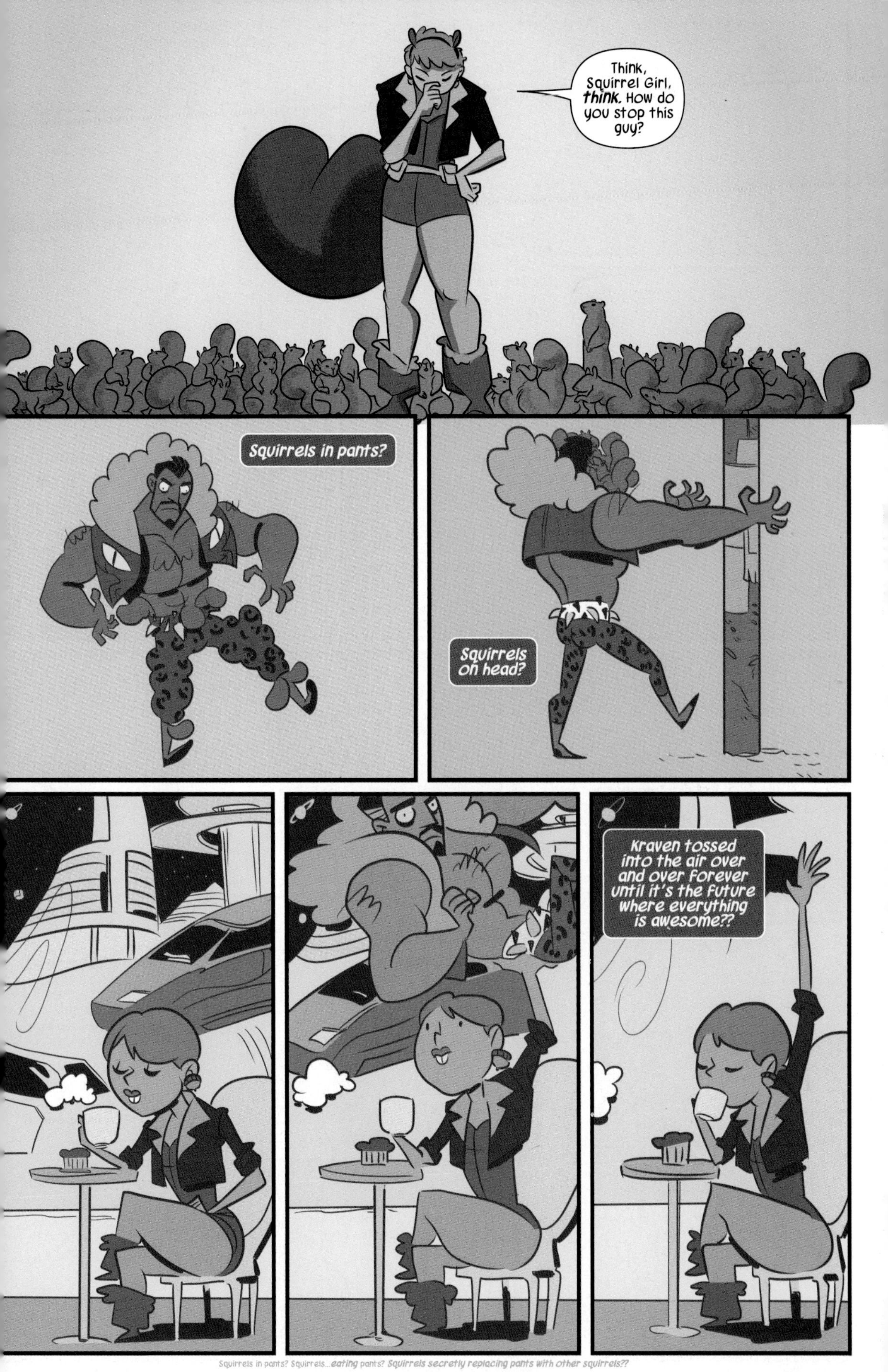
Think, Squirrel Girl, think. How do you stop this guy?
Squirrels in pants?
Squirrels on head?
Kraven tossed into the air over and over forever until it's the future where everything is awesome??

Squirrels in pants? Squirrels...*eating* pants? *Squirrels secretly replacing pants with other squirrels??*

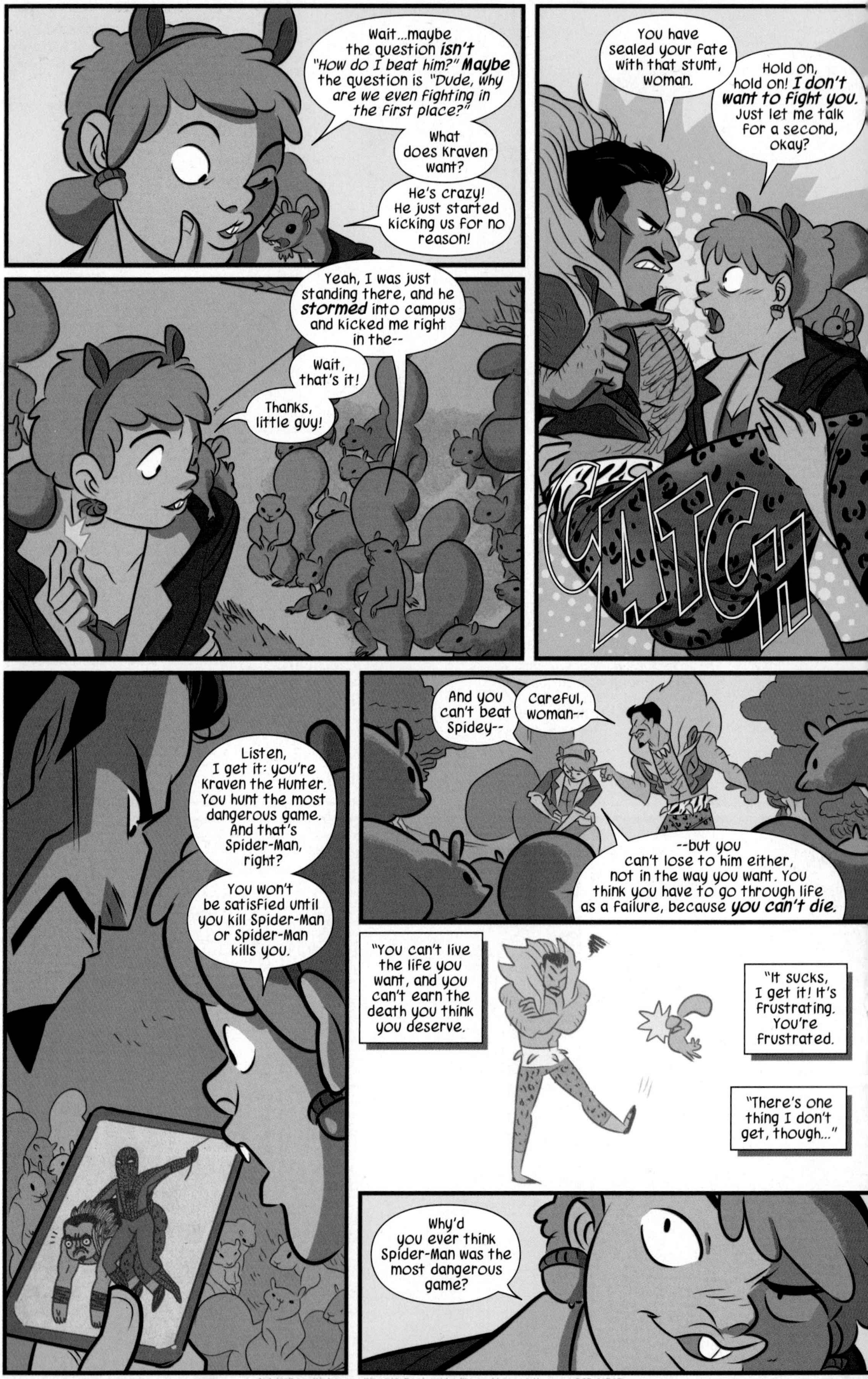
Wait...maybe the question *isn't* "How do I beat him?" *Maybe* the question is "Dude, why are we even fighting in the first place?"
What does Kraven want?
He's crazy! He just started kicking us for no reason!
Yeah, I was just standing there, and he *stormed* into campus and kicked me right in the--
Wait, that's it!
Thanks, little guy!
You have sealed your fate with that stunt, woman.
Hold on, hold on! *I don't want to fight you.* Just let me talk for a second, okay?
CATCH
Listen, I get it: you're Kraven the Hunter. You hunt the most dangerous game. And that's Spider-Man, right?
You won't be satisfied until you kill Spider-Man or Spider-Man kills you.
And you can't beat Spidey--
Careful, woman--
--but you can't lose to him either, not in the way you want. You think you have to go through life as a failure, because *you can't die.*
"You can't live the life you want, and you can't earn the death you think you deserve.
"It sucks, I get it! It's frustrating. You're frustrated.
"There's one thing I don't get, though..."
Why'd you ever think Spider-Man was the most dangerous game?

And don't say it's because it's on his Deadpool trading card because those are *non-canon.*

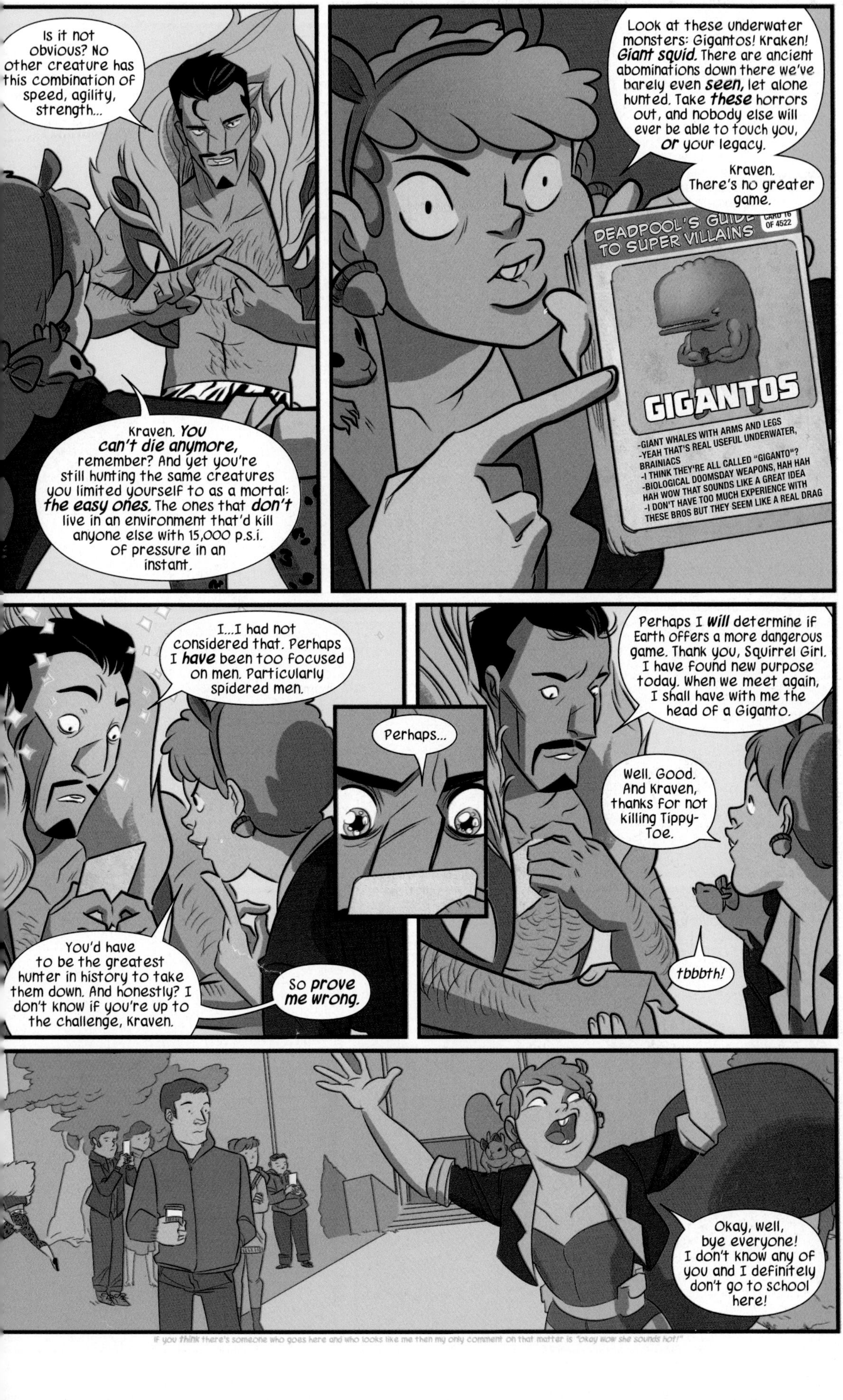
Is it not obvious? No other creature has this combination of speed, agility, strength...
Kraven. You can't die anymore, remember? And yet you're still hunting the same creatures you limited yourself to as a mortal: the easy ones. The ones that don't live in an environment that'd kill anyone else with 15,000 p.s.i. of pressure in an instant.
Look at these underwater monsters: Gigantos! Kraken! Giant squid. There are ancient abominations down there we've barely even seen, let alone hunted. Take these horrors out, and nobody else will ever be able to touch you, or your legacy.
Kraven. There's no greater game.
DEADPOOL'S GUIDE TO SUPER VILLAINS
CARD 16 OF 4522
GIGANTOS
-GIANT WHALES WITH ARMS AND LEGS
-YEAH THAT'S REAL USEFUL UNDERWATER, BRAINIACS
-I THINK THEY'RE ALL CALLED "GIGANTO"?
-BIOLOGICAL DOOMSDAY WEAPONS, HAH HAH HAH WOW THAT SOUNDS LIKE A GREAT IDEA
-I DON'T HAVE TOO MUCH EXPERIENCE WITH THESE BROS BUT THEY SEEM LIKE A REAL DRAG
I...I had not considered that. Perhaps I have been too focused on men. Particularly spidered men.
You'd have to be the greatest hunter in history to take them down. And honestly? I don't know if you're up to the challenge, Kraven.
So prove me wrong.
Perhaps...
Perhaps I will determine if Earth offers a more dangerous game. Thank you, Squirrel Girl. I have found new purpose today. When we meet again, I shall have with me the head of a Giganto.
Well. Good. And Kraven, thanks for not killing Tippy-Toe.
tbbbth!
Okay, well, bye everyone! I don't know any of you and I definitely don't go to school here!

If you *think* there's someone who goes here and who looks like me then my only comment on that matter is "okay wow she sounds hot!"

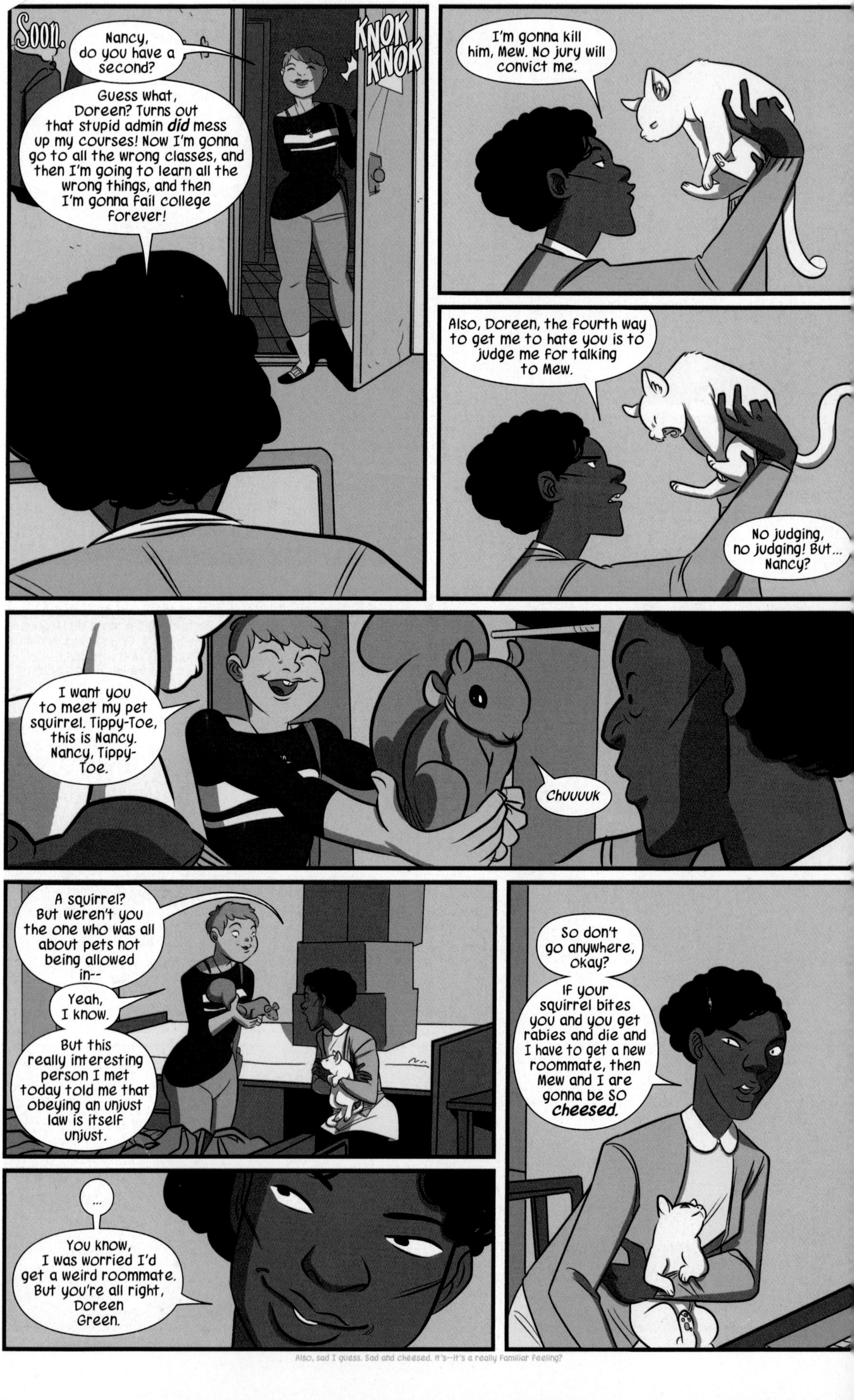
Soon.
Nancy, do you have a second?
KNOK KNOK
Guess what, Doreen? Turns out that stupid admin *did* mess up my courses! Now I'm gonna go to all the wrong classes, and then I'm going to learn all the wrong things, and then I'm gonna fail college forever!
I'm gonna kill him, Mew. No jury will convict me.
Also, Doreen, the fourth way to get me to hate you is to judge me for talking to Mew.
No judging, no judging! But... Nancy?
I want you to meet my pet squirrel. Tippy-Toe, this is Nancy. Nancy, Tippy-Toe.
Chuuuuk
A squirrel? But weren't you the one who was all about pets not being allowed in--
Yeah, I know.
But this really interesting person I met today told me that obeying an unjust law is itself unjust.
So don't go anywhere, okay?
If your squirrel bites you and you get rabies and die and I have to get a new roommate, then Mew and I are gonna be SO ***cheesed.***
...
You know, I was worried I'd get a weird roommate. But you're all right, Doreen Green.

Also, sad I guess. Sad and cheesed. It's--it's a really familiar feeling?

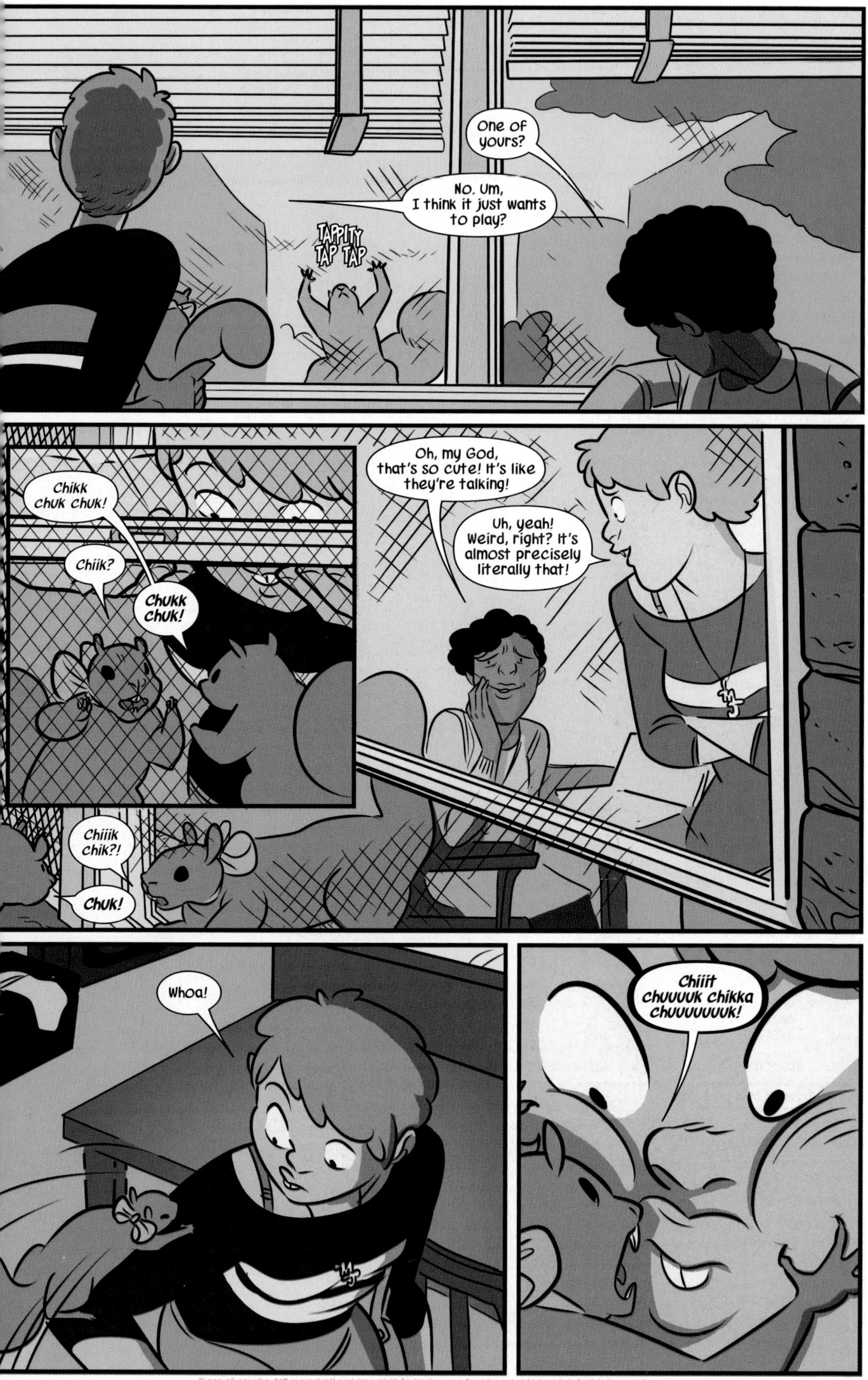

One of yours?
No. Um, I think it just wants to play?
TAPPITY TAP TAP
Oh, my God, that's so cute! It's like they're talking!
Uh, yeah! Weird, right? It's almost precisely literally that!
Chikk chuk chuk!
Chiik?
Chukk chuk!
Chiiik chik?!
Chuk!
Whoa!
Chiiit chuuuuk chikka chuuuuuuuk!

Those of you who *can* speak Northeastern variant Squirrelese are freaking out right now, but don't tell anyone!
Keep it a surprise for the rest of us who have to read the next page to find out what the deal is, okay?

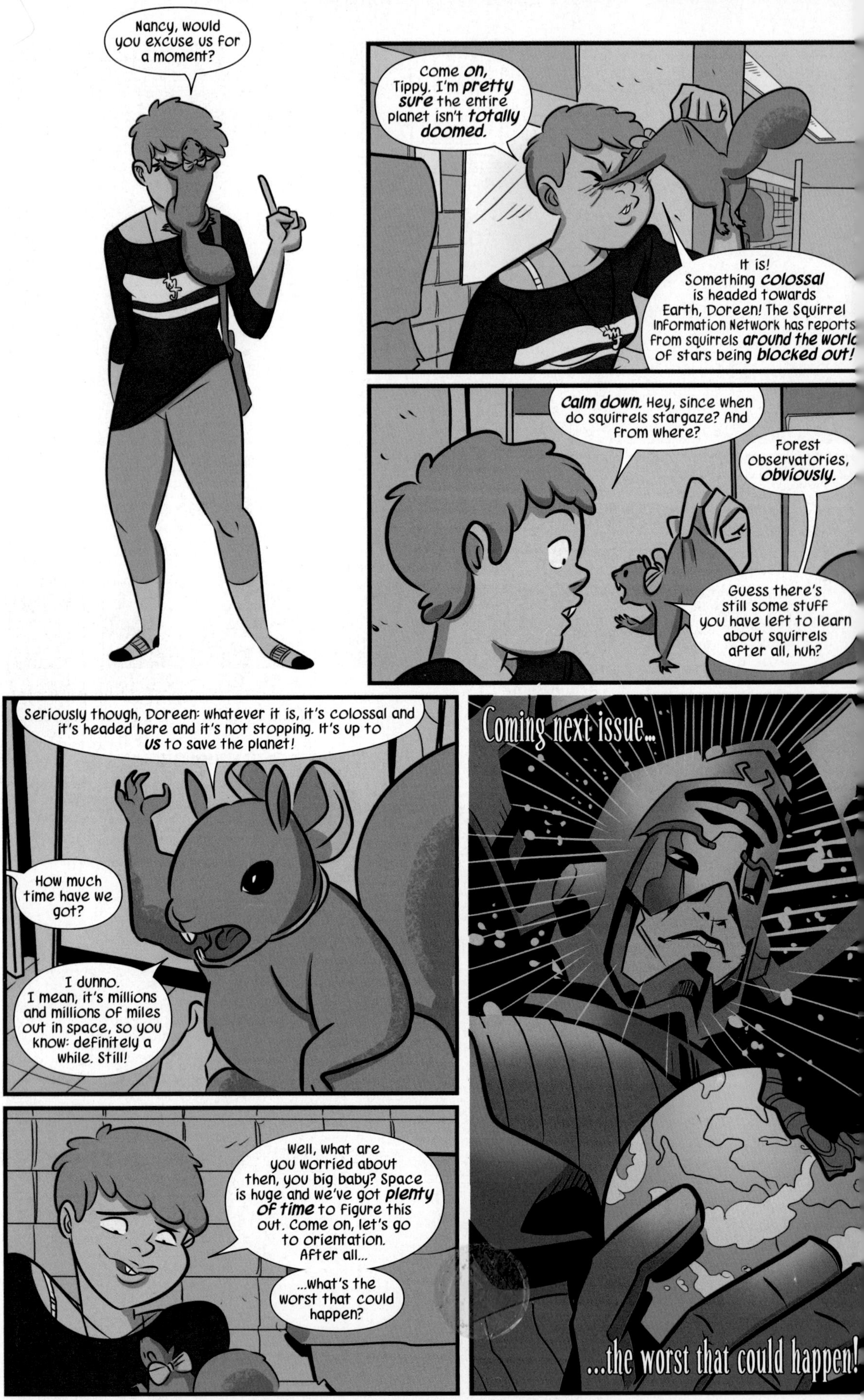
Nancy, would you excuse us for a moment?
Come on, Tippy. I'm pretty sure the entire planet isn't totally doomed.
It is! Something colossal is headed towards Earth, Doreen! The Squirrel Information Network has reports from squirrels around the world of stars being blocked out!
Calm down. Hey, since when do squirrels stargaze? And from where?
Forest observatories, obviously.
Guess there's still some stuff you have left to learn about squirrels after all, huh?
Seriously though, Doreen: whatever it is, it's colossal and it's headed here and it's not stopping. It's up to us to save the planet!
How much time have we got?
I dunno. I mean, it's millions and millions of miles out in space, so you know: definitely a while. Still!
Well, what are you worried about then, you big baby? Space is huge and we've got plenty of time to figure this out. Come on, let's go to orientation. After all...
...what's the worst that could happen?
Coming next issue...
...the worst that could happen!

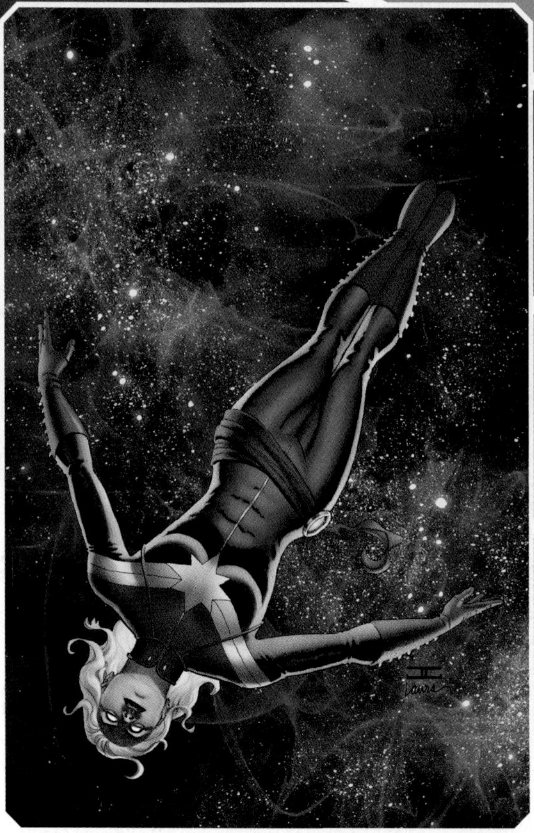

CAPTAIN MARVEL #1
Variant by John Cassaday & Laura Martin

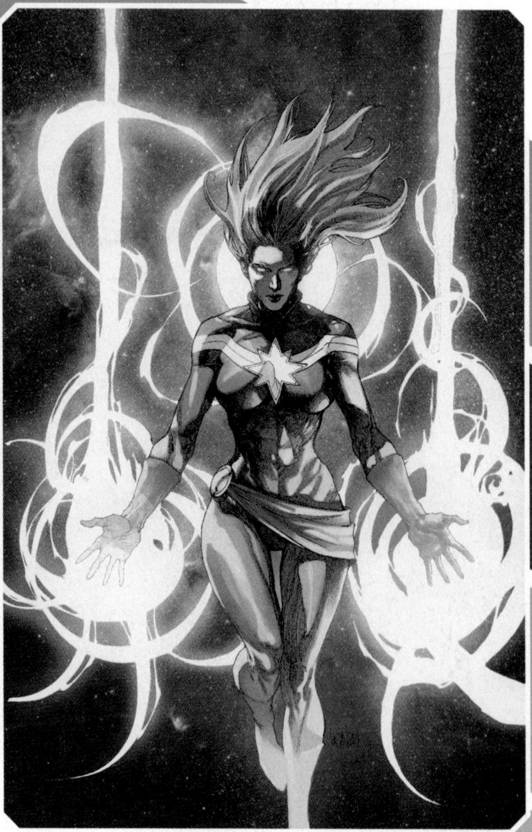

CAPTAIN MARVEL #1
Variant by Leinil Francis Yu & Sunny Gho

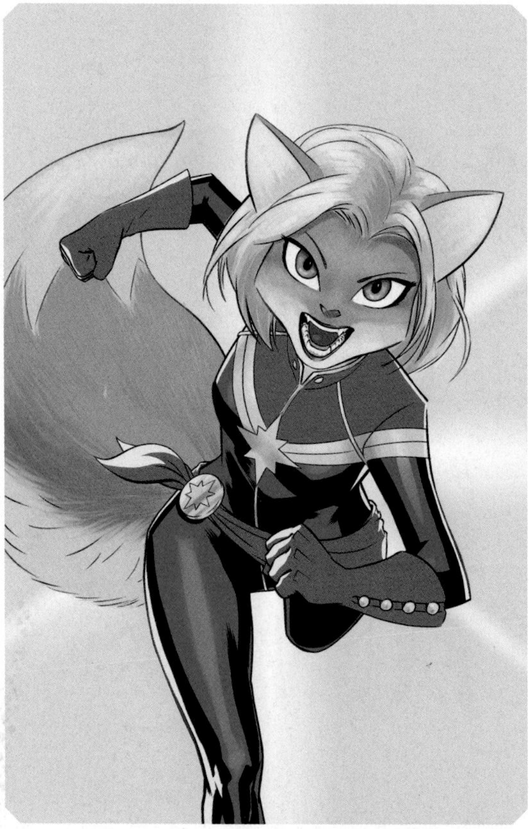

CAPTAIN MARVEL #1
Variant by David Lopez

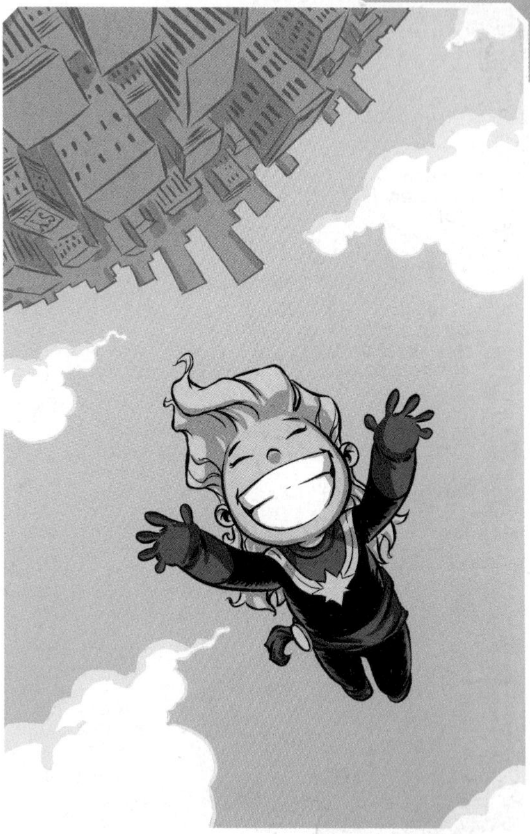

CAPTAIN MARVEL #1
Variant by Skottie Young

MS. MARVEL #1
Variant by Arthur Adams
& Peter Steigerwald

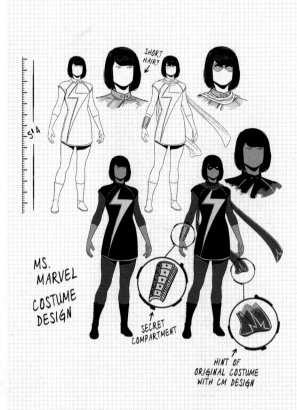

SHORT HAIR?

5'4

MS.
MARVEL
COSTUME
DESIGN

SECRET
COMPARTMENT

HINT OF
ORIGINAL COSTUME
WITH CM DESIGN

MS. MARVEL #1
Variant by Jamie McKelvie

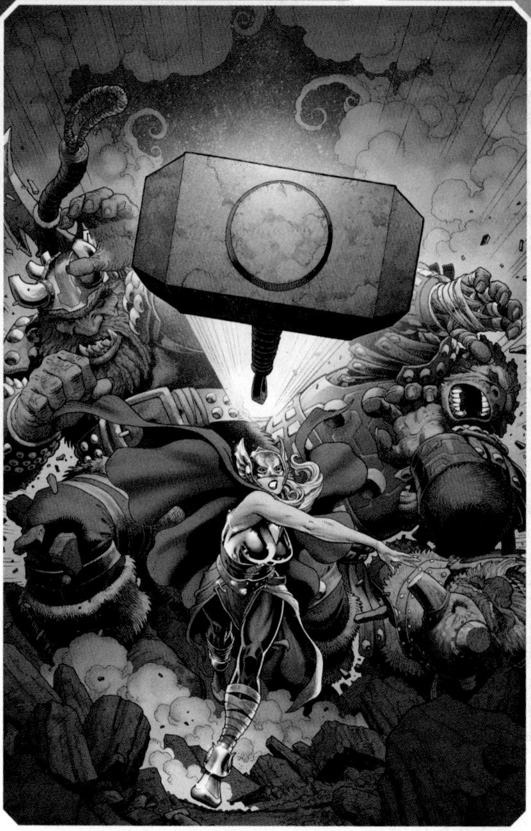

THOR #1
Variant by Arthur Adams & Peter Steigerwald

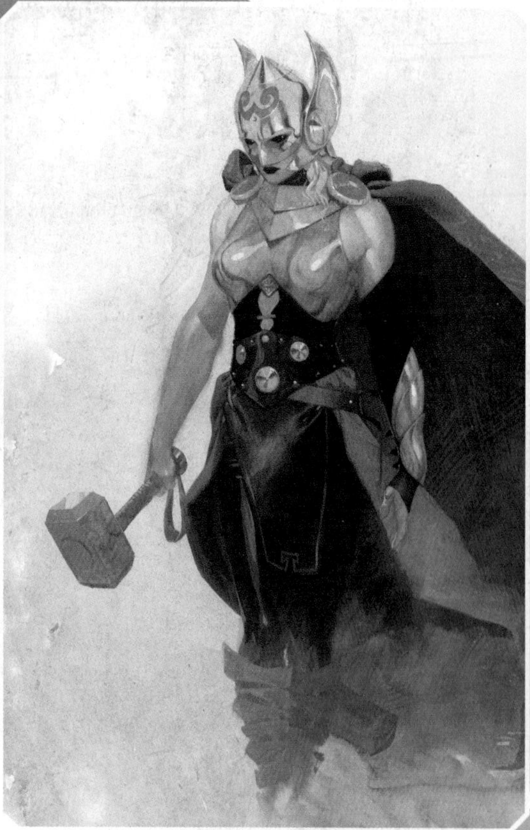

THOR #1
Variant by Esad Ribic

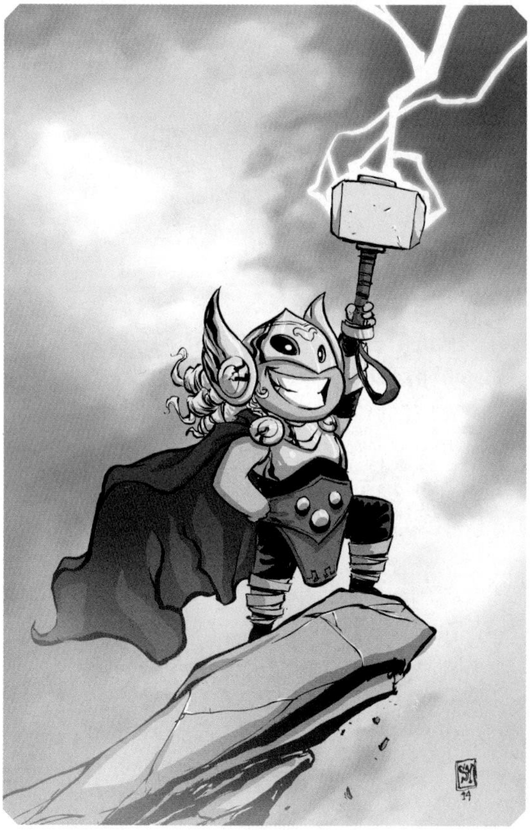

THOR #1
Variant by Skottie Young

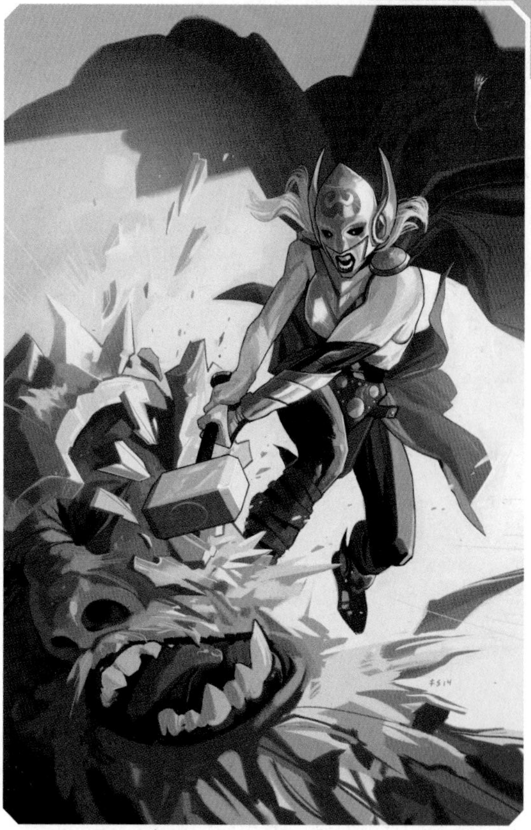

THOR #1
Variant by Fiona Staples

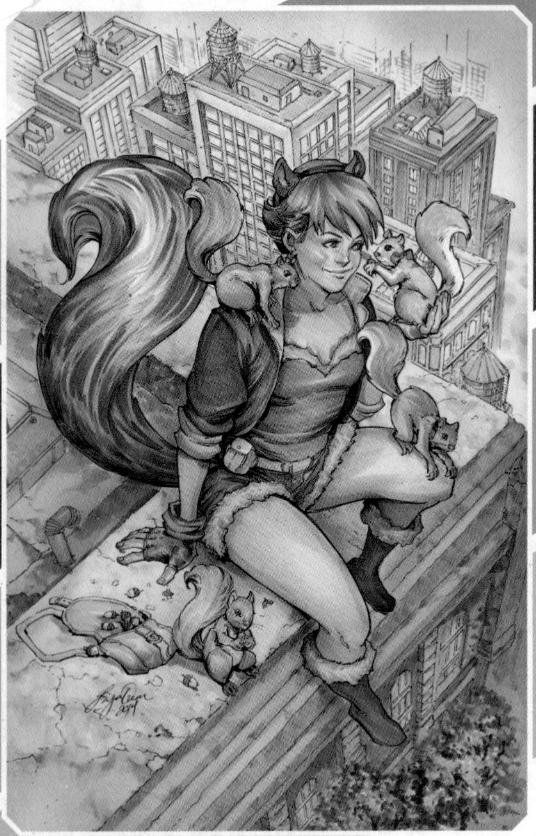

THE UNBEATABLE SQUIRREL GIRL #1
Variant by Siya Oum

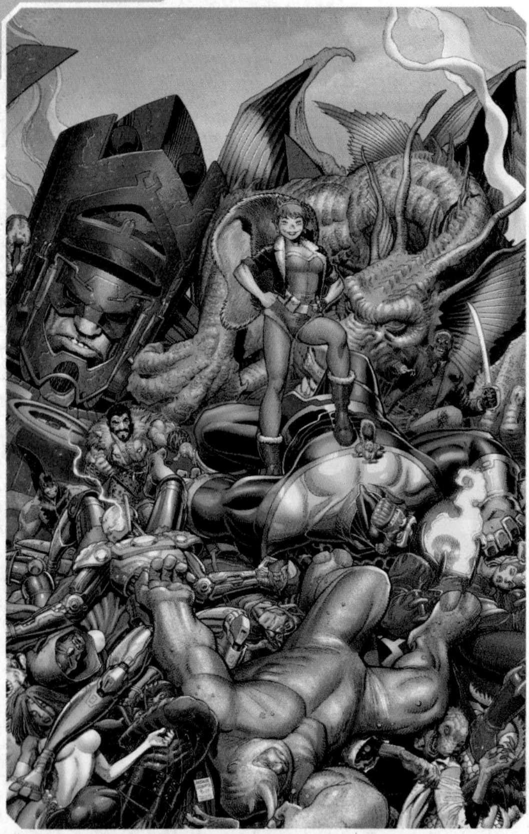

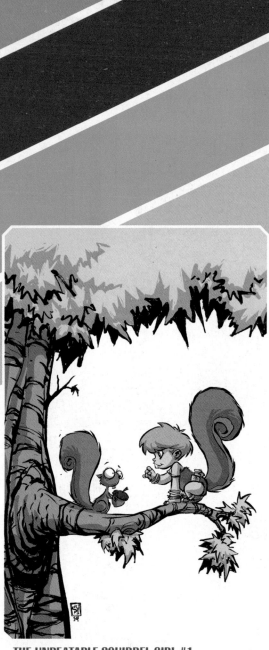

THE UNBEATABLE SQUIRREL GIRL #1
Variant by Arthur Adams & Paul Mounts

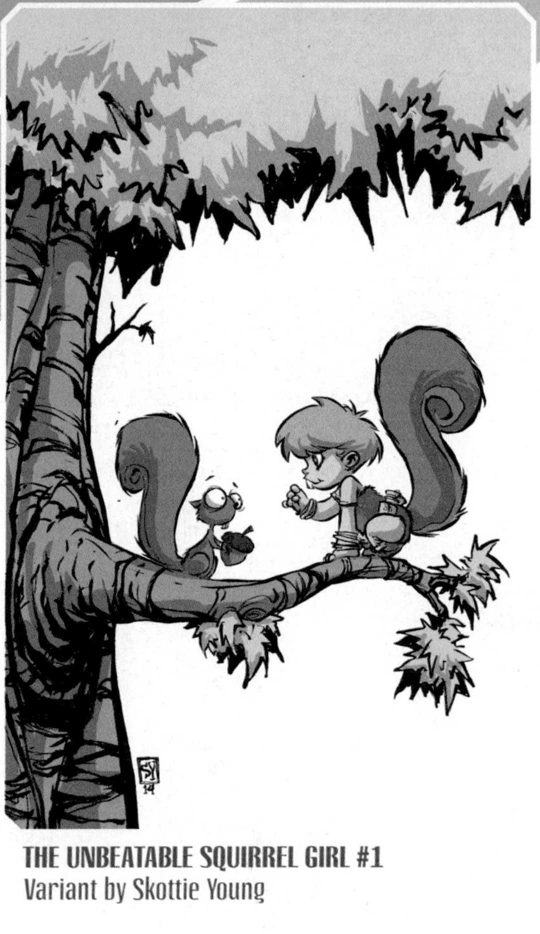

THE UNBEATABLE SQUIRREL GIRL #1
Variant by Skottie Young